--- ★ ---

There was no light, but that was definitely a scuba suit. Donnie could make out the tanks and belt as he got closer. But the rubber suit fluttered loose, like a black leaf waving in the murky tossing water near the bottom. He grabbed a lip of the rock wall with one hand to steady himself; with the other hand, he eased his lamp forward to turn the hood of the scuba suit. He blinked, wasn't sure if he'd seen right. He jerked his right hand back and fixed the light on the suit. The hood stayed turned toward him. Inside, covered with a light patina of brownish slime, was the pale staring face of a skull.

--- ★ ---

RUSS HALL

BLACK *like* BLOOD

WORLDWIDE®

TORONTO • NEW YORK • LONDON
AMSTERDAM • PARIS • SYDNEY • HAMBURG
STOCKHOLM • ATHENS • TOKYO • MILAN
MADRID • WARSAW • BUDAPEST • AUCKLAND

BLACK LIKE BLOOD

A Worldwide Mystery/November 2006

First published by Five Star.

ISBN-13: 978-0-373-26583-1
ISBN-10:   0-373-26583-2

Printed in U.S.A.

BLACK like BLOOD

ONE

TILLIS MACRORY STEPPED INSIDE the door and flipped on the light. The chill-bared teeth of the night outside behind him were black, with silver, slanting layers of rain whipping around in the gusting wind. He closed the door. Each bone inside him seemed to ache individually. Water poured off his slicker onto the carpet. He pulled off the slicker and dropped it beside the mat, onto the brown Spanish tiles of the foyer. A flash of lightning shot through all the windows of the northeast side of the house. Then, two seconds later, came the muffled roar of thunder.

"Two miles away and heading this way." He was used to talking to himself when alone.

He tugged off his boots and left them by the door. His socks were damp and his feet hurt. His pants were wet to his knees and dripped as he went through the room, turning on lights as he did. A small framed picture of a snow-covered bridge appeared in a wash of light. It was one Claire had hung, and he'd never gotten around to taking it down, though he'd had the opportunity. What was it? Four years now? Why anyone would want a picture like that this far down into Texas was beyond him, as was why anyone would leave it hanging there when he didn't have to. He looked away from it, and shrugged, wondering if it was snowing wherever she was now. It was just one more ache to add to the others, the physical ones from a fourteen-hour unproductive stakeout of a pawn shop in a useless effort to backtrack a throwdown 7.65mm found by the body of Hoel's Dam's mayor, Denny Spurlock, a week ago. Hell, it wouldn't be much of a throwdown if it was traceable—the lieutenant'd said that himself when he passed along the request from the sheriff for help. But you gotta do what you gotta do. Tillis moved on through the living area.

By the fireplace, he paused and pulled four mesquite logs from the knotty-pine bin, making sure he got ones with bark. He laid them across the andirons, close enough to each other for a good start, but with enough room between them for a hearty fire. He shoved in one of the presoaked starter sticks and lit it with a big red-tipped kitchen match from the box on the mantel.

The fire was still sputtering and flickering to life behind him as he followed the bend in the room that led along the row of floor-to-ceiling windows beside the dining area and kitchen. He looked out at the tossing limbs and whipping sprays of white swirls of rain. Past the trees he could see a slice of the lake, its surface a rippling sheen. A mercury vapor light on the far side of the lake cast a single beam of bluish white across the tossing surface. He was reaching for the light switch, then stopped. There was a single dark break in the beam, then it was solid again.

He felt his forehead tightening, knowing his concentration showed itself as a frown, had anyone been there to see it. Tillis grabbed for the latch to the sliding door that led out onto the porch, tugged it open, and went outside to listen and peer. Rain beat hard on the porch's roof. He had to strain to listen. Barely, above the smash of the downpour and a diminishing rumble of thunder, he heard the low burble of a motor. He stared hard at the dark lake. But there were no running lights. Damn.

The nearest phone hung on the breezeway between the kitchen and dining area. He used it to make the call.

The phone barely got out half a ring and was snatched off the hook. "Where the hell are you?"

"Here," Macrory said. "Home."

"Oh, it's you. What do you want?" The anger, hysteria, whatever had been in Logan's voice, was gone.

"What's got you wound up like a cheap watch?"

"You call me to ask that?"

"No, to tell you someone's out on the lake."

"And?"

"In the middle of a thunderstorm. No running lights, going slow so as not to make much noise."

"Why don't you call the sheriff?"

"Or someone who cares?"

"You know what I mean. Eldon'd feel he has to go through channels and ask for Ranger assistance anyway, and this is probably something so routine one of the deputies could handle it."

"Come on. It's happening right now."

"Haven't you gotten into enough trouble for leaping into things without waiting for clearance?"

"What're you saying?"

"That you're always half-cocked, that you think you're some kind of knight-errant ready to go off and get involved nine-tenths of the time when you shouldn't."

"Why do you think that is?"

"Because you live alone, telling yourself you're some

kind of happy hermit, thinking you're married to your work, and you don't have a single thing at home to make you want to stay there some nights like you should."

Tillis felt his face get warm, and he should have paused before he spoke, but he said, "Look, I'll make you a deal. You don't tell me how to do my Rangering and I won't tell you how to raise your daughter."

The silence on the other end told Tillis he'd hit a nerve.

"Come on," Tillis said after a minute of quiet. "What happened to the Logan I knew in Korea, who was, if anything, the one everyone thought was a little too gung-ho?"

"It's not a good time."

"It never is."

"I'm pretty all in."

"I know. I'm tired too."

"Why don't you relax? Just this once, be a normal, uninvolved citizen."

"It isn't in me."

There was a half-minute of silence on the other end. After all these years, he knew Tillis wouldn't let up until Logan was miserable or in trouble too.

"You know, you're a manipulative sonuva ... pea thrasher."

Tillis laughed. He knew he had him.

"Okay," Logan sighed out a long low breath. "I guess. How long?"

"I'll meet you at the ramp in ten minutes."

THE BOAT BOUNCED over each wave set, while unrelenting sheets of rain hammered down on its pebble-grained, no-slip fiberglass surface. The rain came first from one direction, then from another in silvery sheets.

Water sprayed up from the bow and sent needles of cold into Karyn's face. The top, snug hood of the wetsuit covered her neck, ears, and most of her forehead. But she had the sensitive skin of a lightly-freckled redhead, and the water stung. The hard sprays of rain pounding them from the downpour stung as much as the spray from the bow. She didn't like being so close to lightning when they were wet and on the water. For that matter, she didn't like going with no lights. Inside she quivered, and it was less from the rain and cold than from the idea of a night dive in pitch-black water. She was scared of the dark, though if she admitted that to Donnie he would've left her behind, and he needed her here. It took everything she had not to turn to him and ask him to head back. But this was nothing new. Everything she had ever accomplished so far in the short eighteen years of her life had been achieved by heading directly into the face of her darkest fears, and this was no different.

She looked over his way. Donnie sat in the seat beside her, bent slightly forward and squinting ahead into the gale-force slaps of rain sheets that buffeted them. On either side of the lake, the cliffs were getting steeper, higher. She could no longer see the homes of the well-off folks nestled high on the slopes, though she did see an occasional flicker of light filtering down through the storm. Each was only a glimmer, confirming that people were at home high up there and experiencing the same storm, but from inside their cozy homes. Thinking that way only made Karyn feel colder and more alone. She huddled in her seat, looked down, and tried to think of anything else. The boat seemed to take forever to get there at this pace.

"You'd better get ready with the anchor."

She looked up at Donnie. He nodded toward the bow. She peered ahead, could barely make out the outline of the dam. "Shouldn't we get closer?"

"Can't. The tow'll suck the boat right over the lip. As it is, we've gotta make real sure the anchor gets a good hold here." The concern on Donnie's face didn't make him look any older, even as he winced while staring out into the storm. He was twenty-three and lean, but with rounded cheeks, clear skin, and pale blond hair. He got carded when buying beer in any store outside the county. His face, like hers at the moment, showed as a pale round moon surrounded by the black rubber of his scuba hood.

She looked at the boat's dash. The only light showing was the glowworm-green face of the radar screen. She could see the shapes of fish low in a hundred and ten feet of water. Closer to the dam, she knew the water went to two hundred feet. But, what was stuck in her head, haunting her even now, were the images they had seen on the radar screen when they had gone back and forth near the dam in daylight a week ago. Big shapes had filled the screen—fish that looked as long and as heavy as a man. Catfish probably, or a few carp and gar, but they had made her shiver then, even in the sunny daylight. Thinking of them now, as they got ready to dive in the black down among them, was doing her no good at all.

"Watch for logs," Donnie yelled.

"What?"

"Logs. They've opened the dam at the other end." His words were nearly tugged away by the gusting, rain-filled wind.

Lake Kiowa was only eleven miles long, and less than half a mile wide in most places. It was part of a series of flood-control lakes that led all the way to Austin.

Karyn couldn't see to the shore on either side, and she could only spot dark shadows around the boat. The rain was coming down too hard to make out more than a blur for each log. But Donnie was going slow enough to brush by most of them.

"Get ready," Donnie said.

"Now what?"

"To drop the anchor."

She rose and moved up to the bow, picked up the anchor, and looked back for his signal. It had been warmer sitting down than she realized, now that she was standing up and could feel the sprays of rain slapping at her. She heard the motor gurgle to a halt, then heard Donnie's, "Now."

Karyn let go, and well over a hundred-and-fifty feet peeled off the pile before the rope slowed, then stopped. She let a few more feet ease out, so the drag would set the anchor, then wrapped the rope in a couple figure-eights over the front cleat and topped it off with a half-hitch. The anchor caught and the boat began to swing around in the current.

She turned and almost ran into Donnie. He had come forward to help, but gave an approving nod instead and moved to the stern to get on the rest of his gear.

Karyn squinted through the rain toward the downriver side. She could barely make out the string of buoys over fifty yards away. The dam was beyond that.

"How come we're this far from the dam?" she asked.

"Tow," he yelled. "I already told you. It'd suck the boat right over the top in this, if the anchor lets go."

None of this made Karyn feel better. A ripple crawled in a cold, slimy ice-cube trail up her spine in a way that had nothing to do with the rain needles hitting her face. She went to the stern of the boat and calmly started to pull on her diving belt and tanks. Her fingers felt cold and brittle as she clasped the tanks in place and felt to confirm that the air line to the regulator was where it should be. They had done this often enough before, but in daylight, bright, sunny, warm daylight.

A bolt of lightning knifed apart the black night and lit up a power line tower that rose high above the dam. It shimmered like a Christmas tree on fire through the wavering lens of the downpour. Karyn shuddered inwardly as the thunder vibrated through her. She reached for her mask. Donnie was already sitting on the port gunwale by the stern, waiting to roll backward into the water.

She spit in her mask, rinsed it, and tugged it on before sitting down beside Donnie. As soon as she did, he made a backward roll into the lake's dark surface. She pushed with her fins and followed him.

Diving at night was like being swallowed whole. The water was cool on her face for a second; then she actually felt warmer than she had on the surface, being buffeted by the rain and wind. The water around her was black, and now felt as warm as blood. Donnie's light clicked on, and she could see her bubbles. She turned on her own hand light and moved closer. He held his hand in front of the light and gave her a thumbs-up. Then he bent at the waist and straightened again, with his head pointed down. He began a slow kick toward the bottom and the dam.

Karyn followed as close as she could without being kicked by his fins. She didn't want to lose sight of the beam of his light. The water was cooler as they went deeper, and blacker. There was a current too. With this much rain, the River Authority almost always opened the dam to generate power while running water down into the lakes in the river chain below. The flow tugged them forward, pulling them toward the dam. That wasn't good, because they would have to come back pulling against that current.

She had been in a cave once when the guide turned out the light to show everyone total darkness. Her bones had tried to crawl right out of her skin then. But the black surrounding them now seemed darker, more sinister.

There was nothing to see around them but black. Occasionally, a small darker shape darted across the extreme range of her vision—a fish, she hoped. She moved closer to Donnie, even felt his fin touch her shoulder a couple of times. She could tell they were getting closer to the dam. The current was getting stronger, and swirled in places. One minute she was following Donnie closely, the next she was yanked away and tumbled end-over-end by a sudden surge of current. She almost lost her own light, but gripped it tighter, straightened, saw the fading beam of Donnie's light, and kicked in that direction as hard as she could.

Just as she got up to him, the beam of his light swung back as he checked on her. His face was lost behind the glaring sheen of her own light catching his face mask, but he turned back and continued to kick forward, confident that she was behind him, and never aware of how close she had come to being swept away.

They were deep enough now for their lights to sweep across the muddy tumble of rocks and objects scattered across the bottom. There was what looked like a silt-covered refrigerator, on its back with its door open. A few feet away was a washing machine, an almost unrecognizable form covered by mud and rust. Who knew what all had been dumped down here?

They honed in on each shape and looked closer, their lights probing. She wasn't sure what to expect—a boat, or maybe a box-like shape. They'd talked about it enough, and it was why they were out here on a night like this. Donnie seemed so sure.

She felt the current grabbing at her as it rushed toward the dam. She raised her light, and could make out the pale, flat gray of the concrete wall. Then something moved. A huge black shape lifted off the muddy bottom. She jerked, almost dropped the light. To her right, there was something as big. A blacker shadow as big as a person moved slowly by. She spun toward Donnie. He was kicking harder and moving forward with the current. His light was fading, growing dimmer.

Don't panic, she thought, just as an underwater wave of current snatched her and tumbled her completely over. Her fingers slipped on her lamp. She snatched at it, barely grabbed it, and clutched at it like it was a lifeline. She rolled end-over-end in the wave, heading toward the cement wall of the dam. The massive slab of cement seemed headed toward her, like a giant fly-swatter. But what bothered her more were the huge dark shapes lifting and moving in the flickering rays of her tumbling light.

She spread her arms wide, to break her tumbling, and she kicked as hard as she could, using the power of her fins the way a race car driver accelerates into a curve. She shot upward in the water, straightening until she was swimming directly against the current, feeling it press against her face mask, making her work her legs hard. She angled into the current, headed the way she thought she had been going. She kept kicking hard, until she knew she had full control again. Then she looked around. She could see no other light. She was by herself, all alone.

THE TRUCK PULLED into the lot beside the ramp, towing the boat on its trailer. Macrory climbed out of his car, reluctant to leave the running heater. He went over while Logan rolled down the window.

Logan was nearly the same age as Tillis and had the unsmiling, squared-edged Semper Fidelis face of an ex-Marine, which he was. Hell, they'd been in the same outfit together, except Tillis didn't think he'd ever picked up the jarhead look himself. Logan's hair was crisp, three-quarters of an inch long, and gray with traces of pale red. He looked like he might run to fat if he ever let himself go, which he hadn't. He wasn't smiling, but Tillis hadn't seen him smile all that much since his once-cheerful wife Heidi had lost an extended battle with depression and then cervical cancer two years back. But tonight his serious look had even darker shadows to it, some caused by the sky and the spray of water whipping now and again at his face through the open window.

Tillis leaned closer to the truck's open window. "I'm not too keen about this kind of shit in my own back yard."

"You mean the boat, or our late mayor, Denny Spurlock, getting wasted?" Logan wore rain gear too, the badge on the outside since his jacket covered the olive drab uniform.

"Both. And, Logan, no one says 'wasted' anymore."

"That's why I'm the game warden and you're the Texas Ranger. What d'you think we have here, anyway. A little drug action?" Another spray of rain hit his face and his eyes squinted beneath thick eyebrows that were still dark red.

Macrory let out a short huff of wind. "This far out, folks think you get a kick out of Alka-Seltzer Plus. I doubt if even the left-over potheads go for anything stronger than what they can grow themselves. This isn't Miami, for God's sake."

"Maybe a little B&E action? Easiest way to get into a waterfront property and leave no tracks. But, no, you wouldn't have called me if you think that. Poaching?"

"I don't know what the hell we have. You just have the boat. What'ya say we get it in the water." He went back and climbed into the boat, unhooking the ring that held the bow to the trailer.

Logan backed the green truck and boat trailer down the ramp until the boat popped free. Macrory started the motor, backed it away, and brought it around the dock and slid over into the passenger side while Logan parked the truck and trailer. There were no other vehicles or trailers in the lot. Logan climbed into the boat. The motor idled very quietly. As he watched Logan settle at the controls, Tillis asked, "What's got your shorts in a bunch? We've all had a long day."

"Nothing." There was more snap again to the way he said it.

"Is it Karyn?"

"Let's just go, okay?"

"Is she out somewhere? Didn't she come home? Or …"

Whatever Tillis was going to ask next was lost in the roar of the motor as Logan pushed the throttle forward and they pulled away from the dock and started down the lake. Logan stared straight ahead into the storm.

DONNIE SWUNG HIS light along the slope at the very bottom of the dam. The cold here was intense enough to feel all the way through his wetsuit. And the pressure squeezed at him. He couldn't tell what the dark shadows were. They always moved away before his light reached them. Inside he could feel his heart hammering, even harder than the flutter he'd felt on the way out here, and he shivered in a way that had nothing to do with how cold the water felt. He couldn't believe how calm and confident Karyn had seemed about the whole thing. He would've turned back in an instant if she'd shown the least bit of waver.

His light swept over what looked like part of the bow of a boat. He kicked closer, saw it was a broken and water-logged tree. The current shoved at him, tried to slam him toward the base of the dam, now just a few feet away. It reminded him that Karyn was a lot lighter than he was, more subject to these gusts of current. He turned and swung his light back to check on her. Nothing. Where she had been there was only the black of the water.

What the hell? Where was she? His heart seemed to be trying to crawl up inside his throat.

He spun all the way around and kicked furiously, looking for her everywhere. But he saw no sign of her light. He cast his beam toward the dam again, tried to estimate how far a light would go before it couldn't be seen. Visibility looked to be twenty feet or less, maybe as little as ten. It was hard to tell where she might be.

Donnie tried to be logical, and started to kick his way through the dark, making progressively larger circles from where he had last seen her. He gave that a few minutes, but didn't see a trace of her light. Then it occurred to him to let himself go, see where the current would take him. It swept him up, first bounced him toward the dam, then abruptly tossed him to his left, up along the rocky wall of the left cliff that rose fifty feet out of the water above the lip of the dam. He kicked and did an underwater reverse tread that kept him from slamming into the rock. The current lifted him upward from the darkest bottom layer toward a ledge. He was watching for a light, but caught just a glimpse of a scuba suit.

He fought against the current now and pulled himself to the suit. There was no light, but that was definitely a scuba suit. Donnie could make out the tanks and belt as he got closer. But the rubber suit fluttered loose, like a black leaf waving in the murky tossing water near the bottom. He grabbed a lip of the rock wall with one hand to steady himself; with the other hand, he eased his lamp forward to turn the hood of the scuba suit. He blinked, wasn't sure if he'd seen right. He jerked his right hand back and fixed the light on the suit. The hood stayed turned toward him. Inside, covered with a light patina of brownish slime, was the pale staring face of a skull.

TILLIS SPOTTED THE other boat first and reached over to tap Logan's shoulder. He pointed it out, where it swayed back and forth on its anchor line. The downpour had not let up, and sheets of rain came down as hard as before. A bolt of lightning lit up the sky off to their right. Tillis counted three seconds before they heard the thunder. The storm was moving away, but the rain was still coming down. From a distance, with no running lights, the other boat was just a long dark shape on the surface. As their boat got closer, Tillis could see that the anchored boat was empty.

Logan eased close, shifted the motor into idle, and reached to grab the gunwale of the other boat. The current sought to tug the boats apart. So Logan looped a bit of rope from cleat to cleat on the boats, holding them together. "Now what the hell?" he said.

Tillis was standing in his seat and ran a flashlight beam across the inside of the boat, spotting some of the diving gear. "Whoever it is hasn't been too worried about breaking every other law. I doubt if he'd put up a diving flag."

"You think someone's underwater in a mess like this?" Logan swept the beam of his light across the tossing white-capped surface. The beam didn't penetrate far through the swirling sheets of the downpour.

"That or we have a drowning on our hands." Tillis could barely make out the cliff on the nearest shore when the swirling sheets of rain cleared in that direction. When he looked the other way, he could see nothing except rain and the dark.

"There's something about this boat."

Tillis looked back at Logan, whose flashlight beam had fixed on the boat's motor. "What's that?" They were shouting back and forth at each other over the storm's noise.

"I think I know this boat."

"And?"

Before Logan could answer, there was a splash on the other side of the boat, near the stern. Logan's light fixed on the sheen of an oval face mask.

Logan lowered the beam of his light, and the diver tugged off the mask. "Is that you, Donnie?"

"Of course it is."

"I thought this was your father's boat." It sounded to Tillis like Logan had almost said "late" father. The boy glanced at Tillis, who so far hadn't said anything. Logan said, "What the hell're you doing out in this?"

"There's no law against diving at night." The boy's face swung back to Logan. His voice was high, stressed, though he was trying hard to seem calm. Donnie's glance snapped around, covering the lake's surface around them. Rain beat down on the half-foot waves. It had let up a bit, but not enough that it was easy to hear over the noise.

Tillis watched Donnie's head whip about. The boy was a tough one, had weathered his father's death better than Tillis had expected. Donnie had been a football player, and had played hurt a number of times without showing it. But something was all over his face now. Tillis wondered what it might be that was twisting the boy into such knots.

"There *is* against running a boat at night without running lights," Tillis said, not as if he planned to make anything of it more than a bargaining chip for more information.

"You don't know where my daughter is, do you? I thought she might be with you." Logan leaned closer, though not to reach out and pull the boy into the boat.

"Well, Mr. Rainey, to tell the truth …" Donnie stalled, his head still making rapid bird-like movements, checking the surface of the water around them. His voice was nearly a squeak.

Tillis watched Donnie's face. The water was too cool to see if it was flushed, and the rain still beat down. But Donnie sure wasn't his usual stoic self.

"Where the hell's my daughter?"

Logan's yell startled Tillis, who was leaning too close.

"You aren't saying she's still down there, are you?" Logan began tearing off his jacket, ready to dive in if he had to.

Tillis reached to put a calming hand on his shoulder, but Logan swept it away.

Donnie's mouth opened and closed, and he looked all around on the surface, though visibility was limited because of the pouring rain. "I ... I ..."

"Speak up. Now's not the time to go stupid on me," Logan shouted. He wadded his jacket into a lump and threw it down into the boat. The uniform shirt he wore was instantly soaked and pressed to the skin of his fit torso.

Before Donnie could answer, a light grew brighter, heading up toward them. Logan and Tillis both leaned closer to that side of the boat to peer down into the water.

The arm holding the hand light pushed to the surface in a boil of foam and shot all the way out of the water; Karyn Rainey's head and upper body bobbed up after it. She yanked off her mask, tossed it in the boat, her head snapping to Donnie, then to Logan and Tillis. It was Logan at whom she, in the end, yelled. "Daddy, there's a body down there."

TWO

TILLIS CARRIED TWO MORE mugs out from the kitchen to the living area that was still lit only by the dim lights from the foyer and kitchen as well as a soft flicker of flames from the fire. He'd kept the lights low, hoping for an atmosphere that was cozy, even confessional. Donnie and Karyn both huddled in blankets in chairs they'd pulled close to the fire. They held the cups of hot chocolate he'd made for them first.

He reached to hand one of the coffee mugs to Logan, and Logan nodded him in closer. Tillis' head bent close enough so just he could hear.

"You think you ought to clear this chat with the sheriff first? He may want to be part of this."

Tillis gave a curt head shake, straightened up again, and carried his own mug over to the small table by the big leather chair. In deference to it being his place, the others had all made other seating arrangements. The kids had two captains' chairs from the breakfast nook, and Logan had the other leather guest chair.

Karyn and Donnie were staring into the fire. Logan had shifted to staring at the back of Karyn's head, a mixture of concern and suppressed anger wrestling on his face. Tillis blew across the lip of his mug and took a sip of coffee. He didn't know what to make of the look on Logan's face. Tillis had been involved in enough cases where parents had been the powder keg and their kids the fuse. Logan had a temper too. But he was either doing a good job of controlling it, or had something else on his mind. Of all the dark mysteries Tillis had uncovered as a Texas Ranger, the thoughts and emotions of others were the hardest for him to comprehend, even with someone like Logan, whom he'd once thought he knew like a brother.

He looked down at Donnie's bowed head. "You intend to say anything?"

Donnie slowly shook his head. Tillis glanced at Logan, who didn't seem surprised.

Tillis put his mug down and turned to the girl. "You said there was a body down there, Karyn. Tell me about it."

Her head swung toward him, made a hitch as she panned past Donnie's face. She held her blanket close to her neck, her long red hair hanging straight down along the back of the blanket where it could dry.

"I couldn't tell if it was male or female," she said.

"Male." The voice was Donnie's. "I saw it too." He realized he'd spoken in spite of himself. He looked right at Tillis and then his mouth clamped shut and he turned to look back into the fire.

Donnie had the same trait as his father—an inability to speak to anyone without looking directly and intently at the person. It had been an endearing trait in the father, one that led to his becoming mayor. In the boy, it signaled some of the same sincerity, and that he was struggling with knowing more than he was going to let himself say.

"Go ahead, Karyn," Tillis encouraged.

She turned back from Donnie and looked at Tillis. "It was in a black scuba wetsuit, with tanks, everything. But it must've been down there a while. There was no face, just a skull." She gave a delicate shudder that even the blanket and fire didn't prevent.

"What about you, Donnie? Anything to add?"

Tillis watched the boy shake his head again. He could be a stubborn one. His father had been. But Denny had been a good man too. It was too soon to know how Donnie would turn out. His appearance was clean-cut, to the point of seeming chiseled out of marble—his dad, too, had looked far too young for his years. Donnie hadn't said more than a dozen words since they'd gotten the boats off the lake and the kids inside, though sometimes expressions flitted quickly across his face before they were suppressed.

"You're going to have to talk sometime, Donnie. Does any of this have to do with what happened to your dad?"

That had been some crime scene only a week ago. Tillis got there when the Medical Examiner and crew were zipping up Denny and hauling him out to the meatwagon. Blood and the throwdown gun were the only signs on the scarred hardwood floor that there had been a human in Denny's living room moments before. Now, in the dim interior of Tillis' living room, the boy's head lowered, settled into a fix on the flames. But the girl's head flicked toward Donnie, then turned away.

Tillis looked at the girl. Karyn was a lot like her mother, enough to make whatever was causing Logan to twitch in his chair affect him all the harder. Heidi Rainey had been very smart, way too smart to live out here in such a small town, so far from all the things she'd grown up with in Houston. But living in the country, wife of a game warden, must have sounded good once. Twenty-seven years of it had been too much, at least for a woman who discovered she craved something that wasn't out here. Raising Karyn had helped. As soon as the child was old enough not to need her as much, the depression bouts started. Then they got worse. The sheriff's deputies found Heidi in her car, which was still running in the garage, and rags had been stuffed in the cracks along the door to seal it. They'd gotten there in time and had saved her, only for her to die a slower and more painful death weeks later from the cancer. Logan had been a while getting over her death. Karyn might not be over it yet.

Tillis had seen Karyn grow up, the way you do, looking up each time surprised at another spurt of growth or awareness. She had slowly matured into a young lady, and even when she started dating Donnie, Tillis had seen none of the visual transformation that had been so obvious with Selma Granite's girl Sandy, when, at sixteen, she'd started sneaking in to town to spend nights with that gambler Morgan Lane, a man in his forties. Tillis had watched Sandy's tiny face shift from the blossom of youthful innocence to take on a harder, more knowledgeable look within weeks. Everyone knew what was going on over there at Lane's place. But Selma wasn't one to go to the law. The two oldest and biggest of her boys, Rocky and Stone, had gone over to pay Lane a visit. The two boys were locally-feared bullies, each hard-muscled and over six feet. But they both ended up in the hospital, Rocky with a broken collarbone in addition to abrasions, Stone in a near-coma.

"What made you two go out there on a night like this, Karyn? No lights on the boat, diving at night. I know you didn't want to be seen. But in a thunderstorm like that, why, you could've both been killed." Tillis watched the girl.

She glanced toward Donnie, who still forced himself to stare into the fire.

"Go ahead, tell Tillis, honey." There was a burr of emotion in Logan's voice.

She looked from her father to Tillis, who said, "If this has anything to do with Denny Spurlock's death, you've got to help us. That's a murder investigation."

Tillis watched her face, sensed she was getting ready to speak. She kept sneaking glances to Donnie for direction, but got none from him.

"I'm not supposed to …"

"You tell him, and quit stalling around here. This is more serious than you think." Logan's face was flushed pink again, and he leaned forward, while struggling to hold himself back.

Donnie jumped upright to his feet, abrupt and flushed, the blanket falling back onto his chair, and what was left of his hot chocolate splashing out onto the flagstones in front of the fire. His face was pink, and his voice full of emotion. "We don't have to say anything. Don't you let them get to you, Kare. It's…it's…they can throw us in the slammer if they like. Remember what we agreed."

She was looking up at him, and Tillis watched her mouth tighten shut. Normally, Tillis might push. But he'd done enough of these interviews to know when he'd hit the wall. He glanced at Logan, who looked as exasperated as Tillis felt. Tillis shrugged and stood. Well, that was probably that, for now.

Karyn was making a conscious effort not to look at him, and that stung a bit.

Logan got to his feet and came over to stand close to Tillis, so he could speak low enough that neither of the kids could hear him. "What's with you? You're not leaning very hard on that boy at all. Either you think this relates to Denny Spurlock's death or you don't."

For the barest part of a second, Tillis thought he might be kidding. But there was the slow clenching and unclenching of Logan's jaw, as if softly chewing something that was very tough.

"I'm not sure that it does," he said.

"Then why all the questions?"

"It's what I do."

"You sure you're not being soft on him because he's prone to pull the jacked-up kind of stunts you might have done as a kid? Hell, that you'd still do?"

"It did take some brass to dive down there on a night like this."

"Don't forget, he did it with my daughter along. He risked her life too."

Tillis studied Logan's face, watched the set he hadn't seen since some pretty dicey times in Korea. "She's got some brass too, or she wouldn't have gone along—must've inherited it."

"Don't try to butter your way around it. That's my daughter, my only…" The scratch in Logan's throat slowed him until he stopped and glared, his eyes glittering with just a touch extra moisture.

"They got out of there all right. Doesn't that count for anything?" Tillis said.

Logan spun away from him, waved for Karyn to follow. Tillis knew he had been near the place where anyone who wasn't a parent dared not go.

THE HEADLIGHTS OF a pickup that passed Logan heading the other way caught the red-bronze highlights of his daughter's hair. Karyn's face was turned away from him, looking out the truck's passenger window. She'd been silent since they had gotten the Spurlock boat into its winch at the marina and his game warden's boat back onto the trailer. Most of the irritated rage Logan had felt at her not coming home on time had slipped away, and he felt more spent now than anything. The lights of the other truck faded in the rearview mirror.

Off to the right of the road, in the splash of light his headlights made, stood three deer. Logan eased off the gas, and the truck slowed. The two does stayed bent and feeding, the spike buck looked up at the truck. Their hides showed sandy tan to pale brown in the light. "Don't you dart in front of me," Logan said softly. When he was past them, he accelerated back to speed. Their place was seven miles out from town. It had been one of the issues with Heidi, one he wished he'd been more sensitive to earlier. He glanced at his daughter.

"Whatever you're up to, you should tell Tillis. He's investigating a murder, one the two of you should care about more than whatever's going on in your own petty world."

She turned to him, and gave her long red hair a brush back so it was away from her face. "Don't you think, Daddy, that Donnie has a right to care about what happened to his father in his own way?"

"There're other things I care about a lot more."

"Daddy, there's a lot you don't understand about Donnie."

"There's a lot I don't want to understand." He glanced her way.

The look on her face was more patient than her years should have let her possess. The expression, accepting of his faults, but firmly trying to defend her own perspective, made him think of Heidi. Karyn was enough like her mother, especially when calm in the face of his own inner rage, to make him feel as if his insides were piled all the way to his throat with broken glass. It was a pain he'd felt before, and about which he would say nothing.

He looked back at the road, at the steady blips of white lines coming at him down the center. There was nothing else he felt capable of saying for the rest of the way home.

IT WAS DARK in the cab of Tillis' truck, lit only by the eerie green of the dash lights, as he rounded the top of the hill and started down into the sleeping town of Hoel's Dam. The boy, Donnie, sat still as a stone beside him.

The street lights and a gas station or two were all that lit the town of seven or eight thousand. Would it have mattered more, Tillis wondered, if Denny had been the murdered mayor of a bigger town?

Hoel's Dam got its name not from Old Bill Hoel, the richest man in this part of Texas, but from Bill's son Edgar, brother of newspaper publisher Herb Hoel. Edgar had been the engineer assigned to build the dam. He had given it his all—literally.

When the dam was built, fifty-one years ago, Bill had pulled strings to get his young engineer son his first big job. Old Bill had those kind of strings, then and now, as one of the bigger soft-money backers of LBJ in those heady days for Texas politics. It was Edgar's first big commission, and he had run into troubles almost at once. There was a labor flare-up—something about bringing in an all-white mostly German and Irish crew from outside—and when that was settled, the tons and tons of concrete being poured in a muggy series of days in April did not seem to want to take a set. Young Edgar was up nights watching the men work,

trying everything he'd ever heard of to start the slow process
of drying. Something seemed to be wrong with the chemical
mix, and some people even hinted of sabotage. Leaning far
out over the scaffolding one night, Edgar fell into the pouring
cement and became part of the dam. But the cement had,
oddly enough, suddenly shown a willingness to take a set.
The completed dam had become something of a monument
to Edgar. He was in there somewhere yet.

The town was a cozy and small one, the kind where
some folks from the First Baptist Church had erected an un-
authorized sign at the city limits that read, "THIS IS
GOD'S COUNTRY, SO DON'T SPEED LIKE HELL
THROUGH HERE!"

Tillis wove his truck through the dim streets, past the
feed store and down a cul-de-sac to the older Victorian home
where he'd been only a week ago on the murder investigation of Denny Spurlock.

He let the engine idle, and turned to Donnie. The boy,
because he was who he was, had to look directly back at him.
It was the only way any Spurlock could be.

"Did your being out there doing that hare-brained dive
have anything to do with Logan being the one doing the patrolling of the lake more than usual lately?"

Donnie gave Tillis a start by responding, "He's an awfully
intense man, isn't he? Karyn keeps telling me he has a warm
side, but I sure haven't seen it."

"I've seen it. You just have to remember he lost his wife
not too long ago."

There was a noticeable pause in the truck until Tillis said,
"I'm sorry. You lost your own father just a week ago. I
shouldn't have said that."

Donnie looked down, but didn't get out of the truck. There seemed to be more he wanted to share, and Tillis waited, hoping the kid would open up a bit more.

"You're friends with him, aren't you?"

"We were best man at each other's wedding."

Tillis didn't go into the part about their drifting apart, or his moving out to Hoel's Dam with one thought being to try and spend more time with Logan. But he'd come at a bad time. Heidi was dying. When he'd later tried to comfort Logan, his friend had said the cruelest thing anyone had ever said to Tillis. He'd snapped, "You think moving out here's what made your Claire leave, don't you?"

"Mr. Macrory?"

"Yeah?" Tillis realized his mind had drifted a bit.

"You were married once, weren't you?" The boy's wide blue eyes were candid, and fixed on Tillis.

There was a short, stunned silence while Tillis organized his thoughts.

The boy went on, "I mean, what was it like?"

"Being married?"

"Yeah."

"Fine. For a while."

"I … I probably shouldn't be asking you all this, should I?"

Tillis felt himself shrug. But the gesture was probably lost in the dim light of the truck's cab. Who else was the boy going to ask?

"What happened? If you don't mind my asking," Donnie said.

"Won't tell me a thing all night about something that matters," Tillis said, "and now you're a regular chatterbox."

"Sorry."

"It was change."

"What?"

"People change. When you're your age, you don't think you ever will. But we all do."

"That's why she left?"

"She left," Tillis sighed, "because the new her liked someone else more than the new me."

"That'll never happen with Karyn and me."

"I hope you're right, son. I really do." Tillis' head shook in slow doubt as he said it.

"Do … do you miss her?"

Tillis thought about it. He did. But it was odd stuff. He missed the way she kissed. Claire had been a terrific kisser. He recalled the way her eyes fluttered beneath her closed lids as she kissed. He missed that more than the bed, though that came up sometimes in his thoughts too, mostly about waking up to find her there. But he missed talking to her, over dinner or riding together on their trips, though he doubted if he'd ever mentioned it to her.

"A bit," he said.

"You think you'll ever get back together?"

"No." There was a hard ring of finality to the word. "Some things are truly over." But Tillis wasn't thinking about himself. He was thinking about the boy's father, Denny Spurlock, who was as dead as anyone ever gets.

The dark house was a solid, old building, one Denny had spent a lot of time keeping fixed up. He'd gotten a quiet joy from tinkering, even mowing the lawn.

Thinking about Denny, alive like that, made Tillis ponder the resiliency of youth, or whatever it was he was witnessing. If he'd been Donnie's age, he wondered how he would act after his father was killed. Would he be thinking about his love for some girl? Maybe. Who knew what kids think these days?

Donnie looked over at him with that unflinching sincerity that was his own, as well as his father's, trademark. "Don't think from this talk about Karyn that I don't care about what happened to my dad."

Tillis looked at the boy's sincere, wide eyes.

"I do care," Donnie said. "More than you can know. A lot of people, yourself among them for all I know, think he must've been up to something, something no good if it ended in him being killed over it. My way of making sure everything Dad did wasn't a total waste is to carry on for him, maybe even have children that bear his name, the kind of kids he would have wanted as a grandfather." The boy's voice was getting louder, more shrill. "I intend to do that, right after I've done what I need to do. You'll see."

He spun and walked up the dark walkway in the rain that had now settled into a drizzle. His shoulders seemed hunched into a proud and determined set that would have worried Tillis a whole lot more if a bigger worry wasn't getting home without falling asleep at the wheel.

THREE

THE SKY WAS PALE BLUE and Tillis couldn't see the tiniest scrap of cloud in any direction. It was hard to tell there had ever been a storm. Here and there a trickle of moisture was working its way down the sides of the cliffs on either side of the dam. But it was far enough into the day that the heat had burned off much of the effect of the previous evening's storm. Tillis glanced toward the horizon at the far end of the lake, hoping for a cloud of some kind. It was going to be a scorcher.

His white cowboy hat gave his face a bit of shade, but the round silver badge pinned above his pocket glittered in the sun.

A crowd of cars had pulled up on the hills on either side of the dam, and some folks in the finer houses were out on their porches to look down at the half-dozen smaller boats around the red and white rescue boat from where the divers worked. Tillis and Sheriff Eldon Watkins were in one of the sheriff's department boats watching and waiting, but keeping out of the way.

Tillis heard a splashing. His head snapped to Eldon, who stood at the edge of the boat with his uniformed back to them.

"Eldon," Tillis said, "there're all kinds of people up there looking down here. Couldn't you hold that in? Why didn't you take a leak before we got out here?"

Eldon didn't stop. He looked up at the cliffs around the dam. "You ain't the one who drank four cups of coffee."

"Well, maybe they can't see much from way up there." Tillis tried to take some of the snap out of what he'd just said.

"I don't mind 'em lookin'," Eldon said. "I just wish they wouldn't laugh out loud."

"Maybe you could yell up at them that they've got their binoculars wrong way around." Tillis fought to keep from smiling when Eldon glared over his shoulder at him.

Tillis looked across the water to the half-dozen other boats with various official markings that were spread across the area where Donnie and Karyn had spotted the body. The other boats bobbed in the small waves of the chop that a wind gusting to fifteen miles per hour was causing.

"What the hell you suppose those kids were doing out here at night in a storm anyway?" The sheriff looked off at the biggest of the boats, where the divers with their gear were taking turns going down.

"From what I can make out, they want to get married, but can't until Donnie straightens out what happened to his father."

"I wouldn't let anything like that get in the way of me porking some sweet young thing like that."

Tillis said, "I'm glad Logan's in one of the other boats and not here in earshot of your sentiments."

"Yeah, he has a touch of temper, that one, if I remember rightly." Eldon turned to look directly at Tillis. Eldon's rounded and weathered face was topped by short, thinning, bristly hair. The graying hair in his ears and nose was thicker and longer than that on his head. When he squinted in the sun, it gave him a mean look, like a tough kid whose toy had been taken away.

"What's come over Logan anyway, Tillis? You know him as well as anyone. Hell, he used to hunt and fish like the rest of us. He wouldn't even go out dove hunting with me this year. Then that sting operation he set up along the highway nabbed three guys I know all too well. If I'd of seen a ten-point buck like that standing in a field beside a road just waiting to be plugged, I might've taken a shot at it myself. And, if that don't tear a plank off the back barn, he's been patrolling the lake like a madman almost every day. Tore out every unmarked trotline he could find. Cost my nephew Rudy damn near fifty dollars in trotline gear."

"You know unmarked trotlines, especially ones from the shore, are illegal. Beside, I think you know what's bugging him. Just give him some time."

"You weren't too easy on them kids, were you, Till? I mean, no one's accused you of being a bleeding heart, but you probably didn't get out the rubber hose, brass knuckles, nothin' like that." The sheriff's head tilted a quarter to the right, to underscore that he wasn't really being funny.

"They're kids."

"But they still know something. More than you do yet. Let me ask you again, in case you kinda wanted to skip over it. Do you think *you'd* have come all the way out here and done a night dive?"

"It's hard to say what you might do if you were obsessed enough."

"But to come out here in the middle of a goddamn storm, and with no running lights." Eldon shook his head slowly.

"They sure didn't expect anyone else to be stupid enough to come out and find them here then."

"They didn't know you."

"No, I guess they didn't, Eldon." Tillis watched one of the divers come up at the side of the diving boat and gesture urgently. Two other divers shot off the side with a cable in tow. A man on the deck of the boat cranked the spool holding the cable, to send line down with the divers. The diver who had surfaced and started the sudden activity spotted the sheriff's boat and started swimming toward it.

Tillis watched the strong strokes as the diver came closer, and was surprised to note as the diver came in range that it was a woman. He doubted if he could swim as fast as she was going, and she had on full diving gear.

When the diver was all the way to the side of the boat, she grabbed the gunwale with one slim brown hand, then tugged the mask back from her face and held it by the strap as she grabbed the gunwale with both hands. Her face gave Tillis a start. It was a startling, exotic face, and showed some Hispanic background, maybe a touch of Indian too. But it reminded Tillis more of carvings he had seen of Olmec jaguar gods. The lips were thick and sensual, with a slight downward curve at either end. The eyes were a penetrating brown. The nose looked like it had been broken once and set by someone who didn't particularly care how it came out. She looked like she didn't much care either. The face was almost animal-fierce until she spoke.

"Found the body," she said. Then she smiled. "I hope you didn't have one of your big breakfasts, Eldon."

What a smile, Tillis thought. It was like a different person. There was a mischievous twist to the grin, like someone in on a personal joke about which only she knew. This one spends a lot of time alone, too, he figured.

"Oh, yeah, Tillis, this is Gala, my newest deputy." Eldon rubbed an awkward finger along the line of sweat on his forehead and looked out across the water. "I don't believe you've met her yet—only been on six weeks, but turns out she's got more diving experience than all my other deputies combined. Gala, this is the Texas Ranger I mentioned would be hanging around, bugging us."

Her brown eyes flickered an irritated wince at the scrap of flattery. But that was gone by the time she turned back to Tillis.

Tillis ignored Eldon and bent to shake the hand she held out. It was a firm, strong grip. Those penetrating brown eyes laughed back at the puzzled look that must have shown in his glance. She had that damned smile going again, and he couldn't think of a thing to say. She seemed to know just how long it'd been since he'd seen a woman's wet face like that, with the black hair swept back like she'd just come out of the shower. Whatever she knew seemed to amuse the hell out of her, Tillis thought.

"It's been a long time, you think?" he finally managed.

"I'll bet."

"I mean the body. It's been down there quite a while?"

She winked. "This one will hardly smell at all. But he's a sight, all right. Wait'll they get him up. But they've gotta go slow or he'll crumble. He must've been buried down there for a long time, only come loose in a recent storm or the current. Otherwise, he'd have been beaten apart a long time ago."

"What makes you think all that on first glance?" Eldon said. Forensics had never been his long suit, and some of the background new deputies brought out to the county often seemed to surprise, even irritate, him.

"Wait'll you see his gear." She gave Tillis another wink, a slower one this time, and lifted her diving mask and slipped it back on. Then she spun from the boat with a wave of one slim brown hand and dove back in to help.

"What do you…"

Whatever Tillis was going to ask was cut off by the sheriff twisting the key and starting the motor.

Eldon eased the boat around a couple of the floating red with white-stripe flags, over closer to the diving boat, until one of the men on the boat reached out and grabbed the tender Tillis held out. The man, who still wore the bottoms of a diving suit, lashed the tender from the sheriff's boat to a cleat on the diving boat; and then he dropped over a couple of white tubes of polyform boat fenders on cords, so the sheriff's boat could swing around in the current and come to beside the bigger boat, without scratching paint on either vessel.

Eldon climbed over the gunwale into the diving boat, and Tillis followed. They kept out of the way, but were handy when the body came up. The two men working the winch reached for the steel cable and helped lift their load out of the water and swing it over onto the deck.

Gala climbed up the stern ladder, tugged off her mask with one hand, tossed her fins onto the deck, and dripped over to stand beside Eldon and Tillis. Tillis got a momentary satisfaction when he realized she was no more than five-foot-two or so. But she glanced up at him with such a look of penetrating intelligence and, yes, a touch of mockery, that he squashed that thought.

The men stepped back away as they lifted the cable clear from what they had brought up. Tillis took a step forward and bumped into Eldon. They both stared at the aged black diving suit that was slumped over the rust-covered metal chest that was half the size of a footlocker, but looked much stronger. The shapes of loose bones were visible under the black rubber drape of the suit, and in places a brownish, moss-covered bone stuck out from the suit that seemed barely able to hold together.

"Good Lord," Tillis said. "That's World War II diving gear, or maybe Korean conflict at best."

"And would bring a good price in some antique shop if it wasn't in the shape it's in," Gala said.

Eldon took a step back and bumped into Tillis again. When Tillis glanced at him, the sheriff's face had washed whiter than usual. His mouth hung open a half-inch, and he seemed to be trying to swallow but had forgotten how.

"This one's going to be harder'n hell to ID," Gala said. She leaned closer to gently lift the hood. The mask must have long ago been lost.

"I don't know about that." Tillis still stared at the sheriff.

Gala followed where he was looking. "What's the matter with you, Eldon? I wouldn't have figured you for the squeamish type. This one's been dead too long to smell. Hell, it might've even happened before you were sheriff."

"Who is it?" Tillis asked. Gala looked at him, then realized he was talking to Eldon. Tillis nodded toward the sheriff and said, "He knows."

Eldon Watkins wasn't looking at either of them, or what was left of the diver, for that matter. He stared off at the sheer wall of the cliff that went up from the dam on one side of the lake. A few yucca plants and some yellow blooming prickly pear cactus dotted the otherwise blank wall of stone.

His words came out like a hollow echo. "There's only one person that could be—Hugh Spurlock."

"Denny's father?" Tillis asked.

"No, Denny's older brother."

"Better give me the whole story." Tillis sighed, looking over at the limp diving suit.

"Lemme check something first." Eldon went over to the

body and pushed one of the divers to one side. He lifted the suit with a careful finger and was staring at the box.

"That'd better wait until we get this to the lab, hadn't it?" Tillis said. He'd eased up to Eldon's side, and Gala came along up closer with him.

"Get me something to have a go at opening this box." Eldon glanced at one of the divers, then held out an expectant hand, as if he were a surgeon waiting for a scalpel. He stared at the lock on the box, and the double length of chain that had rusted to it. The diver hustled down into the boat's hold.

"I think we should wait, Eldon." Tillis looked from Eldon to Gala, but both still stared at the box.

"Hell, he's been down there since before the damned flood. Give your city scientific crap a break for a second here."

"What's that his arm's stuck in?" Tillis asked.

Eldon looked up at him, and Tillis hadn't often seen this level of intensity in him before. "That, young man, is a bear trap."

It was clear to Tillis then. He looked at Gala and realized she'd already figured it out. "How long ago you think this happened?" The words came out stilted and slow, the way Tillis felt.

The bear trap had been set on the metal box and held in place, concealed to one side, by a double wrap of chains. When the diver had swum down to it in the dim light of water that deep, he'd grabbed the box to bring it up and had been grabbed by the bear trap. The whole thing was too much weight to take to the top, or it'd been held onto the bottom, chained to a wooden boat or something that'd long ago rotted away.

It was an awful, awful way to die, Tillis thought, trapped down there and waiting for the air to run out. He moved closer and saw the cuts through the suit and across the bone he expected and feared he'd find. Near the end, the diver had made the final try. He pulled his diving knife and got to the worst of it in a last-ditch try. He sawed at the arm, trying to cut it loose from the box. But it'd been too late. He was out of air, or energy, or something. Anyway, he'd been down there on the bottom for a long time.

"There's a local yarn, goes back a ways," Eldon seemed to be talking to make idle conversation while waiting, "that Hank Spurlock died out on this lake, went down with his boat."

"When was this?" Tillis figured he could play along. He glanced at Gala, who watched the sheriff.

"Oh, forty years ago, or so. Well, when young Hugh here—at least I'm pretty sure we'll find that that's who this is—had wrapped up his play in WW II, with a silver star and a couple of purple hearts, and diving skills he'd gotten over there somewhere doing the kind of diving those kind of guys do, he took his act on to Korea, the same as you and Logan. Only he was there from Pusan to Chosin, in the thick of the worst of it, and was one of the ones who got a taste and had to keep at it."

"Of killing?" There'd been a few flare-ups when Logan and Tillis were there, though it'd been years later, but he left that alone.

"Of whatever it is in war that gets under the skins of some men that young. Hell, maybe it was the camaraderie, though I doubt it. When Hugh came home, he was full of all that training and an adventurous itch. He was somebody nobody wanted to mess with, that's for sure."

One of the divers brought over a crowbar, and Eldon bent over the box and used it to pop the chains in half. They parted with brittle, sharp cracks. He levered one end of the crowbar between the sides of the box at the lock and twisted, shoved, then pushed down hard. The lock separated with a softer, tearing crunch.

"What about the father?"

"He was missing, like I said. Everyone thought he'd gone down, boat and all, out here. There were even one or two witnesses who claimed they could see through the storm, though, truth is, I doubt if either could see their hands in front of their faces the way everyone talks about that storm. Why, some folks even said …"

"Can we get back to Hugh and Hank?"

"Well, excuse me all to roller skate. The short version, if you're in such a damned hurry, is that Hank was missing and Hugh spent a lot of time trying to find out where he'd gone. Then Hugh disappeared."

"Until now."

"Sure looks that way."

Eldon bent forward, and levered the lid up off the box. Tillis and Gala leaned forward too, and the other divers crowded in. The inside of the box was filled with water to the top.

"Get some of that water outta there."

The box was too heavy to tilt, so the divers bailed at first, then tilted it to let the water pour out from one corner.

"Careful there. Just the water." Eldon was leaning over, getting in the way more than helping. One of his boots and the pants cuff got wet, but he didn't seem to notice.

The divers set the box back down, and the sun was bright enough to poke through as the muddy water settled. Eldon reached in and grabbed at a handful of what looked like loose gravel. He lifted it, looked closer, then tossed all of it back into the box but one of the stones. He rubbed it at his shirt, looked closer and frowned.

"What is it?"

He turned to Tillis and gave the stone a casual flip overboard. Tillis watched the stone plunk into the rippling blue surface and disappear. He repeated, "What is it?"

"Gravel. Just gravel."

"Hugh Spurlock died over a box of gravel?"

"That's sure enough what it looks like."

THE RIDE IN to Fearing, the county seat of Kiowa County, was a long one for Tillis. Eldon had decided to have Rudy, one of his deputies, tow back the department boat and had invited himself along. He sat in the passenger seat, slumped down and staring ahead, apparently deep in thought, and such a thing was possible, despite the rural look and manner he cultivated. Tillis drove.

The radio speaker below the dash cracked and a voice came through. "Ranger Macrory?" It wasn't the usual voice he got on the radio.

Tillis reached for the speaker and pressed the button on its side. "Go ahead."

"Is Sheriff Watkins with you?"

"Yes."

"I'd like to speak with him, if I might."

Tillis passed over the speaker to the sheriff. "Must be something warm, for you to be tracked down this way."

He shrugged. "New dispatcher. Still a bit over the top," he said. He keyed the mike. "Go ahead."

"Eldon? That you?"

"Yeah. What you got?"

"There's a fellow here to see you, a Don Cinco Hernandez. He says it's *muy importante*. That's all the lingo I can make out from him so far."

"You need to pick up a bit of Spanish, or get him on your wavelength." When Eldon let go of the key this time, he grinned over at Tillis.

The radio voice crackled on, "I doubt our wavelengths are going to connect at this moment. I could use a hand from Gala, if you can't get right to him."

"She's busy, but should be heading there soon. Do what you can. Use that investigative mind of yours."

"And in the meanwhile, you can get that growth on your neck checked."

"What growth?" One hand went involuntarily up to feel each side of his neck.

"I mean your head."

Eldon sighed, waited a tick or two for his cheeks to get a lighter pink, before he keyed the mike. "Tell him to cool his heels a bit. I'm headed that way."

He handed the mike back to Tillis, who glanced his way. "Breaking in a new dispatcher is always a treat. This one's still a bit rough on the edges. Been out of society a while, and I'm easing her back in."

"Why that's unusually decent and altruistic of you, Eldon."

"Humpf."

"What happened to the dispatcher you did have, that good-looking Betty Lou?"

"That's just the thing. Wife got a glimpse of her."

ESBETH WALTERS SAT and quietly stewed in her chair in front of the sheriff's department radio. Heat was rushing in small, pulsing waves up the sides of her neck. On her very first day on the part-time job, with just enough instruction for her to get her bearings about everyday procedures, she'd been left alone, high and dry in the command module. It made her feel responsible, nervous, and, for the first time in quite a long spell, inadequate.

Not even having enough time herself to fully unpack in her new home didn't bother her as much as the feeling of being out of her usual comfort zone. She'd not lived out here long enough to get a glimmer of anything going on in the town, and Eldon sure hadn't helped with that. She was more sure than not that Eldon's hiring her had been to keep track of her and to keep her out of the way, rather than to use any of those detecting skills he'd been so full of flattery about, when he'd said she was able to give a jaybird the first two pecks and still beat it to the bug.

She knew no more about Denny Spurlock's death than she'd read in the papers, and now it seemed there was another body to deal with, about which she knew less. Coming to a new community made it harder for her to catch the pulse and rhythm of the place, its elemental hum that, when off-beat or out-of-tune, told her where to start nosing. In Austin, big as the city was, she'd had more of that. Here she was a virtual outsider, knowing no more about the locals than she did the fellow sitting so meek yet so full of dignity in the chair along the wall.

In a small town or rural county area, there is one person— or even two people, most often male in Texas—who blatantly, or behind-the-scenes, runs the town. With the mayor dead and no other prominent citizen to consider, Esbeth hadn't quite figured out how things worked out here in her newly-adopted hometown. All she could be sure about was that the person wasn't this pleasant *paisano*-looking gentleman seated along the wall.

Occasionally she'd seen people who carried the entire history of their race carved on their faces, and this small but stately specimen was one of them. In her orienting trips around town, she'd detected some sense that prejudice was alive and well in the area, people with dirt beneath their own nails still willing to use not-so-nice words, like "beanos" or worse, to refer to the Hispanics in town, to complain that "they" had taken jobs in auto repair garages and doing lawns that could just as well go to others.

She wasn't one of those so politically-correct types herself that she'd made the quick leap to saying "Latino" instead of "Hispanic." All that made as much sense to her as the fellow who'd studied Latin because he planned to visit Latin America. There just seemed something wrong and mean-spirited about name-calling, ever, though she wasn't without stain herself, especially when driving. Maybe it was guilt, she reasoned, that makes some people want to do right.

There weren't all that many people like this kindly fellow in the town, and even fewer blacks. She supposed many of the smaller towns had settled into demographics like this, while the larger cities provided far more opportunity for anyone whose skin was the color of a worn saddle, the way this man's was.

If faces could talk, his could sure tell a story. He was no taller than Esbeth, which put him somewhere around five-foot-three, but his upright bearing, even when seated, made him seem much taller. What a study in contrasts. He looked humble, but passionate: a servant perhaps, but someone accustomed to leading. It was an odd mix. His clothes didn't help the confusion either. The boots and pants could be those of a common laborer, but the shirt was of an uncommon, white, silky material. The hat seemed new as well, perhaps worn especially for a meeting with the sheriff. The wrinkles on the mahogany of his weathered face placed him at Esbeth's age or beyond, yet the glittering twinkle in those dark eyes could have come from a man in his twenties.

He saw her looking at him and spoke. *"Abuelita?"*

"No. I'm not even a *señora.*" She tried to take the edge off that with a low chuckle. You couldn't teach high school in Texas for over thirty years without picking up *some* Spanish, no matter what she'd shared with Watkins. She said, *"E tu? Un abuelito?"*

"Sí." His smile was slow to come, as if there weren't many of them. But when it came, it was the sun breaking through the storm clouds.

He started to reach for his wallet, then stopped. The smile slid away.

"Fotografías?" she said.

"No. Lo siento."

That was the last he said for a while, which was just as well for Esbeth, who'd used up about all the Spanish she had, asking him if he had photos of his grandchildren.

He seemed to know that too from her faltering efforts. He sat quiet, waiting, like all the patience in the world in one place.

When he did look her way, those brown eyes—sad, yet with sparks of low fire—looked at her in ways she couldn't begin to understand, yet another mystery in a county where, too often so far, an irritating number of matters felt out of touch or over Esbeth's head.

The worst of it was that in her former dealings with Eldon and Tillis, the former schoolteacher side of her had resisted their efforts to pick her brain by saying, "If I told you everything, you'll never learn anything." Now she was on the other side of that, and it didn't feel all that pleasant, she had to admit.

She got busy with two calls of locals just being nosy and some radio traffic for a few moments. When she looked over in his direction again, he was gone, the chair empty, as if he'd never been there.

ELDON CROSSED HIS arms and looked out the window on his side of the truck, making a point of not talking for a few miles. There were times, Tillis recalled, when Eldon could be a veritable cornucopia of borrowed wit and country-flavored sayings. But somehow, he thought, it was occasions like these, where Eldon shared long stretches of hard silence, that seemed to give him any real character.

"What was supposed to be in the box?" Tillis finally asked, as they came into the outskirts of Fearing traffic.

Eldon sighed. "Diamonds."

"Diamonds? From where?" Tillis was picturing the faceted and glittering pile of stones he'd seen once, spilled out from a small pouch onto a black velvet surface, after the loot from an upscale Houston jewelry store robbery had been recovered.

"Native Texas diamonds."

"There aren't any diamonds in Texas."

"Yeah, you think there ain't such an animal. Well, that's what I thought too," Eldon said. He frowned and kept his face pointed straight ahead.

That was the last Tillis got from the sulking sheriff until

they pulled into the gravel lot by the sheriff's department and jail building. Eldon's dark mood seemed to lift a bit as he unlocked the door and they slipped into the air-conditioning. There he had the familiar setting of his office and staff surrounding him.

Tillis had been to the building often enough before. The walls were dark green up to four feet off the floor and then were light green the rest of the way up and across the ceilings. Someone in the administration before Eldon's had read that green was a relaxing color. The furniture was a mix of gray metal and older oak mismatches that filled the single room where the sheriff's desk was off against the wall in the corner. There was a window where, if he chose, the sheriff could lean over in his chair just a bit and look out enough to catch a corner of the parking lot.

In the middle of the room were two other desks the deputies shared when they needed to do reports after their shifts. They were usually out moving around the county, so there wasn't much call for sitting around in the department's office. Though if any of that *did* need to be done, Eldon preferred to do it himself.

The sound of the dispatcher's radio squawked softly as they came into the open office room from the long hallway. A couple of things were different from the last time Tillis had been here. Where the air had smelled of stale smoke before, now it was clear, with perhaps a touch of air freshener. The other thing was the shape of the woman who sat at the dispatch desk with her back to them as they came in. This time there were rounded shoulders on a squat, low body, topped by a round puff of white hair.

Eldon caught Tillis' stare, and the sudden hitch in his

steps. His grin had none of the mischievousness of Gala's. It was a grin that confirmed he enjoyed seeing Tillis squirm, especially when the woman turned on her squeaking oak swivel chair to look at them.

"Where's this Don Cinco, this fella you were in a lather for me to see?" Eldon asked Esbeth.

"Why, it's Esbeth Walters," Tillis said.

The rounded face of the seventy-two-year-old former reluctant amateur detective looked back at him, the head tilted an inch to the right and the smile more polite than sincere.

"How're you, Mr. Macrory? Still Rangering, I take it." She turned to Eldon, "He took off. Skedaddled. Gone like a speckled bird. He said something about a banana, or that could have been *mañana.*"

"You get you one of them there Spanish phrase books, Esbeth, and you pick up a few strings of words. Or get a boost from Gala. Might come in handy sometime."

Tillis was as surprised by the strained politeness coming from the sheriff as he was by finding Esbeth Walters, of all people, working as dispatcher.

Esbeth wore jeans and a white blouse. Tillis was mildly glad she was not required to wear a uniform. On one corner of her desk was a pile of newspapers, among them copies of the *New York Times,* to which Tillis recalled Esbeth subscribed by mail. There was a story above the fold, Tillis could see, about Senator Martinez, the only congressional former member of Delta Force, saying the U.S. still needs a domestic counter-terrorist squad, in response to the FBI saying the country already has what it needs. There was no one like Esbeth for wanting to keep up on every detail of crime or law that might in some way connect with something in which she was nosing around.

"Kinda surprised, ain't you?" the sheriff said. Eldon wore a smirk at Tillis' apparent discomfort as he eased himself into his own swivel chair, and hooked a straight-backed chair with the toe of one boot and slid it toward Tillis by way of invitation.

"Always humble and ready to take an occasional steer from anyone who knows more than I do." Tillis managed a smile toward Esbeth as he sat. She was still turned in her chair, watching him.

"I want you two to get along now," Eldon said.

"Why shouldn't we?" Tillis nodded at Esbeth.

"I don't know. She kinda helped you out of a spot once. I know you got a reputation as being willing to take help from whichever direction it comes. But some folks aren't as good at that as they say."

"I'm fine with it," Tillis said. He tried to make the words sound not too mechanical.

"I hired her 'cause she has a good nose for this sort of thing, and she's a good dispatcher too." Eldon gave the matter a curt nod.

"Not to mention, as I just learned, that his wife made him fire Betty Lou. I was the least threatening person out there willing to take the job," Esbeth said.

Tillis had seen Betty Lou, and had reason to recall that Eldon had described her once by saying, "I'd rather watch her walk than eat fried chicken."

There was a squawk from the radio and Esbeth turned to tilt closer and catch the string of numbers.

Eldon's smile slipped a tiny bit. "Now what the hell?"

"Just means her location's at headquarters now." Esbeth turned away from the ten-code list she'd tacked to the wall earlier and reached for a button on the corner of the desk. There was a buzz, then the sound of the outside door opening.

"Damn numbers. I used to know 'em back about thirty-two years ago, when I was a rookie just out of academy. I don't know why she asked the deputies to try using them."

"If it helps, some of those ten-numbers are different from department to department. Only a few are APCO standard." Tillis was sorry he'd said anything at all, as soon as he was done. He watched the flicker of color wash across Eldon's pale face.

"No, it doesn't help."

"Oh, let me have my rookie moment," Esbeth said. She was turned back around in her chair now, facing them. "Besides, it confuses some of the nosy locals, sitting around listening to the police bands on scanners."

Eldon frowned at her and said, "I didn't hire someone with your experience to have rookie moments."

"What's the matter with you, Eldon? You sure are all a'grump today." Gala came through the hallway and walked across the room. She was in uniform. Her black hair was short and swept back from her tanned-looking face, which still had more than a bit of a feral, feline look to Tillis. But he found it exotic. She eased herself onto the corner of a desk, and it was also hard not to notice that she had the athletic thighs of an ice skater or ballet dancer. Tillis forced himself to focus on Eldon.

"I'd have thought you'd be pleased," she said. "You took swift, decisive action, and soon the reporters'll be here from all over, to share with your voters the level of competence you bring to the job." She shared another of those mischievous smiles.

"Speaking of which, that reporter Thirsty Mills called."

Esbeth glanced over at a note she had on the log. "He wants you to call him back."

Eldon glanced at the clock. "Hell, if I was of a notion to call him, it's almost noon. Who's to say that he'd be sober at this hour?"

"I'd be careful of underestimating him," Esbeth said. "He was Ivy League once."

"Yeah, and I was young and had hair once," Eldon said.

Gala frowned. She had a few more laugh lines than frown lines on the toffee tan of her face, but both seemed to work equally well when called upon. "You really are a regular grump today. Why aren't you more chipper?"

"Because I've had a can of worms opened on me I'd have as soon kept closed."

"This business about the diamonds?" Tillis said.

"What diamonds?" Gala said, close enough to be an echo. She leaned forward and her brown eyes glittered.

"There are no diamonds, never were any diamonds. I'm telling you, that's my last word on the subject."

"I don't think so, Eldon." The Ranger's eyes narrowed. "You're better at telling tales than this."

"Hell, the statute of limitations probably ran out on Hugh Spurlock's death."

"There's no statute on murder. Even if there was, Denny's death is recent enough. If I can show the glimmer of a connection …"

Gala and Esbeth's eyes tracked the two men like a crowd watching a tennis match. Tillis realized he had stood all the way up, and Eldon was halfway out of his chair.

They both stopped at the same time, and slowly straightened.

"I think," Eldon said, "it being lunchtime and all, that you and me oughta slip over to the Bluebonnet Cafe for some biscuits and gravy. What d'you say, Tillis?"

"I guess I could stand some lunch." He watched disappointment show on the faces of both women.

"You can't just go off and leave us hanging like that, Eldon," Esbeth said.

"You will find, Esbeth, that in fact I can, and that I often will." He spun on one boot heel and led the way to the door.

"You can't do that," Gala called after him.

He spun and stared at her. "Do what?"

"It's not right to cut your staff out like that, Eldon. It's not fair."

Eldon grinned at her. "The fair comes to town once a year, and you can always tell when that is, because you'll spot the Ferris wheel." He turned and started out again.

Tillis followed. He didn't know what to make of the look on Gala's face as he went past her this time.

He heard her mutter, "Men."

But her frown shifted to stark, open, brown-eyed surprise when Tillis winked at her this time.

THE MEN HAD been out of the room a good five minutes, with Esbeth quietly grumbling to herself, before Gala looked up from the report on which she was working. "What's up with you anyway, Esbeth?"

"What do you do when you're not working, Gala?"

Wow. Esbeth watched Gala's face shoot through a gamut of emotions, starting with startled and settling on defensive. Gala's eyes widened, alert, a little concerned. Then they narrowed just enough to form a mild threat. For a few seconds her face took on a nearly Asian cast, inscrutable.

Esbeth could hear the slow, regular tick of the large-faced clock on the wall, and a ripple of static that came from the radio's speakers. She gave a quick shake of her head. "I mean, you're almost as new to this place as I am. Have you found anything to do? I mean, anything that makes you feel more connected to this place?"

"Oh, you mean volunteer work?" The white teeth of her smile were striking against the tanned tone of her skin.

"Like that. Helping pick up trash in parks, reading to kids, helping old folks—I mean, folks even older than me."

"You're just feeling a bit cut out ... because Eldon's not sharing. You thinking being involved in the community could help more?"

"Couldn't hurt." Esbeth paused, watched Gala relax just the tiniest bit in her chair.

"I know how you feel," Gala said. "I was a bit out of sorts myself when I first got here. But, you'll settle in."

"I miss some of the people I knew, even the ones who didn't care much one way or the other about me. And, I miss Carol Bean's Mean Baking Machine—best pie in Austin and only a block and a half from where I used to live."

"I expect Eldon knows a pie place or two. The rest will come with time, Esbeth."

Esbeth nodded, then remembered. "There was a fellow in here to see the sheriff, a Don Cinco. You know him?"

"Oh, what did he want?" It sounded casual, but wasn't.

"I guess just to be listened to. Wanted to see the sheriff. He couldn't speak much English at all. Well, no English that

I could tell. I know only a handful of words in Spanish, and that's including *Como frijole?* How you bean?"

Gala's smile shifted to her mischievous grin. "He comes in here again, you let me know, Esbeth. I'll help you with him."

Esbeth took the full measure of the suppressed eagerness on Gala's face. "Okay," she said. "I'll do that."

FOUR

ELDON PLOPPED INTO ONE side of the booth and reached for a menu, even though he'd already said what he intended to order. One of the waitresses, Phyllis this time, came over and slid down two ceramic mugs of coffee with the spoons already in them. Tillis gave his head a half-shake, while Eldon still looked down at the menu. Phyllis put her pad back into the front pocket of her apron and shoved the pencil up into her red-dyed hair. She hustled off to another couple of rancher types who had just sat at a table by the door.

"Why'd you have to go and hire her?"

"Who?" Eldon looked up from the menu.

"Esbeth Walters."

Eldon rubbed a finger across his upper lip, perhaps to mask the beginning of a smile. He'd squawked about Esbeth too once, about her even thinking she might help a trained professional like a county sheriff. The trouble with that was that she *had* delivered the goods, and saved both himself and Tillis some embarrassment. He'd been as reluctant then as Tillis to show any appreciation, though now it seemed to tickle him a bit that the idea of hiring her irritated Tillis. He worked most of the expression off his face and said, "She moved out here, got some kind of little retirement place or other. Sure, she's no spring chicken, but she's good at this kind of stuff. Hell, you should know, though you probably resent any kind of help makes you look like you need help, no matter what you always say about yourself on that subject."

"It's not that. Finding her here and working for you isn't what's rattling my cage."

"What is it, then?"

Phyllis came back to the table, and they stopped long enough to order. Eldon ordered his biscuits and gravy, a breakfast dish, but you could get breakfast all day here. Tillis went for the liver and onions and some deep-fried okra.

As soon as Phyllis had turned and started off toward the kitchen, Tillis leaned closer across the table. "Tell me about the diamonds, Eldon."

Eldon got that country-sly look he could do stretched across his face. He leaned back and lifted his coffee cup. Before he took a sip, he said, "Catch me up on what you got on Denny Spurlock's murder first."

"I've got the tip about the pawn shop."

"You got that from Thirsty Mills, a reporter on that Hoel's Dam version of a *Daily Planet,* a newspaper I wouldn't use to wipe myself with half the time."

"Except when you're running for re-election," Tillis said. He caught the twist of Eldon's mouth and skipped to the subject of the pawn shop. "Well, the place is missing a few pages from its register. Thirsty even said he had it from a source he refused to name that assault weapons had been sold out the back door at night from there."

"But you got nothing about any 7.65mm throwdown gun being sold out of there, or bought in the first place?" Eldon pinched the tip of his nose with thick, blunt fingers and thumb.

"Nothing on that but vagueness from Tony, the owner, or

James, the thirty-year-old kid who works most of the hours at the place. Not to mention the fire that started at the place and could have eradicated anything like evidence."

"You know, Tillis, when you start talking about someone who's thirty as a kid, it kinda says something, don't it?"

"Are you going to just ignore that fire?"

"Hell, that could be one of them seren—dinkity sort of things Esbeth likes to talk about."

"I believe you mean serendipity."

"Anyway, that fire went out on its own-hardly did no damage. You could have all the evidence you want there, if there was any. I think your boss, Lieutenant Comber, came up with that piece of busy work for you, said stake the place out, so you're staking it out. I got no beef with you Rangers about that."

"You want this or not?"

"Oh, go ahead." Eldon drank the rest of his cup and waved the mug over his head until Phyllis spotted him.

"That's all of it. I staked the place out for fourteen hours. Nothing."

"And you think that's worth trading over."

Phyllis filled their cups and scurried off.

"I'm not asking for a trade, Eldon. I want to know what you know." Tillis sat very still on his side of the booth and let no emotion show on his face.

Eldon glanced around at the other tables, then leaned back and looked at Tillis with what the Ranger thought was a brooding scowl. The sheriff had just tilted forward and looked ready to speak when Phyllis came hustling to the table with their plates. She futzed around, filling their coffee mugs before leaving. Eldon tore one of his biscuits apart and poured gravy across it. He was adding pepper when Tillis prodded again. "Eldon."

The sheriff shoveled in a bite and chewed. He looked up at Tillis, and held up one finger. He seemed to chew in anger, which shifted to a satisfied smile in spite of himself. When he finished the bite, he glanced around again and leaned a bit closer. He waved the gravy-covered end of his fork while speaking. "I'd hoped this whole damned thing was all done with, that we'd heard the last of it. It'll crop up every now and then, and I'm always glad to see it go to bed again for a few years."

"You're going to have to be more specific than that, Eldon."

The sheriff took another bite and worked on that. With a partially-filled mouth, he said, "You better eat while your food's warm."

For a while they both ate, Tillis stealing looks at the sheriff, who seemed able and happy to focus on his food. The piggish glee of Eldon eating his rasher of bacon was nearly enough to make Tillis think cannibal.

But, for all his enthusiasm and size, Eldon had very good table manners, for the most part, and even had a dainty way of dabbing at his mouth with a napkin between bites. There were some people Tillis had watched dine, who should be made to spend their eternity paying for their ways by having to watch themselves eat. He was grateful Eldon wasn't one of those. He was tolerable to watch, though by no means a joy.

Eldon wiped up the last bit of gravy with a crumb of biscuit and finally pushed away his plate, which looked empty and sparkling enough to have just been washed. Tillis was done with his meal as well. Eldon waited until Phyllis had filled their coffee mugs and whisked away their empty plates before leaning forward on the table, his thick forearms rested against the table's granite surface and his hands half-curled into contented fists.

Eldon tilted his head an inch to the right. "You moved out here to Hoel's Dam what? Four or five years ago?"

"Yeah, about that."

"You maybe only heard a scrap or two of this, but quite a while back, we had a kind of mess out here that I don't want to get started again." Two rows of flesh wrinkled into lines on Eldon's forehead.

"You've got two bodies in a little over a week. I'd say that's a mess too."

"Hell, one's too stale to count," the sheriff said.

When Macrory started to respond, Eldon cut him off with a frown.

Tillis made a brisk hand-sweep for Eldon to go ahead, though the gesture looked more irritated than he intended.

"Okay. Okay." Eldon leaned another half-foot closer. "A few years back we had us a real cow-teat-in-the-wringer tango around here—the kind I don't want to repeat. It happened before I was sheriff, and, like I said, way before you were around here. But it was sure a hornet's nest I don't want you or anyone else stirring up. Got me?"

"I thought it was a can of worms."

"Don't patronize me. I can mix my metaphors with the best of them, and play the country fool of a sheriff while doing it." There was a bit of an aggressive edge to Eldon's otherwise cheerful smile.

"Sorry."

"That's a start." Eldon lifted his coffee cup, found he'd already drained it. He glanced around for the waitress.

Tillis sat watching Eldon try to do anything but tell this story. It would have to be a good one.

Eldon looked back at him, his expression almost embarrassed and awkward this time. "It's about the diamonds."

"The ones not native to Texas."

"I *know* that. But you have to remember that all this happened over forty years ago. Things were different then. We didn't have this Internet, a hundred TV stations, and books and magazines on everything but weaving armpit hair."

Tillis nodded in what he hoped was an encouraging way.

"Anyway, the dam being built, and the lake covering up farming and cattle-ranching land the way it did, changed a lot of things around here. For ten years or so, things were kind of in an upheaval, until everyone got settled again. And just about the time they did, ten years or so after the dam went in, there started to be talk of diamonds being found. Hank Spurlock was the one finding them, or so everyone said. His wife, Sadie, was a natural gossip. Hank himself wasn't much of a talker. His boys could vouch for that, if either of them was still around."

Eldon paused, seeming to remind himself that it was Hank's two sons who were found dead in the past few days.

"If it wasn't for Donnie, that'd be the end of the Spurlock clan, wouldn't it?" Tillis said, more to be making conversation than anything else.

"Yeah, and that's a big deal, because families are sure enough clannish out in these parts, and in their own strange ways. Hank Spurlock was one of the worst. Don't know what he'd say about young Donnie courting a girl who's not related to another Spurlock."

"And you say Hank's the one who allegedly found diamonds?"

"So the word trickled out from Sadie. It does sound a bit like tall tales on the Texas frontier, don't it? But the trouble it started was real enough."

"Where was he finding the diamonds?"

"That was part of the big secret. Hank never said. Didn't even tell his wife, though we know now why he didn't."

"Why's that?" Tillis wondered if Eldon was making the story hard to follow on purpose.

"Because of all the trouble."

Tillis sighed. "What trouble?"

"Well, you let the hint of a thing like that get out around here, and it could be like those tales of the Lost Dutchman mine area in Arizona, or Jim Bowie's lost silver mine here in Texas."

"I'm afraid I don't know much about them."

"Every few years someone thinks they've got wind of one of those and starts digging around where they shouldn't."

Tillis didn't want to interrupt any flow. But by now he was beginning to suspect that Eldon might be the worst story-teller he'd ever heard. "What trouble?" he said again.

"You know how a rumor is, especially about something like a gold mine, or, in this case, a diamond one. Those kind of rumors had people stampeding across America to California once, and Colorado, and even Alaska. Silver had them turning cartwheels in Nevada, even a bit here in Texas."

"But diamonds? Here?"

"It don't matter if it was real, or if it wasn't, Till. Don't you see that? It had people laying for each other and family stirred up against family."

"You make it sound like the Civil War."

"It was more like the Johnson County War."

"Where ranchers battled each other and hired guns were brought in?"

"Or, the Hatfield-McCoy feud."

"Like you say, this was quite a while before I ever lived out here. I've heard a historical ripple or two, but never much more than that."

"That's kind of the way the community'd like to leave it, Tillis. Are you getting that through to that thick Ranger skull of yours?"

"Maybe that decision isn't yours and the community's to make. You ever think of that?"

"You know, I don't really have to tell you all this."

"Eldon, we've worked together a number of times, especially since Claire and I moved out here, and you never stonewalled me before."

The look on Eldon's face as he leaned back in his side of the booth showed more than he intended. It seemed to make light of anyone whose wife would leave him. Eldon was too much the politician to normally share so much. As soon as he realized what Tillis must be seeing, the look flickered away from his face.

Once he had his stone-man face back on, Eldon stared at Tillis another minute, then sighed and leaned closer again and took on what he seemed to think was a storytelling tone. "First of all, you have to remember that when everyone lived down there in the valley that's flooded over with Lake Kiowa now, they were cut off from the rest of the world."

"And?"

"Like I hinted at before, there was quite a bit of inbreeding going on down in the valley in those days. Hell, it was bad as Dalmatians."

"What do you mean, Dalmatians?"

"You know, how they've been inbred so much they have twisted personalities. Some of the people around here got like that, only the people didn't end up with a movie."

"You're forgetting about Deliverance."

Eldon's face took on his nasty scowl again. "Don't make me regret telling any of this to you."

"Okay. Sorry. Go ahead." There was a little friendly antagonism in any of Eldon's professional relationships. He seemed to respect other people best when they dished it back and forth with him, the way Esbeth did. But Tillis knew you had to be careful to know how far to go.

"You know what I mean." Eldon's thick, stubby fingers swept through his short-cut hair as he shifted in his seat and looked around at the other people in the restaurant. "We still got a few folks who resemble each other too much, and there's the recessive chin trait."

Tillis could have commented that Eldon's chin was a bit recessive, at least one or two of them. But he kept quiet and looked interested.

"In addition to the few clannish families around here that didn't socially mix or intermarry much, there's also the fact that everyone likes the idea of getting rich quick, too. As soon as there was any talk of real money, the sides, that were already getting far too rigid, lit into each other."

"Over diamonds, you say," Tillis said. "Anyone end up dead? Seems like the scraps I've heard of point that way."

"Fourteen people were killed in a little over three weeks," Eldon said.

"That's not a feud. It's a small war. And this little place swept all that under the rug?"

"As much as anything, from embarrassment. Turns out, according to the tale I've always heard, that there never were any diamonds."

"Then what was everyone fighting over?"

"The idea of them, I guess. Things got started and then they accelerated. I wasn't old enough to be taking notes then either. I just know it's a damn-all tender point around here."

"Well, if it's got anything to do with Denny Spurlock's murder, it's a boil that's going to be lanced, to throw in yet another metaphor for you."

Eldon just made a low, grumbling sound.

"What do you think, Eldon? Were there any diamonds, or weren't there?"

"No one knows. The only one to claim to see them was Hank Spurlock. His widow said he had a whole strongbox of them. But she'd not seen them herself."

"So it may've been just rumor."

Eldon shook his head slowly, and started to push himself to his feet. He gave his belt a short tug and leaned closer so he could speak in a near-whisper. "Whether there were or not is only part of it. But I'll tell you what started all the fighting. It was nothing less than native raw greed."

THE TWO OF them sat in the room waiting. They had little to say to each other. Thurston Mills looked down at his square-edged fingernails. There was still a smear of ink inside the corner of the right ring-finger's nail. He started to reach for his small penknife, then thought, "What the hell?" He'd leave it for what bit of character it gave him. At a tick of noise, the reporter, who the locals called "Thirsty," looked up at the closed door as if at any moment a waiter with a tray of drinks would come through. He wore the pants to a Hickey Freeman suit, to which he had long ago worn out the jacket. His long-sleeved shirt was his last unfrayed, white one, open at the collar. He'd learned to go without a tie the first week he lived in Texas. It might only be an hour and a half drive from Austin out here, but it might as well be on the moon, as far as any past link with so-called civilization went.

Thirsty's tired eyes quit scanning the room, and he said, "'Though patience be a tired mare, yet she will plod.' Henry the Fourth."

"Why don't you just give that a rest?" Selma said. "I honestly wonder if you don't enjoy for people to think your education isn't nothing more than an albatross around your scrawny neck."

She stared at Thirsty with almost no expression on her face, although someone coming new to the two of them might suggest she wanted to bite him.

Coming out to live in this puddle in the road town, allowing himself to be lured out here by the need to have a job of any kind, had been a mistake. He'd told himself he didn't need people the way others did, those weak and nonintellectual clods who knew only rough-eating and mating, the legacy of beasts. Half the time, in the mundane quotidian drag of each labored day, he forgot even what it was he wanted. Perhaps it was to have one halfway intelligent conversation; or, it could be as simple as just wanting to have the money to start over somewhere else, without having to work.

The worst thing of all for him was realizing he had the learning and acumen to know what greatness was, while also being clever and aware enough to know that he did not possess the raw talent to ever rise above a mediocre state.

It would be far better to have never known at all, to be swept along in the idle silliness of those who dream and try and never, never have a heartbeat of a chance of any breath of success. And they wondered why he drank a bit.

He certainly couldn't expect understanding from the likes of someone like Selma. When her face flickered toward any emotion, Thirsty thought, it was with desire for power. He'd been around people with aspirations long enough to sense this woman's frustration with just being a city councilwoman. She was the type who butted in, from the county library to the school board, to reconfigure their decision processes. No committee could form and meet without her wanting to be on it, and running it. She was a small-town control freak, and there were her detractors who felt she might best have shown more of that bent at home, what with a daughter like Sandy, who everyone knew could no longer be surprised by any physical mysteries life might offer, and the even more delicate Pebble, who was a "special" student and had to be bussed to another county where preschool teachers were better trained to deal with manic mood swings in a girl who Thirsty felt had an I.Q. slightly lower than a cabbage.

Selma had lived in Hoel's Dam all her life, had been there when Mills arrived ten years ago. He knew he was pretty seedy-looking even then, with his hair streaked with gray in a ponytail, and he had a beard some wild goat might have thought twice about growing. Folks thought it was his way of saying he didn't care, that all he seemed to want was enough money for beans and beer.

"Well, that's all right with me," Selma'd said. "If that's the kind of product Dartmouth College wanted to spit out, and the sort of reporter Herbert Hoel, the newspaper's owner, wanted to inflict on the community, fine with me."

The hell it was fine. She knew, as did too many others, that Thirsty had bounced around on a dozen newspapers before finally landing in their town. It was a dead end for someone with the problem that had given him his nickname, a tag that had started out in a jocular way but by now had more than a bit of nasty edge to it. He was as aware of that as any of them.

Selma broke the silence first. "I don't know why they don't just make me mayor and be done with it."

Thirsty pulled his eyes away from the door and looked over at her. There was no surprise at all on his face, nor did he hesitate to consider the comment serious. Coming from Selma, of course it was. The calculating gray eyes behind the thick lenses of his glasses barely moved.

"Being Denny's opponent in the coming election doesn't automatically make you next in line. What it does do is make you a prime suspect in his killing. You, or one of your boys." His voice was an uninterested monotone. His eyes swept around the room with the narrowed and suppressed glitter of an awakened barn owl trying to look toward the sun.

"My boys been in some scrapes, but they wouldn't kill anyone, especially Denny, unless he needed it."

"I'd be careful of talk like that right now," Thirsty said. He went back to watching the door. They were waiting on Morgan Lane. The room they sat in was the back room, where every Thursday night Morgan held a table stakes poker game, one at which it was rumored the sheriff himself occasionally sat in and played. The table was an eight-sided cherry wood affair, with a top that lifted off to reveal a felt-covered center and eight places to hold poker chips and beverages. Thirsty knew all about the table, even though he had never been to any of the games. He'd seen the cars parked in a row outside, including the sheriff's personal vehicle sometimes. It was one of the town's obvious secrets, as solid as the table itself, and the matching chairs they sat on now. The rest of the room was done in hunter green and dark paneling, with a small wet-bar against the far wall. That's where Thirty's eyes strayed most often, though he was self-aware enough to know what a sad cliché his life had become.

"You ever do a background check on Morgan?" she asked him.

He looked across the table at Selma. He'd been at the hospital when they brought in her two sons, had seen the look on her face then. How she could be around the man the way she was now was beyond Thirty's powers of understanding. He was here too, although he knew he was here because at bottom he was as weak, and maybe as greedy, as she was.

He waited, hoping the question would drift away like a trail of smoke. But her squinty hazel eyes were still locked on him when he looked up from the table. "Yeah, I poked a bit. Then a couple of guys showed up, checking on me. That killed my curiosity quicker than whatever got the cat."

"What kind of guys?"

"The ones not afraid to wear suits in a tiny cow-flop town like this. Not from here and not concerned with who knows," Thirsty said.

"They threaten you?"

"They did the minute I saw them, without their having to say a thing. You know the type—eyes like the deep-burned sides of a well."

"Like Morgan's?"

"Yeah, like that."

"But they didn't rough you up, or say anything threatening to you?"

"Guys like that don't have to."

"Some folks around here think my Rocky and Stone are like that."

"Selma, your boys are tough nuts all right, but you know they're not quite in the league I'm talking about."

"Yeah, Morgan's league." There was a sour twist to her words.

It was quiet in the room for a few minutes. Thirsty saw a poker chip lying half-hidden under the edge of the wet-bar's counter. He had a notion to pick it up, but realized it was worthless to anyone who didn't play in the games. After a few minutes, he looked back at Selma, whose thick-featured, wide-pored face showed every one of her fifty-five years. Her hair was a ratty yellow, even though Thirsty knew it was dyed and done up at the little Mane Attraction beauty shop that was the highest-priced beauty restoration spot the town of Hoel's Dam had to offer. Though, to appearances, it had been wasted money. Selma wore a dark blue dress that looked like a Donna Karan to Thirsty's eye, though he had to work from memory. But it might as well have been a grain sack for all it did to Selma's doughy figure. After a minute more of looking at her, more than he really needed, he suppressed a shudder and spoke again.

"How'd your family make its pile, Selma?"

"You mean, all the old money around here that's just a little moldy to the smell."

"I'm just asking."

"Haven't folks told you?"

"I heard a bit of gibber about a gold mine back on his old spread that's now underwater. Your ex, Slim, was gone when I got here."

Selma let out an unwomanly snort. "Oh, you know all about what really went on. Everyone around here has an idea. Slim's daddy, Old Man Granite, made the money growing dope," she said. "Marijuana. Any good digging would uncover that. But he went legit way back 'fore I was born. None of that'd do you much good now."

Thirsty nodded. He'd done his own homework, but wasn't as motivated for a hot story that'd upset this small pond of a town as some cub reporter might be. There were a lot more things he didn't say in print than he did. Herb Hoel didn't believe in making waves, especially when it came to any story that might involve the few truly rich folks in the county, among whom his father, Old Bill Hoel, was richest.

Selma barely acknowledged his nod. "Oh, sure. Slim's daddy always had a notion there was gold on his place down there in the valley. But we'll never know. Like everyone knows, it's all underwater now."

"How long's he expect us to wait?"

Selma took a deep breath. "Maybe he's out bumping off someone who he thought cheated at cards."

"Don't even kid about stuff like that, Selma."

The door opened and Thirsty's head snapped in that direction. He wondered if Morgan had waited outside the door and listened, then shrugged off that. A guy like Morgan Lane didn't need to know if people were afraid of him. He had to know they were.

His eyes swept over the two of them, and they were the

kind of eyes you see in the shadow of a cleft of rocks just after you hear the rattle. Thirsty thought his own emotions had long ago cauterized, but he felt an irrepressible, chilly slime of fear oozing down along his spine. He straightened a bit in his chair, as if his shirt was soaked in sweat and was sticking to the chair, though in the brisk air-conditioning of the room that couldn't be so.

"I'm not sure how smart us being together right now is," Selma said. "What we should …"

There may have been more she was going to say, but when Morgan's slow-moving head swung to her, she stopped, and she was a person used to dominating a room.

Thirsty watched her mouth close and the belligerent look on her face shift slowly to as little expression as she could manage.

No one really knew where Morgan had come from, although there were all kinds of interesting and unfounded rumors. He spoke a fluent Spanish that some of the local Hispanics had told Thirsty was an erect Castilian. They understood it, but it was elitist even to the more laid-back of them. Thirsty had been in a room once, when Morgan was asked to speak with a visiting Frenchman. The man had later said that Lane's French was pure Parisian. How did a man like Morgan, harder than flint as well, come to be all the way to hell and gone out here in this armpit of Texas? Thirsty often wondered about that, but not out loud.

Morgan eased down into one of the chairs at the table, and for a few seconds it was easy to imagine he was scoping every corner of the room with his peripheral vision. Then his eyes focused with their full intensity on Thirsty and Selma, and it was this unflinching intensity that most made him stand out in a sleepy burg like this. His stare was like lasers cutting through steel.

Selma stirred in her chair. "What's this about? I thought we weren't going to meet like this unless something …"

Whatever was in Morgan's look, as his face swung to her, stopped her cold.

"You think their finding another body will stir up things. It needn't have any impact on us, should it?" Thirsty said.

Morgan's now-expressionless face made a slow pivot to the reporter. "It might start them on another round of questions. That's my concern."

Thirsty started to say something, but stopped himself. After a few seconds of Morgan's staring, he swallowed, then said, "What do you want?"

"What I want … what I asked you here for," he said, "is to ask if either of you've had a second visit from the sheriff, or a first visit from that Ranger."

"No," Selma said.

Thirsty shook his head.

"Well, you probably will."

"I hope you didn't call us here, giving us that 'step lively' crap, just to tell us what we already know …"

"Selma," Morgan interrupted. "Shut up. What have you heard from the sheriff, Thirsty?"

"He doesn't actually confide in me. The sheriff, that is." He was thinking that if he was the law looking into a murder, Morgan would be high on the list of people who stuck out in this community.

"What is all this? We suddenly have to answer to you? I thought were all in this on an equal footing."

"No one cares just this second what you think, Selma. I was speaking to Thirsty here."

"You never did say why we're here. This goes against everything we agreed on."

"Shut up a minute, Selma. Now, Thirsty, did you have anything to share with the Ranger or the sheriff?"

"Just what you said, what we agreed on, about that pawn shop, the back-door trafficking stuff as well. Though I'm getting a lot of pressure on that now, because it's a murder case."

"You've said all you need to. Add nothing to that. Now, Selma, how about you?"

"How about me what?"

"What exactly did you tell them?"

"That Denny Spurlock's death was a terrible tragedy."

"Tragedy?" Thirsty let out a harsh snap of air. "What a farce calling Denny's death a tragedy. A true tragedy only occurs when there are noble intentions. Try finding that in this town."

"Thirsty?"

"What?"

"Shut up."

Thirsty lowered his head, felt the beginning of a warm flush along his temples. Alice, his ex of eleven years ago, would sure get a kick out of all this. She'd always said that what Thirsty really craved was being a martyr. She'd yelled something about ashes and sackcloth as she'd pulled away in the packed Volvo station wagon.

Morgan gave the stare a couple of ticks and turned back to Selma. "Now, what did you say to the sheriff?"

She hesitated, glanced at Thirsty, then back to Morgan. "What you said. What we agreed."

Thirsty sat up a bit straighter. "The box they found was empty, but we're here, having anything to do with the likes of you, because we believe that somewhere around here there still is a box of diamonds …"

"Why don't you hold that thought a sec, Thirsty," Morgan interrupted, with a warning glance.

Selma let out an almost-relieved puff of air. "We could have just said we were together. That would have given us all solid alibis for Denny."

"That's exactly what I don't want you to say," Morgan said, and his eyes had narrowed a bare quarter-inch. Thirsty started to say something, then stopped, but not Selma.

"Why?" Selma insisted. "We could always say it was a discussion about how to get me elected."

"No one would buy that."

Thirsty wouldn't have wanted to be stared at the way Morgan was glaring at Selma. Morgan was about the last person you'd ever want to cross, and that idea flickered across Thirsty's mind because he was giving strong thought to crossing him.

"Thirsty, you know why we can't do that, don't you?" Morgan said.

Thirsty sighed. "Because we don't want to draw any attention to us as a group, what we know."

"Oh, crap," Selma said. "We could have been playing cards. No one has any idea about anything." She said it in a way that made Thirsty think of thin ice.

"That's not the point. We just weren't together, then or now. Got it?"

Selma said, "There just had better be some goddamned diamonds."

Morgan's eyes narrowed even more, and glittered from the tight slits. "There are, just not where we thought. This is a blessing, really. It eliminates that."

Thirsty scooted an inch more upright in his chair. He glanced at Selma.

She said, "None of us trusts the others a hell of a lot. We got that out on the table, right?"

Selma's hard matter-of-fact oblivious tone stung Thirsty's sensibilities. Things like this were better to sneak up on, not bull toward, right through the tall grass. He looked closely at her face, as if the open pores and rough skin had something to do with her thinking.

The diamonds were the last thing he wanted to talk about too much, even though it was the flimsy thread that held them together. He'd done too much digging to share everything, or, for that matter, anything, with these two.

"We couldn't have done this by phone? I don't like this being together right now at all," Selma said.

"Selma, there is so much you don't know or understand here. Why don't you give yourself a break and listen for a bit? Trust me on this."

"What do you think, Thirsty?" Selma's prune-like eyes had fixed on him. "Do you picture Morgan here as someone we might actually trust?"

Thirsty was fascinated by the way Morgan was looking at Selma, like he wanted to break her in half like a used match.

Anticipating how much Selma was getting to Morgan gave Thirsty misdirected confidence. He almost grinned at the councilwoman when he said, "We could just ask him, Selma. He's right here."

Morgan's head pivoted slowly from Selma to fix on

Thirsty. It seemed to take an hour for him to pan across and lock eyes. Thirsty knew, for the first time, what it felt like for a deer to be transfixed by headlights.

"What did you say?"

"I…"

"What…did…you…say?"

"Nothing."

"I didn't think so. It just seemed like something there for a second."

The wave of fear and self-loathing that washed through Thirsty was palpable to him. It was what he'd been hiding from all his life. Knowing he had a good education but had amounted to squat bothered him some. But worse, he'd always pictured himself as standing up under a crisis, under real pressure. And now he knew, as he'd always known, that there was no spine or sand in him. Thirsty felt the prickle of a pink flush sweep all the way across his own gaunt, time-hardened face this time. He would let this man, or any other who wanted, take whatever he wanted from him. The awareness sucked every bit of manhood out of him.

"Why don't you go home, Thirsty," Morgan's words were softer, though no one would confuse them with tender, "and put a nipple on that jug of yours?"

FOR SOME INCONCEIVABLE reason, Esbeth was thinking about pie—not just any pie, a Carol Bean's Mean Baking Machine Granny Smith green apple and cranberry pie, heaped high, with a towering shortbread crust all browned into a crispy…

"Are you drooling, Esbeth?" Gala had looked up from her paperwork.

"No." Esbeth dabbled at the corner of her lips with a tissue.

Across the room, a slim figure stood in the doorway. It was that Cinco fellow again. He stood with his straw hat in both hands while peering through the room, looking for the sheriff again, Esbeth figured.

"Gala," Esbeth said.

The deputy was on her feet and hurrying toward the door, talking a rapid string of Spanish Esbeth couldn't begin to understand.

"Shouldn't he wait for the sheriff, Gala?"

"All Eldon will want to know is if he's here to confess. Otherwise he's of little interest to the sheriff."

At the door, Gala waved back to Esbeth, and with the other hand ushered Don Cinco outside.

Esbeth sat staring at the door that closed behind them. "Now doesn't that just scald your preserves. People are shooting around here all over the place like greased bars of soap, and I don't have the beginning of an idea what it's all about."

WHEN ELDON AND Tillis came into headquarters again, Tillis glanced around the room, and saw only Esbeth turned at the dispatch station, looking back at him with a stare that was the opposite of eager pleasure at seeing them return.

Gala was gone, though Tillis could still picture her quite clearly. Hers hadn't been a beautiful face, not by conventional standards. But it was a haunting one. Not that it mattered to him, he told himself a couple of times while he crossed the room behind Eldon.

"She's not here," Esbeth said to him.

"Who?" Tillis felt his face flush a bit in spite of himself. Eldon just shook his head and plopped into his squeaky wooden swivel chair. Tillis eased onto the corner of the nearest desk.

Esbeth's round, puzzled face still stared at Tillis.

He said, "I hope we can get along?"

"Why shouldn't we?" She was still far from smiling.

"I didn't detect any cartwheels for joy when I showed up."

"I got the impression you weren't doing any cartwheels to see me again, either."

"Your intuition's working overtime."

"At my age, my intuition's lucky to get up when I do. You men are a lot more obvious than you think. Ask Gala. She could tell you the same thing."

"You're a touch crankier than your usual grouchy self, Esbeth. What's got you riled at the moment?" Eldon asked. "And where the hell is Gala?"

"She bustled out of here with that Don Cinco who was here to see you earlier."

Eldon glanced toward the door, started to take a step, then shrugged.

"That's sure a real good way to make a new deputy and dispatcher feel. You and the Texas Ranger here going off to have a private chat. How're you going to get any help on Denny Spurlock's case, if you don't open up a bit?"

"Why? You have an idea of where Tillis here might be better spending his time than staking out some pawn shop?" Eldon scratched the rounded part of his shirt front, where the biscuits were buried.

Tillis pushed back a small wave of resentment. Eldon had a way of making it seem Tillis was thrashing around a bit, when he had barely started on what was turning out to be a pretty screwy mess.

Eldon squinted at Esbeth. "You got some way of knowing what ole Denny was thinking?"

She looked thoughtful, reluctant to answer. In the past, she had been slow to offer advice to either of them. The retired schoolteacher in her had always told them that they would never learn anything, if she told them everything. At the time, Tillis had thought she had just been kidding, until she had been right enough about aspects of the case that only made sense to him in hindsight.

Esbeth finally said, "No one can tell what another person's thinking. That's for sure. But if it was me, I'd be talking to someone who did know what Denny was thinking."

"I've made myself unwelcome with all of his family and friends," Tillis said.

"Then maybe you can try someone who used to be close, but isn't anymore—his former best bud, Pudge Hurley."

Eldon's eyebrows shot upward. "You know, Till, that isn't such a bad idea."

"Pudge Hurley. He's the dam manager, isn't he?" Tillis asked.

"And according to him," Eldon added, "the best dam manager around."

"I DON'T KNOW what to do."

"You could hold me," Karyn said. She sat on the far side of the car. They both looked out over the deep end of Lake Kiowa at the lower dam end. The windows on both sides of the boxlike 1951 Dodge Meadowbrook were open, and a vigorous breeze up this high on the cliff pushed through the car. It wasn't that cold, but Karyn didn't feel like sitting so far away, especially after the past few days. The inside of the car was like being inside a small, square room, though made more cozy by the leather seats that had replaced the cloth ones. It was the first time she'd ever been in it. When she'd dropped by Donnie's place, he was inside the car, removing the seats to look behind them, even though he hadn't really expected to find anything, since his father had been still looking too. The car was Denny's tinkering machine. He'd replaced all the fabric inside and had the outside painted a dark teal green. Classic car enthusiasts wouldn't like what he'd done to the car, but Denny had never been one to care too much what others thought. The car had belonged to his older brother, Hugh, and had sat in the garage for years, until finally even Denny had given up on his brother ever returning. Donnie had never been allowed to drive the hobby car before. Now it was his, so he'd asked Karyn if she wanted to go for a ride. She'd gone, hoping it'd take his mind off everything for a while, but here they were parked where earlier in the day the idle curious had watched the law fish out what remained of Hugh Spurlock.

"I'm sorry." Donnie moved closer and lifted an arm. She snuggled in under it. He said, "I was just thinking. I'm kind of stuck about what to do."

They had been a long time getting to this arm-around-the-shoulder stage, and he didn't seem in a hurry to rush much further along, which was one of the things she most liked about him. Some of the other kids, when they'd been in high school, thought Donnie lacked ambition. But Karyn knew he could be more obsessed than any of them. For years, they had been mere acquaintances at school, then pals, and finally best friends. They'd gotten there by accepting each other's foibles. There was some sexual tension between them by now, but neither seemed inclined to push it, though her father would probably neither believe nor understand that, even if she explained. He seemed to anticipate the worst. But Karyn didn't expect anything to happen with Donnie, until the whole mess about his father was cleared up for him.

Donnie gave her shoulder a soft squeeze, but still stared ahead. She looked up at his face. "You could let the law do its job. Or at least tell them more than you have."

Even though the sun was at its hottest, the air whipping through the car chilled her bare arms. His arm around her felt good to Karyn.

"You've been around here long enough to know that's sometimes just going through the motions. Besides, there're still one or two things maybe only I can work out."

The radio played softly in the car. It was an old tube-driven model that took a while to warm up, but had a rich sound to it. For all she knew, Denny had upgraded the speakers. The tuner was set on an oldies station, and she could make out Joe Cocker singing, "Don't let me be misunderstood."

"I wish you wouldn't be so stubborn and try to do things on your own. You're just like your dad. If it hadn't been for his friends, I doubt if he'd have been mayor."

"I don't know about that. I just want to do something."

"Well, you get that honestly enough." She rubbed one hand across the leather of the seat and looked at the glowing face of the big radio. The Spurlocks' house, this car, and a lot of other things told her the family was one caught up intensely in the threads of its own history.

He didn't say anything, but gave her shoulders another soft squeeze.

She said, "I know you're upset about your dad. But part of it's the diamonds, isn't it?"

"Yeah. That's part of it now."

"You don't think they're down there now?" Karyn watched the wind form patterns in the low ripples of waves.

"No. All those divers. Somebody'd've come across something."

"But you were so sure before."

"That was guesswork, based on what I'd heard Dad work out."

"You need more than guesswork now."

He nodded and stroked her long, smooth red hair where it ran down past her temple.

"What next?" she said.

"I don't know. I wish I did. But I don't."

TILLIS PARKED IN one of the only open spaces in the gravel lot beneath the tall, turbine buildings beside the dam. All the Texas shade hounds had gotten to the good parking places first, by the time he'd driven all the way back to Hoel's Dam from Fearing.

He crunched across the lot and climbed the metal steps up to a door with no other markings than a stenciled, "Employees." He pushed it open and went inside.

The room was a wide and tall open area with steel girders painted a flat battleship gray. In the distance, there was the deep, angry whir of turbines at work. A walkway led to a set of offices with wide windows and blinds that could be closed. He could see one or two people inside, moving around in usual workday office slowness.

Tillis opened the door to what passed as a reception area.

A woman was bent over an open lower file drawer. A man with about the same build as the sheriff leaned against the doorway that went to other offices. He saw Tillis, but didn't say anything.

Both of them could see the white hat and badge, so he didn't have to waste time with that. Tillis said, "I'd like to see Pudge Hurley, if I could?"

The woman looked up at him. The man in the doorway turned and yelled back into the offices, "Pudge, better hide those girlie magazines. It's the porn police."

The woman straightened up and frowned at the man who'd yelled. "Will you quit fooling around?"

The man grinned with a false sheepishness that seemed to delight him a lot more than the woman. He turned to Tillis and held out a hand. "I'm Pudge Hurley," he said.

Tillis reached out and shook a very firm hand. On closer inspection, Pudge was not all that pudgy. He was a hard slab of country man who cultivated that look, and was probably a lot more clever than the bumpkin he appeared to be. He grinned at Tillis with real enthusiasm, but seemed to be appraising him at the same time. His long, square face on his oversized head looked like it had been carved, somewhat hastily, from the local rock. It was also too tanned and weathered to belong to someone who spent all his time in the guts of the dam's inner workings facility. Tillis imagined the man got outside every chance he could.

Pudge led the way back into the offices and, when they came to his, he entered and waved to a chair. He sat on the desk and looked down at the Ranger. It was a strategic position, and he knew it. But it didn't bother Tillis. He put his white cowboy hat on the desk and tilted back in his chair, so he could look right at Pudge. He crossed his legs and waited.

The office was like any other government-furnished one; the desk and cabinets looked like they went back to the Eisenhower era. On one wall was a plaque of various kinds of barbed wire, from the early days when Texas converted from free-roaming plains. On another wall there were three framed photographs of Texas cutting horses in side profile. A trophy with a horseshoe on top was in front of a row of flood plain atlases on one of the bookshelves. Another plaque behind Pudge's desk was a little less serious. It was for bull throwing, and was made to look like a rodeo award. But it was dedicated to Pudge from his staff, and the wording made it clear he'd never won it in any sawdust-sprinkled rodeo arena. Tillis had enough time to inspect the office.

"This about Denny?" Pudge finally said.

Tillis nodded. "Have you got any ideas?"

"About who killed him? Why, I'd give worlds to know. I would've sure enough told the sheriff if I knew." Pudge was using a poker face, though not a good one. Any really good gambler would be able to pick up half a dozen telling tics from him.

"He already talk to you, did he?"

"Of course."

"Figures. Did Denny have any of what you'd call enemies?"

"Hell, the man had gotten into politics. That means that about half the area didn't like him, or thought they could do better, or would have done whatever he did differently."

"You know what I mean. Was there anyone in particular?"

Some of the silly farm-boy grin slipped a bit on Pudge's

face. "You mean like his opponent, Selma Granite. What're you fishing for?"

"I don't know. You're Denny's former best friend, I hear."

Pudge's wide, thick body slumped for a second, and his face that seemed carved from stone turned away from Tillis. He looked off at nothing in the corner of the room. His face showed nothing, though his upper lip quivered for a second before he snapped his mouth shut.

"You guys grew up together, didn't you? What made you fall apart the way you did?"

"Oh, hell. That hardly matters now. We disagreed once over something …"

"What?"

Pudge hesitated, then shrugged. "I gamble a bit. Denny didn't think I should. He thought it might reflect on him, but I insisted it had nothing to do with him. It was a monkey on my back, not his." Pudge's head, that would have been too large for any other body than his, swung slowly back to Tillis, and the bleak look in those eyes was nothing to wish for. "If I could tell you," Pudge's words quivered a bit this time, "what it was like helping haul Denny's casket out to the cemetery, knowing that I was never going to be able to patch up things between us …" He stopped, and looked away. One rough, thick hand reached up to his face.

Tillis looked down at his own boot. He reached out to pick out a piece of gravel where it was wedged between the sole and side of the boot. He'd have gone on doing other chores, but Pudge's face turned back toward him, as if surprised and a bit irritated to find him still there.

Tillis said, "I was hoping you could tell me something, maybe even if you think Denny's death's in any way connected to the body of his brother we just pulled out from in front of your dam."

"Oh, that."

"There's something more in the way you said that."

"Well, Denny and I may've not of been as close as we once were. But I kept track of him, tried to be supportive even when I … wasn't around anymore."

"What was he up to? The election?"

"No. Denny couldn't seem to get caught up in that this time. He didn't much care if he won or lost. At least that's what the folks I talked to said."

"What was bothering him?"

Pudge blinked and looked up at whatever it was in the empty corner of the room that attracted him. After a minute, his low, rumbling voice filled the tiny office. "He was obsessed about his brother, about Hugh."

"Who Denny's son Donnie just helped locate under the lake out there."

"The boy won't talk, though, will he?"

"Nope."

"Denny was the same way. It's a wonder he ever communicated enough to get elected."

"Maybe that was a plus—what the voters wanted."

"Could be."

"What do you know about what happened to Hugh? Did you ever get anything out of Denny about that?"

"No. But I heard plenty about Hank."

"So, tell me. What do you think happened on that dark and stormy night?"

"Which one?"

"The one where Hank Spurlock, the father, disappeared."

"I know what others in town know, but don't like to talk about. Hank Spurlock was supposedly coming across the lake at night in a boat, in a storm as bad as that one the other night. It was a helluva storm. I don't know that anybody could have really seen anything through it."

"And?"

"Folks say that's where he was last seen."

"What do folks say about the box of diamonds that he was supposed to have with him?"

Pudge's head stayed rigid and still, staring at Tillis. It was supposed to reveal nothing, but it showed as much as if his head had snapped up. After a minute, he realized it too and said, "If they know what's good, they don't say anything."

"That's true enough. I'd never heard anything about these ghost diamonds before."

"Ghost diamonds?" Pudge made a sound like he was warming up to spit. "Oh, there were diamonds all right. Hugh and even young Denny saw them—almost enough to fill a strongbox."

"What happened to them?"

Pudge's shrug this time was a touch over-elaborate.

"Where did Hank get them?"

"He couldn't say, of course. He was supposed to stake a mineral rights claim, and when he did, the land around wherever it was would shoot through the roof. But none of that ever happened when Hank disappeared."

"Do you think all of this ties in with Denny's death?"

"Like I said, I'd give worlds to know."

"And you don't have a single idea who might've killed him."

"No. No I don't. But I will tell you this, for what good it is to you, though I doubt it'll be worth much. If I had to pick one mysterious stranger in this whole town for you to focus your efforts on, it'd be Morgan Lane."

"Don't you play in his game?"

"Not anymore."

"Just since Denny's death?"

"I should have quit before that. But I didn't, and that's just the way that is."

"But you wouldn't mind if I could hang Denny's death on Lane?"

"I don't want you to hang the death on anyone who didn't do it."

"But if some harm comes to Morgan, you wouldn't mind that, would you?"

"No. That I wouldn't mind. I wouldn't mind it a bit."

FIVE

Esbeth stared down at the lined pages of the old, worn composition book on which she had written a list of names, the citizens of the county who interested her so far. Beside the names of some, she had only the sketchiest of notes.

Denny Spurlock, mayor, dead.
Donnie Spurlock, son.
Hugh Spurlock, brother, dead.
Hank Spurlock, father, dead.
Pudge Hurley, Denny's former best friend.
Selma Granite, watch her, control freak.
Rocky Granite, son, gotta love these names.
Stone Granite, son.
Sandy Granite, daughter, linked to Morgan?
Pebble Granite, special ed. student.
Morgan Lane, wary rumors, gambler, bad ass?
Don Cinco Hernandez, maybe nothing?
Old Bill Hoel, rich, reclusive.
Jorge and Estaban, Bill's top two hands, dangerous?
Edgar Hoel, son, dead engineer who built dam.
Hoel, son, newspaper editor.
Thirsty Mills, reporter.
Logan Rainey, game warden.

Karyn Rainey, Logan's daughter, goes with
Donnie Spurlock.

Well, it was all one fine mess. She had starred the location of houses on a rough drawing of the county, most nearer Hoel's Dam, a few in Fearing, and some at points between. She'd even drawn a few rough family trees, but that didn't tell her much either. There just wasn't much to make of any of this yet for an outsider like herself. If it all came down to something as simple as a feud, she still didn't have the beginning of an idea about who was on which side. She closed the book and slid it into her purse.

Esbeth turned to look at the clock, and her chair squeaked. Eldon lifted his head slowly from the pile of paperwork on his desk to glance over at her. "You're not off for twenty more minutes, young lady, so calm your jets."

"And you wonder why I'm cranky."

"You were cranky before you came to work for me."

"I'm not the way I am by choice. It just turned out I ended up living alone. Is your life so perfect?"

"Well, no. It's not."

"You talk about diamonds, and tell me nothing. Then there's this Hispanic fellow who comes and goes, roaming in and out of here like the ghost of Hamlet's father. You've got a dead mayor and now a body dredged up from the lake after lo these many years. And I'm told nothing about any of this."

"Do you recall telling us once that if you shared everything with us, we wouldn't ever learn anything?"

"I was recently refreshing myself on that."

"How's it feel?"

"Like a boot on the butt."

"Good."

"Oh, come on."

"Payback's hell, ain't it?" His grin was genuine and just as short of evil as Esbeth had ever seen him wear.

She intended to hold back, but couldn't. "You know, there's something to be envied of people with their roots in an area who know every nuance of it."

"Sometimes." His slow nod seemed to tire him until he stopped.

She turned back to her desk, and he let her stew a few minutes before he spoke.

"What do you have so far?"

"What makes you think I've even been poking?"

His blunt fingernails scratched at the taut, starched uniform material across his stomach, making a sound she could hear all too clearly. He stayed leaned back in his chair and grinned. "Oh, you give a cat a ball of yarn, or leave a raccoon in a room with a jar of marbles, and you can tell just what's gonna happen. Your nose has been twitching in real earnest the past couple of days. Now, what you got?"

"The sum of about all I know is that Hoel's Dam is thirteen-and-three-quarter miles southwest of Fearing along a two-lane state road. The town's adjacent to the dam that formed Lake Kiowa, and the gas stations charge about three more cents a gallon than here. That's it. You happy?"

"Now, how did you manage to find all that out?"

"You know how. I drove down, looked around a bit, asked a few questions of people who acted like they wished I wouldn't, and then drove back."

"That's some fierce detecting work you've been doing there."

Oh, she was mad enough to crush a grape, and she nearly

told him so. But he surprised her when he lowered himself and reached across his desk for a pencil, which he fiddled with a moment before saying, "Don Cinco's just a disenchanted ranch hand from around here. The diamond business is something I'd just as soon everyone forgot, especially. It's never caused anything but trouble. If there's anything I come across where I can use that investigative brain of yours, I won't hesitate to call on you."

"Oh, frog piddle. I still think you hired me more because there's something going on you don't want me to know about."

"Really I just wanted someone around who made me look sweet-tempered." He took the edge off that with a twist of a smile.

All the time Esbeth had been thinking and thinking about all of this, the whole thing seemed a bunch of mish-mush as far as she could see. But his seemingly flip remarks made her look at Eldon in a different way. You can't be sheriff in an out-of-the-way county like this, she thought, without knowing a whole lot more than you can ever tell. He was an expert, when he wanted to be, at playing the bumptious rube with a badge. But he was nowhere near like that when he let his guard down. He was as razor-edged a lawman as she had ever come across. Yet there had to be things that compromised his job, people so powerful an elected official could never dare cross them himself.

For the very first time Esbeth began to realize how very clever Eldon might really be behind that good-old-boy pose. She played back a quick newsreel in her head of every contact the sheriff had with the Texas Ranger as well: the nudges, the reverse psychology steers. Maybe he was manipulating the Ranger too, without saying so. She'd seen

Eldon in action before, dealing with the wealthy owner of a lot of land and a vineyard in the northern part of the county. He'd been careful to a fault there too, letting the Ranger take any risks that needed taking. A lot of things made a whole lot more sense suddenly than they had before. But there was still a lot for her to find out.

"I'll bet what's really bugging you right now is you're peckish, and that you're already thinking of what you'll have for dinner." He gave her one of his best countrified smiles.

"You'd win that bet," Esbeth said, willing now to roll with the obvious change of subject, the wash of understanding still rippling though her. Her frown relaxed and she said, "I'm going to pan fry two chicken breasts and have them with fresh-made cornbread and black-eyed peas."

Eldon dropped his pencil and leaned back in his chair, as if he could savor her dinner now. "Hmm. Hmm. And for me it's meatloaf night, though my favorite is chicken and dumplin' night."

"She ever change things around on you?"

"Yeah, once she had some white bass fillets with chutney on a Thursday, and I forgot to come in to work Friday morning, 'cause that's the day when we always have fish."

Someone keyed the mike of a walkie-talkie twice, and Esbeth reached to buzz the door open for Gala, who came in seeming small compared to the much taller and slightly bent man who came in behind her, looking like some blue heron wading to land from the edge of swamp water. Thirsty Mills was glancing around at the room in a way that seemed to miss very little.

Gala was still in uniform, trim and showing that mischievous grin of hers.

"Look what followed me in, Chief. Can I keep it?" she said.

"Don't know what you'd want with the likes of a reporter from the town of Hoel's Dam's Daily Squeak," Eldon said. "And that's Sheriff, not Chief. I don't care where you worked before."

Thirsty wore the pants to what had once been a quality suit. His white shirt was stained in three or four places with sweat. His shirt collar was open, and one of the collar points had curled. The temperature had been in the nineties all day. His long, lean face above the unkempt, goatish beard had a pale gray tinge that somehow went well with the long, graying hair tied back in a ponytail.

Esbeth could smell the reporter as soon as the door closed behind the two of them coming in. He smelled like an ashtray nestled in a pool of stale beer, but didn't look quite as inviting. Gala didn't seem bothered, and was more amused than annoyed.

Though Esbeth had been the one he'd spoken to on the phone, Thirsty zeroed in on the sheriff as he came across the room. He was pulling a ringed pad out of a back pocket and fishing a pen out of a side pocket, as he came across and sat down in the straight-backed chair beside Eldon's desk.

Esbeth watched Eldon manage a political smile as he held out a piece of paper to Thirsty. "Got the report back early this time. Should save you a lot of questions."

"That was unusually quick." The puzzled response on Thirsty's face got a real smile out of Eldon this time. The reporter looked up. "Death by unknown causes? What the hell is that? The man drowned, didn't he?"

"You know Doc Tallon. Unless the man's got a lungful

of water in a real autopsy, he isn't gonna say drowning. Of course, we can assume…"

Thirsty sighed, and gave the sheriff a baleful look while he shifted to pen and pad in hand. "What's your opinion of what happened, Sheriff?"

"Why, you know, Mills, that I can't speculate. If you want to say you thought he drowned, and that's just your opinion, why go ahead."

Esbeth thought the sheriff was getting a lot of joy out of making Thirsty's job harder than it needed to be. Though Esbeth could still catch that faint whiff of yesterday's beer past the stale tobacco smoke, the reporter seemed to be sober, though that might have been because he'd been working all day on this story. Still, that in itself wasn't enough for the sheriff to be treating the reporter the way he was.

Thirsty's lips pressed tighter together. Esbeth could almost see him repressing whatever he was tempted to say. Few people could be as aware of the public's perception of him as he had to be, and he channeled it as well as anyone she had seen. Little towns had broken men with bigger intellects, and he looked determined to come out ahead in the end, wherever "ahead" was.

Thirsty's face seemed weary, but a flicker of attitude began to show. He said, "You know, when this goes out on the wire, with the business about the bear trap and all, and that time-preserved corpse being Denny's brother, you're likely to have more than some retread reporter like myself sitting in front of you. You'll be blinking into the camera lights of three networks, and some slicked-up reporters, in suits better than you can afford, will be putting questions to you."

"Well, that'll be quite different than dealing with you,

won't it?" Eldon looked at the reporter as if he was something gummy he'd just scraped from his boot heel.

Eldon was sure a study to Esbeth. She had watched how he'd reacted the minute the reporter came in the room. Eldon could be the tough guy with a teddy bear inside waiting to come out, or he could be completely around the other way, the way he was with Thirsty. Men, to Esbeth, sometimes acted just like dogs in packs, though without the polite sniffing of each others' butts, though that might be part of it too, for all she knew. But they could sense who of them was wounded—and if they wanted to turn and snap, just to make a dominant point, they would. Eldon's teeth were showing now—a forced smile, but Esbeth had always heard that it wasn't polite to smile at dogs, since they couldn't tell if the gesture was hostile or not. She glanced at Gala, saw her perched on the corner of a desk, with an amused, closed-mouth smile.

"'Never did mockers waste more idle breath,'" Thirsty said.

"And what's that one from?" Eldon said, with less interest than the question implied. They'd played this game before.

"Midsummer Night's Dream," Esbeth said before she caught herself.

Gala had to suppress a laugh at the look of raw anger Thirsty shot at Esbeth.

"We've got some iced tea made up, Mr. Mills," Esbeth said, trying to make up. "I could get you a glass. You're probably parched after the day you've had."

His head moved back to her as if she was someone who'd taken a kick at him. He looked at Eldon, and said, "Whatever happened to that Betty Lou that worked here? Weren't you a bit sweet on her until the missus found out?"

The sheriff's voice took on none of the defensive edge Esbeth expected. "As you can see, we've gone with a more mature and experienced lineup. But I'll tell you something. If you think that's taken all the romance out of the office, you're wrong. 'Cause now I've got eighty-year-old Floyd Bettles getting drunk, just so he can come in here and make moon eyes at Esbeth there while he's getting booked. And you know how pitiful it is to see an old bird try to swim in the soup, especially over some love's labor lost. The man doesn't do anything for you, does he, Esbeth?"

Esbeth shook her head slowly. She'd felt the beginning of a blush, a bit of whatever was showing in Thirsty's face.

Gala spoke from her perch. "One has to admire your winning ways with the press, Chief…Sheriff, but you do recall that next year's election year, don't you?"

"That's right," Thirsty said, his tone conversational, with a tiny tinge of the sarcastic. "Same year as the presidential race. There's even some talk of a Hispanic presidential candidate—maybe that Senator Martinez. You think that'll ever happen?"

He was looking at Eldon, but Gala replied. "Probably not next year," she said. "And, if it was up to this county, probably not ever."

"Come on, Gala. I hired you, didn't I? That's fair, isn't it, Thirsty? I'm not so certain that as much prejudice exists around here as you think."

"Now, Eldon. That smacks of the same kind of logic we got from Horse Calloway three weeks ago, when he told us that screwing his fat little brother wasn't the same as incest." Gala's face showed the first bit of impatience.

"Had him for worrying sheep the time before that."

Eldon winked at Thirsty and chuckled, seeming to try hard to miss the point.

Gala said, "I think you should move this stirring interview along. The reporter's probably eager to get back to his paper and put this story to bed."

Whatever tone was in her voice, and it did have a spin to it that made Eldon straighten in his chair, was new to Esbeth. She gave the deputy an admiring glance.

The junkyard animosity that had been on Eldon's face was gone.

Thirsty seemed as surprised as Esbeth that Eldon would take any guff from someone on his staff.

Eldon gave Gala only a quick glance, then turned back to the reporter. Eldon's smile was nearly genuine this time. "You probably do have a legitimate question or two," he said to Thirsty.

Esbeth thought Eldon suddenly looked more like an elected official in whose head the gong had gone off that next year was indeed an election year. Any reporter in a small town has some power, even though the locals knew that all anyone with clout had to do was convince Herb Hoel. He could, and probably had, squashed Thirsty's stories before.

"Sorry we got off track there, Sheriff," Thirsty said, with just the shadow of something suppressed easing across his face. "Can you tell me what led to Hugh Spurlock's body being found?"

While Eldon rehashed the events, in a version somewhat favorable to himself, Esbeth watched the two men go through their motions. They'd both settled down like two dogs, once the hairs on the backs of their necks had flattened. She glanced at Gala and saw her openly expressing the way

Esbeth felt. Men. Their eyes met and agreed on the subject without having to say anything.

Eldon wound down, and Thirsty was scratching notes on his pad, quite unlike the reporters of today who shove a hand-held recorder into their victim's face.

At Eldon's pause, Thirsty looked up and leaned forward in his chair. For the first time, there was anything like a predator's glitter in his eyes. He said, "Now then, tell me more about what was in the box."

TILLIS EASED UP and parked in front of a house that stood on one of the highest hills in the town of Hoel's Dam, the back side of which went down in a deep cut to a creek that carved a bigger and bigger gouge into the rock until it led all the way down to the waterline of the lake. The house wasn't waterfront, but he imagined the view was killer from up there.

He sat in his truck for a few moments with the windows open and the afternoon stir of a breeze off the water waffling through.

He sighed and reached for the cell phone and punched in a number. After only one and a half rings, his boss, Lieutenant Tim Comber, answered.

"Glad you could check in. I'm about to face a press conference here."

"That bad?" Tillis could hear the hum of other voices in the background. He could picture the cluster of microphones and cameras waiting.

"Just tell me what you have so far."

"There's the throwdown gun, and the pages torn out of the registration book at a pawn shop, followed by that fire at the pawn shop. I haven't seen any of that assault weapon trafficking out the back door we heard about."

"You think it's worth staking out that place?"

"You know what interests me about that? I've been getting a lot of people going out of their way to say nothing. I get a tiny scrap of something, even if it's normally something we wouldn't rise to, then I'm willing to give it a night or so. If it weren't for that bit of a fire, I wouldn't bother. Something must've been worth trying to burn the place down, to erase the whole place."

"I've known you too long, Till, and known your record too well for me to tell you not to try to solve anything with busy work. Just don't do anything crazy. You remember the Pearson case."

"Which we solved."

"And for which I'm still mending fences. You stepped on a lot of toes there. But, what the hell. Stake out the damned pawn shop if you want. Just don't run up a lot of overtime on me."

"I doubt this'll break the State. I don't expect much, and I expect I'll tire myself out on this pretty soon."

Tillis heard Comber's not-so-patient sigh on the other end. "Anyway, the throwdown gives us probable premeditated on Denny Spurlock's death. There was no blowback, so we know he didn't fire a gun, and there were no powder burns. It's this business about the bear trap and his brother's death that's putting on the pressure. You know how the media love a story with gritty details."

When Tillis didn't respond, Tim asked, "Where'd you get the pawn shop lead in the first place?"

"The reporter, Mills, said he'd seen a gun like it there recently, and the records for that gun's sale were included in the pages torn from the registration book. Then there was the fire. Like I said, all that could mean a lot, or very little.

It's hard to say, especially with the reporter refusing to disclose his sources."

"What'd the reporter say when you asked him what he was doing at a pawn shop?"

"He said he was pawning stuff."

"Anything else?"

"Afraid not."

"Let me know when you have something. I could use a bit of heavy, concrete detail to throw to these wolves."

"There's the dam. It's both heavy and concrete."

"Till, you're not helping." The phone clicked as Comber cut the connection.

Tillis watched the uppermost dark pink pom-poms of a mimosa tree sway in the breeze in a lawn across the street. He shook his head. If all that fancy detective work wasn't enough to make him wonder about his career, he now also had a tale of some damned diamond mine or other. It was too soon to share that with the media, or even Tim. There were days it was hard to feel like a fully-trained professional, and this was getting to be one of them.

He got out of the truck, put on his white Ranger hat, and started the long walk, first across a small wooden bridge, and then up a winding walkway made of limestone flagstones that led all the way up to Morgan Lane's house. In all the time he'd lived in Hoel's Dam, he had never bumped into this man. Maybe it was time he did. Every town has some little business—a whorehouse or, in this case, a regular poker game—that some of its citizens think is a tiny cancer eating at the community. But enough of the ones who complain have their own domestic differences, indiscretions, or blatant hypocrisies that nothing much is done about the place, unless it calls too much attention to itself.

The flagstone walk wove through a couple gentle switchbacks, until Tillis came to a carved wooden doorframe around a heavy solid-oak door. The downstairs of the red brick house was skirted by hedges, and each window had a decorative, but sturdy, ironwork grill added. It could easily have been a bank instead of a residence. Gold filigree surrounded a pearl button, which he pushed. He could hear no chimes ring though the thick door. The place might be soundproofed, for all he knew.

The door opened, and Morgan Lane stood there, about half a foot taller than Tillis, though a bit of that could be the half-step up into the house that seemed designed to make visitors trip, or to keep out the handicapped.

"Yes?" He was focused on the round badge pinned above Tillis' pocket.

Tillis said, "I'd like a few words."

Morgan turned and waved a hand for Tillis to follow. The gambler wore black dress slacks with an impeccably starched and ironed white long-sleeved shirt. When he turned to lead the way through the house, Tillis was grateful that at least there was no black vest with a back of pearly gray silk. Still, Tillis had to imagine that if locals came to the place with expectations of playing poker with a professional, that Lane was doing his best to dress the part.

The framed art along the wall looked real, and, even if they were just good replicas, the Miró and a Klee among them were probably meant to signal to anyone coming to a game that Morgan had money to lose—that is, if the poker player was the optimistic type.

They went down a hallway and turned into a small den and office. Tillis was disappointed he hadn't been taken right to the poker table, for effect. This room was all hunter green and dark-stained wood, with oxblood red leather chairs. A green banker's light, that Tillis could see was a genuine one and not one of the many imitations, lit the dark sheen of the desk's surface. The drapes to the room were all pulled shut, leaving it dim as some daytime bar. Two of the leather chairs were close together by an empty fireplace. A reading light lit one of them. Lane waved toward one of the chairs, and sat in the other. Tillis expected to get the light beaming into his own eyes, but realized as he sat that it would be shining on Morgan. But he soon realized why the gambler had made that choice.

Lane didn't offer any refreshment, or get into the polite social chatter that usually accompanies a first-time visit to anyone's home. His movements so far had been those of a strong and purposeful person. Now he leaned forward in his chair, still a bit taller than Tillis, and let the light catch the intensity of his eyes as he asked, "Is this a fishing trip? Or do you feel you have a legitimate reason for calling?"

"I think the reasons are legitimate enough, and I'm the only one I have to account to for that."

"Do you now?" Morgan leaned just a bit closer.

Whenever Tillis looked right at Morgan, he found his eyes locking automatically. There was something off and hypnotic there. First, there was the shape of his eyes—almond-ended, and at a slant, but tilting the opposite direction of an Asian's eye. Then there was the color, or lack of it. Lane's irises were the color of pale Mediterranean ice, more like glass than not. That, and he never blinked, or at least did so rarely that Tillis found himself staring back into that vacuum, waiting on any kind of twitch or blink. The man must be hell to sit across from at a poker table. Tillis looked away.

"I wonder, in a small town like this, if there's the usual backwash about cleaning up the sore spot here and there?" Tillis glanced around at the room. The furniture in the room was worth more than his own home and land—had to be.

"Wouldn't that be within the bailiwick of the local sheriff?"

"Unless maybe he was compromised."

"Now look here."

Tillis glanced back at Morgan, and found himself locked in once more to the whirlpool eddy of those strange eyes.

Morgan said, "If you have something solid, say it. If not, maybe you'd best peddle papers elsewhere. Unless this is your version of rounding up the usual suspects."

"No. This isn't as random as all that. I came to find out how you and Denny Spurlock got along about the idea of gambling in a tiny town like this."

"Like I said before, if I was doing something against the law, don't you think the sheriff would drop by and have a talk with me?"

"No."

"I suppose you want to know where I was the night Denny was killed?"

"In fact, I do, unless you're too busy acting like a B-movie extra to answer a few questions."

"People usually try one of two things when they meet me. They either try to take me as seriously as I take myself, or they try to laugh me off, as you've chosen to try and do. And I'll tell you something else for free. Your poker face isn't nearly as good as you think it is."

Tillis was aware it would take more than a few words to get this man off-balance. He said, "I've been told that. I guess I'd best not play at your table. But we're not sitting there now. Where were you that night?"

"You're serious?"

"Yes."

"It was a Thursday, wasn't it?"

"It was a Wednesday. You know that."

"Then I guess I don't have an alibi, especially one involving the sheriff himself."

"I didn't think so."

"Are you going to take me in now, or do you actually need more than something as flimsy as that to go on?"

"Everyone seems to know more about procedure these days than me."

"I wouldn't let it keep you up nights. A lot of people aren't particularly good at their jobs. But, the old pay slip comes along each payday just the same."

"You've been in town what, a year and a half now?"

"And no one's run me out yet."

Lieutenant Comber had once noted that one of Tillis' investigative strengths was knowing when he could expect neither straight answers nor substantive ones. Tillis took a deep breath and looked away from Morgan's growing smirk and gave the room one more once-over, then let his gaze settle again on Morgan.

"You know, you're not very likeable in the first place, and you don't grow much on one."

"I don't much care if people like me. Does it worry you?"

"Only a bit." Tillis stood up. "I find it hard to care about you at all myself."

TILLIS STEPPED OUT into the sun, now at the peak of its daytime powers. It was like coming out of Dracula's basement, and blinking in wonder to find the peaceful little town right where he'd left it.

He went down to the street and was unlocking the truck when he saw a small figure jogging up the hill. The familiar confidence of the stride was what stopped him for a moment. As the figure came closer, he saw it was Gala. The coffee con leche brown of her skin glistened with sweat. She wore shorts, running shoes, and a thin light-gray Everlast shirt. Tillis could detect no bra, though he told himself he hadn't been focusing on that.

She smiled at him, always disarming coming from her. She slowed to a walk and came up to him. He kept his face locked on hers, to avoid seeming to stare at her athletic sweatiness.

"You look kind of surprised to see me in street clothes," she said. "You know I'm not always on duty."

Tillis misunderstood that as an invitation and said, "I guess you've only been around a few months and don't know many people. Would you like to share dinner sometime?"

"Sorry. No. I don't want to falsely encourage anyone." Her smile had even more of that "humor to herself" that told him she was her own best counsel most of the time.

"I didn't mean …"

"Oh, yes you did. But never mind. What are you doing up here?" She waved a tanned arm at the surrounding houses, sweeping past Morgan's place.

"I don't get up this way much," he said. "I was just nosing around."

"You solved either of the murders yet?"

"Not quite. I'm still grabbing at straws like the pawn shop stakeout."

"But you don't need any help. Is that it?"

"You know how the Rangers work. We cooperate with local law enforcement. We're here to supplement forces already in place these days."

"The Rangers. That's where they put middle-aged DPS lawmen out to pasture these days in Texas, isn't it?"

His mouth opened, then closed.

"Is that why you're so open and fair with all the staff, like Esbeth and myself?"

"I'm just going through channels."

"You know, in a perfect world, that'd be all you'd need to do."

"Are you saying Eldon Watkins is bent?"

"I'm just reminding you how the team concept works."

"You think I need it?"

"You need something. All I've heard about you so far is how you're the one Ranger willing to take help from wherever it comes. But all I'm seeing is this Lone Ranger posture. That's not to impress me, is it? I hope not."

For a moment, Tillis was out of things to say. He looked down, but caught a glimpse of where her sweat-soaked shirt was clinging to her chest. He looked up and around at the houses, took a bit longer on Morgan's place.

"You been up there talking to him?" she asked.

Tillis looked back at her, conscious of whether he stared too long at her lips or her brown eyes. "What's Eldon say about him?" Tillis said.

Gala laughed. "He says the man never bluffs, ever."

"And?"

"Eldon admits sometimes that Morgan gives him 'the willies.' "

"I can understand that."

Gala's laugh was a lower, sarcastic chuckle this time. Tillis didn't know whether to find it sexy or embarrassing.

"You know, you men aren't nearly as tough as you like to act." She spun, waved, and took off jogging down the street, her sweat-covered skin glistening in the light of the fading sun.

He couldn't decide if she'd been referring to Morgan or himself.

THIRSTY MILLS SAT behind the wheel of his car with the worn leather notebook in his lap. The street was quiet, and he watched the sun sink lower in the sky toward the trees. He looked up and down at the houses on either side, especially the taller Victorian place where the Spurlocks had lived for generations. The front windshield was cracked in a jagged, spidery line where a rock had flown up from the road, and he had to lean to peer around it. His hands tightened and loosened on the softening sides of the notebook. Damn the whole bunch of these hillbilly hayseed cowboys, all of them. They'd see how this all shook out in the end.

He looked back down at the pages of the diary, or journal, whatever it was. At first, it had been hard to make out some of Hank Spurlock's cramped scribble. The later entries, in Hugh's handwriting, were as bad or worse. But Denny Spurlock had a nice hand, though not much insight to add to the obsession that had haunted this family. After he'd read and reread the entries many times, he had almost every word down. Still, there was a lot to figure out. He looked up and sat watching the light dimming in the sky, casting dark shadows around the house. When it was too dark to read, he closed the notebook and slipped it into the glove compartment. There was a half pint of unopened Napoleon brandy in there, but he left it where it was. He would let the anger he felt at the whole damned town feed him for a while.

"Home is the hobby. Home is the hobby." He muttered and stared at the house. Hank had written the phrase an unnecessary number of times, and Hugh had underlined it and had jotted a note in the margin, "Fishing?"

But Hugh had been wrong. Thirsty's finger had traced another line where Hank's barely-legible scrawling hand had written, "Most folks think I'm a fishin' fool. But I only do it to get to my real passion, which is sittin' and starin'."

Now, who would write dribble like that in a notebook of this kind unless it mattered somehow?

The porch—that's where Hank had surely done a lot of that, too. No one had thought of the porch. It had to be that, under there somewhere.

Night slowly settled on the little town of Hoel's Dam. The sky faded to pink, then orange, with streaks of purple. Finally it was dark enough for the lights to come on, including those of the Spurlock home.

Thirsty sat in the car and stared. To hell with it. The place wasn't going anywhere. He started the car, and reached toward the glove box.

AT THAT SAME moment, Tillis was easing his truck into the back gravel parking lot behind an auto repair and tire shop across the road from the pawn shop. Out this far, the main street of Hoel's Dam had settled into a road leading out of town, with only a small, darkened business or strip mall here and there, between the still-open and brightly-lit gas stations. He eased into a location where he could see the pawn shop, but the truck would look like just one more vehicle waiting for repairs, which was a bit closer to the truth than Tillis liked to think about.

On the seat beside him were a couple of Styrofoam containers of coffee, a package of beef jerky, and a twelve-pack of Diet Coke —stakeout food, much the same as his road warrior cuisine. He reached up to turn off the dome light for the inevitable trips outside the truck that all the liquids would necessitate. Out here behind the repair shop, where the edge of the parking lot ran to a chaparral of young live oak, mesquite, and a bit of prickly pear cactus, all of outdoors was a potential bathroom.

As the night grew darker, and the family autos and sports utility vehicles on their various ways home transformed into pickup trucks shuffling between bars and eighteen-wheelers rolling through town only because they had to, Tillis finished off his coffees as well as the beef jerky, and then started on the warm Diet Cokes while wishing he'd brought along some dental floss. He stared at the town and its traffic, and played back the last few days while staring at the pawn shop, where nothing happened, nor did he much expect it to. This wasn't one of those procedural deals mandated by the kind of orders from headquarters he'd gotten in his rookie year. It was a raw hunch, and didn't make himself feel much like a veteran of eleven years as a Ranger. But that didn't really matter. There wasn't anything to do at home but watch television or read one of the books he'd already read a couple of times. The cell phone on the seat beside him was silent. In the distance, he heard a siren heading the other way. His radio wasn't on, and he didn't turn it on. Probably just a fender-bender out on the highway.

His window was open and the breeze came through the truck. He heard cicadas making a racket in a stand of trees on the next lot, and the whiz of tires going by. He glanced at the luminous hands of his watch; just a bit before three a.m. Whee. He opened the door and got out of the truck, went over to stand near the brush and do an Eldon Watkins on a prickly pear plant. It was too late for snakes, and his boots were proof against scorpions, so he glanced across the road. From this angle, he could see all the way to the other side of the pawn shop. He saw a large dark shadow shoot across the open lot and then freeze beside the building. He zipped back up, hurried over to the truck, tossed his hat in on the passenger seat, and grabbed the long-handled black metal flashlight that was better than a club. He reached down and felt for his side holster that held the 9 mm service automatic. Then he bent low and circled around the tire shop to head for the pawn shop from the other side.

When traffic cleared, he ran across and tucked close to the building, then started around toward the back. The building had no spouting, and rainwater had fallen off the sides of the roof often enough to form an indented gravel row along the sides of the building. He stepped a bit outside that onto scruffy Bermuda grass, as he eased along the side of the building.

Cars and trucks went by on the road, and their headlights swept past the front of the store, and though he could see the traffic, he doubted if any of the passengers or drivers could see him in the shadow of the store. He made almost no sound, but could hear the crunch of gravel of careful steps around the corner. His focus was on those slow steps. He gripped the flashlight like a club and eased closer to the corner. He'd seen only one shadow running across, but it occurred to him there might be more than one of them. He glanced behind him just in time to see in the flare of a passing car's headlights a bulky shape right behind him, and an arm holding something coming down toward his head. He lifted an arm and ducked. The pipe, or whatever it was, came down hard on his forearm and grazed the side of his head as it smashed into his shoulder.

The clip along his head was harder than he thought. His vision blurred, and though one hand reached for his holster, he felt himself tumbling to his side to sprawl across gravel and grass. He could barely make out the dark shape of a man, and even though a truck came by from the other direction, all the lights caught for him was the toe of a Red Wing boot with a smile across it where the owner had kicked something hard enough to reveal the steel toe inside. Oh, great, a kicker. He could think it, but not react. One whole side was numb, and he had to struggle with all he had not to pass out from the blow he'd taken to the head.

He watched the foot move back, prepare for the kick that would come for his face. Then he heard the skid of gravel as a blast of bright lights blinded him. The door flew open on the vehicle that had pulled off the road and slid to a stop, and he heard a strong female voice shout, "Freeze, right where you are."

The man did the opposite, spun and darted around the corner of the building. Tillis tried to lift himself and collapsed back onto the gravel. He heard the footsteps running in pursuit. Then he heard a shot, probably a warning shot. He could see the red and blue swirling lights sweeping rhythmically across the siding of the building.

After a while, steps crunched back to where he lay. A face lowered until it was inches from his own. It was Gala, and she was in uniform this time. She put her gun back in its holster and reached to lift him upright to a sitting position. He helped as much as he could, which was very little, but she was strong. She eased him back until he could lean against the building. Then she crouched down to look at him.

"They get away?" His voice came out like a croak.

"Yeah. Wasn't much I could do about that. They ran pretty well for guys wearing ski masks. One of them had a truck running just on the other side of the draw."

He reached up with his right hand to feel the side of his head that was throbbing. There was a bit of blood, but not as much as he expected. "You just happen by?"

"Thought you might need looking after."

"That's all you saw, two guys in ski masks? I was hoping you'd get a better look at either of those two thugs than I did."

"No. But I know who's got a couple of young men like that right in her own family. What about you? You okay?"

"My pride's a bit scuffed up, but it's wash and wear."

"Come on, help me get you to your feet. We'd better get you in and have someone look at that." Her glance at the side of his face showed only a little sympathy and told him she'd seen a lot worse.

But he could feel the flesh around his temple swelling. He'd been lucky only to be grazed. If that pipe had connected directly, he'd be in a lot worse shape, or feeling no pain at all. She tugged and he pushed until he stood upright on wobbly legs. He leaned against her and she tucked his arm across her shoulder. He let her support some of his weight as they moved toward the still-flashing cruiser. She was as solid as grabbing a post, a real hardbody. She glanced up at him, and her eyes were big and brown as she flashed that smile of hers that had first intrigued him. "What do you make of it?"

"It tells me I might be on the right track after all."

SIX

TILLIS' WHOLE LEFT SIDE ached and his head throbbed, as he climbed out of his truck where it was angle-parked in front of the newspaper building, a single-story sprawling affair made of orange and red brick. He was younger than a lot of the Rangers; feeling he might be getting too old for the job didn't do him much good. He glanced at his watch—not quite ten thirty a.m., though the sun made it feel like noon. It was a good time to visit a newspaper office, he figured; they'd be as busy as they ever get. Sometimes people talk better when they're trying to get rid of you.

The building was located in the center of town on the main street passing through Hoel's Dam. Traffic was picking up, and Tillis had been lucky to find a parking spot so close to the building. He caught a glimpse of himself in the mirror of the door glass as he reached for the handle. His reflection had a white patch at one temple and a spreading purple bruise along the side of his face. He didn't look or feel lucky.

The inside of the building opened into a wide room, with most of the desks on the divided part of the room marked Advertising. Four people were busy in the advertising section, bending over chest-high, tilted art tables with X-Acto knives, reaching for strips of paper coming through waxing machines. It gave Tillis a better feel for the newspaper's state-of-the-art than he expected. One of the advertising women at a desk looked up at him, but the hope eased from her face when he pointed back to the news area. Only three desks were on the other side of the low wooden barrier, and at one of them sat Thirsty Mills, pecking away at a keyboard while staring at a computer screen. Either the light coming off the screen or the fluorescent panels above gave a macabre tinge of green to the silver sheen of the gray hairs that were tied back in a ponytail and sprinkled through Thirsty's scruffy beard. His face had a nearly-matching greenish-gray pallor to it. A phone on a nearby desk was ringing, which he ignored. He looked up, saw Tillis heading his way, glanced at the wall clock, then looked back at his screen to finish a sentence. He did, frowned at it, then moved the mouse and hit the Enter key before hopping to his feet to face the Ranger.

"I'd been hoping to track you down," he said. "Looks like you saved me the bother. I've got folks calling from all over for more details, and a chance to string for a wire service here." He glanced toward the corner office, knowing that anything he sent out on the wire would have to go by Herb Hoel first to be approved.

"That's the Texas Rangers, nothing but eager public service," Tillis said.

Some of Thirsty's native sarcasm nearly showed in the response on his face, but went away as he looked more closely at Tillis' head. "What happened to you?"

"Had some problems with plumbing." Tillis looked for a place to sit. He reached for the swivel chair behind an empty desk and dragged it over beside Thirsty Mills' desk. He lowered himself into the chair, inwardly groaning a bit until his aching left side was settled.

Thirsty stood looking at him, reaching into a pocket for a pack of cigarettes. An ashtray like a wide crystal candy dish was piled high with butts on his desktop. That's the thing about small towns, Tillis figured. They haven't pushed a lot of the rules about the work environment that have city office workers huddled outside the doors of buildings in all kinds of weather to grab their nicotine.

While Thirsty lit up with a plastic disposable lighter, Tillis looked around at the office. The building looked sturdy, like it had been built for something else, maybe some kind of mill or factory, maybe even built for the newspaper itself back during its hot-lead days, before computers replaced the heavy, cumbersome Linotype machines. In converting it to its current use, the ceilings had been lowered and the brick walls painted. But instead of making it cheery, it gave even the wide, open space of the newsroom a claustrophobic feel. It would be a tough place to show up every day and work, especially for someone of Thirsty's height. That could be why his upper body had taken on a bit of the lean and shape of a question mark. It looked, from Tillis' sitting position, as if Thirsty was ducking beneath the hanging ceiling, though that could be just the head tilt Thirsty was giving him. The cigarette in the corner of the reporter's mouth stuck up at a jaunty angle as he sucked hard at it. Then, spears of smoke shot from both nostrils as he eased back down into his chair and looked at Tillis from beneath eyebrows that could use a bit of trimming.

"Have you wrapped up these little whodunits, both old and new?" Perhaps without realizing he did it, Thirsty pulled over an open, ringed pad and placed a pen across it, in case the Ranger said anything the inquiring minds of the public might need to know, providing it clicked with what Herb Hoel thought they should know.

"It's the older case that kind of intrigues me," Tillis admitted. "I've never worked on one quite this stale before. I dropped down here because I thought you might be able to help me."

Tillis waited to see how Thirsty would react. A less sophisticated reporter might be flattered. As it was, Mills sucked on his cigarette and stared through the smoke at the Ranger. Then he took what was left, and snuffed it out in the crammed ash tray. He managed to be looking with a sideways glance at Tillis when he said, "You've got to know that anything that long ago happened way before I was here. It'd be no more than of historical interest to me, even with the skeleton thrown in. Now, the death of the mayor, that did happen while I was here, right here at the newspaper office."

"So you've got an alibi?"

"'Murder most foul, as in the best it is.'"

"You're not Hamlet. How about that alibi?"

Tillis knowing the source of Thirsty's quote seemed to irritate him more than any question asked so far. Here was someone with a lot of suppressed rage. Small-town life wasn't clicking with this one.

"Yeah, boss Hoel was here working late himself, so I've even got a witness."

"But you got there pretty quick."

"I heard the squeal on the scanner. Sure, I was one of the first ones on the scene, if that helps." Thirsty didn't look like someone who wished to be helpful. He slid the pad over closer and picked up his pen. He glanced at the clock on the wall, then at his computer screen. "You've locked up both

Tony and his hired hand James from the pawn shop. What's going on there? Are they suspects in the mayor's murder?"

"You're the one as much as fingered their place, with information for which you still haven't shared your source. You shouldn't be asking me about them. I should be putting the vise grips to you about that."

The wry smile half-buried beneath Thirsty's face fur showed more disdain than fear. "I'm not one of your locals who just rolled off the back end of the turnip truck, so don't try that strong-arm stuff with me. Did you arrest them, or what?"

"They're not locked up. They were taken in for questioning. The place'll be open again by now. You'll still be able to pawn more stuff. As for suspects for Denny's murder, we're still shopping. Any suggestions?"

Thirsty shrugged off the question. He looked like he was going to reach for another cigarette, then didn't. "Since I'm pushing a deadline, I hope you don't mind if I make the most of my asking you a few questions about these murders."

"You'd better go with what you have. I don't have any answers just yet. I only have questions myself. What I'm here for is to find out more about Hugh Spurlock."

"I told you, that's way before my time."

"You're an enterprising reporter, Mills. If you were me, and you were in a newspaper office, where would you go to find out about what was going on forty years ago?" Tillis glanced around, but didn't see any old newspapers piled around.

Thirsty didn't quite manage to suppress all of a smirk. He nodded toward the corner office door. "I think you'd better see the boss. I'm sure he'd kind of like to field that sort of question himself."

Having learned he'd get no help with his story, and having made it clear that any information exchange was on a *quid pro quo* basis, Thirsty turned away from Tillis and squinted at his screen again. He got his bearings and started tapping away at the keys again, as if the Ranger was no longer there.

Tillis eased his aching frame up out of the chair and went back to the open corner door. He peered inside, saw a thin man in a gray suit sitting behind a desk smoking a pipe. That explained some of the relaxed rules about smoking. Tillis tapped on the open door and Herb Hoel looked up from what looked like a copy of the *New York Times*. The story Tillis could make out once more featured Senator Martinez, this time hammering home another of his platform issues. This time the pitch was that America needed to clean up its own lingering civil rights issues before taking on those of the world.

"Yes?" Herb Hoel lowered the paper and politely folded it without losing eye contact.

"I'm the Texas Ranger working on the two Spurlock cases. Do you mind if I come in and ask a few questions?"

"That's politely put, young man. Come on in and settle. What's on your mind?"

The room was big, and had tinted windows that looked out onto both of the major streets of Hoel's Dam. The desk was teak, or some equally dark wood, and was as big as all the reporters' desks together. Both walls without windows were lined with bookshelves. The carpet outside had been a dull gray. Inside the office, the carpet was a thick burgundy that gave beneath his steps and went well with the off-white textured wallpaper on the wall space not covered by shelves. The room set a tone that said there was a difference in people, as did the air-conditioning, set ten degrees cooler than the newsroom so boss Hoel, who looked to be in his early sixties, could wear a suit jacket that looked tailored.

"This is my first forty-year-old murder," Tillis said as he crossed the room. "I was hoping to do some research here. Maybe you can even tell me what went on back then."

"Oh, I'd have been too young to know much of what was going on, and people don't talk about the past as much around here as you'd think, at least not to me."

On the surface, it was one of the most absurd things Tillis had ever heard. He had yet to meet a newspaper man who didn't have an itch to know every little thing, all the way down to the smallest corpuscle of someone's blood. And Herb wasn't too young, though he might have been on an extended toot at the time, given some of the rumors he had heard about the man. He was being stonewalled, and he knew it.

"Do you have some of the old papers that go back that far?"

Herb Hoel took the straight-stemmed briar pipe with a medium round bowl out of his mouth and carefully set it in the marble ashtray with its own pipe rest. He sighed, or tried to. He seemed the kind of person who found it hard to show emotion, even mock regret.

The publisher was lean, upright, and had a careful way of doing every little thing, even to picking up a pipe tamper and starting to clean out the bowl of another pipe he took from a drawer, this one a stained meerschaum. Tillis would have guessed military, if he hadn't heard somewhere that Old Bill Hoel had paid good money to see that Herb hadn't gone that route. The rigid mannerisms could come from an Ivy League background, though that contrasted with Thirsty Mills' ways, and Tillis knew Mills'd gathered up a sheepskin back in one of those dusty Ivory Tower schools. No, it had to be old money. The Hoels owned this town, and that was the belabored care of movement he was seeing in Herb, the easy-going but controlled way he folded his hands on the desk when he was done fiddling with the pipe.

"Let me show you something." Herb rose slowly and went over to one of the bookshelves. Tillis creaked to his feet and followed. He could hear computer keyboard keys clicking away out in the newsroom. Outside, the world went on with its frantic urgency, but here in the calm of Herb Hoel's office, it was as if time had stopped.

Tillis was surprised to find he was an inch or two taller than Herb, once he came up and stood beside him. The publisher's posture had fooled him into thinking he was a much taller man.

Herb reached up and, from a row of large folders bound in light blue cloth, pulled out the first one in the row and carried it over to a stand beside the window that looked like a pulpit. He put the book on the stand, that Tillis could now see was for standing and reading. Maybe Herb had something wrong with his back that made him such a rigid pole. Tillis could understand standing to read, though, since his own banged-up side hurt every time he sat.

Herb was flipping through the pages, and Tillis leaned closer.

"There." Herb stepped back and pointed. He'd turned all the way back to the first newspaper in the folder, and it was only half there. Big chunks were missing, and black rings and edges left where part of that paper had been. The date on the paper was only twenty years ago.

"A fire? You're saying you had a fire here and there's no record of the papers before that?"

Herb was nodding slowly at him, wearing a sad smile that had just a touch of contentment to it.

DONNIE WALKED ACROSS the wide, open center of the Hoel's Dam Library and approached the desk where a woman was breaking the "Shush!" sign above her head by talking loudly on the phone, something about a casserole. She was one of those young women who already looked and dressed as an older woman—maybe thirty, but acting twice that old. Donnie looked over at Karyn and she gave him a reassuring smile.

The woman glanced at them and frowned. She said into the receiver, "I'll have to get back to you, Grace." She hung up, reached for a clip-on gold earring, and put it back on her right earlobe before turning to Donnie and Karyn. "Now, what can I do you for?" She tried for a cheery, helpful tone, but didn't quite hit it.

The librarian had her hair pulled back in a tight bun and had a way of pursing her lips in disapproval of almost everything. It was a real stretch for her to try to act civil and interested.

"We were trying to look up some old newspaper stuff on the microfiche machine," Donnie told her, "and they only go back so far. Are there more of them someplace?"

The woman frowned at him, and it was an intensely personal frown, as if she'd caught him masturbating in the stacks, or something. "The back issues were stolen some time ago, even before I worked here. People ask about it all the time, but there's nothing I can do about it. A lot of stuff moves out of here like it had wheels. You wouldn't believe the stuff people steal from a public library that's just trying to do a good thing."

She looked them over and fixed on Karyn's small purse, as if it might be full of library property.

"You mean there's no other place we can look back that far?"

"That's what I'm saying. We try to do what we can here, but people just don't understand what …"

Donnie had already spun and started with brisk steps toward the door out of the library. He felt Karyn's hand grab at his elbow. His first instinct was to shake it loose, but he wasn't irritated with her. He glanced at her and saw her long red hair lifting out as she hurried to keep up with him. He slowed down. "Sorry," he said.

"Over there." Karyn nodded toward a back table, where a roundish woman with white hair sat with a litter of books, open atlases, and folders in front her. She was waving for them to come over. Karyn tugged on Donnie's arm, though he was in the mood to just get out of there. But he let her lead him over to the table.

The woman didn't get up. The composition book she'd been jotting in was open in front of her. The page was half filled with the kind of handwriting Donnie had only seen in some old Palmer-style handwriting books, though his Dad had written kind of like that. The atlases showed the area around Hoel's Dam, as well as Lake Kiowa.

She looked up at them with an intensity Donnie was surprised to see in an older person. Her face had concern and interest on it, expressed in a candor that again reminded Donnie of his father.

"Sit down," she said in a library-soft voice. "Maybe I can help."

Donnie glanced at Karyn, who was already easing into a chair. What the heck? They didn't have anything else on their dance card, and they were only getting nowhere so far. He sat down too.

"You're Donnie Spurlock and you must be Karyn Rainey. I'm Esbeth Walters. I work at the sheriff's department when I don't have a day off, like I do today."

"Are you working on a case?" Karyn leaned closer to see what Esbeth had been writing in her notebook.

"No. I'm just one of the dispatchers. But I'm not from around here, so I was trying to catch up on some of the background here. The whole mess is confusing to me, and I'm the type of person who has to get her head straight about things, if I'm to be able to sleep nights."

"We've been a bit confused ourselves," Karyn said. She looked at Donnie, who gave a short nod, like he ought to say something. But he was too cautious, and a little uptight. Women will pour out their souls to some stranger on a bus. He had never even seen this woman before, and he'd lived here all his life.

"I take it you hit a dead-end over there with Florence." Esbeth nodded toward the counter where the librarian once again had the phone to her ear and was talking loudly into the receiver.

"People say they want to help," Karyn said. "But…"

"I understand. What are you looking for?"

Karyn looked over at Donnie. She was going to force him to speak.

"We…" He glanced to Karyn for reassurance. "We've been trying to find out some things that happened a long time ago."

"To your family."

"Yeah, exactly."

"Wasn't there a family Bible, any kind of journal? Your father was a pretty literate man, I hear. He even wrote some things before he got busy being mayor."

Donnie looked down at the table, let his eyes follow the line of the lakeshore on the map to where it led to the town of Hoel's Dam.

"Some things were missing, weren't they?" Esbeth said.

His head snapped up to the woman, to see if she was giving him that mind-reading look the fake fortune-tellers use. But she was looking at him as if going over some things in her mind, sorting them out.

"Yeah," he admitted. "There were a few things missing, maybe a journal that'd been in the family for as long as I can remember. But there were a lot of people coming in and out of the house. I thought … well, I thought the sheriff might've taken it. I didn't want to say anything."

"I understand. But I think you can rest easy there. He's not the kind of person who'd do that without asking. He may seem a little slow to you, but he's not. He just works in mysterious ways his wonders to perform, though you didn't hear that from me. He kind of plods his slow way to Bethlehem."

"What?"

"Oh, nothing. Just an old person's way of talking, one who's read too many books. Besides, there's no way of knowing that the person who killed your father didn't take some things. Oh, I'm sorry to talk about your father that way."

"That's okay. I'm more used to the idea of him being gone forever now, than I was at first."

"Do you think something like a journal might've been

what the person was after?" Esbeth's round, sincere face was full enough of genuine concern to keep him talking.

"I hadn't thought about it. But maybe that's so. Nothing else makes sense. People liked or disliked Dad, but not enough to kill him. At least I didn't think so."

"What else could there be that might've been that valuable to someone, valuable enough to maybe kill for it?"

"That's what we don't know." He looked at Karyn, but she didn't quite know how to respond to this lady.

"Someone took all the old microfiche copies of the newspaper too, we think," Karyn said. "Fearing didn't have a newspaper then, and the library there didn't store the Hoel's Dam in either paper or microfiche."

"Is that what Florence said?"

Donnie nodded.

"She's kind of new here, relatively, that is. Maybe she doesn't know everything."

"Or care enough to help," Karyn said.

"Some people ignore their fellow man without knowing they're doing it. I know I've been guilty a few times myself," Esbeth said. She pushed at the arms of her chair and stood up. Donnie kept expecting her to rise some more, but she was done getting up when her head was still even with his shoulder. Esbeth closed the books and atlases and picked up her notebook; then she tilted her head and took off in a slow deliberate walk toward the back of the library. She paused at a drinking fountain where she bent and took a short sip while they caught up to her. She stepped a bit closer and said, "A lot of people don't come back this way much. There's an annex built on to store stuff they just didn't feel like pitching. Up north, they'd have stuff like this in a cellar. But you know there aren't many cellars in all of Texas. I doubt if Florence comes back here much, and I know she doesn't to dust."

Donnie followed her, as surprised at himself as Karyn must be. But there was something about Esbeth that made him relax and open up. He doubted if he could explain it, or even if she could herself. It was a manner that told him instinctively that she was there to support and instruct. But she was one of those people who nudged other people to discover things themselves. He bet himself she'd been a teacher once, and a heck of a good one.

Esbeth led them down a long, narrow hallway to a room that was crammed with older books and magazines. This was where they kept the thousands of yellow-spined *National Geographic* magazines, now that there were computers out in the big lobby that could read the CD-ROM versions. Books were squeezed into all the available shelf space, and boxes of magazines, and black buckram-bound copies of *McClure's Magazine* and *Harper's Magazine*. Esbeth seemed to know right where to head. She eased around a row of shelves and went to the far back corner, reached low, and drew out a wide and tall cloth binder. She carried it to a low shelf, where Donnie noticed there was no dust. She'd been back here looking before. He watched her flip through the pages back to an issue that was all about the dam being built.

He read the headline and the first few paragraphs before he asked, "What's this have to do with anything?"

"That's when the trouble started," Esbeth said.

Donnie looked over at Karyn, but she was still reading. When she looked up at Esbeth, she said, "It tells about how the River Authority had to compensate people for the bottomland in the valley it was taking from them, when it filled the valley with what's now the lake. But that wouldn't affect the Spurlocks. They've always lived up here in the hills."

"Exactly." Esbeth said it as if a star pupil had just performed well.

"Yeah, our house's sat right where it is, long before the town of Hoel's Dam ever formed. I always understood the town was just a place for the workers on the dam to live, while the construction was going on. There's all kind of talk about how lawless it got for a while, with hookers and everything else. There's even a plaque over by the dam that kind of brags that only thirteen men died in the building of the dam."

"And that includes Edgar Hoel, who's now part of the concrete mix," Esbeth said.

"But what about…" Donnie stopped himself.

"The diamonds?" Esbeth said.

"How could you possibly know about that?" Karyn looked at her the way Donnie had, when she'd known about the missing journal.

"That's what seems to have everyone standing on their ears." Esbeth pointed down at the pages again. "But finish the story. It's all part of what shapes up later."

She stood back a couple of steps and let them read through the story. Donnie glanced up and caught her smiling when they hesitated and reread the table of land ownership of the big spreads that were going to be relocated in the highlands.

When he and Karyn looked up at last, he said, "A lot of this is common knowledge. Everyone knows that the Hoels were the biggest spread. The Granites had a big place too, but nowhere nearly as large as what Bill Hoel had."

"I'm not saying there are any pat answers here," Esbeth said. "You have to follow the story along for a ways, before any of it forms a bigger picture."

She bent low again and pulled out two more folders. These, Donnie noticed, covered ten years later. She opened them and spread them out.

Donnie and Karyn started reading again. Karyn, who read more quickly than Donnie, looked up after a while and said, "It's kind of hard to tell what was really going on. But it seems like Bill Hoel was doing a lot of complaining that the land they'd given him wasn't nearly as good as what they'd covered up with water. He wanted compensation, but it doesn't sound like he got any."

"You're ready for the final one of these," Esbeth said.

They had to skim through about a month's worth of the papers, though it looked like three weeks of it had been a pretty hot time. Donnie was the first to look up this time. "Sure seems like a lot of people ended up dead."

"Fourteen, by my count," Esbeth said.

"One or two of the Granites, even more of the Hoels. Then some other people who just got involved on one side or the other. What the heck was going on, some kind of feud?" Karyn said.

Donnie looked over at Esbeth. "It doesn't say what started it all, or share anything, really. Except that Bill Hoel isn't complaining anymore. But where's the talk about any diamonds? These stories make it sound like some temporary madness passed over the town, one that went away again after a while and a few people were killed."

"That's the thing about reading this kind of thing. It's only one source, one perspective. You have to read what's not on the page as much as what is." The look on Esbeth's face was as enigmatic as some stone Buddha.

"At least you didn't call either of us 'Grasshopper' when you said that," Karyn said.

"But it's a riddle, all the same," Esbeth admitted. "I haven't put it all together myself. But you have to remember who's running the newspaper by this time."

"I caught that," Donnie said.

"And that's all you have?" Karyn looked at the yellowed pages of the newsprint.

Donnie was watching Esbeth more closely. She showed genuine excitement, a thrill of the hunt in digging through this old stuff. She'd been pouring over atlases and finding all this stuff everyone else thought no longer existed. But, why? In a way, it seemed useless and fruitless digging. But he knew he was just as excited, but only because he was pulling at threads that led all the way back to his own grandfather, Hank Spurlock. What made someone like Esbeth work at it so diligently on her time off? He couldn't understand it, but he had to admit that it attracted him, that it was the kind of thing he wished he was better at. For the first time in a long time, he thought about going to college, learning to do real research.

Esbeth was putting away the folders. When she straightened, she gave a short huff and shared the kind of look a teacher does when class is over for the day. They started out of the room and were going up the hallway, when Karyn turned and spoke softly to Esbeth.

"Is it that unusual for it to be so hard to find out what happened a few years back?"

"You must know that no one loves their history like

Texans—just love it. About every town has some small museum—all, that is, except this one. No county history that's survived has been written in detail, except a small blurb in the *Texas Handbook* that Herb Hoel may well have written. Almost all records for Hoel's Dam, even at Fearing, have clean skedaddled. No, that's not normal, dear."

"Do you think someone stole the microfiche copies of the paper, thinking they'd destroyed some of the city's history?"

Esbeth smiled. "It's possible. Think of it this way. A city without a history has an opportunity of rewriting it the way they'd like it to be."

"Who do you mean when you say 'they'?" Donnie asked.

Esbeth's eyes lit in an amused sparkle. "There, my young friend, you've touched the needle on the nub of the issue."

SEVEN

"YOU THINK HE KNOWS something just because of the way he's been sniffing around? Hell, it's his job to do that." Morgan held up a hand and looked closely at the manicured nails. Selma watched him the way she'd watch a snake when she didn't have a long stick.

"I think the sonuvabitch knows something. You take him too lightly. I checked on him, and he's got just about the best record of all the Rangers for solving cases." Selma sat in what she called her reading chair and scrutinized the gambler, who was still absorbed in looking at his own hands.

"Then why isn't he a lieutenant at least by now? And where'd you get that about his record?"

"I've got a few connections myself."

"I have yet to meet one of you small-town high-steppers who doesn't think he or she has a poker all the way up the governor's ass."

Selma reached for her highball glass. There was just a trickle of bourbon left at the bottom, with ice melting onto it. She tilted the glass back until the ice rattled against her teeth.

"From what I hear," she said, "he's the kind who likes to keep up a humble front. But in the end, he uses whatever it takes to solve more cases than anyone else. But he's no politician, and he's stepped on the wrong toes a lot of times in the past, too many times to go up the ladder as he should've. That doesn't mean he won't be a problem for us."

"Maybe his goals are different than yours and mine, less tangible to him," Morgan suggested. He looked up at her, and gave her a dose of those eyes that even she found disturbing. "I know he doesn't have a wife or family, nothing to make him vulnerable."

"Everyone's vulnerable." Morgan said it in a firm and unflinching tone that made her shudder. "Everyone."

"Even me?"

"Rumor has it you used your husband worse than a servant, more like a woman, in ways I needn't spell out, and that he finally left you for another man."

Selma's normally squinting eyes narrowed to squint even more, until her eyes were two glittering slits between pressed pale flesh. "That's as juberous a splash of sheep dip as I've come across in a while. But, even if true, what's your point? You think that might be used against me, come election?"

"I'm just saying there's surely something on someone like that Ranger."

"Well, there're sure some things I'd like to ask him."

Morgan's head was turned toward the window. "You'll get your chance soon enough for that. Unless I'm wrong, that's his truck pulling up out there."

Selma slammed her glass down onto the end table and shoved herself to her feet. She went over to the window to look through the lace curtains, where Morgan could look out at the road.

"That's a helluva notion." She looked over at Morgan. "Maybe you'd better not be here when he comes in."

"I'll go out the back way." He rose slowly, took his glass with him, and left it in the kitchen sink on his way out.

Selma busied herself with freshening her afternoon beverage, while he went out onto the back porch. Usually she only had one at this hour. But today was turning into at least a two-drink afternoon. She carried the full glass back to her table, then went to answer the door when the doorbell chimed.

She opened the door and took in the Ranger standing there. He was a solid six-footer with a face that looked like it wasn't always so serious. There was just a bit of Indian blood showing in the higher cheekbones, one of which was still sporting a fading purple bruise. His hair, what showed beneath the white hat, was lightly sprinkled with gray, and a white bandage covered his left temple. He wore an open-collar blue shirt over Docker slacks. The Ranger badge was pinned above the left pocket in the accustomed fashion. His Cordovan Lucchese cowboy boots looked like he'd had them a while and gave them a polishing every month or two, whether they needed it or not.

She said, "You might as well come in out of the heat before you shrivel up."

Tillis followed her inside and to the room where she'd just been talking with Morgan Lane. He took off his hat and sat in the same chair where Morgan had sat. She saw him glancing at the ring of moisture where Morgan's glass had been. This one doesn't miss much but, hell, he's a detective.

"Can I interest you in a beverage? I've got a Walker's and water here myself."

"I'd be grateful for just the water."

She went to the kitchen and came back with a glass of iced well water. She set it down on top of the moist ring she should have mopped up before she let him in.

"Nice spread you have here. What is it, about seven hundred acres?"

"Yep. Same as my family had on the valley floor once, but it's not the agricultural land we had there, so I'm told. We've had to switch over to cattle to make do. We put out a number of head each year, but nothing like Bill Hoel's numbers. He's one of them even the big boys call a big boy. But you didn't come all the way here to catch up on the Granite family's doings. What's on your mind?"

He reached up and ran a finger lightly over the bruise on his face. "I was wondering how your two boys are doing?"

"Does that have anything to do with that mouse you're sporting? 'Cause I'd have figured if it was my boys, they'd have left a more distinctive message."

"Whoever it was, they were interrupted. I guess since you've got your thumb on the pulse of this town, you know I was jumped last night."

"So, it was two fellows, and you immediately thought of my sons." She reached for her glass and drank down a healthy inch of it, wishing she'd put in just a bit more bourbon.

"I didn't say that. But I would like to speak with them, if they're around."

Selma felt herself squinting at him and made herself stop. Tillis seemed not to notice. He picked up his glass and took a sip, then put it down in the same spot. "Texas well water," he said. "Nothing like it."

She reached for the phone on the table beside her drink.

One of them'd have his cell phone. "What're you fellas doing? Well, come into the house. There's a Texas Ranger here'd like to have a few words." She paused, listened closely, and then smiled. "Tell him that yourself, if you like."

She put the receiver back on the hook and they waited for a few minutes. He talked about the weather a bit, and she mumbled a few of the standard responses to that.

A few minutes later, the two of them came in through the back. Both of them had on work clothes, and from the dust and dirt on them, it was clear they'd been out working the fence line like they'd set out to do that morning. Both had their leather work gloves tucked into their back pockets.

Every time she saw them, especially all grubby from work like that, it made her think of Slim, their father, though neither boy had his build. They'd clearly taken to her side of the family, where the men ran to the beefy and sullen model. Rocky was the taller of the two by half a head, but both, side-by-side like this, looked like a tag team in professional wrestling. Rocky had short, dark hair and a chew puffing out one cheek, though she'd told them again and again, no spitting in the house. She watched him make a short swallow and glare at the Ranger. He hadn't shaved and there was a dirty smudge across his low forehead. Stone was blond and the looker of them. He'd let his wavy hair grow out, until it came down to his collar. It was brushed back over his ears. She'd worried about him for a while, after he'd come out of the coma that time. But he'd gotten into a scrape only two weeks later and had the kind of vanity about himself that meant getting a tooth capped that was knocked out in that scuffle. Rocky was still missing a lower tooth, but he'd let it stay that way, and thought it added something when he gave the kind of dog-yard grin he was starting to show now. Most mothers might be a bit distressed having a pair like that to feed and raise, but she was prouder of them than the two girls. She knew they might cost her a few votes in an election, but that didn't seem like such a big thing now.

Selma looked over at the Ranger, saw him looking down at the boys' boots, then up at their faces.

"Either of these boys look like the type to be sneaking around in the night trying to waylay anyone with a pipe?" she said.

"I don't think I mentioned there was a pipe involved."

"You didn't have to. I'm on the inside of things around here, as you pointed out earlier." She turned to the boys. "How about it? He's probably gonna want to know where you both were last night."

Stone was usually the one to do the talking for them. But this time it was Rocky who spoke first.

"We was at a church social, or something, wasn't we, Stone?" He grinned at his brother, let the gap in his lower teeth show in a look she'd seen him use just before letting go with a sucker punch.

"Yeah, I guess that was it," Stone said, making no attempt to hide his contempt for any lawman.

"Now, remember, boys. He's a guest in the house right now."

"Is that all?" Stone asked. "Or you want us in profile, or something? We got a lot of work to get back to."

"You boys go on and get to it. I just wanted the Ranger to have a look is all."

They glanced at each other, then went back out the way they'd come in.

"You must be very proud," Tillis said.

"I am. You know, I truly am."

"You've had your hands full, raising a family and running a ranch this size. I'll say that."

Selma was taking another drink and would have laughed if her mouth wasn't full. She put the glass down and grinned at him. "Does that take care of all your questions for today?"

"I've heard a bit about some gold mine or other, back when your spread was down on the valley floor, before you were relocated up here. Was there anything to that?"

"There's been some silver found in Texas, up in San Saba County, from what I hear. But no gold to speak of. I doubt, if there was any gold down there on that valley spread, that old Daddy Boy Granite would've given up the place. That story might've just been spice to get a fair shake, when it came to the land he got up here. This place did turn out to be better pastureland than what Old Bill Hoel got, may his soul rest in hell some day."

Tillis looked out the window, ignoring her for a second. He seemed to be sorting out something in his mind.

"You know, my two boys aren't the only so-called thugs around these parts. Even as short a while as you've been here, I'm sure you've heard about the two destroying angels Old Bill Hoel has up there at that place of his."

Tillis looked back at her. "I'd heard something about them."

"You hear he bailed them out of some Mexican prison, where they both wore murder jackets?"

He smiled at her attempt at lawman's language. "Yeah, I guess I'd heard that. Do you think that might be just some smoke to keep folks away from his place? I hear he's something of a recluse up there on that spread of his."

She let out a snort before she could catch herself. "Old Bill's no recluse. He's just like everyone else around here. He just wants to be let alone, without everyone stirring things up."

Tillis got to his feet slowly, and she noticed he did a pretty good job of not showing a wince when he did.

"You might remember, Selma, that it's not lawmen who're stirring things up around here. It's two Spurlocks turning up dead. That's what's given this rotten old beehive of a town a nudge." He nodded and headed toward the door.

She stood up, only because that was the way she was raised. "I suppose you're right," she said. "I just suppose that's it."

Selma watched out the window as he climbed back into his truck. She lifted her glass and finished the rest of the drink. The second drink was never as good as the first. She could hardly taste the bourbon. As his truck started up and pulled away, she said out loud to herself, "But as far as I'm concerned, the fewer Spurlocks in this town, the better."

ESBETH'S FEET WERE starting to feel like two clods of cement as she went down the street. Going back to work at her age, even at a part-time job, was a challenge. Most days she went home and flopped into bed. Today she was still going, but on borrowed steam, and she had yet to drive home from Hoel's Dam.

The tree-shadowed lawns around her were getting darker, and her car was still a block up the street, the only place she'd found to park near the library.

She recognized the parked copper-with-black-trim car, with its box of red and blue lights across the top, just as the passenger door swung open in front of her. Gala was leaning across the seat, and waved her inside.

Esbeth slid into the seat and shut the door. "Not too far to go," she puffed. "But I can stand a break. Thanks."

"What are you doing all the way over in Hoel's Dam at this hour?" Gala said.

"I could ask you the same."

"But I asked first."

"I heard there was a bakery over here worth finding. I miss Carol Bean's Mean Baking Machine something fierce, though I could really stand to do without the sweets."

"There is a bakery back there, Sweetheart Sue's, though it's likely closed at this hour."

"So I noticed." Esbeth's breath was still struggling to get back to normal after the hike from the library. She caught Gala's quick sideways glance at the big house up on the hill across the street. A number of cars and trucks were parked along the street near it.

"How about you, Gala? Isn't your double-shift about over?"

"In a bit."

"You weren't here for a bakery, were you?"

"No. Not for one that's been closed for three hours. Though I do hear from Eldon that the cheesecake is to die for."

"Is it really good?"

"Eldon claims it'll make you cry."

"But, in a good way?"

"So I hear. You aren't nosing around in anything else over here, are you, Esbeth?"

"Who me? What about you? Did you learn anything from that nice Don Cinco? Have you heard from him again?"

"Don't you worry about him."

"Okay. Guess I won't." Esbeth watched Gala's brown eyes slide away and look up the street. "Well, I've got my wind back. I'd best be heading home, before I turn into a pumpkin."

"Esbeth, you didn't really answer the question."

"No. No, I guess I didn't." Esbeth slid out of the patrol car and shut the door, then waved at Gala as she headed up the street. The deputy stared after her for a minute, then went back to watching the house on the hill.

JIM EDDY FISHER had something of a reputation in the Hoel's Dam area. It ranked a bit behind the Granite brothers, since messing with either of them meant taking on the whole family, and, much to his recent chagrin, he now ranked behind the more recently-arrived Morgan Lane. Jim Eddy had gotten his reputation when, in a scuffle in some late night honky-tonk parking lot, he'd bitten out the eye of his opponent. "I only meant to bite him on the skull," he always explained, "and sucking the eye out just came to me." His tossing it off lightly as a moment of temporary insight and genius didn't inhibit the growth of the reputation that now surrounded him. Jim Eddy may well have lost as many fights as he won in his life, but no one wanted to fight him after that story had circulated.

He was one of the ones sitting at the poker table when Tillis was ushered into the room. Jim Eddy's head made a sheen in the light that hung over the table as it pierced the stubble of his buzzed flattop. He wore a short-sleeved charcoal turtleneck shirt that showed off his gym-conditioned body. Why short sleeves on a turtleneck shirt? Tillis didn't know shirts like that existed. The sleeves were rolled up two turns to showcase biceps and triceps Jim Eddy had spent a lot of time building.

The other three men at the table looked up at Tillis. A couple of them he knew. One was Eldon Watkins; another was Pudge Hurley, the best dam manager in town. Pudge first looked embarrassed, then his head tilted and he seemed to be taking in Tillis, who was without his hat or badge, in a whole new light—the lawman as a potentially flawed and maybe bent individual. Tillis didn't know the other man, but he looked like he had the kind of money it took to play at Morgan's table. He looked at Tillis with indifference, but Eldon's scowl more than compensated.

"Hello, Eldon," Tillis said.

The sheriff just gave a curt, faintly irritated nod.

Sometimes when the going is slow, or you hit a stone wall, you have to be a bit unorthodox, see what kind of a bastard people really think you're capable of being. Tillis looked around, registering the looks on the faces—sure a lot less surprise than he'd have expected.

"You know, if your call is in the least social, you might as well sit in and play a few hands." Morgan smiled in as unfriendly a way as Tillis had ever seen. He was certainly in the lion's den here.

"We have one too many law officers playing as it is," Jim Eddy said. He stared at Tillis, who could see the muscles rippling beneath the shirt in a display he felt sure he was supposed to see.

"Hey," Eldon said. "I'm sitting right here." He gave a half-hearted chuckle.

"That is," Morgan said, "if you're good for these kind of stakes."

It was that kind of situation where if you have to ask, you can't afford it. Under normal circumstances, Tillis would have never accepted. But he was feeling run around by everyone, Eldon included, just enough to want to make a point, though he'd have been hard-pressed to say what that point was as he reached for the chair Morgan offered. He slid the open chair back and slowly lowered himself into it.

Morgan took three matching stacks of blue, red, and white chips and put them in front of Tillis. As he leaned over close, he said very softly into Tillis' ear, "Think you might just be thrashing around, hoping to stir up whatever you can since there's nothing really solid to start on?"

Tillis looked up at him, but Morgan was still the better starer.

Morgan sat down and picked up the deck, offered a cut, then started dealing around the table. Everyone tossed in a white chip, so Tillis matched the ante.

"Five-card draw, pair of jacks or better to open," he said.

Tillis watched his hands. He was good enough to be a mechanic, and Tillis felt the same tinge of envy he always felt when watching the best dealers at Vegas make their living. It was like watching Fred Astaire dance. But he also watched for any unusual movement: dealing off the bottom, something like that. As near as he could tell, Morgan dealt a fair hand.

A game of poker among men can be as revealing as a couple dancing for the first time together. If you knew where to look, and got the least glimmer of a chance, you could learn a lot. Tillis hadn't really scratched the underbelly of the community in which he lived yet. But he sure felt he was there now, fleas and all.

The man to Jim Eddy's left opened, and Tillis picked up a white chip, having no idea of their value until he heard Eldon say, "See your hundred and raise two."

Tillis looked at his cards. He had kings and twos, and was almost certain Eldon had three of a kind to raise like that. But Tillis raised back.

A shadow of doubt showed on Eldon's face. Jim Eddy's shirt jerked about in subtle, but obvious muscle twitches. That was his tic. Tillis saw Morgan catching it. Morgan tossed in his cards, when it was his turn.

Jim Eddy stared at Tillis, hesitating. Then his muscles relaxed and he tossed in his hand.

Pudge tossed down his cards, muttering something about, "... not a hand, it's a foot." He seemed to be taking Tillis in from the corner of his eye, the look of embarrassment now replaced with a hint of resentment, like a man on the wagon caught in an all-night speakeasy by his wife.

"Bet's to you, Phil," Morgan said to the man who'd opened. He sat looking at his cards. He called, then he pitched one card.

Eldon took two new cards, but didn't raise.

"I'm good," Tillis said. He slid a blue chip onto the pile with the blundering poise of a beginner, unaware it was bad form to bump the bet so high.

"Well, damn," Jim Eddy said.

Phil folded. When the bet came around to Eldon, he looked from his cards to Tillis, then back to the cards. Then he turned over the cards and tossed them onto the pile. He frowned at Tillis. "I guess you buy this one."

Tillis tossed his cards down and reached for the chips.

Jim Eddy shot to his feet and grabbed for Tillis' cards. But Tillis' hands landed on the back of Jim Eddy's and slammed them to the table. "You want to see them, you pay to do so."

Jim Eddy flushed red and a ridge of flesh rose across his

forehead. But before he could do anything, Morgan said, "He's right. Sit the hell down, Jim Eddy."

Jim Eddy's head pivoted that way.

Morgan just looked at him. "I said…sit…the…hell… down."

All the tension went out of Jim Eddy's shoulders and he slid his hands out from under Tillis' and lowered himself back onto his chair.

"We can at least see his openers, can't we?" His voice was more sulky than demure.

Morgan glanced to Tillis and nodded.

Tillis reached and turned over the two kings. Then Morgan gathered up the rest of the cards, careful not to show Tillis' three down cards. He shuffled the deck once in a crisp snap and handed it to Jim Eddy, who picked up the cards.

"At least I won't make a payoff by dealing anyone a pat hand," Jim Eddy said.

It was a mistake, Tillis knew, as soon as he said it. But when he looked at Jim Eddy, he saw that crafty pitch to his head that said he'd done it on purpose, that he wanted to test the man.

Morgan's voice sounded like a gravel shirt being slowly ripped in half. "Don't you, or any other sonuvabitch, ever call me a cheat."

It was the gong Jim Eddy had been waiting for. He leaped out of his chair and grabbed at Morgan.

Tillis had seen a lot of men in fights, some of them professionals, and others among skilled and young amateurs. But he had never in his life seen anyone move as fast as Morgan did. One second, he was watching Jim Eddy leap; the next second, Morgan stood behind Jim Eddy with one hand twisted up behind his back as far as it would go and the other hand clenched on Jim Eddy's Adam's apple. First Jim Eddy was red, and struggled feebly. Then the struggling stopped and he turned purple. When he went limp, Morgan opened his hand and stepped back. Jim Eddy fell to the carpet like a wet sack of cement.

Tillis was half out of his seat, but he eased slowly back into it.

Eldon said, "I hope you haven't killed him, Morgan."

"He's not dead."

"Good. It'd be a damn sight of paperwork I don't want right this moment."

Eldon reached down to the floor beside his boot and picked up a walkie-talkie. He turned it on and spoke into it.

Morgan walked across the room, then brought back a matching cover for the poker table. Everyone's chips stayed right where they were, and the cover went over the table.

"I suggest we all take a beverage break while we straighten this out," Morgan said. He reached and touched a button. Tillis heard a bell ring somewhere else in the house.

Eldon looked across the table at Tillis. "I knew you'd be some kinda distraction."

A girl came into the room from the dim hallway, blinking at the brighter lights of the poker room. She had pale blond hair, almost peroxide white. But it was natural and wispy. Her face was round and soft, with pale blue eyes set in the soft skin that made her look about twelve, although Tillis knew she was now seventeen. Everything about her looked fresh and innocent, except her eyes when they swept across the men in the room with a touch of disgust and settled on Morgan with a look Tillis could only think of as raw lust. She wore a thin, white camisole—one that did little to hide her barely-developed body—along with matching white slippers. Sandy Granite ignored the other men in the room and focused on Morgan with an obedient puppy look that made Tillis shudder, when he realized he was picturing the two of them together doing some of the things they must do. The air of decadence and corruption in the room increased for Tillis. Sandy's eyes were a bit bleary, and she looked as if she had been interrupted from the beginning of a nap, or from watching too much television.

Morgan tilted his head toward the wet bar. "See what the men want to drink and mix up a round," he said.

She went over to the bar and started setting up some glasses. Those who wanted drinks got them, with Tillis getting a tall glass of ice water with a single shot of Scotch in it. The idea of his drink being mixed by someone so underage didn't do much for the gritty feeling he was having about himself. Sandy put away the bar things and left with as little fanfare as when she had entered.

All the men had glasses in front of them on the table when the uniformed deputy came in. It was Gala, and she nodded to Eldon, but her eyes showed a second of surprise when she took in Tillis. He gave her a quick half-wink. Her eyes swept on around at the others; then she went over to Jim Eddy.

"You got here plenty fast enough," Eldon said, but she just nodded.

She and Eldon got cuffs on Jim Eddy, who was just coming to. They helped him stand and led him outside to the patrol car. He didn't look at anyone in the room while he was being led away.

When Eldon came back in, he said, "Well, I guess we can get back to it."

Morgan had already removed the drinks and was lifting the cover back off the table.

They played for another half hour before they hit one of those pots where everyone had a betting hand.

Tillis had won enough to hang in with the betting, though it took him down to his last chips. He didn't let himself calculate how much he'd owe if he lost. For all his earlier reminders to himself what he was up to, he was caught up for the moment in a rush of adrenaline, and the exhilaration of the game, the fact that as much, or more, could go wrong as right.

Morgan stood pat, the others all drew cards, and Tillis asked for one card. He didn't need a card. He already held four jacks. Asking for a card would make the others think he was drawing to two pair for a possible full house, he could only hope, unless they were second-guessing him as he was them.

The others eventually all bowed out during the betting, and it was just Morgan and himself. Tillis said, "I'm going to need more chips."

Morgan smiled, and asked Eldon to bring another stack of blue chips. Eldon grumped, but got them, and put them down in front of him while looking at Tillis as if wishing the Ranger considerable harm. The entire stack of chips was just enough for Tillis to match the final bet.

"What's that place of yours out there worth, Tillis?" Morgan asked. His eyes locked with Tillis' then opened slightly wider, for the first time Tillis had ever seen them flinch in a stare.

Morgan lowered his hand to the table, showing four sevens. When Tillis put down his four jacks, Morgan didn't sigh or show any emotion. While Tillis racked in the little mountain of chips, Morgan drew the cards together and began to shuffle.

Tillis said, "I think I'd like to cash out now."

Eldon started to say something, but Morgan held up a hand. He reached for Tillis' chips and counted them out in stacks.

"Check be all right?"

"I'd prefer cash."

Morgan rose, went out of the room. He was back in just a little over a minute with a stack of bills. He put it down in front of Tillis. "You want to count it?"

"Do I need to?"

"You want a bit of advice?" Morgan's eyes were like two lasers.

"Not really."

"I'll offer it anyway. Spend that as quickly as you can."

"I'm disappointed." Tillis pushed himself to his feet, folded the money, and shoved it into his jeans pocket. He looked at Eldon, then back at Morgan. "I thought you'd be more original than that."

TILLIS WALKED OUT into the cool night breeze and, now that he was out of sight of the others, he stretched some of the tension out of his shoulders. It hurt to do so. The residential area had street lights staggered every half block or so, and they only dimly lit the street. He could look up and see stars. He'd had to park his truck half a block up the street. Tillis stepped out into the street and started that way, keeping an eye on the bushes on both sides as he walked. No one made a move out of the darkness toward him, as he halfway expected. He was almost disappointed. But someone small and solid was leaning against the side of his truck waiting for him. As he got closer, he could make out Gala's distinctive features, her brown eyes catching what little light made it down through the leaves of a sycamore tree to his truck. She wore street clothes now: khaki shorts and a snug dark blouse with sandals on her tanned feet.

"Thought I'd see if you made it out all right," she said.

"Have folks disappeared who went in there?"

She shrugged and turned, started walking. She waved for him to join her. "I got off right after I got Jim Eddy to where he can rest for the night. I kind of wondered what you were doing in a place like that. Have you got an idea?"

He caught himself looking down at her lips while she spoke. He looked up and away.

She sighed. "Oh, what the heck. Want to join me for a nightcap? I'm staying right up this way."

Tillis took a few long strides that caught him up to her, then had to walk briskly to keep up.

Her place was an older, wooden two-story house almost at the end of the street. She went in first, flipping on the lights. The furniture was overstuffed sofas and wing chairs, each with a doily on the arm rest. The rest of the furniture was all antiques. An upright piano that had been around before Tillis was born was nestled against one wall. The framed photos along its top looked like daguerreotypes of people long dead, standing in front of carriages and old buildings that were also long gone.

"Place came furnished," she said. "But I like the museum effect it gives."

She went over to a secretary, tugged the cork from a half-empty bottle, and poured red wine into a glass. "What's yours? Scotch?"

"Yeah." He was having trouble talking, watching her move so gracefully through her home.

She poured an inch-and-a-half of Glenlivet into a tumbler. "Water?"

"Straight will be fine, since it's single-malt."

She brought him his glass, then settled into a corner of the couch and patted the middle cushion. He didn't have to be asked twice and sat down beside her, a little too quickly. His sore side let him know. But he kept from wincing, though he did catch her looking at the bruise on his face over the top of her wine glass.

He took a sip of the Scotch, then another, before reaching to put the glass on the coffee table. When he sat back beside her, she reached out to touch the side of his face.

"Still a little tender?" Her fingers were soft, and lit on his skin like a butterfly.

He turned to look at her, and caught himself staring at her lips. He looked up into her eyes and the next thing he knew they were kissing. She was a very good kisser, and that wasn't just because it'd been a while for him. Part of it may have been all the anticipation since the first time he'd seen her.

He could taste the wine, and could imagine she got a sample of the Scotch, but he doubted if it was the combination of those two giving him a tingle all the way up his spine.

They pulled apart after a few minutes, and she reached for her wine glass and finished the bit in it. "How'd it go in there?"

"Okay, I guess." The wad of bills in his pocket was pinching him. He pulled it out and put in on the table beside his glass.

"You plan on leaving that on the dresser like all the sailors?"

"No, I ..."

But she was grinning that mischievous grin of hers.

"You got a favorite charity?" he said.

"I guess anything connected to law enforcement's out. How 'bout a fund that helps immigrants out? I know of one that Senator Martinez heads."

"You know him? He's sure been in the news a lot."

"He's from this state. I've met him. His fund could really use a boost."

"Fine with me. Morgan'd be proud, and I know Eldon'd be tickled."

Back while he'd been playing poker, posturing with the other men, he'd felt silly. Right now, plopping the money down in front of her, like some cat bringing a dead bird to lay on the pillow of its owner, he should feel even sillier. But he didn't. He felt more awake and alive than he had in a long time, as if tossing back the covers of a long slumber.

He took a sip of his drink and looked at her. If he really stretched, he might even read some concern in her look. "You sure you know what you're doing?" she asked.

"A lot of people want to know that. I wouldn't let it worry you. You're young and you'll recover from whatever happens with this."

"I'm not so young. I'm forty."

"You're in damn good shape for forty."

"And you?"

"Forty-three."

"I'd have taken you for thirty-four or -five."

"You like your men younger?"

"I like chocolate. But I don't let myself have any. I do allow myself to have an occasional man."

"Lucky me." He put his glass back on the table and turned to her.

She was unbuttoning the top buttons of her blouse. He watched her slim brown fingers undo each one. Then he leaned closer and they were kissing again while he fumbled with his own buttons.

She pulled back and stood, reached, and held out a hand. She led him down a hallway, each of them dropping clothes along the way.

The bedroom had a dim night light of Tiffany glass glowing in the corner beside the four-poster bed, complete with a canopy. She turned to him and dropped the rest of her clothes to the floor and let him look at her as she eased back onto the bed. Her stomach was rows of hard-ridged muscle, the thighs every bit as firm and as athletic as he'd thought. She didn't seem to mind him looking over the peaks and valleys of her stretched-out naked body while he tugged off the rest of his clothes, and let them fall to the earth he knew not where. She had interesting tan lines, the pale places small enough he wouldn't mind knowing where she did her sunbathing.

He slid onto the bed beside her and reached for her. She was warm and soft-skinned over that hard body.

"Don't make this into more than it is. We're a couple of lonely people stuck in this place," she said.

"Oh, I won't." Make it any more than it is, he thought. Then they were done talking for quite a while.

He woke either in the middle of the night, or early in the morning. His watch was off, and that arm was tucked under Gala. The dim night light that glowed orange, red, and blue from the Tiffany lamp lit the room enough for him to see the sheets worked down and to show the muscles of her back down to her waist. With his free hand, he softly rubbed the skin and began to work her trapezia muscles with his fingers.

"Hmm," she said. "Don't stop."

He stroked the firm muscles of her back down to where her hips were softer. She made soft responsive noises for ten minutes or so, and finally rolled on her side to face him and draw closer to him.

"You know your problem?" she mumbled into his ear.

"What?"

"You're a giver."

"Is that a problem?"

"It is for most men. In the manly bullshit world you live in, it's a sign of weakness. So you've got to go around hiding it the way you do, wearing loose shirts to hide these pecs." She cupped his pectoral muscles the way he would a woman's breasts.

It made him uneasy for a second, but he said, "Don't reduce me to an object."

"I intend to do just that," she said, and her hands slid down him, where she found him responsive.

There was something else he didn't share with her, and not merely because he was distracted. He wasn't good at being casual—he was likely to end up caring about her.

She rolled him onto his back and climbed across him to sit upright and straddle him. She looked down at him and said, "I just wonder if you know what you're up to."

"Yeah, I wonder about that a bit myself."

EIGHT

ESBETH WAS A LITTLE AHEAD of schedule. It was six forty-seven a.m. by the time she had walked the fourteen blocks from her little cottage to work, and that was good time since Texas towns, even a county seat like Fearing, don't have half as many sidewalks as they need. The sky was lightening and still a little overcast, though she expected that would burn off by mid-morning. She spotted the sheriff's car already in the lot beside the cruisers. She buzzed into the building, expecting to find Luke, the night dispatcher. Instead, she found Gala sitting at the dispatch desk.

Gala spun in the chair, grinned at Esbeth, and wagged a cautionary finger back to the desk where Eldon was bent over a couple of open folders. Before Esbeth could respond or even put down her purse, the sheriff looked up at her.

"I suppose you're in a cheerful damn mood too."

"Always am after a day off." Esbeth worked through the cause and effect cycle quickly. Yesterday was Thursday, poker night in Hoel's Dam. The cards had probably not been very kind. She turned to Gala. "You worked a double-shift yesterday, didn't you?"

Gala nodded.

Gala stood up, and Esbeth sat down in the Dispatch chair. She looked up at Gala. "You're sure here early, then. That should have tuckered you."

"You're a bit early yourself."

"Something was gnawing at me."

Gala grinned to herself. "Nothing like I had."

Eldon had gone back to his paperwork. He looked up at them. "Ladies. I don't want to hear about it. And, oh, Esbeth, on that subject, Floyd Bettles is back there locked up and pining away for you. He got himself liquored up again last night in hopes of seeing you again."

"Oh, shoot a bug." Esbeth glanced toward the hallway that led to the cells.

"Now, if we can move on from the subject of romance."

Esbeth was looking back to where the eighty-year-old and drunk Floyd was housed. "At my age, romance isn't dead, it just looks that way."

"Can we get to work?"

"Why don't you try being some of the other dwarves some days? You're wearing Grumpy out," Esbeth said.

Eldon clamped his mouth tight and went back to work.

Gala was humming to herself as she unlocked her locker, took out her gun belt, and strapped it on. "There was another one back there last night. But we let him go, once he'd cooled down."

She watched the sheriff, but he was scribbling away, reading and signing reports.

"The media's on the way, too, Esbeth. Get ready for that dog-and-pony show."

This time Eldon's head snapped up again, and he frowned.

That's what's put the real burr under his saddle, she thought. Esbeth straightened the piles of paper on her desk. When camera crews came all the way out from Austin, it put the hot seat under Eldon, who from the look of it hadn't slept all that much or that well.

Esbeth glanced at the clock and made a note in the log. "Well, I doubt there's very much to learn at this point. Everyone seems to be going at this like the cowboy who hopped on his horse and rode off in all directions. Those media crews will leave here, knowing no more than they came with, and that should leave them the grouchy ones at the end of the day."

"Yeah, there's that," Eldon said, and a partial smile struggled onto his face. The thought seemed to please him somehow.

WHEN THE OLD classic Dodge pulled up in front of the house at ten fifty-three a.m., Logan was up onto his feet, off the rocker in seconds. But the car door slammed and the car was pulling away by the time he had stepped out around the thick clumps of wisteria that sheltered a corner of the porch. Karyn came running up the walkway to the house, her long red hair streaming out behind her. She looked up and saw him, then slowed to a walk.

"Is this what being grounded means?" Logan had to fight to keep the quiver of anger out of his voice.

In the past few hours, he'd driven all the way in to Hoel's Dam, where he'd searched all the spots he thought Karyn might've gone, even the Spurlock boy's house. He'd only succeeded in whipping himself up into a more irrational frenzy. He'd known that while sitting out on the porch, and he'd tried to talk himself down from it.

"I was only at the library again, Dad. I was up early this morning. It isn't like I was out all night."

"But you were with the Spurlock kid."

"His name's Donnie. You know that. Why're you being like this?"

"If your mother was here…"

"Don't use her like some playing card. I loved her too. So don't bring her name up every time you can't think of what to do on your own."

If he hadn't worked himself up into such an emotional and jittery mess, he might have admired the flash and sparkle of spirit in her green eyes.

Logan felt the red line of flushed skin pass up along his throat and climb across his face until it swept into his hair. What made it ten times worse was remembering the one or two times his temper had gotten the best of him with Heidi. He'd broken a favorite vase of hers the second time, and he'd have bought her a hundred vases to replace it if she'd only have let him. He couldn't shake the look that'd been on her face either, and that had stayed there for the two weeks she had avoided speaking to him. He hated his own temper, and that just made it worse.

"Get in the house." He turned from her and started a slow walk, down a half-mile on the road and then back. A couple of pickups and a car or two went by, one of the drivers waving at him. He forced himself to wave back—must look silly, a game warden in uniform out walking up a road by himself.

He wasn't much calmer by the time he got back to the house. But he figured he was fit enough to talk to Karyn now without snapping at her. He went to her room, but she wasn't there. Then he checked the rest of the house. She was gone.

He couldn't believe it. He went through every room again, checking. Where could she have gone? He walked back to her room and stood looking at the made bed, the pictures along her dresser, including her prom photo with Donnie, the small, worn, brown bear tucked by her pillow. He put a hand on his hard stomach. It felt like a large, jagged hook had his entrails and was pulling them out, a ripping wound. "What have I done?"

If his own irrational guilt about Heidi's death wasn't so great, would he feel this bad? Hard to say; he had no point of comparison. But there were folks who beat their kids. At least he hadn't struck Karyn. But she had seen him struggle with all he had not to swat her. What to do? What to do?

He walked back out onto the porch and then to the road, looking either way to see if he could see her walking. Then he got in the truck and drove. He drove everywhere, even to the Spurlock house again, where no one was home. When he finally pulled up at his home again, he was emotionally exhausted. His hands trembled and the steering wheel felt clammy to him. That's when Tillis pulled up in his truck.

Logan sat there, so Tillis climbed out of his truck and came up to look in at him through the driver's side window.

"Hey, you okay?"

"Sure. Sure, fine."

"You don't look it."

Logan turned to look at him. "What do you want?"

"I'm headed over to beard the lion in its den."

"What?"

"I'm driving up to see Old Bill Hoel."

"And?"

"I wanted to know if you could go with me. I checked with your buds at work and no one's seen you today."

Logan just looked at him.

"Well?"

"Well, what?" Logan felt queasy. Maybe if he checked her room again.

"Can you go?"

"No."

"No? No, why?"

"I've got problems of my own here."

"I'll go alone, then."

"Fine. Go, then. It sounds just like the tom fool thing you'd want to do."

"I don't get it. You're going to let me go up there by myself?"

"Why, you scared?"

"No."

"Well, you should be."

THE ROAD THAT led up to and past the Hoel spread was maintained by the county. It was only two lanes wide, and patched in spots. There was even a one-lane bridge where Tillis slowed to make sure no vehicle was coming in the other direction before he crossed—not much traffic came out this way.

He knew he was getting close when he came to the fourteen-foot-high deer fence with razor coils of wire looped all the way along the top. The fence posts and trim were all a freshly-painted green. That was one expensive fence, and Tillis knew it went all the way around the place, which at thirty-five miles by thirty-five miles, and over twenty-two thousand acres, was half as big as Yellowstone Park. It was land given him in compensation for what was now underwater. The Hoels had owned most of the valley.

The gate was a long expanse of cemented rock, leading to a sliding steel set of bars across the only road Tillis knew of that led into Hoel's place. The gate was shut, and locked with a pair of padlocks. Nestled into the rock of the right side of the gate was a covered phone. Tillis pulled over, got out of the truck, and felt the sun and heat of midday slam into him while he walked over to the phone. There was no dial, but as soon as he lifted the receiver off the hook, he could hear ringing on the other end. It rang seven times before someone answered.

"What?" The voice was rough and harsh, like some irritated person interrupted in the middle of a coughing jag.

"This is Tillis Macrory, with the Texas Rangers. I'd like to come in and talk with Bill Hoel."

"Go away."

"What?"

"You heard me."

"I can come back with a warrant, if I have to." By now Tillis had figured out he was speaking with Old Bill Hoel himself.

"What'ya want to talk about?"

"I can come back with the INS too, if that helps." It was a long shot.

"Hell, they done been here. You're shooting with blanks there. Go away."

"I'm working on two murders, and if you don't think I can come back and get inside, you're wrong."

"Who's dead?"

"Denny and Hugh Spurlock."

"Hell, that ain't murder. There oughta be a bounty on Spurlocks."

A trickle of sweat ran down the back of Tillis' neck, and ran all the way down his back to his belt. He wished he'd put on his hat. "Quit fooling around and open this gate, or I'll come back and have it knocked down."

"And you'd pay for it, too."

"Goddamn it, Hoel …"

"Aw, hang onto your star. I'll have the boys come out and let you in."

By "boys" he meant Jorge and Estaban. At least that's who Tillis figured they had to be. Both, he'd heard, looked like enough miles of hard road to have been doing time in a Mexican prison for murder. They drove up in a pickup and pulled up, blocking the gate from the other side.

As soon as the truck pulled up, men stood up in some of the brush on the other side of the fence. Tillis could make out two down along his left, and at least three to the right. Each held a weapon, semiautomatics it looked like from here. The faces were all Latino and sullen, as if blaming Tillis for their having to be out in the scrub like that, though Tillis imagined there was some kind of guard all the time. Old Bill Hoel might be just a tad paranoid.

The one in the passenger seat got out and went to the gate, unlocked both locks, and slid the gate open just wide enough for Tillis to walk through. He wore a red long-sleeved shirt, jeans, and a gun in a side holster. It looked like a Colt .45 single-action to Tillis. The Wild West was still alive and thriving out here.

"Leave the truck, and any guns with it," he said, with a heavy accent and with the practiced sound of someone not used to using English much, having to think out the words and rehearse them.

Tillis went back, slid off his holster, and put it and the gun into the glove box. Then he locked the truck. It wasn't blocking the gate, but he wished it was.

The one in the red shirt had the face of someone who had

been beaten at least once, perhaps more—beaten and left to heal on some hard cement floor. Hard sticks or ax handles had broken even the deep bones of the skull on what was now an imperfectly-formed head. But, if those beatings were meant to break his spirit, they had failed. There was spirit left, plenty of it. Black sparks glittered from the slits of his eyes as he stared at Tillis while trying to show no emotion, but seeming to be a copper-tinted statue to hate itself, though Tillis couldn't tell if it was because he was looking at a Texas Ranger or if he just hated everyone. When they got to the truck, he got into the back seat of the extended cab. Tillis sat in the passenger seat and didn't much care to have one of them behind him in a blind spot. He turned sideways in his seat until he could see them both.

"Estaban?" he said to the driver.

The driver just nodded to the back seat as he put the truck in gear, and that covered all of the conversation all the way to the house.

Jorge drove in a slow and deliberate way. He wore the same clothes as Estaban, except his shirt had been faded by bleach or the sun. The gun on his side was some kind of automatic, a 9mm Tillis guessed, maybe a Glock, something like that. He didn't want to lean closer and find out.

Tillis could only catch Jorge's face in profile, but it was a complete contrast to Estaban's. Jorge's was nearly angelic, youthful and devoid of expression. Yet it somehow seemed the sort of angel that might tear the hearts from small children with more zest than required.

The drive was several miles long, and wove through open cattle land. The live oak trees all had the flat-trimmed bottoms that come from cattle rounding out their diet by pruning the lower branches. Much of the mesquite and other scrub had been cleared off in routine burnings, so most of the hills were rolling and covered in grass. They passed a number of drives that led off in other directions, and a couple of times Tillis could see clusters of buildings in the distance, some shaped like houses. They finally climbed a hill with winding switchbacks, until they came to a surprisingly humble ranch home up on the top of the hill. He doubted if it had more than half a dozen bedrooms. It sprawled in a U-shape around a courtyard of red brick-colored tiles. Crepe myrtles and oleanders bloomed in the corners of the courtyard. They were old plants that hadn't been trimmed recently and had gotten as big as small trees.

A cedar fence, that had aged in the sun until it was silver, ran around the house. The house was old mission stone and stucco, with orange curved tiles on the roof. It was nowhere near the mansion he expected. Meeting Old Bill would be like coming face-to-face with history. All he had heard of him were stories like Old Bill being one of the main financial backers who helped LBJ into office so long ago.

Jorge led the way inside, and Estaban trailed behind. They worked it so someone was always on either side of him, herding him down the hallway into an open back room where the sun came in through the windows that lined two of the walls. A dining table, old and scarred, with a couple candle holders and partially-guttered candles, was in the center of the bright room. Old Bill Hoel himself stood over by the window, looking out across his estate.

Bill turned and started across the room, waving toward the table. Tillis felt either Jorge or Estaban nudge him that way.

Tillis lowered himself into the offered chair, didn't stand and wait for the handshake that didn't look forthcoming.

Bill could barely walk. His jeans-clad legs were bowed, and each step came down on the inside of a worn cowboy boot. His face was set in a concentrated frown, and it was a face that'd seen a lot of sun and was as wrinkled and as worn as an old glove. The barely-combed hair still had a thatch of black at the top, though the sides were white as a snowy egret.

Old Bill Hoel lowered himself into a chair with an effort, one hand gripping the table and the other the back of the chair. He didn't ask for help from either of his men, and they stepped back. Bill waved a hand at them. "We don't need you two hanging 'round. *Vamos*. Send Marie in with coffee, though."

Bill wore a denim shirt that hadn't been ironed, and the wrinkles went with the dark tanned lines that covered his neck and face. He turned to Tillis. "I heard you're finding dead Spurlocks all over the place like Easter eggs. What the hell's that to do with me?"

Before Tillis could answer, a matronly Hispanic woman carrying a tray with a round Thermos pot and two mugs on it pushed her way through the swinging doors from the kitchen and carried it over to the table. She was as deferential as anyone Tillis had ever seen, her eyes never going near Bill Hoel, though she gave Tillis a quick look.

Bill thanked her in Spanish, and Tillis noted that Bill spoke Spanish very poorly, with a heavy American accent, making no effort to get the sound right. But everyone seemed to understand him so far. They made that extra effort, and he seemed the sort to expect it.

Bill poured himself a cup into one of the white ceramic mugs and let Tillis fend for himself. While Tillis filled his own cup and tried not to think about it being almost a hundred degrees outside by now, Bill asked, "What's the other guy look like?"

Tillis looked up at Bill, saw him looking at the bruise before locking stares. Bill had a penetrating stare, but nothing like the one Tillis had experienced from Morgan Lane. "I'm hoping to find that out."

"Come again?"

"Two guys jumped me while I was on a stakeout."

"And you just naturally thought that Old Bill Hoel has a couple of guys like that, eh?"

It surprised Tillis to hear Bill call himself by the same appellation all the town people used. It hinted that he was pretty aware of what went on down below in the real world.

"I've heard they're hard cases," Tillis said. He'd heard locals refer to them as the "hands of darkness."

"Maybe by local standards."

"I guess."

"If I was to bother to send a couple of my beanos down to give you a message, it'd been a damn sight more thoroughly done than whatever little love tap was laid on you."

"These two were interrupted."

Bill shrugged.

Tillis looked out the window at the sprawling fields dotted with cattle. In the distance, he could make out little villages, all within the confines of the fenced-off land. "This is a huge place. How do you manage to take care of it all?"

Tillis looked back at Bill, found him frowning even harder. "You come here to talk cattle or ask me about those dead Spurlocks?"

"Denny was probably just a boy to you, but you probably

knew Hugh, and you certainly knew Hank. What can you tell me about Hank? I gather Hugh was trying to track down his steps when he disappeared."

"If you've come for a history lesson, you've come to the wrong place. You do your own homework. Hank's been missing or dead all these many years, and Hugh almost as long. I don't even know why you're fussing around, wasting taxpayer dollars."

Tillis was taking a sip of coffee. He lowered the mug and let it bang down on the table. He leaned forward, seemed to see a glitter of amusement behind Bill's frown. "Now you listen. I've been getting the runaround about this all over town, from that priggish newspaper son of yours to almost every man and woman on the street. But don't think that's going to slow me down. I'll get to the bottom of this, if I have to subpoena every one of you hilljack cowboys into court and pound it out of you. Now, do you hear what I'm saying?" Tillis felt heat rippling through himself, and it was more than just the coffee.

Bill cocked his head just a fraction of an inch. "Yeah, I hear the words, and know what you're sayin'. Long as I've cattle farmed, I've even stepped in it a time or two."

Tillis rose and turned to walk out of the room. Jorge and Estaban were waiting in the hall. Neither waited to hear from Old Bill. They just walked Tillis to the door and out to their truck.

As they were going back out the drive, three pickup trucks, each with the cab full and a half dozen unsmiling Hispanics in the bed, crossed from one road to another. That INS crack earlier hadn't gotten as much of a rise out of Old Bill as he'd expected. But then, that old cowboy wasn't the kind to show too much that was in his hand. Tillis looked off into the distance, where earlier he'd seen small clusters of buildings, like villages on the property.

He climbed out of the truck at the gate and went through when Jorge opened it enough for him to pass through.

Tillis couldn't tell if he was just heated up himself, or if it was sun that made beads of sweat pop out on both his temples. He waited until the gate had closed and the truck started back down the lane toward the house before he took out a blue handkerchief and wiped at his forehead.

He climbed into the truck, twisted the key, and lurched off with an irritated little scratch of gravel.

He hadn't gotten much, that was for sure. But, as he drove away, Tillis was thinking about Jorge, and his boot, the one with the smile on the end of it where he'd kicked something hard enough for the steel toe to show through.

IT'S A DAMNED thin line between celebration and despair. Thirsty Mills took careful steps as he wove through the stacks of magazines and discarded books of his that he'd sorted through and decided to leave behind in this armpit of a community. No, armpit wasn't strong enough. Years ago he'd seen a scrap of graffiti— "If the world needs an enema, they'll stick the tube in here." That fit Hoel's Dam better. He knocked over a small stack of CDs, didn't pause to pick them up, merely kicked them out of the way. His one-bedroom flat was on the second floor above the Mane Attraction beauty salon that had long ago closed for the day.

He looked for, and found, a flashlight. He checked it, put in fresh batteries, then took it over to put in the small canvas duffel, along with the green folding trenching shovel he'd gotten at a surplus store. The leather Spurlock family journal was already in the bag. He had about everything he needed, and the rest of his possessions he planned to take with him were already packed and in the trunk and back seat of the car.

Each move he made was slow and deliberate, putting each tool in the bag so it wouldn't clunk, even though no one was below to hear him. He rode a righteous little buzz and moved with the absorbed concentration of a DWI driver trying to stay within highway lines. He was down to a last half-pint of brandy and three beers, which he'd put in a bag for later. He didn't want to be over the top and unable to do one final little chore.

When the last of the gear was together in the bag, he zipped it closed and looked up and around at the rest of the place where he'd spent too many years. His look lingered on the shelf where he'd removed the small row of individually-bound Shakespeare plays. The rest of the worn paperbacks could stay. He'd trimmed down to only what he could carry and felt he must have. If everything went as he expected, he'd be able to replace everything else with leather-bound sets, if he liked.

He carried the two bags down to the car, leaving the door to his place unlocked and partially open. He put the bag of gear onto the passenger seat of his tired-looking Dodge and the bag with the beers and brandy on the floor. He closed the door and stood looking around at downtown, metropolitan Hoel's Dam, population 7,567, soon to be 7,566. The street was quiet, and the lights lit up the same scene he had viewed too often. Several storefronts were closed, with "Out of Business" signs demonstrating in harsh reality that too few people formed sound business plans before making their entrepreneurial leap. His own plan was far simpler, and he went around to get into the driver's seat to execute it.

Seventeen minutes later, he eased his car into a parking spot half a block down from the Spurlock house. The lights were out in the old Victorian house, but he sat and waited for another half hour before he got out of the car. He carried the bag of tools and eased along the sidewalk until he could slip closer, letting a large japonica bush shield him from the dimly-lit street.

At the side of the house, he hugged the paneling closely and took careful steps until he was at one end of the porch. He eased to his knees and looked at the cross-hatch of wooden slats that ran from the edge of the porch down two feet to the ground. He reached for his tool bag, took out a claw hammer, and began to quietly loosen the nails that held it in place.

When he had enough of the nails loose, he pulled the edge of the wooden cross-hatch loose and bent it outward. It was old and weak. Suddenly it gave, and a loud crack froze him in place. He looked around. There was no one on the street or on the neighboring porch. Thirsty took out a flashlight and slithered in under the porch, dragging the bag of tools with him. Once he was under, he laid the flashlight down, careful to let it make only a small spray of light that pointed away from the front of the porch. He took out the trenching tool, unscrewed the knob at the top of the handle, opened the shovel's small blade, and screwed the knob back into place. Then he began to dig.

Three holes later, he was covered with sweat when the tip of the shovel's blade clicked on something hard and hollow. He was clearing away the rectangular surface when he heard a small noise, then felt something hard press against his lower left ribs. A voice said, "Drop that shovel and back out from there slowly." He had never felt the barrel of a gun prodding him before, but a ripple of adrenaline went through him as he realized that the barrel of one was what was poking him now.

As he stood slowly, once he was out from under the porch, Thirsty felt bits of dirt falling from his beard and sweat running down in a trickle along his spine. The breeze that swept down between the houses gave him a brief ripple of shudders.

As his eyes adjusted, he looked at the one pressing the gun to his stomach now. "Oh, it's you."

Though he had no way of knowing it, Thirsty was about the make the last and most serious mistake of his life. But being kicked around, just finding the box, and then being interrupted was all too much. All of Morgan's emasculating words came back to him, and his fist was slowly tightening. Every time Herb Hoel had killed one of his stories, each time he'd had to take the disrespect of every one of these country bumpkin Philistines, and on top of that, finding the box. Dammit. He'd found it, and he wasn't going to let it slip away.

His fist all the way tight, his shoulder dipped and he started his upward swing. Something hard slammed into the back of his head, and he crumpled slowly, first dropping to his knees, then sprawling out across the dirt and grass beside the porch.

LOGAN HAD BEEN muttering to himself all the way back on the drive from Fearing to Hoel's Dam, and he was still doing it when he turned his truck around the corner and the lights swept across the darkened front of the Spurlock house.

Two figures stood over to one side of the porch. He could just make out the dim shapes as he slammed on the brakes, threw the door open, and ran toward the house. He slowed as he got closer, realizing it wasn't Donnie and Karyn. The two figures turned and ran. Logan started after them, but tripped and fell. He started to scramble to his feet, then realized he'd fallen over a body. He stopped and leaned closer until he got a look and a whiff. This sure wasn't Karyn or Donnie either. He got up slowly and brushed himself off. The men were long gone. He went back to the truck, pulled it off the street, got out the flashlight as he should have in the first place, and went back to have a look.

He took in the torn side of the porch and the loose dirt in piles under it, and he swept his light across the body and bent down to feel for the pulse that wasn't there, just as he expected.

The relief that still flooded through Logan that the body was not Karyn's, or even Donnie's, made him giddy for a moment.

"Well, Thirsty," he said, "looks like we're going to have to get us a new town drunk."

NINE

ESBETH WAS PLODDING HER way toward her cottage home at ten minutes after ten that night. Her legs felt as if made of lead, and she'd made the walk home on automatic pilot, thinking over the chaos of the day—or rather, trying not to think of it. She'd been held over by the late arrival of the media crews, and it had been a sullen and unproductive visit by them, until just as they were packing to leave. That's when the call came from Logan about finding Thirsty. Those media jackals were happy then, almost as happy as Sheriff Eldon was unhappy, even though she knew he didn't care a fig for Thirsty. Each lift of a leg now was a concerted effort, and she stared down at the sidewalk where there was one. The fourteen blocks seemed to stretch on forever into the darkened streets.

A mockingbird scolded her from a persimmon tree, and, half a block later, she heard the single sharp squawk of a scissor-tail flycatcher. Either call on a normal evening walk would have had her looking up into the dark clusters of leaves in the trees, wondering what the birds were doing moving around so late. She even ignored a neighbor's yappy little dog that crashed against the chain link fence of that yard in a way that usually gave her a start. Tonight the little annoying furball didn't even succeed in making her miss a single, plodding step. It would be a good night for a diet. She wouldn't even bother to fuss over making dinner. She could picture her bed and planned to head right for it and climb right in, and the only positive to the whole mess was knowing she didn't have to go in to work until noon tomorrow.

She turned left and wove along the final winding half-block until she came to the small crepe myrtle bushes she'd planted at the end of her walk. They were drooping a bit. She'd water them in the morning. Esbeth went down the walk, staring at the flagstones, too tired to lift her head and see if the bougainvillea she'd put in along the edge of the porch was coming along. She picked up the newspaper that lay across the doormat, creaked back upright, and had the key in her hand reaching for the door when someone appeared out of the dark a couple feet to her left and said, "Pssst."

She jerked and spun. Karyn and Donnie stood in the dark shadow of the porch. "Great gobs of grits. You just scared me out of three years of growth," she said.

"Sorry. We're kind of in a jam and want to see you," Karyn said.

"Didn't know you'd be this late," Donnie said. It was still a little hard for him to get started talking.

The tremble was still rippling through Esbeth. The start had almost awakened her. But even that wasn't enough, tired as she was. "You might as well come in," she said.

She opened the door and flipped on the lights. They followed her inside.

"You sure have a lot of books," Donnie said.

"The better to ... oh, the heck with that. Why don't you two sit down and tell me what's on your minds." Esbeth dropped her purse and plopped the unread newspaper down beside the easy chair in the room, her power spot. She eased down into the cushions, wondering if she'd feel like getting up again, or if she'd sleep right here, as she had once or twice in the past.

Donnie started to sit on the couch, but when Karyn stayed standing so did he. That was fine with Esbeth, as long as she got to sit. "Go ahead, tell me what made you almost scare the gizzards out of me."

"Someone was waiting outside Donnie's house," Karyn said.

"Two of them," he said. "One was in a car, waiting, the other around to the side of the house."

"Who?"

"We couldn't see." He glanced at Karyn, but she was still fixed on Esbeth.

"It was dark," she said.

"The two of you coming in late like that, to Donnie's house, where he lives alone. What were you up to?" Esbeth was comforted to see the question flustered them a bit, Donnie as much as Karyn.

"I'm ... I'm not supposed to be out. Dad grounded me."

"Karyn," he cautioned.

"It's okay, Donnie. We can trust Esbeth."

"But you can't count on me to harbor you while your dad is going frantic, looking all over the place for you."

They were looking at each other, and her tone as much as her words made them both snap back to her.

"But, Esbeth, I'm eighteen. He has no right," Karyn said.

Donnie said, "I thought we could trust you."

"I don't know about kids today, but when I was growing up we always had a kind of rule about that, one so automatic we could all understand. It went like: 'As long as you're putting your feet under my table, you'll abide by the rules of this house.'"

Karyn's face flushed as if she'd been slapped. "Just because someone is feeding you doesn't mean they own you. It means they love you."

"You've put the whole thing more eloquently than I could, tired as I am. Now, do we call your dad and try to make peace with him?"

They glanced at each other, sharing their disappointment. When Karyn turned back, she nodded slowly.

"And you, young man, need to talk with the Texas Ranger."

"I won't." His head tilted and he looked at Esbeth. "I don't get it. One minute you're our friend and helping us, then you want to rat out Karyn and make me talk to that Ranger. This is the only place we knew to come, and now you …"

"I know, I know. I'm tired and a little cranky, but you might understand if you let me finish. You two were right to be leery of going into Donnie's house. Someone was killed there tonight."

"Killed?" Karyn went pale and lowered herself onto the couch. Donnie sat down beside her.

"Who?" Donnie could barely speak.

"A reporter. Thirsty Mills. Thurston Mills, really. Everyone just called him 'Thirsty.'" Esbeth got no pleasure from their shocked expressions. She knew they hadn't known the reporter, at least more than to hear about him, maybe meet him once or twice. But to her, Thirsty's death was the capstone of pity that summed up the tail end of his sad life. She watched their faces wash pale. The kids' brush with their mortality hit them hard, but no harder than did Esbeth's sadness at anyone with Mills' potential who had come down in the world to his level, only to dip lower in death.

"How did he ... what killed him?" Karyn asked.

"Someone hit him over the head hard enough to do the job. They may not have meant to kill him, but the sheriff and Ranger Macrory think whoever did it knew enough to pull the punch if they'd wanted to."

Esbeth watched their faces for a minute. She knew she would have to call Logan Rainey in a minute, and maybe arrange a place for Donnie to stay until it was safer for him to sleep at home. Finally, she said, "The reporter was digging around under your porch, Donnie."

"What for?"

"He'd found a box and was digging it up. Any idea of what was in that box?"

"Yeah, Spikeroy."

"Spikeroy?"

"He was our Boston Terrier. Died about three years ago and we put him in a box and buried him under the porch because he used to like to go under there to get out of the heat. I always complained about having to shovel back the dirt from the holes he made getting under the lattice, until he was gone. Then I kind of missed the chore."

"Hmmm." Esbeth looked down at the carpet for a minute, too tired to make sense of any of it right then. She heard Donnie say something and looked up. "What?"

He said it again. "Why would someone dig up Spikeroy?"

ESBETH WOKE WITH a jerk at a little after five a.m. She lay waiting to see what sound had awakened her. But it was her heart slamming away, and the events of the previous evening reeling past like some anxiety dream, the kind she hadn't had in years. She knew there was no use in trying to get back to sleep, so she pushed off the covers and got out of bed. Besides, after missing supper she was hungry.

When she was cleaned up and dressed, she made breakfast. It was a wrestle not to call the department office to see if there was anything new. That would be being nosy.

She'd been real glad last night that Tillis came along with Logan to keep him calm, and that the Ranger had agreed to take the boy home and have him camp there until they were sure the Spurlock house was safe. Logan had barely spoken three words, and if Karyn hadn't assured Esbeth that he'd never touched her in a disciplinary way, she'd have figured that Karyn was in for a lively time at home. That would have made her feel worse than she already did about ratting on the poor girl.

She concentrated on scrambling three eggs to go with the three slices of bacon and toast. Then she carried the plate over to the table and rounded up the newspaper she'd been too tired to read last night. She read while eating, but there was little to add to what she'd already heard and witnessed at closer range. The couple of copies of the *New York Times* that had stacked up while she'd been distracted had even less on the local scene, but she did what she could to catch up with that perspective of the country and world too.

When she was done eating, she piled the breakfast things in the sink, too recharged and full of energy now to labor over washing up the plates. She knew what she had to do next, though she didn't look forward to it.

She was ready to go by eight a.m., but she knew the liquor store didn't open until ten a.m., so she had to wait, knowing that narrowed her window if she was to drive to and from Hoel's Dam and still be at work by noon.

It was already getting hot by nine forty-seven, when Esbeth started for the store. She waited a minute for them to open, took the looks in stride of someone her age buying a fifth of Old Overholt the minute they opened, then headed for her car.

Esbeth had seen the address often enough on the blotter recently, so it was just a matter of finding the street. She felt conspicuous walking down the street with the bottle in its sack, the end of the brown paper twisted in the prescribed spiral. Anyone seeing her would think she was off to an early morning toot, which she figured was at least partially true.

The streets narrowed to some of the older streets in town, where now, with cars parked on either side, there was just one lane down the middle. No one cared much, and gave way when they had to get cars up and down to the homes. Way at the back, near the dead end sign, stood a small, gray, wooden house all by itself. The lot was almost an acre, but the house probably had less than eight hundred square feet inside. Lots of people used to live in even less space. Esbeth's cottage wasn't a whole lot bigger.

She went down a long walkway where hedges of sage had grown up. She could tell they had once been trimmed, but had been let go and had lost whatever shape they'd had so long ago. They lined the walk to guide the visitor to a house that didn't look visited much. Along the sides, Esbeth saw flowerbeds that had run to weeds, and even those had been beat down to a yellowish tangle by the sun and neglect.

There was a three-by-five card Scotch-taped by the doorbell that said in blockish printed letters that the bell didn't work and advised her to go ahead and knock. She held the neck of the bottle in its sack and gave the door a couple of firm taps with the bottom edge of the bottle. It was a bit like christening a ship, only the gray and weathered house didn't slide off into the ocean, although it looked like it wanted to, and would if the chance came along.

The door swung slowly open, and there stood Floyd Bettles in a long, blue, terry bathrobe with a look on his face of mingled surprise and delight. It made Esbeth even more sorry she had come.

"Come in, come in. You're sure a sight for sore eyes."

"Your eyes are sore because you're drinking too much."

"I know, I know. It's a weakness. But I..." He let that hang.

But Esbeth sidled past him where he hovered by the door. He clutched his robe about him tighter and snugged up its belt, for which she was glad.

"Take a seat and I'll be back out in a sec," he said.

She looked around. There was, of course, a favorite chair. It was a worn cloth-covered wing chair, with an ottoman between it and the thirteen-inch television that sported a rabbit-ear antenna. There was barely room to walk between them, but Esbeth wove through and sat in a rocker that must have once belonged to the late Mrs. Bettles. A small, antique-looking floor fan swayed slowly back and forth, stirring the air through the room that would get warmer as the day wore on. The room was a whole lot more comfortable than it had looked at first glance, and Esbeth settled into the rocker, clutching her purse and the bottle, waiting on Floyd to reappear.

He came back into the room and his hair was slicked back, what there was of it, and that was gray and stringy.

He'd put on a light blue short-sleeved shirt that was too big for him now, though it had probably fit once, and he had on khaki slacks and worn but polished loafers without socks. It was as dapper as he could get. Floyd was a tall man, or had been. Now his stoop took him to about six feet, and his bony arms hung out from the short sleeves with occasional little scabby spots and liver marks. He had a long, narrow face with only a single nick where he'd shaved too close. His eyes were red-rimmed and sad, even when he looked eager, as he did now. He came across and lowered himself into his power spot chair. He worked up a smile and his expectant eyes swept across Esbeth in a way that made her even more uncomfortable, until they landed on the bag she held.

"What's that?" he asked.

"Oh, I brought you a little something."

She pulled the bottle out of the sack and held it up. Years ago, she'd watched a man trying to put a shoe on a mule. It had given a jerk and kicked him briskly in the stomach. The man had dropped the mule's foot and reeled back, the look on his face not too different from the one Floyd wore now.

"Oh," he said.

"Is it the wrong brand? I thought you drank rye."

Those sad eyes of his got a whole lot sadder and welled up. A drop started down from the center of each sagging eye, and he looked away while digging in his pocket for a large white handkerchief. He wiped at his face with it.

He shoved the handkerchief back into his pocket and pushed on the arms of the chair to stand slowly. He went over to the small window that looked over his back yard. Esbeth had no idea what he was seeing out there, but it didn't seem to cheer him up much.

"I suppose," he said slowly, "that the fault is mine. I went about this all wrong."

"What?"

"Trying to get you interested in me this way."

"How's that?"

He turned to face her. The light coming in through the window made it hard to catch his expression. "Truth is, I don't really drink."

"You've been doing a pretty fair imitation of it, then."

"I guess I have that coming. But, the fact is, I just thought if I could be around you, let you get to know me, that, you know …"

"Sparks would fly?"

"Well, not that at my age, or yours either for all that, though you're a chunk younger than me."

"You thought I'd find a guy ten years my senior more attractive, if he was lying around sleeping off a drunk in a jail cell?"

"Look, I said I wasn't thinking as clear as I like." There was the first bit of edge to his voice, and Esbeth found that heartening.

He went back across the room and lowered himself into his chair again. One hand rubbed across the other in an unconscious way. He looked at her. "Look, you came here for something. What is it?"

"I was hoping to ask you some questions."

She had put the sack containing the bottle on the floor beside the rocker where she sat. He glanced down at it, and though he didn't shudder, his expression registered the same effect.

"And you've read those stories where the detective liquors

up the drunk and he spills his guts before passing out. Then the detective leaves."

"Yeah, I suppose that was the sort of script I had in mind." Esbeth didn't feel too sanctimonious now herself. "But I'm not really a detective. I'm more of a busybody."

"Same difference."

"I guess. But what I'm having trouble with is figuring out what went on around here as much as forty or fifty years ago. I wasn't around here back then. But you were."

"Hell, I was a dashing young man about town then."

"Well, I'm having a hard time getting anyone to talk about what happened."

"I'm not surprised. It was a damned embarrassment."

"In what way?"

"That's why it's so hard to talk about. Stuff just happened, and then, when it was all over, no one really cared to stir it up again much."

"Were you involved?"

"Me? Oh, everyone was. But the really bad stuff? No, not me personally. Most of what happened was among the big families."

"The Hoels, Granites, and Spurlocks?"

"That's the heart of the lineup."

"What started it?"

"My own hunch is that there's always been a curse on the area."

"Oh, come on."

"No, I mean it. And I don't mean like voodoo, or none of that. But there's always been a get-rich-quick cloud that hung over everything around here and kind of spoiled anything good sooner or later."

"What do you mean?"

"Well, it goes all the way back. You sure you wanna hear all of it?"

"Don't leave out a thing."

"It goes back to the valley first. All that used to belong to the Indians. Them Kiowas had one of their biggest villages down in the valley. I guess that's why they call it Lake Kiowa now."

"But we white folk came along and pushed them out."

"The attitude way back then was that it was like free land, and the more of it you could grab, the richer you could be. The Indians already being on the land was just a wrinkle to work out, and to people wanting to get rich quickly without a lot of work, killing a few Indians didn't weigh much."

"And the ancestors of the richest of the local time-honored families were the best grabbers?"

"Mostly the early Hoels and a few of the Granites ended up with the bigger chunks. There were some others, but once the Hoels got going, the land seemed to just turn itself over to them until they had almost everything. Those Hoels, they were world-class champion grabbers."

"They run out the others?"

"That's what everyone thinks. It was too early for me to know anything about that. The Hoels were just there. I was born down in the valley, you know, and in those days the Hoels were everything."

"Things haven't changed much. What about the Granites?"

"They were the only ones too stubborn to give ground, and they were hardy pioneer stock, good shooters too, I understand."

"And the Spurlocks?"

"They weren't in it then. The Spurlocks were hill folk, always have been highlanders. Their place was right where their house still stands. They didn't have anything to do with the gold fever, or any of that."

"Gold?"

"Yeah. Old Slate Granite started turning up nuggets on their place. It made quite a stir for a little while. Oh, Esbeth, you can't begin to know what a strike and the idea of gold being in a place does to people—that it's just lying there on the ground in nuggets or dust to be scooped up. Whole parts of America have been swept up in that kind of madness, and besides the miners there're the dealers, providers, fancy women, everything that goes with it. The valley had a little taste of that, and you'll never know the kind of things that led to."

"I'll have to stretch, but I get the rough idea. Was there a mine? And why didn't anyone find gold on the Hoel spread? It had to be a lot bigger than the Granites' land."

"Now you're getting to the touchy part. You see, there never was any mine, leastways as far as anyone could ever figure."

"Where'd the gold really come from, then?"

"I'm not saying you couldn't have found part of a word or two on any of them nuggets, maybe a piece of 'In God We Trust,' or the bend where the nugget was once a ring or some other smashed and reshaped bit of jewelry. The dust was harder to trace, but must've been harder to make, too. Everyone suspicioned that the Granites were making their fortune as highwaymen, burglars, robbers one and all. Then they'd grind down, or melt down, the coin, jewelry, whatever, and find it as nuggets. Or, so they said."

"These days we'd call that money laundering."

"All I can say is that no Granite ever did time, and the law never put a finger on who was doing some of the stealing and robbing back then. The valley was a pretty isolated place, with no train or other way in and out. Damming up the river and filling in the whole thing was one of the best things ever happened to that crack in the earth."

"But the diamonds, and all the killing later? What was that about?"

"You recall that everyone in the valley had to be relocated."

Esbeth nodded.

"Well, the Granites made the transition better than the Hoels. They switched over from agricultural crops…"

"And robbing."

"And robbing, to spend more time raising cattle. Slim Granite, the head of the household and Selma's husband, didn't hold with a peaceful life like that. Some folks think his restless boot heels just carried him off one day to where he could get back to the kind of work he liked and was suited for."

"How do the Spurlocks fit in?"

"They were up here on the hill all the time, and they started to feel crowdy when the dam was being built, and Hank was never too keen that all that land was given over to the Hoels, especially when the diamond business started."

Esbeth stopped rocking and leaned forward. It was hard not to show her eagerness. This was what she'd been waiting for.

Her look encouraged Floyd.

"You may know that the Hoels owned most of the valley. They were given a wonderfully huge spread up on the hill. Why, it sprawled all the way into the next county. But the land wasn't near as good as what they'd had down in the valley, or so Bill Hoel said. He was young then and as hard a man as there was around. But he couldn't get cattle to go, like below. There wasn't the water, and he had a lot of other stuff he squawked about. But most folks thought it was just the rising cost of labor to run a big spread like that. Wasn't no new thing. Even the King Ranch had troubles like that, and it's big enough to make the Hoel place look like someone's hobby."

"Did the troubles peak about ten years after Bill Hoel got the new land?"

"That's about right." If it bothered Floyd to have Esbeth butt in while he was telling the story, he didn't show it. "It was all kept pretty quiet, but the rumor was that Hank Spurlock had located a diamond mine. He wouldn't say where, and most folks didn't believe it anyhow. But one or two tried to follow him. But they were never able to track or trail him to his so-called mine."

"Your story made a jump there. You know more than you're saying, Floyd." She hadn't batted her eyes, or done anything to falsely encourage him, but she could see he was wrestling with something. "You don't have to tell me, though. I don't want to pry anything out of you like this," she said. She put her hands on the arms of the rocking chair, ready to push herself upright.

Floyd's eyes got that rummy, regretful look again. He sat up straight in his chair and then leaned over closer, looked intently at Esbeth. "Oh, don't go, Esbeth. I'm telling you as much as I think I should, as I dare."

She didn't say anything, but he must've seen something in her face.

"Okay. I'll tell you something I never told anyone before. Hank swore me not to, but he's pushing worms himself now, like I will be soon enough myself. So, what's it really matter? Anyhow, he—Old Hank—took me along a time or two to help him. Hugh was off to the war then, and Denny, why he was just a little sprat. I wasn't never very bright, and Hank kinda knew that, figured if he could trust anyone, he could trust me. He made me swear…" Floyd looked away and swallowed. "I had to swear never to tell. But, like I said…" He didn't try to finish that, just stared off to where the seam of the corner ran up to the ceiling. A cobweb tossed in the current of the floor fan.

"And you found diamonds? Where?"

"I'm not supposed to tell you this, even now. I can't."

Esbeth tilted her head at him. It was tempting to flirt her way to more information, but she knew he had buttons she could push and she had to fight herself not to go that way.

"I … I really can't, Esbeth. I mean, I swore."

"That's okay. What was it like finding them?"

"We had to go up into some of the highest country around. There were a couple long stretches to hike, then small mountains of rock to go up."

Esbeth was getting an idea of where that might be, but she chose not to press.

"There was a hill we had to climb, and up on its top the hill dipped back in, a bit like a volcano, but it wasn't. Hank said the geology was all wrong for a volcano. There was Precambrian rock, he said, but no fresh lava, nothing like that. All of his chatter about that was in geological time and way over my head. He knew a bit about this kind of stuff and had been prowling around looking for the right signs all over the county, ever since topaz was found off a couple of counties from here. He'd been up there to where we went before, and had almost always been run off. But then he started finding diamonds. And it was true. They were there. I found some myself. You could rake through the dirt and uncover them here and there. If we'd of had equipment and some running water up there, we could've uncovered more'n we did. But we got run off ourselves. We had to cut out and hide our stash. The owner—the one who run us off—was trying to sell off some of the land then, and we were on part of it he wanted to sell—worthless rocks and other hillsides that could never take cattle, or if it could, you couldn't get them outta there."

"Why didn't you just buy the land?"

"Hank was set to, and I was having some dreams about being rich myself and buying some. But then everything changed and the owner took the land off the market."

"He say why?"

"I can only suppose it had to do with making more money off the land somehow."

"You think he found the diamonds?"

"I don't know."

"What about all the ones you and Hank found?"

"They were still up there, stashed away. Trying to get them out's what started all the shooting."

"I gather the Granites got involved, somehow."

"They've always had a nose for making money, them Granites, especially easy money. You recall what I said about people when gold was mentioned. Well, you oughta seen folks around here when diamonds came up. Oh, God, it was ugly there for a while, Esbeth. I was scared to death to mention I'd ever had anything to do with it, still am, for all that. Don't you ever tell anyone, or my life won't be worth spit."

Esbeth said, "You can trust me, Floyd."

He gave the door a nervous glance.

"The scorecard I charted out had several Hoels killed, while the Granites also lost quite a few," she said.

"And don't forget that Hank Spurlock came up missing about then, too."

"What about you?"

"That's when I took a serious disinterest in anything having to do with land and everything else around here. I took off and didn't come back until everything had settled again. That was almost two years later. Truth is, Esbeth, I'm something of a coward."

"And that's the last you ever heard about the diamonds?"

"Except for the version that has Hank going across Lake Kiowa with the strongbox full of diamonds and disappearing out there somewhere."

"Anything to that?"

"Young Hugh Spurlock must've thought so."

"But what about you?"

"Come on, now. I've worked hard all these many years not to think a thing about that. I married Vivian and worked my days and kept my mouth shut like everyone else, and watched as most of the ones who knew or suspected anything died off one by one. Aren't too many of us left that actually know anything about what really went on. And, until today, we weren't talking. I'm not sure who started that talk about Hank and the box of diamonds being lost in the lake, but that's all it was, just rumor, and a flimsy-enough one. Few enough people wanted to even mention diamonds at all."

"I'm glad you opened up and told me, Floyd."

"But it don't mean much. What can you do with it?"

"It's information, and the kind I didn't have. So I appreciate it. I'm the kind doesn't sit well with a mystery hanging over her head." She glanced at her watch. "Oh, great horny toads. I've got to get scampering."

She creaked up out of the rocking chair and stood up, left the bottle on the floor. She didn't want it, and Floyd was still focused on her. She doubted if he wanted it either. Maybe the visit would cut out his drinking bouts. If so, all the better.

Floyd was looking at her with those sad eyes again. "So, we're not gonna date?"

"No. I don't think so. But we can be friends, and talk. Is that okay?"

He nodded, slowly at first. Then he worked up a reluctant smile.

Esbeth went to the door. But Floyd shot up out of his wing chair and headed toward the door to open it for her. The heat from outside hit her like the slap of a frying pan as soon as she stepped into the sun outside the doorway. She turned and looked up at him. "You mind if I ask you one thing?"

"What?"

"What did you see in an old coot like me anyway?"

"First, you gotta remember, I'm an older coot."

"But it was more than that, wasn't it?"

"You didn't know Vivian, did you?"

"No."

"She passed on before you ever came to town."

"I'm sorry."

"Don't be. It's as natural as rain, and we'll all get a turn at it." He grinned, and if it hadn't been for her slowly cooking out in the sunlight while he stood inside the shadow of the doorway, Esbeth would have smiled back at him. "The truth is, you look a lot like her."

"It's a reason for a lot of foolishness, but never the best one."

"I know. I see that now. But I miss Vivian so much. She was a lot like you."

"Like how?"

"Well, maybe I shouldn't put it this way, but Viv was a round little butterball."

"Oh."

"I used to look forward to holding her each night, hanging onto the round softness of her. We'd talk then, cuddled up like that, and catch up on the day."

"You must…"

"Yeah." Floyd got choked up for a second and looked away. When he looked back at Esbeth, his eyes were red and watery again. There was a quiver in his voice. "I miss her so much."

"I understand. But you know it's not going to be like that with us. For one, I'm more the prickly porcupine type than the teddy bear type."

"If you say so. I hope we can be friends."

"Sure, why not?"

"I'm glad we kinda got this out in the air. Truth is, I was awful tired of drinking like that. I never come to it natural, and it was gonna be the death of me."

"I'm glad some good came from this."

"It sure helps to talk things out."

Esbeth glanced at her watch and knew she'd have to get a move on. Besides, she could feel the clammy sweat forming around her neck from standing out in the sun. She said, "You know, with most of the problems of the world, and in ninety-five percent of all television sitcoms, the issue is almost always some kind of breakdown in communication."

Floyd looked at her, then lowered his head. Oh, now what, she thought. When he raised it to look at her, he said, "You know already anyway, don't you?"

She hesitated, then slowly nodded. "Sure, the diamonds you found were on Old Bill Hoel's place, weren't they? And I'd almost guess it was on land once owned by Hank Spurlock, on which he made money when it was bought by the River Authority people to give to Bill Hoel."

Relief and fear were in a tangle across his old tired and long face. Then he relaxed. "Maybe it's for the best."

"Oh, nothing's going to happen to you, Floyd."

He shrugged, an elaborate and bony version of a shrug, like someone shaking off all the cares and fears of a lifetime in one concentrated gesture. He said, "Oh, something will happen, all right. We all die, Esbeth, sooner or later."

Esbeth wanted to say something reassuring, but she was out of time. She turned and went off. She would have to scurry now to get to work on time. The lather of sweat around her neck had already turned into a small trickle running down the small of her back. Above her, the sun was blasting down on Hoel's Dam. But she was beginning to be more fully aware of the shadow of fear that had hung over this cursed little town for all these many years now.

TEN

TILLIS CLOSED HIS BEDROOM DOOR, then flipped the switch that lit an amber-shaded floor lamp in the far corner of the room. Gala sat on the corner of the bed, leaning back with her weight resting on her elbows. She was looking at him with that amused smile he'd been thinking about, while his head was crowded with the tangle of this increasing mess. The floor lamp was an old one, antique perhaps—one Claire had bought and he'd been surprised she'd left behind. It cast a soft glow over the exotic lines of Gala's face. She had her black hair tied back in a short ponytail that looked casual, but made more of her cheekbones and those oversized brown eyes.

"You always enter a room that way? You're liable to get yourself killed some day." She wore cutoff jean shorts, sandals, and a creamy off-white silk blouse.

"You always sit around in the dark like that?" He kept his voice low as he could get it. "The boy's right outside on the couch."

"You tuck him in real good? I know you probably did. It's so like you to think of others."

"How'd you get in?"

She waved a hand in a vague sweep across the room that encompassed the house. "This crackerbox?"

"Did your basic training include B&E?"

"Let's see. To be a Ranger you've had a minimum of eight

years commissioned somewhere in law, and at least four of those with the Department of Public Safety."

"I was a trooper first, and later an Austin police detective. What's your point?"

She seemed to be checking his face closely, whether to note that the bruise there had faded quite a bit or not he couldn't tell.

"Just seems like for someone with your experience, your methods seem a tad strange."

"You mean my investigative style, or us?"

"The 'us' is pretty much a small thing, in light of what's going on. The 'us' isn't even happening, as long as no one sees us together."

"Don't think just because I'm a Ranger that I haven't been trained to work under covers," he said, and managed not to grin.

Her head tilted a quarter-inch more to her right. "You think you're up to dealing with the likes of people like Morgan?"

"I've had a bit of experience."

"With guys like that who have no limits?" She sure didn't blink much.

"He's that over the top?"

"Have you ever beaten a woman?"

"At what?"

She had to chuckle at that. Then the smile slipped away. "What are you playing at?"

"You'd better be more clear than that."

"I can only imagine that this has been a frustrating case for you." She slid one hand, in what seemed an unconscious gesture, along a taut brown thigh before putting it behind her for support again.

"Frustrating, like how?"

"All this happening in your own back yard, involving

people of the community you've adopted as your own, yet no one is talking."

"The not talking's common to most cases."

"Then there are at least three deaths, and the natural tendency is to think that they have something to do with each other, when, in fact, they may not. That they were done by the same person, when that's not a likely, or at least a necessary, conclusion."

"What's your point?"

"It took me a while to understand why you'd even want to stake out that pawn shop. Just a few missing pages in the register and rumors of assault weapons being sold at night—there seemed to be nothing to it. Yet it stirred up something."

Tillis reached up to rub at a fading bruise. "Consider the source. Thirsty hadn't ever said an original thing in all the time I'd known him. Someone put the words in his mouth."

"To lead you in the wrong direction."

"The attempt to burn the place down and to rough me up were supposed to give credence to the lead."

"Too bad Thirsty isn't around to explain."

"Yeah. Too bad."

"But it did stir things up, like you barging into a poker game."

"I did do that."

"Seems to me you've tried all the normal investigative steps and realized you needed to do something different here."

"I don't think anything I did led to Thirsty being killed, if that's part of what you're implying."

"It's not. I'm just trying to make sense of some of your fancy footwork here."

"Maybe I am, too."

"There's that."

"You think I'm bringing a whole new style to Rangering?"

"It's like it's still emerging, and not as native to you as it might be. Kind of like some partially-clumsy butterfly wrestling its way out of its chrysalis—the same as learning for the first time to take some things more lightly, to laugh at them, to laugh at yourself."

"Thank you, Dr. Freud."

"Don't get me wrong. I think it's cute. I like it, and will probably like it more when it's all the way grown up."

"You think I'm really taking some aspects of this whole thing too lightly?"

"No. But I've never heard of a Texas Ranger doing anything covert. You seem to have an unorthodox approach, and I do mean the investigative procedure."

"Now you're starting to sound a lot like Lieutenant Comber. Isn't it kind of early for an expert opinion from you?"

"Do you think all this is happening by accident? That every few years this area winds up and just goes nuts?"

"I haven't landed on someone to take the fall, if that's what you mean."

"Does the boy know anything?" She glanced around the room, rubbed one hand across the bedspread. He was glad he'd made the bed that morning.

"No."

"He knows about the diamonds, and what Thirsty thought was in that box."

"But he knows all Thirsty got was dog bones. Old Spikeroy."

"Why do you let those two kids run around picking away, then?"

"What would you prefer I do, book them for not

sharing their adolescent ideas? Your colleague, Esbeth, told me once when I was working on another case that everybody has to learn, sometimes their own way, and at their own pace."

"You've really taken to living in a small town like this, haven't you?"

"What about you? You think you could ever learn to?"

Gala sighed, but her Mona Lisa smile wasn't full of despair, and her eyes caught the amber glow of the light and seemed to glitter. "Don't talk anymore," she said. "You're going to need your strength." She started to unbutton her blouse.

TILLIS WOKE AND there was an empty, warm space in the bed beside him. He could still smell her and feel the smooth softness of her skin that contrasted with her firm muscularity. Outside his bedroom door, he could hear young Donnie Spurlock up and stirring around in the kitchen, making coffee or doing something that made enough noise to cause Tillis to push off the covers and head for the shower.

When he got out to the kitchen, Donnie was frying country ham. That, and a pot of fresh coffee filled the kitchen with smells that should have reminded Tillis of Claire, but didn't. He sat at the table in front of one of the two place-settings Donnie had already put on the table. It would have worried him if Donnie had set places for three. He must not have heard Gala come and go. The woman moved like a cat.

Donnie set a plate of eggs, with an oversized piece of thick Texas toast and a slice of the ham, in front of Tillis. He glanced at the badge already pinned in place on Tillis' shirt.

The Ranger reached for his fork. "You're going to make someone a good wife, Donnie."

Donnie looked across the table at him, with the eyes-open-wide, honest stare that was part of his heritage, and said, "I used to fix for Dad, and I kinda miss that."

The boy went to pick up his fork, but hesitated, wrestling with a lump in his throat while looking down at his plate.

Tillis was sorry he'd asked. They ate in silence, and he had Donnie just leave the dishes in the sink to soak instead of doing them right then like he wanted. Tillis leaned on the counter until Donnie stopped futzing around at the sink and stared at him.

"I've been taking it kind of easy on you, Donnie, trying to respect the fact you just lost a father."

"I appreciate that."

"Are you ready to tell me anything now?"

"I can't."

"Why?"

"I can't say."

"Too much has happened for me or the other law enforcement people to roll with that."

"Am I guilty of anything?"

Tillis started to say something, then stopped himself. Instead, he said, "We need to get into town and let the sheriff have another turn asking you questions."

On the ride into Fearing, Tillis glanced at the boy, who sat with shoulders square and staring straight ahead, as if going to an inquisition. Tillis said, "You know, Logan Rainey's my best friend. His daughter's like the niece I never had. All this blows over, you're going to marry Karyn, aren't you? Make an honest woman of her?"

Donnie's Adam's apple bobbed and he turned to look at

Tillis. He just couldn't help himself. "We never…I mean, well, I shouldn't have even of said that."

Tillis kept himself from laughing, but only barely. Donnie was a virgin. There was something about the reticence of a boy who wouldn't tell the law anything he didn't have to, when it came to helping them solve his father's murder, but he would open his heart and tell this most revealing and intimate thing on himself. As Eldon might say, it was enough to make a cat laugh.

He was just pulling into the slower, bunched traffic at the edge of Fearing when he glanced over at Donnie. "I know you've got some kind of agenda about your dad. But any ideas about home-style justice you have ought to go out the window. You may not care what happens to you, but what if something happens to Karyn?"

"I've … we've talked about that. All I want to do is find out what happened. She wants to help me with that. I know you think I'm meddling, but that's just the way it's gotta be with me. Okay?"

"You're taking risks, with your life and hers—ones you may not understand. Two people died at your house. If you think this is the kind of situation where the police will put up a protective ring around you and your home, you misjudge the area where you live. Those kind of resources aren't available." He didn't add that neither were the skill levels in towns this size. If someone wanted to get someone, that person usually could.

"That Walters woman told us the same thing. But it hasn't stopped us."

"Esbeth is helping you with this?"

Donnie's innocent face was twisted into a sour-taste look. "She's someone I misjudged. I thought she was our friend."

"Sounds like you've still got her wrong. But that's not new. Don't be too quick to form an opinion about that feisty old gal. She's a lot smarter than you can imagine."

"Smart's not the issue."

"You think she betrayed your trust, yours and Karyn's?" It was hard to drive and look at Donnie, but Tillis knew that the slender thread of getting this boy to talk involved the trust of as much eye contact as he could manage.

Donnie made a small noise low in his throat.

Tillis said, "You may find she's a lot more on top of things than you imagined. I took her a little lightly once myself, but no more. You've got to remember that she has teaching deep in her blood. She's not so worried about your short-term opinion of her. She's focused on how you'll come out in the long run. I was fooled by her, and then I learned a bit myself. You may not know where, but let me tell you, that old gal is headed somewhere."

Donnie said, "It's just that with Mr. Rainey down on me, I could've used a friend."

"I know Logan'd never bring this up, and maybe he's never even told Karyn. But he was more than a friend back when I needed it. This's back before you were born, to a time you might not understand, but your Uncle Hugh would. He was in Korea too. Our outfit took quite a hammering once, and the only one not injured real bad was Logan. He got us out, one by one, then made the copter wait and went back in and brought out even the ones who didn't make it. He came within an ace of getting the Congressional Medal of Honor, but he didn't because there was only one witness who'd been conscious, and that was me."

"I don't know how his being some kind of war hero's

supposed to make me like him more, after the way he's been to me."

"I'm not trying to help you like him, just to understand him more."

Donnie just nodded. He was quiet the rest of the way to the Sheriff's Department office.

When they were buzzed inside, Tillis led the way and saw Eldon back at his desk, not doing paperwork, but sitting on the corner of the desk and watching them come in while he talked on the phone. Logan, in uniform, with his daughter Karyn on another straight-backed chair beside him, sat beside the sheriff's desk. Logan nodded to Tillis, but ignored Donnie. Tillis could tell from his tone that Eldon was probably talking with one of the many journalists to call, though he was barking at everyone by now. When the media has someone kill one of their own, every J-school grad with a pen, camera, or microphone within spitting distance will be down on an area.

Eldon finally wrapped up and banged the receiver back onto its hook. He glared at Tillis. "I've had deputies out all night bothering the two most influential families in the county…"

That would be the Hoels and Granites, Tillis figured. He noticed how the Spurlock clan had faded to a third-rate power, now that Denny was dead.

"…and I have alibis on one set of heavies, but can't even find the two Granite boys. I've called out every deputy I could," he glanced over at Gala, "the ones I could find, anyway, and we still haven't treed that pair. It's been a madhouse here all night, and with a crew that couldn't track an elephant in four feet of snow. Now I've heard from just about every S.O.B. in the fifth estate today, including Herb Hoel twice."

"I think you might mean fourth estate," Tillis said.

"You apparently aren't familiar with the way Thirsty went about it. Everyone in town knew he'd been known to drink more'n he could walk with. Now, to hear it, the man's a saint. I knew that low-life was going to cause me problems someday."

"By getting himself killed?"

"It don't exactly clean up my plate now, does it?"

Tillis glanced at Logan. This wasn't very confident talk in front of Donnie, or Karyn either, for that matter.

"What say we get started with the talks you wanted to have with Donnie and Karyn here?" Tillis nodded toward the back, where a small interrogation room was wedged between the front offices and the back holding cells.

Gala came into the department office, and she said to Eldon, "You've got television trucks pulling up and a couple of guys in rental cars who look like the kind of reporters who are on really good budgets. I'd say you have about an hour or less before you've got to face them. You want to set up a conference or take them one by one all day?"

"Conference," Eldon snapped. He looked at Donnie and Karyn. "We'll have to make this quick." To Tillis he said, "You're lucky you've got the Lute to speak to the press on behalf of the Rangers. Which reminds me, he's called twice already, trying to talk with you. Did you knock your phone off the hook, or something?"

"Maybe. Any more people get killed out here, and it'll be the Captain talking and Comber'll be out here busting my chops to wrap this up," Tillis said. "Maybe I'd better skip this séance and get over to the Granite place."

"I've got Rudy over there staked out now. He'll let us

know if anything stirs. You'll get your chance to take a lap in that pool soon enough."

"You really think Rudy'll find them? Or handle them if he does?"

"I think he has less chance than a grasshopper in a chicken yard. But I've gotta use what I've got."

Gala went over to use one of the other phones. Eldon pushed himself up off the corner of the desk and stood upright, brushing some crumbs off the top of one pant leg.

Esbeth had been turned to the dispatch desk, talking into the phone. When she hung up and spun her chair around, Tillis saw the way Donnie looked at her. Karyn's look was less bitter, but wasn't cheerful. It was Esbeth's expression that most surprised Tillis. She managed a smile, but it was forced, and he'd seen the brief flash of pain first, when she caught the two kids' attitude toward her.

"Come on." Eldon waved a hand for Donnie to follow him. "And you'd better have something solid to share this time."

"I don't," Donnie said.

Eldon whirled and said, "You mean to tell me you don't have the foggiest idea why a reporter'd be killed digging a hole under your own front porch?"

Tillis tried to catch Eldon's eye, to steer him and the rest of the conversation into the interrogation room where it belonged.

Donnie's head hung a bit, and he shook it.

Esbeth cleared her throat, then spoke for the first time. "Maybe you'd better tell them about the journal."

A FLAT, HARD wind was blowing in from the west with uncharacteristic energy, kicking up red dust devils of dirt across the Granite ranch and making the wooden house creak. Selma watched a cone of the reddish dirt lift and then settle, like some miniature cyclone trying to get up the nerve to get bigger.

She turned and there they were. They'd come in the back way. Rocky, thick and slightly slumped, carrying a paper sack and showing no more expression than the bumper on a truck, while Stone had the beginning of a nervous grin that didn't quite show his dimple.

Rocky stopped and leaned in the door jamb, trying to look relaxed and unconcerned. Stone sat down on the couch and clutched a red can of Tecate beer in both hands. He looked more pensive.

"Where the hell have you pissants been? Do you know every lawman in this county is poking around looking for you two?"

"We had to loop around the back of the spread and come in that way. Rudy's out front in one of those sheriff's cars parked up about half a mile. It was nothing to dodge him," Stone said.

Rocky said, "We got you something you might want."

He walked over and dropped the sack onto her lap. It made a small thump. He went back to lean against the door jamb.

Selma opened the sack and looked in. "Well, shit."

She looked up at them. Stone had made it all the way to a grin now, though it had a touch of sheepishness to it.

"Just what the hell were you lunkheads thinking?"

"A minute ago it was pissants," Stone said. "Which is it gonna be? Lunkheads or pissants?" He ran the fingers of one hand through his blond hair and swept it into place at the back, where it covered his collar.

"You can be the pissant and he can be the lunkhead, for all I care." Selma pointed to one, then the other, and felt the flush of color shooting up the sides of her neck. Rocky was staring off past her out the window, where the wind was still kicking up. "You listening to me?"

"I hear you." Of the two of them, he was least like Slim, maybe more like his famous grandpa who'd once terrorized the valley. But there had been stark cleverness in those earlier Granites, a fox-like cunning. Neither of these boys seemed bright enough to hit the floor if they fell out of bed.

Rocky pushed away from the door jamb and began to rub his back against the corner. With his thick slightly-hunched muscularity, his cropped, short hair, and his dark furriness, it made him more than a little like a bear.

"Well, hell," he said. "He was digging and it looked like he knew what he was doing."

"You finished him off over dog bones?"

"We thought it was the diamonds. And I didn't mean to hit so hard, but he had a head like a robin's egg, all brittle-like."

"And we did get you what you wanted. He'd been holding out on you." Stone lifted the can. It was empty, but he was using it to spit tobacco into.

She slid the leather journal out of the paper bag without looking at it. She clutched it in both hands and let the paper sack fall to the floor. "Oh, hell, you two just don't get it, do you? You're as worthless as Democrats."

"Hey, now. Lunkhead and pissant is one thing. Democrat is another whole thing altogether." His face matched the mocking tone in his voice.

"Shut up. Both of you. Can't you see I'm not kidding around here? We've got to think."

"Sheriff Eldon's nothing you can't handle. He's gonna be

tied up with these film-at-eleven guys, buzzing around in their little satellite vans."

"I'm not worried about him, or even that Ranger. It's Morgan."

"You were gonna cut him in before; just show him the damn thing. See what he can make of it."

"If someone clever like Thirsty couldn't get to those diamonds using this," she waved the journal, "what makes you think any of us can? I need time. Don't you see, I never was gonna cut him in on nothing. We can shake off the law, but I don't fancy dealing with Morgan, once he knows I've got the journal. He's almost certainly planning to cut us out, just like I was him. Morgan's as clever as he is mean, and I don't mind telling you he's a worry now that there's just the two of us. I was the one brought Thirsty into that mix just for a bit of insurance."

"And it looks like Thirsty was trying to do to both of you," Stone said, but she ignored him.

It was quiet inside the house, and she could hear the wind outside scratching and rasping at the sides of the house.

"We could always do for Morgan," Rocky said.

"Yeah, like before?" She didn't mask her own mocking tone.

"Except we got something different this time, something he don't know about."

"What's that?"

"Jim Eddy Fisher."

"What about him?"

"He's ticked off at Morgan. Maybe we might could use that."

Selma looked down at the journal. The leather was

scratched with lines of wear, and the hinges crackled with age. "No," she said, "I'm not sending you boys that direction again. You're gonna have to get out of town and lay low for a while. Don't worry about Eldon, either. I said I can handle him."

"But we'd have the element of surprise with Morgan," Stone said.

She sighed and looked up at them. "Knowing Morgan, I think you'd best throw out any notion of surprising him at anything."

"I WANT YOU to repeat what you just said." Eldon glared at Esbeth.

She had her back up too, and snapped when she spoke. "You heard me. I suggested he tell you about the journal. He's right over there. Don't yell in my direction."

Eldon turned to Donnie. "Well?"

The boy couldn't avoid looking right at the sheriff, but his lips became a thinner line. "No. I'd rather not."

Whatever had been building up in Sheriff Eldon Watkins through all this so far shot the rest of the way, and he exploded. His face went red and he spun to shout, "Gala, get that front door locked and don't let another sonuvabitch in here."

"Hey," Logan said, though Tillis was sure Karyn had heard him say worse.

"Tillis, tell Donnie here whether or not I can book him for obstructing justice." Eldon was glaring at Esbeth while he spoke.

"He can." Tillis couldn't remember when he'd seen Eldon so animated, even including the time spent losing money at cards.

"And tell him whether I will," Eldon snapped.

"Almost certainly."

"And that goes for you too, Esbeth," Eldon said.

Her eyes popped open wider, but, for the moment, she had nothing to say.

"She'll tell you like she told us both a number of times, that if she gives you the answers, you won't learn anything," Tillis said.

"She pulls that, we're going to be without her services as a dispatcher." Eldon swung toward her, almost knocking into Gala, who was coming over to be closer after locking up. Eldon pointed a stubby finger at Esbeth. "The whole point of me hiring you, Esbeth, was so that you can't stonewall me. Now, tell me what you have. You can use small words, or large. I just want it, and I want it now."

She hesitated, then said, "You know what they say, that sometimes you have to be careful of what you wish for. Some of this stuff you know and could have chimed in a bit about earlier yourself."

Tillis enjoyed the way she was looking at the sheriff. Though Eldon said, "Now don't get your tail up over your back. Just tell me what you know. Someone around here's going to start the talking, and it might as well be someone on this staff." He glared at the young Spurlock boy.

Esbeth poured some coffee from her Thermos into her mug. Gala sat on the other corner of the desk on which Tillis sat. Their eyes connected for a brief second. Tillis, though, caught Logan's expression as he saw her look at him. Logan's head rocked back a half inch as he stared toward Tillis, then Gala. He'd been Tillis' friend too long to miss anything.

"It seems this town has a history, and a messy one, that goes all the way back to the valley, to what I'll call the gold fever days," Esbeth said.

"There wasn't any gold," Eldon said.

"You going to listen, or butt in every other sentence?" Esbeth fixed him with a look that would've made any school-boy squirm. Eldon just waved for her to go on.

"There wasn't a mine, but people didn't know that, and whatever normal greed there is in a place got out of hand. This was down in the valley days. People were killed. When all those folk were forced to move up on top of the hill, and I'm speaking mostly of Granites and Hoels, they came into contact with the Spurlocks."

Donnie jerked upright in his chair. But Eldon held a hand toward him. "You had your chance, son. Keep a cork in it until she's finished."

"The natural, feuding clannishness of those valley people just got a fresh infusion when the Spurlocks joined the mix, and some already-touchy chemistry got a tad livelier."

"Who told you all this bullwash?" Donnie Spurlock was on his feet and Tillis hopped over to go calm him, but Karyn beat him to it and got the boy back into his chair.

Tillis was thinking that there seemed to be some significant holes in the story Esbeth had chosen to skip over in her Reader's Digest version. But Donnie seemed to know exactly what she was talking about.

Logan folded his arms across his chest, and pink spots stood out on his cheeks, but he didn't say anything.

"Most of this is stuff I've pieced together, and some of it's conjecture, so no one need put a lot of stock in it. But it makes a first step toward explaining some of what's going on around here." Esbeth scanned the faces of the others. "Is it all right if I get on with it?"

"Please do." Eldon didn't look as cordial as he managed to sound.

"The rumor that lit the fuse was that Hank Spurlock had started to find diamonds in the area, but he wasn't saying where. This was at the same time Old Bill Hoel was grousing about the land he'd been given to replace what was taken from him on the valley floor. He said the new land wasn't working for him. The grass wasn't as good, and the labor costs of providing water and hay were ruining him. He was trying to sell. The leap of faith some people made was that the diamonds were on Bill Hoel's spread, because there he was whining away, and then suddenly Bill quit squawking."

The phone started ringing, but Eldon waved for Esbeth to ignore it and go on with her story. Someone started ringing the buzzer outside too, but they all ignored that.

"The Granites had, in their time-accustomed way, been trying to horn in on Hank Spurlock. They started putting the same kind of pressure on Old Bill Hoel and his people. The tension built up from at least three directions. That's when some real fighting broke out, with Hoel and Granite corpses making up most of the dead count. Then the fighting stopped, and almost as quickly any talk about diamonds went away. It didn't hurt during the hush-up that Herb Hoel was running the only newspaper in town. Somewhere during all the confusion Hank Spurlock also came up missing."

"I'd be careful where you're going with this," Eldon cautioned.

"I'm not going anywhere. In fact, I'm done talking, for now." She reached for her mug and took a sip.

"That's it?" Logan said, unable to keep quiet any longer. "I've had cafeteria coffee stronger'n that."

"I'm not asking any of you to think anything, or believe anything. I'm just saying some of the things that led to where we are."

"But what was all that about the journal?" Eldon frowned at Tillis.

"Don't say anything, Esbeth, please." Donnie was half out of his chair before Gala helped push him back down.

Esbeth tried to smile his way, but didn't hit it. She said to Eldon, "The Spurlocks kept a journal. It's missing, and I think Thirsty had opportunity to come up with it."

"But where is it now?"

"Look, you're pumping all this out of me against my will. I didn't say this bread was all the way baked. Left to my own devices, I wouldn't be sharing any of this."

"You think whoever killed Thirsty has it now?" Tillis asked. She nodded.

Eldon looked as puzzled as the others. "But who do you think killed Denny?"

"I don't know."

"And Thirsty?" Gala said.

"You've got two guys at the scene there. That's as much as I know."

Tillis let out a breath. "And Hugh?"

"I haven't gotten that far yet."

Eldon shook his head. "Well, I'm sure as bob-wire not going to open any press conference with any of that."

"You can do what suits you. Now, are you going to book me for obstructing justice over that little bit of dribble I've gathered?"

Eldon shook his head reluctantly.

"The same should go for Donnie too," Tillis said. "He was only doing research."

"Diving to the bottom of the lake in a thunderstorm was research?"

"But they did you a favor and found a body."

"You think that's a favor?"

"Come on, Eldon. It took a lot of courage to make that dive, and to keep trying to dig up something about his father."

"We don't want vigilantism."

"And that's not what you're getting. Everyone has a right to find out about a family member. I'm not saying he has to be so bullheaded about not telling us everything he thinks he knows. But I can't see how he's obstructing anything now."

While he spoke, Tillis watched Logan. Whatever was on Logan's face slowed him. "Anyway, you've got a press conference and I've got to pitch in with your deputies to find the couple of thugs who Logan saw near Thirsty's body." He caught another glance from Gala and was sorry that Logan seemed to be taking it in as well.

"If it's all right with all you, I'd better get back to work too," Esbeth said. She turned around toward her desk and reached for the phone just as it started ringing again.

Eldon waved for Donnie to follow, and he and Gala went off toward the interrogation room.

Logan stood and tugged at his uniform pants until they slid down over his boot tops.

Tillis could almost feel the crackle of angry electricity coming from him. He rose and went to the far side of the room, so Esbeth and Karyn wouldn't have to hear whatever it was Logan looked ready to unload.

"I suppose you like that little sonuvabitch because he's like you."

"I haven't thought about it," Tillis said.

"You went to bat for him, when you know how I feel about him."

"I just don't know why you feel that way."

"And you probably never will."

"What do you care if he puts himself in danger?"

"I don't. But there's Karyn."

"Well, even if my standing up for him a little bit was wrong, Karyn's still an adult."

"Maybe you're too busy pumping that Spic deputy to know how anyone else feels."

"There's no call for that."

Logan stepped closer, until his intense jarhead face was almost touching Tillis'. "Then don't you try to talk about something you know nothing about."

"WHERE THE HELL you going?" Rocky said. He sat low in the passenger seat of the truck with a straw Western hat tilted forward, covering most of his face, so no one on the street could make him.

"Jim Eddy lives out this way." Stone had taken as many back streets as possible when they passed through the town, and now was steering them along a two-lane road that wove out through some pretty chaparral-strangled hillside country.

"Momma ain't gonna be happy." Rocky took the hat off and tossed it back into the extended cab now that they were out of town.

"She's never too happy, or maybe you haven't noticed

that. Get me one of those pieces from the glove box. Keep the Magnum for yourself, if you like."

"How do you still feel about that time Morgan took us?"

"He was just lucky."

"Lucky, hell. He took us apart like a rotten willow stump."

"What you think this time?"

"We need two things. One's the element of surprise."

"What's the other?"

"Jim Eddy. Remember? You do want another go at this fancy gambler, don't you?"

"Nothing could be better, and…we do owe him, owe him large."

ELEVEN

FIRST THERE WAS A distant bell, then the hammering on the door. Esbeth sat up in bed, realized the racket was coming from the front of her own little cottage.

She stepped into fuzzy slippers and pulled on her thick, red chamois robe, then stumbled through the house, barely missing an end table and getting to the door just as the hammering picked up its pace.

Through the peephole she could see the glimmer of a uniform splashed alternately by blue and red sweeps of light. That couldn't be good.

"Good gobs of pollywog poop," she snapped, unlocking the door. "Now what?"

She swung the door open and Rudy, one of the deputies, nearly fell inside. Behind him, Eldon Watkins stood in civilian clothes. His eyes still had some sleep in them, so he'd been awakened too. The sky was still dark, with a haze of lighter sky off to the east.

"What in tarnation?" Esbeth barely got it out of her mouth before Eldon waved her quiet.

"Your car. It's your car."

"What?" She stepped out onto the small porch, and could see the yellow lights of a wrecker now, as well as the flashing lights of the patrol car. "Where is it?" She looked to the curb where it had been parked.

"Most of it's half a block up," Rudy said. "Some parts are a ways farther."

"Rudy, let me handle this." Eldon stepped around his deputy until he was blocking part of the view.

A dog was barking, and Esbeth could see one or two neighbors coming out to see what the racket was about. "What happened?"

"Near as we can tell, a trash compactor sideswiped it and dragged it down the street a ways." Eldon was watching the wrecker haul the mangled lump up onto the flatbed back of the truck.

"The trash man did that?"

"Well, we don't think so. Someone made off with the truck, kids maybe on a joyride."

"Kids?"

"Well, maybe."

"Joyriding in a trash compacter?"

"Does kind of sound ..."

"Oh, spare me," Esbeth snapped.

"Yeah. I kinda thought so too. Compacter's just a couple of blocks up the street. Took a quick dust for prints on the wheel and dash, but it's been wiped clean." Eldon's eyes didn't meet hers; he turned instead to watch the tow truck driver tossing aside loose parts of Esbeth's car.

Esbeth had been thinking about the deductible on her auto insurance, and of walking to the grocery as well as to work for a few days. Now she thought back to toes she'd stepped on in the past few days, or those of people who she might have been going to annoy in the near future. "You think someone's trying to slow me down?"

"Oh, I doubt that. Maybe ..."

"Yeah. Yeah. Just kids. Right. Just serendipity that it was my car."

"Sure. That's possible." Eldon glanced to Rudy, who didn't look any more convinced than Esbeth.

Esbeth caught something else on Eldon's face. "You think something about this is funny?"

"Well, it's sure enough a no-argument way to get you a bit more exercise. No getting around that."

"Whew." Esbeth let out a hard snap of breath and turned and went back inside, slamming the door after herself.

"Karyn. Karyn."

Donnie walked around the outside of the Rainey house shouting. The sun was up enough to add a patina of sweat to his forehead, supplementing that already there from worry.

Logan's Game Warden truck was gone, and the house was locked. He'd tried calling, but there'd been no answer. Then he'd called the operator, and she'd said the phone was "off hook," which could mean anything. But it probably meant Mr. Rainey had yanked the cord.

"Karyn," he shouted again.

An upstairs window opened and her head and shoulders stuck out, the long red hair lifting out a bit in the breeze. "Aren't you supposed to be yelling, 'Stella'?"

"This isn't funny. Did he lock you in your room?"

"Looks like that. Should I let my hair down like Rapunzel?"

"No." He didn't mean to snap, but she was rolling with this far better than he was. "I can't believe he'd do that."

"Oh, yes you can."

"How about tying the sheets together?"

"I'm way ahead of you there. I was just waiting on my knight in shining Dodge." Her head disappeared, then re-emerged as the end of the tied sheets fluttered out and angled a bit in the breeze as one end of the makeshift rope fell all the way to the lawn.

As he was holding the car door open for her, Karyn slid in and said, "You didn't even say, 'What light through yonder window breaks?' or any of that drippy stuff."

"Don't say that. The man's dead, and he died at my house."

She might not have been referring to Thirsty Mills, but just the thought stifled some of her kidding.

He went around and got in, started the car, and pulled out. Karyn was quiet, and they went a couple of miles before he said again, "I can't believe he locked you up like some kind of … some kind of …"

"Donnie, he did it because he loves me," she said.

"He has a strange way of showing it."

"Well, I won't argue with you on that."

ROCKY RUSHED THE back door, gun drawn and looking mean enough to bite a rattlesnake. Jim Eddy stood along the side of the house by the door holding a crowbar. Stone maintained a shooter's stance a dozen steps back from the door, one hand clenching his pistol, the other steadying it for a shot. One booted foot was planted in a bed of nasturtiums, but he was far nastier than they were. The look of raw eagerness on Jim Eddy's face was awesome to see.

When Rocky slipped inside, Jim Eddy was right behind him, rushing in with the crowbar raised. The screen door had barely closed when glass and metal crashed inside, and there were screams before Stone was halfway to the door. Some of the screams sounded like a woman, and the only one he knew of inside was his sister Sandy.

The screen door flew back open and Jim Eddy came running and stumbling out into the back yard with his hands covering his face, blood running down between his fingers. Standing in the doorway behind him, only half-dressed, was Sandy. She was screaming something incoherent at Stone and waving at him to either rush forward or go back; he couldn't tell which.

Morgan Lane pushed her to one side and stepped outside. Blood splattered his white shirt, but none of it looked like his. He was holding the crowbar now. Stone was raising the gun when Jim Eddy lowered his hands and Stone saw that there were only two red holes where his eyes had been. He shouldn't have looked away from Morgan himself.

He squeezed the trigger but the crowbar slammed at his wrist as he did. Stone felt both bones in his wrist break while the shot went low and into a stand of sage. The gun dropped from his limp fingers. He stood looking at his smashed hand long enough for Morgan to step over and smash the crowbar down with all his strength twice on the back of each of Jim Eddy's knees.

Jim Eddy pushed himself off the ground with both hands and screamed until the crowbar slammed in across his open mouth. He dropped to the ground. Any other sounds he made were muffled.

Stone had bent at the waist to grab at the dropped gun, and was lifting it when Morgan smashed his other wrist. He turned to run, the sound of Sandy's screaming behind him, but it was too late even for that.

LIEUTENANT TIM COMBER sat in his Austin office, looking up at a framed print of John Coffee "Jack" Hays, who made Captain after being a Ranger only three years. One of his Indian scouts in 1837 had called him: "Bravo too much."

The ringing stopped on the other end, when Tillis Macrory finally picked up his cell phone. Tim didn't even give him a chance to speak. "I'm aware that the Rangers have for years prided themselves about the brevity of their reports—cogent, even terse. But I haven't heard a damned thing from you, Tillis. What the hell's going on over there?"

"Oh, just the usual bit of poking around."

"That's what I'm worried about. I'm over here fending off the press in what is turning into the hottest story in all Texas, and I can't get so much as a scoop of kitty litter from my man on the scene."

"You should have told me that's the sort of thing you're after. I can get plenty of that. Facts are another thing altogether."

"I read through all the same forensics reports as you, and still nothing solid."

"Looks like we're on the same page."

"Nothing doing with that pawn shop lead?" Tim could hear the sound of gravel crunching as a vehicle went past outside Tillis' open truck window.

"You know where that led, straight to Bill Hoel. And that's been a dead-end so far."

"That's why I've been trying to get through to you."

"About the pawn shop?"

"No, about Bill Hoel."

"What about him?"

"I want you to go out of your way to soft-pedal it in his direction."

"You telling me to lay off?"

"You heard me. This time, there're some political interests involved."

"You don't think the fact that a couple of Bill's men were hell-bent on knocking the snot out of me is worth pursuing?"

Tim paused. This wasn't much easier for him. "That's what I'm saying."

"Wasn't it you said that a Ranger's an officer who's able to handle any given situation without definite instructions from his commanding officer?"

"Actually, it was the Captain who said that. But I was nodding my head. This is different, Till. You also need to know when to stand down."

"Tell you what. The next time you see the governor, you ask him if that still goes if a steel-capped boot toe is swinging toward his head."

"You know I won't say that."

"You're right about that." Tillis hung up.

When Tim tried to dial again, the mechanical voice of the cell phone operator said the number he wanted was not currently available.

TILLIS LOWERED THE 7 x 50 Nikon binoculars he held and looked down at the cell phone he'd turned off. Back in Korea, it was Logan who'd said that half the trouble in all the world was caused by lieutenants. Tillis hadn't expected that to bite him in the butt the way it had after all these years. He toyed with turning the phone back on, but he caught a bit of movement along the fence line and looked back up.

He had to bend out the side window to see past the stand of sumac and mesquite that hid his truck from the estate.

Through the binoculars, he saw two of the Latino guards come up to the fence at a spot forty feet down the road from the gate. They lay their automatic weapons along the chain links. One of them carried a bucket. They both took out sponges and began rubbing at a large, brownish smear along the fence. It could be blood, but maybe from a deer. There was no telling from this far away. It could have even been put there as a graphic message to him, though he doubted that.

It was getting hot in his truck cab, even though he'd lowered the windows on both sides. Sweat ran down his temple, and the glasses were fogging over. He lowered them and reached and turned on the police band radio. The first thing he heard was Esbeth's excited voice about all kinds of activity. She was using the numbers, but it was hard to miss the chaos. He tossed the binoculars onto the seat beside him and turned to fire up the truck.

GALA CLIMBED OUT of her cruiser and checked the strap across the butt of the 9mm Smith & Wesson semiautomatic in the holster on her right hip as she went over to Rudy's cruiser. He stood outside, waiting, and occasionally glancing up at the house.

"How long ago did they get here, Rudy?"

Rudy had a round face with short, graying mustache, a small barrel of a chest that pushed softly at the buttons of his uniform shirt, and he wore aviator sunglasses—in short, about a bullet or two short of a full gun belt, a negative stereotype of a small county deputy, except he could be a shade less bright. Eldon usually had one or two like him on the force, she figured. She wondered what citizens thought of the bright yellow stress ball he kept wedged up in his windshield by the video unit. Rudy could look hard enough, especially to someone nervous about being stopped for a speeding violation. Right now he looked uncertain, though perhaps only cautious, which Gala preferred over the ones too ready to leap into action. The too-quick ones often caused most of the problems in situations like this.

"When I called for backup," he said, glancing at the house, where something crashed around on the back side.

"That was six minutes ago. Call for more backup." Gala broke into a run.

She had her gun out by the time she sprinted around the corner of the house. Rudy had slowed behind her and was talking into the transmitter on his shoulder.

The first thing she saw was Morgan bent over one of them, dragging him over the door sill into the back of the house.

He dropped the body and stood up, looked at Gala as she slowed. He ignored the gun hanging in one hand, and said to her, "Don't just stand there. Give me a hand here."

Her head gave a jerk toward the corner of the house, around which Rudy came lumbering, his gun out too now.

The body halfway into the doorway was that of Stone Granite. Gala saw no blood, but one arm was completely twisted around in a way that was as far from natural as it could get, both wrists hung loose and broken, and Stone's eyes were shut and his mouth hung open.

"Freeze," Rudy shouted, and went into stance with his gun in both hands pointed at Morgan.

Morgan straightened and slowly raised his hands, locked the fingers, and put them on top of his head. He looked at Gala, but with no expression on his face.

She heard Jim Eddy Fisher before she saw him. He lay

half under a hedge near the far corner of the house and was mumbling a scream as he tried to turn over. He was lying on his stomach. Both knees were bent back the wrong way, as was one elbow.

Rudy kept his gun pointed on Morgan while he slid sideways over to Jim Eddy and bent lower to lift him by one shoulder. As soon as he could see Jim Eddy's face, he let go and Jim Eddy flopped back to the lawn with an anguished, mumbled groan.

"Better send an EMS too, Esbeth," he said into his transmitter, though he had trouble with the words. His stance stiffened.

Gala was bent down to check Stone. "This one's alive," she said.

"The other one inside is too," Morgan said.

Rudy called in the new information, then asked Morgan, "What the hell happened to Jim Eddy?"

"Looks like he fell on a rake," Morgan said.

Gala had seen the face. Both eye sockets were red holes with blood pouring down across the face, and the mouth was an open, smashed wound where something hard and heavy had slammed into his face. She saw the blood-stained crowbar lying in the grass.

Rudy looked over at Jim Eddy and at Stone. "You did all this with a crowbar?"

"A twenty-four-inch wrecking bar," Gala said. Somehow that name for the tool fit better. "I'm going in to take a look at what's left of Rocky."

"Hadn't we better cuff him?"

"He's not going anywhere. Are you, Lane?"

Morgan didn't even look at her this time.

Inside she found Rocky, curled up in a fetal position, his

face turning a little purple from some internal injury, but he was still alive. She checked to see that no blood bubbles were around his mouth or nose, then went back out into the sun. Somewhere in the fear of whatever had gone on, he had voided himself, and the inside of the house was getting ripe. She took a couple gulps of the clear, hot summer air, once she was back out on the lawn.

"They were all inside when it started," Morgan was saying to Rudy.

Gala stepped behind him and brought down his hands one by one and handcuffed him. "Just a precaution," she said.

"Until we straighten this out," Rudy finished for her. He put his gun back in its holster. "You can put whatever you want in your statement."

Gala glanced at the other deputy. He was looking away with tired resignation showing on his face. Maybe he wasn't as slow as all that after all.

From the distance, she could hear the EMS sirens approaching.

"IT'S NICE TO have all this wrapped up in a nice neat little package." Eldon leaned back in his chair with one foot up on the corner of his desk and the other crossing it.

"What neat package are you talking about?" Tillis stood, more at parade rest than at ease, in front of him. His shirt was still sweated through in a place or two, even though he'd had the air-conditioning on while he'd hurried back to town.

"Oh, don't give me that whomper-jawed look. You know what I mean. We've got the Granite boys cold for doing Thirsty."

"You have an eyeball witness? You have this journal

Thirsty was supposed to have? You even have whatever it was that crushed Thirsty's head like a cheap piñata?"

"What the hell's giving you the diaper scoots? We make our first bit of progress, and you're all sour grapes."

"You know, and I know, that Lane's going to walk on this. Three armed men come to his house and one and a half are inside, though he probably drug them there. No matter what they say, when they're able to talk, it's still going to come down as self-defense."

"Isn't that man a piece of work? Three of them, all armed, and he takes them out with the first thing he grabs."

"You skip lightly over the bigger question of why."

"You got Lane figured for Denny's death somehow? Okay. Tell me how? And why for that?"

"I don't have anything figured. I just don't think it's quite as neat a wrap as you do. All you want is something to throw to the media right now."

"Somehow, that's enough for now."

"I suppose it is for you, Eldon. I suppose it is."

"Don't make me sorry I called the Rangers in on this."

"Hell, you did that because you had to. A mayor in your county gets killed, first question the media's going to ask you is why you think you can handle it on your own."

Esbeth, who had been too busy all day to dwell on her smashed car, buzzed in Luke, the evening dispatcher, and stood up to stretch when the men stopped talking. Luke sauntered in, carrying a lunch pail and an armful of newspapers and magazines. "Man, this little town sure made the news today," he said.

Esbeth turned to Eldon and Tillis. "You two make me glad I've got a day off. Maybe you'll both settle down and accomplish something before I get back, instead of bickering."

"He started it," Eldon said.

Tillis turned away, shaking his head. He went over to the desk at which Gala had last sat. The pen she had last used lay across a pad, and he picked it up, and Esbeth thought the way he ran a restless finger across its length was interesting, but she looked away.

"Esbeth?"

"What?" She looked back at Tillis.

"Do you have any idea about the demographics of this county?"

"In what way?"

"The Hispanic population."

"It's kind of light. Always has been. I was surprised at first, but that's just the way it is, I guess. Why?"

Tillis shook his head. "Eldon, okay if I use one of your phones?"

The sheriff didn't look up from the papers he was shuffling around on his desk, just held up a hand and waved for Tillis to go ahead. He eased into Gala's chair, had to look up the number first, and then picked up the phone.

The maid answered this time, and Tillis had to use some of his Spanish before finally getting to talk to the old man himself.

"What the hell do you want now?" Old Bill Hoel shouted into his end of the phone.

"I'd like to come out and talk to you."

"Well, I don't want you to."

"You don't have a choice."

"The hell I don't."

"I'm on my way."

"You come out here and I'll have my beanos explain things to you in a way you'll remember."

"I'm working a murder case here."

"And you've already slapped an arrest on them Granite boys. So don't come out here. The sheriff's already done pissed away enough of my time."

"That arrest just happened. Your sources must be very good."

"You just don't get it, do you boy?"

"I guess I don't."

"Well, you will." Bill Hoel slammed down the phone on his end.

As soon as they were inside the cool of the library late in the afternoon, Karyn nudged Donnie. There, at the same table where they'd last seen her in here, sat Esbeth Walters. She had a small pile of books and magazines in front of her.

Karyn saw her look up and spot them, and then the hurt show for a flicker on her face as she and Donnie scurried past, heading back to the archive room, where she'd showed them how to dig through the old newspapers.

"That wasn't much fun," she said to Donnie when they were alone in the back room. "What she said back at the sheriff's department did help you."

"I had an idea of where the box got buried. Now, I'm just more sure. Come on, hurry. You'll be in big trouble if your dad catches you here, with me."

"I'm already in big trouble."

"But locking you in like that. You're an adult. That's abuse, Karyn."

"I told you before, he did it because he loves me and cares about me."

"Well, it doesn't mean he respects you much."

She didn't have an answer for that. Donnie had the old

newspaper out. When he flipped it open, they saw the place where the pages had been cut out.

"They're gone," Karyn said.

"You think she did it?"

"Who, Esbeth? Of course not. You saw how she was around books and all this. It's like it's sacred to her, or something."

"Well, someone cut out these pages."

"It's the town trying to bury its own history again. Now what?"

"I was just trying to confirm something, and this does it as well as if the pages were here."

"What?"

He turned and put a hand on each of her shoulders, and looked hard at her face. "Karyn, I'm going to have to go in, and I'd better do it alone. You're in enough of a jam."

"Look, if you think I'll dive at night in a lake in a thunderstorm and then back off from something like this, you're wrong. You don't know how wrong you are. Now, listen to me, Donnie. If I mean anything to you, anything at all, then I'm going along."

Donnie was frowning, but couldn't keep it up. He broke into a smile. "That's good. I know I shouldn't say it. But I'm glad."

When they went back out through the front of the library, Esbeth was gone. For Karyn, there was substantial relief in that.

SELMA OPENED THE door to find Sandy standing on the porch with two small suitcases beside her. "Why'd you ring the bell?"

"'Cause I wasn't sure I was welcome."

"Oh, come're." Selma opened her thick arms and Sandy rushed forward to be embraced like the seventeen-year-old she was.

Selma felt the rippling shudders going through the girl. "What is it?" She held Sandy out at arm's length to look at her face.

But Sandy kept her head bowed. "Momma, it was awful."

"What?"

"What he done to Rocky and Stone."

Selma clutched Sandy close again and stared out across the spread. "Oh, my poor boys. Did he kill them?"

"No. I don't think so. Least they was alive when they was taken away. They took Morgan away in handcuffs too."

"That won't last. Man like him'll get out. Self-defense, or some such. We're in some serious do-do here, Sandy. You'd best stay packed," Selma said.

"Momma."

"What?" Selma nestled the small head to her. Sandy smelled good, better than she ever had. Only the smell reminded Selma of Morgan and made Selma catch some of the girl's trembling.

"You shoulda...when he hit Rocky with that steel...I always thought Rocky was like iron, but I heard bones crunching in echoes all through the inside of the house. Momma, it was ... it was terrible."

"I know, honey. I hate to admit a thing like this, but without the boys around, that man makes my bones feel like dry ice."

"He made tapes, Momma, of everything. His bed, the poker room. Me. There're a lot with me in them, naked and such. You think he'll use any of that 'gainst you?"

"None of all that matters a helluva lot just this minute, honey."

Barely an hour later, the doorbell rang.

"Now what?" Selma shambled to the front door and opened it. "What do you want?"

"Just a word or two, if you can spare a moment. Looks like you're busy." Esbeth Walters wore her best casual clothes, none of which either hid or flattered her figure.

"Oh, come on in."

Esbeth glanced around as she wove through the front room. Selma led the way through the open, partially-filled boxes. Nor did Esbeth's sharp eyes miss the fact that a pile of fresh ashes was centered in the fireplace and a can of charcoal starting fluid was on the mantel. "Looks like you're getting ready to move."

"Count on you not to miss that," Selma said. She waved an arm toward the sofa and flopped into her own chair. She thought Esbeth looked a tad tired, but no less sharp than she'd heard.

"Aren't you going to wait until the boys get out of the hospital?"

"That could take a while, from what I hear."

"Haven't you been to see them?"

"Nothing to see yet. Both of them are still out as crossed-eyed-mackerels. That Jim Eddy is twice worse off, though. He'll never whistle at another fat girl, or wink neither. I hear they're gonna let that Morgan Lane loose on his own recognizance."

"Have to. All they have is a clear case of self-defense. Your boys were the ones with the weapons coming into his house."

Selma gave a low snort, and just shook her head. She looked out the window.

"What about the mayoral race? You throwing that over too? That isn't like you, Selma."

"How do you know what's like me? You haven't lived around here all your life like me."

"But you're just going to walk away from that?"

"I am, and as fast as my stubby old legs can carry me. The Granites aren't quitters, but I've had it around here."

"There'll be a trial, you know, over Thirsty's being killed. Your boys have been charged with that."

"I know. You think my boys facing a murder rap is going to help my political chances? I don't. That, and I've stayed here because Granites have always stayed. But I'll tell you, I'm beginning to believe this family's more cursed than the Kennedys."

"You're not going to stay for the trial?"

Selma heard her voice go up an octave when she answered, but there was no help for that. "I said I've had it. I don't care what happens anymore. I'm beaten down by years and years of this. You can't imagine what it's like."

Esbeth nodded toward the fireplace. "Burning that only makes matters worse. You think they can't sort through what's left of those ashes and tell that was a journal, like the one that came up missing after Denny's death, that Thirsty had until his death?"

Selma felt her shoulders sag. Her own voice was husky, hard to recognize. "What is it you want?"

"Was there anything in there that you remember, anything at all?"

"I know it didn't come out and say anything about where the diamonds are. I thought it was just a lot of ranting and raving by the Spurlocks—their family obsession through the past several generations. You know the only thing that sticks out in my mind?"

Esbeth bent forward, her eagerness showing in spite of herself. "What?"

"It was this bit at the front about how each and every one

of them had to swear to never give up on getting back what was theirs, and that they could tell no one, to keep it only among family, the Spurlocks. It practically put a curse on anyone who violated what Old Hank called the Spurlock code. Now isn't that a load of crock?"

"It explains a few things, about Donnie, for instance. But it does sound more like the ravings of a madman than anything someone with any common sense might say. You think there's a vein of obsessiveness in the Spurlocks?"

"I think there is in any of them who've lived here this long, Granites included. I'm clever enough that I shoulda seen it earlier. Now I got sorrows I don't even want to think about or face. You know about Pebble?"

"A little."

"She had spinal meningitis when she was only three years old. Her fever was too high for too many days. She came out of it, but she's never been right since. 'Special' they call it. What a load of crap. That poor girl's head is as empty as last year's bird nest. And you know what?"

"No, what?"

"Here's the really sad thing. Of all of us, I'm beginning, just beginning now, to understand that Pebble might well be the fortunate one. Leastways, she's the only truly happy one of us."

TILLIS ANSWERED THE door with just a towel wrapped around his waist. Every time he saw her now, he was surprised and relieved. The very air of his life had taken on a surrealistic hue, and she had become something of a touchstone, all he had left to believe mattered.

"How did you know it would be me?" Gala asked.

He bent to kiss her at the door, then turned to lead the way inside. "I don't get all that much company. What d'you have in the bag?"

"Burritos."

"Mmm. Classy."

"You have any hot sauce?"

"Of course. What kind are they?"

"Lengua."

"Well, I hope that's not the only tongue I'll be getting."

"Oh, lordy. I've corrupted one of those incorruptible Texas Rangers."

She fussed over getting the burritos out and onto a couple of plates while he went into the other room to dress. He came back, still barefoot, but wearing cutoff jean shorts and a t-shirt that said: "Life's Where You Find It."

"Nice shirt."

"My wife got it for me. Ex-wife. Thought it'd loosen me up a bit."

"Are you uptight?"

"Not at the moment."

She sat on one of the dinette chairs and was pouring on Tabasco and adding slices of jalapeños. "Any for you?"

"Absolutely," he said. "It's the only way to go."

"That's the way I feel." She took a bite out of her burrito.

When Tillis had finished his own last bite, and wiped away some hot sauce from the corner of his mouth, he said, "I want to know what you think's going on."

"You mean with Thirsty's death? Or Denny's? Or what's up with the Granite boys? What're you talking about?"

"I mean at Old Bill Hoel's place."

"You think something's going on up there?"

"I sure as hell do, and it's tied to the Latinos he has

living up there on his big old spread. Do you know anything about that?"

Gala stood and came around to him, cupped his face in her hands, and bent to give him a good, probing kiss, full of hot sauce and a hotter tongue.

The only time he'd ever had a similar experience was with a divorced mother about a year after Claire had gone. The mother and young son had come out to visit a few times, and when Tillis and the four-year-old had played well together, the mother had suddenly opened the emotional gates with a surprising amount of warmth. Tillis hadn't followed up, and the opportunity cooled after a few days. Only much later did he realize he'd passed some sort of test as potential surrogate father material, that she'd been communicating some signal to him, that he'd been given a green flag he'd been too slow on the uptake to realize.

When Gala moved her head back and let him look into those extremely brown and large eyes, he said, "What was that about?"

"I was so afraid you'd missed that. But you haven't missed a thing. You may be smarter than you've been acting."

"Well, thanks. I think. What is going on over there?"

"Later," she said. "I've been thinking about what you said about living in a small town. Let's talk about us."

"What about us?"

"Is there an us?"

"I think there is. I hope there is." Something had been gnawing at Tillis for a long time, and it had gone away in Gala's presence.

"You might be expecting too much," she said.

"I always have."

"What're you shopping for, some sort of Joan of Arc?"

"I'm not shopping anymore."

She didn't say anything, but reached for his hand and stood him from the table and led him down the hall.

Later, in the dark bedroom together, he lay facing the ceiling. Bits of shadows and suggestions of light played across it in distorted reflection from the lake outside.

"You asleep?"

"No," he told her.

"Why do you go about things the way you do?"

"You think I make it harder on myself?"

"You could play the game better, let others at least think you know procedure."

"I know so-called procedure."

"That's right. You did do time as a trooper once."

"Maybe I'm kind of rebelling from that phase. Do you think?"

"Well, you've still got the erect posture."

"That's not my posture you've got hold of there."

"You wanna make something of it?"

He pushed back the covers and rolled toward her.

GALA WAS BARELY out the door the next morning while it was still getting light outside, when Tillis' doorbell rang. He answered it, and there stood his boss, Lieutenant Tim Comber. He was frowning.

"I hope I didn't see what I just thought I saw."

Tillis frowned back at him. He wore a dark blue flannel robe and slippers. He glanced at his watch, saw it was six-thirty a.m. "You stake out my house, you're liable to see lots of things."

"I just pulled up. It was lucky timing, or unlucky."

Tillis waved him inside. On the dinette table was a pot of coffee and an almost-finished rack of toast. "I can make more toast, if you like."

"I didn't come to dine, though I'll have coffee if there's any left."

Tillis got down a mug from the cabinet and handed it to Tim. "I thought you were over in Waco."

"I was supposed to be. That's where we're meeting the press on this little mess out here."

"I didn't know you'd shifted to out here."

"You would if you'd turn on your cell or plug your home phone back in. You know I've had to try to reach you through Eldon Watkins' office. You aren't trying to dodge me, are you?" Ripples of suppressed anger flickered across his face like heat lightning.

"What would make you think that?"

Comber took a sip of coffee and put the mug down on the table. "Tillis, you have one of the absolutely best records for solving cases among all the Rangers."

"Uh, oh. That's the positive spin. Now, what'd you really come to say?"

"Tillis, no one admires those old-time Rangers more than me—Sam Walker, Big Foot Wallace, and Rip Ford."

"You forgot John B. Anderson, who brought in John Wesley Hardin."

"You know where I'm going with this. Just listen. I'm trying to get through to you that the times have changed. I normally leave you alone, knowing you'll come out all right in the end. You've got a lot more experience than most of the other Rangers ... well, hell, you should've been Lute now yourself. But you know what's holding you back."

Tillis wasn't going to have another cup of coffee, but decided to after all. He took his mug out of the sink and poured it full again. "Have there been complaints?"

"You know there have, or I wouldn't be here."

"Whose toes did I step on? Eldon's?"

"That's just one of three directions I'm getting hit from."

Tillis had the mug almost to his lips. He lowered it slowly. "What was Eldon's beef?"

"We were called in on Denny Spurlock's death. But you kind of dragged yourself in sideways on what turned out to be the finding of what was left of Hugh Spurlock's body."

"It's related."

"How do you know that?"

"They were brothers, for one."

"That's not enough, and you know it."

"Okay, who else didn't like the way I buttered my bread?"

"I got another call from the governor's office."

"That'd be Old Bill Hoel's connections."

"Hoel claims you're harassing him unnecessarily."

"You ever get calls like that before, from big shots who turn out to be more involved than they say?"

"Lots of times. But you're being uncharacteristically indelicate with your handling of Hoel. He still draws a lot of water in this state."

"Must be how he keeps a spread that size watered."

"Dammit. Don't be cute right now, Till. I'm getting more heat about this than you realize."

Tillis sighed. "Are there any other complaints? You said there were three."

"There was one more."

"Who?"

"I can't say. But it surprised me. There was talk about you being seen gambling. But even more important, do you mind explaining whatever's going on between you and Eldon's deputy? You're supposed to lend your support and help his department solve its problems, not add to them by planking one of the deputies cross-eyed."

"Could've been worse. It could be Esbeth."

"Tillis Macrory, I'm being as serious as I can be with you. What's the matter with you? Are you going through some mid-life crisis, or something?"

"I might be."

"Well, do it on your own time. You know what being a Ranger stands for."

"I seem to remember hearing of a time under Governor Ferguson back in the nineteen twenties when over two thousand three hundred Special Rangers were appointed, some even ex-cons."

"That's contemptible of you to even mention that, Till. That was all taken care of when the DPS took over. You're kicking sand here, when I'm trying to be serious."

"Well, I don't care much for this business about you taking an anonymous complaint seriously."

"You don't have to like it. Besides, it wasn't anonymous to me, I'm just keeping it that way for you."

"What're you saying? You want my badge and gun?" He glanced at the badge Tim wore over his left pocket, still made out of a Mexican coin as they always had been. Tim wore the cowboy boots and hat, too, that Tillis had not had time to get into.

"Oh, come on now. Are you trying to throw away a nearly twenty-year career?"

"How do you know what I want?"

"Damn you, Tillis, for putting me in this position."

Tillis shrugged, tried to seem calm, though he could feel the blood pounding inside him in throbbing pulses.

"Till, you were selected out of a large pool of people who wanted to be Rangers, in part because you had the dignity and comportment that go with being a Ranger. If your results weren't just about the best anyone could ask for, your attitude would indeed have you on the streets. Why do you think you haven't made lieutenant?"

"I haven't wanted it all that much. What're you really saying here? Have you come to help me out?"

"No, I've come to take over from you." It seemed all he could do to speak as calmly as he did.

"You going to bear in mind that little business about Old Bill Hoel's two men being the ones who jumped me at the stakeout outside the pawn shop?"

"That didn't lead anywhere."

"It wasn't supposed to; it was just supposed to make me think it did, if I survived it, which I may not have been supposed to at that."

"I'll bear it in mind." He bit off each word.

"But you'll go light on Bill Hoel."

"Tillis, you embody the original spirit of 'one riot, one Ranger' as well as anyone I know. But, this is a new era of Rangering, with procedures, backup, and timely information-sharing—all that stuff. We're in times of change, of new sensibilities."

"If it's the butt-kissing of rich landowners you're talking about, that's an older sensibility."

"You're just not going to get it, are you?" Tim's voice got louder in spite of his efforts.

"Am I on probation?"

"No. At least not officially. You're on vacation."

"I don't want or need a vacation."

"Just take some time and cool down; go fishing, hell, fly a kite for all I care."

"I said I don't want time off."

"I'm not asking. You're already on vacation, as of this morning."

"You know, Tim, I hadn't thought about this much, but the essential difference between us is that you have ambition, and I don't."

"That's good, Till. That'll give you something to focus on and mull over while you're on holiday."

TILLIS SAT AROUND the house frittering for a while. He made a fresh pot of coffee and worked on that while staring out the window at the water of Lake Kiowa. A wind out of the west had picked up and put a chop across the water that ran to whitecaps in places. He wandered back into the bedroom and put away the cowboy boots and hat he'd gotten out to wear through a working day. He wrapped the belt around the holster and put away his service piece as well.

He got out an older, worn denim shirt that had never had the star pinned above the left pocket. At the bottom of another drawer, he found some old jeans that still fit. He put those on, along with a pair of Timberline shoes, all of which made him feel as much like a civilian as he had in years. It wasn't an altogether bad feeling.

While he was in whatever atavistic mood drove him, he

dug out a long-neglected pack of Camel filterless cigarettes from a plastic bag in one of the desk drawers. He tried to remember how long it had been since he smoked—ten, twelve years?

As long as he was digging, he dipped into the false bottom of the bottom right drawer of the desk and took out a soft, leatherette case. He unzipped it and took out his backup piece, a Sig-Sauer P220 9mm Parabellum that held nine rounds in its magazine. The serial number hadn't been scratched off, but the gun had no history. It had come to him from a fellow trooper who was dead quite a few years by now. Ben had never said where he got it, through some drug bust or whatnot. None of that mattered by now. Every cop Tillis knew had a backup piece stashed somewhere. It was the card up the sleeve, and in many cases, it was the gun that officers decided to eat when the whole business got too sordid. Tillis checked the action and slid in the magazine, then stuffed the gun in the small of his back. He felt ready—for what, he wasn't as sure. But he was ready.

He went out on the porch. The breeze and the early hour made it fit for sitting and staring. The sun set on this side, and the summer afternoons got far too toasty for comfort out on the porch. For now, he was fine. He sat in an old glider rocker he kept out there that could take the weather. He smoked and stared at the waves and the occasional boat.

I wonder if I've gone too far this time, he thought, if I've gotten to that point where I'm beyond redemption.

He tried very hard to care, but couldn't get there. When he reached for another cigarette and found the pack empty, he crumpled it, stood, and went inside. It was time to do what he'd been putting off for far too long now.

GALA WORE JEANS, boots, and a chocolate brown silk shirt that made her skin seem a pale tan. A fresh tear near the edge of one short sleeve had come from getting through the fence. It didn't seem to bother the two young men who stood facing her.

"Where's Don Cinco?"

"Muerte," the one with red-rimmed eyes muttered.

"Is that true?" Gala could see the machete the other fellow held had been freshly honed to a shining edge.

"Es verdad." His eyes glittered in unblinking fury. He looked away when his eyes could no longer meet hers.

"I want you to hold on. Stick to the plan. Tell the others. Don't do anything crazy, okay?"

He shrugged elaborately and glanced at the other one. They both shrugged, then turned and headed back along the path they'd come.

Gala waited until they were out of sight. She spun and headed back toward the hole in the fence, pausing only to look up at a single bird that turned high in the sky above her. "Well, shit."

TWELVE

TILLIS MACRORY DROVE HIS truck through metropolitan Hoel's Dam—population 7,566 and dropping—and on toward the only slightly larger town of Fearing. A glance in the mirror told him his bruises were almost completely faded away by now, but he didn't much care for the rest of the expression he saw there. He focused on the road, and on the rough country covered with scrub that whizzed past. It was a day full of portent. The sky was the off-chartreuse that can signal the near presence of tornadoes, or, at the least, a coming storm of the kind able to register on the Richter scale.

His white hat hung at home on a peg, and the badge made of a Mexican silver coin was tucked in the drawer where he kept his loose change. The badge had the smooth heft that came from having a bit of lead mixed in with the silver. It was the first time in eleven years he'd gone anywhere on an errand related to work without wearing it. He should've felt lousy. But he didn't, nor did he know exactly why.

IT WAS LIEUTENANT Tim Comber wearing the white hat and silver badge this time in the sheriff's office, when Eldon and one of his other deputies led Morgan Lane out of the hallway that went back to the holding cells.

The gambler was loading items into his pockets from a manila envelope, while Comber took in the clean, starched white shirt and lean, hard build. He'd heard Lane's shirt was spattered with blood when he'd been brought in, but Tim gave only a brief, passing thought to where Lane might've gotten his laundry done while in jail.

"I've heard that those Granite boys were as tough as could be found around here," Tim said. He sat on the corner of one of the desks, watching Lane's smooth, fluid movements, in contrast to the sheriff's banging around over at his desk.

Lane looked up, his eyes half-closed and sleepy, but even more dangerous when like that. "Reputation's a funny thing that way, isn't it?"

Tim shrugged. He looked over at Eldon, but he spoke to Morgan Lane. "Come this Thursday night, do you know where I'm going to be?"

Morgan didn't answer, so Tim answered for him.

"I'm going to be outside your place, and if there's a game going on in there, it'd better be tiddly-winks, or something even tamer, else I'll be coming through that door with half-a-dozen crazed Rangers who make Tillis look like the sane one of the bunch."

"That Macrory's going as wild on you as a peach orchard boar, is he?" Eldon said.

"He's in the right environment for it." Tim stared at the sheriff. "And I'd be careful yourself, or your own re-election chances won't be worth a bucket under a bull."

ESBETH HAD HER hands in the dishwater past her wrists, while keeping a weather eye on the sky out the window above the sink, when the doorbell rang. Something nasty was coming in from the northeast. The wispy ends of clouds were jerked up at the ends like so many cracks of a whip.

The flat pan of the sky was shifting to an odd off-pea color that couldn't mean anything good.

She swung the front door open and said, "Well, what's got you out raising more hell than a catfish in a dry lake?"

Tillis Macrory stood there; he wore no hat, so he didn't have to hold that in his hands. She took in the way he was dressed—no badge, and a short-sleeved denim shirt with the tail hanging outside his jeans. She bet herself he'd have to be careful sitting, since he almost certainly had a gun tucked in his belt at the small of his back.

"I believe you've been around Eldon too long. You're starting to sound a bit like him," he said.

"Oh, don't wish that on a little old lady whose pear shape has gone pumpkin. Don't just stand there. Come on in."

"You know, that kind of humor with someone like Eldon is a bit of a misdirection signal. It usually means a person's got something to hide."

"Maybe I'm just trying to cheer myself up, after having my car smashed." She looked for a response, but he just nodded slowly. He was as serious as she'd seen him.

He settled into the couch and let her have her chair.

"Coffee?"

He shook his head.

"Not in the mood for small talk, eh? I heard about… well, at least Eldon was saying that…"

"I'm not here officially, if that's where you're going with that."

"I gathered that much. You didn't come here to explain why you've been acting weird lately, have you?"

"Weird's such an overworked and relative word."

Esbeth, for a roundish woman, knew she had an almost

delicate shrug, which she shared now. "How's wacky, daffy, unpredictable? What happened?"

"I may be off-duty, but I'm still interested, very interested." He rubbed one restless, wide hand across a jean-clad thigh.

"I don't know why that'd bring you *here*."

"Why do you think Eldon hired you, Esbeth?"

"You don't think it's because I ended up helping solve more cases than he did?"

Tillis' head shook slowly.

"No? Okay, I know better. It was to keep an eye on me, probably."

"You've got superior instincts to him. He may resent that too. You ever sense that?"

"You mean like the time I overheard him say about me that, 'Any blind hog can find an acorn once in a while.'" She tried to say it without any little painful hitch in her throat, and almost made it.

"You think he ever says anything original?"

"Don't matter out here. No one would know if he did. People latch onto things, like a good luck piece. They use the same patches of words every day, makes them feel comfy."

"The way the late Thirsty Mills was always spouting Shakespeare?"

"Education's supposed to be a steppingstone to greater things. But when it's the peak of everything you ever did or accomplished, it's worse than pitiful. But you didn't come here to talk about the flotsam and jetsam that's washed up here, did you?"

He leaned forward on the couch and rested his elbows on his knees. "I want to get back to that part about your instincts, Esbeth. I want you to tell me what you really think is going on."

"Now, why would I do that?"

"Because there's a sense of urgency building that someone like you just has to feel."

"What makes you think …"

"I'm not here to think, Esbeth. Sorry to be harsh, but it's nut-cuttin' time. Now, what do you really think is going on? And don't give me the watered-down crap you shoveled back there in the sheriff's office."

Her head started to snap back half an inch until she realized she was coming close to faking. This wasn't Eldon, after all. "I don't owe that to you, or even any on-duty lawman, no matter what you think."

"If something happens to Donnie or Karyn out of this, I'm going to lay that guilt trip on you all the remainder of your life."

"That's low. I don't think you could stoop to that."

"Look, I envy those kids their youth, their childish intensity, even that they're the kind of people and at the age where patriotism, commitment, loyalty come out of their mouths with a purity of raw innocence I can only imagine. But I'll damn sure use the threat of something hurting them in order to protect them, if that's what's necessary."

"That's still low."

"I can go lower if I have to, so quit stalling."

"You could've dug up some of it yourself, you or Eldon."

"I may have the time. I just don't have the connections, now. Besides, if I know you, you've already done enough groundwork to have a better big picture of this than anyone. And don't say I won't learn anything if you just tell it to me. I'm here to listen and learn, and that's all the discovery I have time for now."

She sighed, looked down at the slightly worn throw rug

in front of the chair, wishing she'd made that coffee after all. Then she straightened and leaned back in her chair. "What do you know about the stock market?"

"I thought we were going to talk about diamonds."

"We'll get there, but we'll cover gold first, too."

His forehead showed a concentration wrinkle, but he was a good listener, and could give an interested and encouraging look.

"The way it is with stocks is that people hear about one that's hot, or get wind of a merger or a new product, and the stock can soar. Sometimes it gets caught in a groundswell of buying and goes higher than the stock is worth. Then a few of those people holding shares sell out and make money, while the others get stung. These days, with a lot of amateur day traders out there, more people get stung than don't."

The concentration wrinkle on Tillis' forehead deepened, but he said nothing.

"The point is that a lot of investment is speculation, and a lot of that happens because of rumor or innuendo. What you have to think about here is a little backwards history lesson. Back in the days of the early gold and silver strikes in the West, a rumor almost always got out, and a little pocket of America would go crazy. And that's just with the rumor. If the strike was real, things got crazier."

"I've read a bit of history, Esbeth."

"Then this pill should be a bit sugarcoated for you. You probably know that the people who make money on a gold or silver strike aren't always the ones who made the discovery."

Tillis nodded, though a touch of impatience flashed in a glimmer across his face before he suppressed it.

"There were nabobs back in the gold and silver strike

days—guys who got rich and spent fast. Most of them were broke a year or two later, some of them in less time than that. There were guys who sold out their whole claim for a bottle or two of cheap whiskey. But the guys that really interest me are the ones on the fringes, those who bought and sold futures, got little, tiny pieces of the mines and speculated with them, kind of like today's stock market. First the miner would get an assay, taking the best possible sample, and then he might sell out shares on the mine, to hedge his bet. He might hit a ledge, or the whole pocket could dry up and he'd have nothing more than what he made from selling the shares."

To his credit, Tillis didn't glance at his watch, but his lips did press together a hair more tightly.

"In addition to the chiselers, dealers, hookers, and all kinds of suppliers that crowded around any strike town, there were those hanging on the fringes making money. A strike lights up a whole area, and people're pulled in from all over."

"Could you localize that?"

"I'm getting there. The so-called gold strike down in the valley, under what's now Lake Kiowa, never was a strike. It was a way for the Granite clan to seem to come onto their wealth. They were simple highwaymen at best—looters, burglars, whatever you want to call them. It's nothing to be too shocked at. I'm sure a lot of family trees have a pirate or a congressman farther down on an earlier limb."

"The Granites?"

"I wouldn't worry about them too much at the moment. Their cannon's spiked for now. But they were part of all this falling into place."

"We going to get to the diamonds?"

"Rein in your horse, there. I'm building to it. I bet you'd

build a house without a foundation. Anyway, you know all about everyone moving up to the top of the valley when it was flooded in and the lake was formed. That left the Granites with slightly better land, the Spurlocks with new neighbors, and Old Bill Hoel with land he wasn't all that happy about, even though there was twenty-two thousand acres of it."

"You think Hank Spurlock found those diamonds on Bill Hoel's land?"

She ignored the question. "Now, I'm going to have to go a whole different direction on you, so don't get your shorts in a wad."

Tillis eased himself back upright on the sofa.

"Most big strikes—the gold around San Francisco, silver around Virginia City, gold in Colorado—all happened in the mid-nineteenth century, except the gold rush in Alaska, which wasn't until eighteen ninety-two. I hope that wasn't a yawn you just stifled. Bear with me if I'm belaboring anything for you here. Anyway, most of the strike areas had the kind of paper-trading frenzy I'm talking about that we associate with the stock market today. People even bought up land at inflated prices. It was a seller's market.

"By eighteen seventy-one, there were some successful mineral rights men in San Francisco who had experience in buying and selling paper like that, trafficking it as far away as London. To name a key handful, there was George D. Roberts, W. C. Ralston, William W. Lent, and Asbury Harpening."

Esbeth was looking up into the corner of the room as she recalled the names, then looked back at Tillis and caught him staring.

"You've got a remarkable memory."

"People think I'm the teacher type. But I'm really a student, have been all my life. It's what keeps me going. Now, are you going to let me finish?"

His mouth tightened shut again.

"These men had all had success with land and mineral speculation before and had become bankers, which set them up just fine for what followed. A couple of dusty prospectors named Philip Arnold and John Slack showed up with a bag full of what seemed to be diamonds, even a few rubies and sapphires. They needed backing to mine the strike they'd located. They were sufficiently coy about seeking the backing, enough to lure the men into a frenzy of eagerness. The potential backers even had the stones found so far verified by Mr. Tiffany himself in New York. The backers were a bit more surprised when they got a glowing report from him. When word of that got out, a lot of others wanted to invest too, but first the backers lined up a mining expert, Henry Janin, and they headed out into the California wilderness to confirm the diamond fields. Arnold and Slack led them in zigzags all over the place until they were someplace up about seven thousand feet above sea level. Then they started through the fields. The dirt was hard and packed, but when the backers and the mining expert scraped, they came up with rough gems of their own. They left one of the prospectors and the rest returned, while backers went to New York to organize a ten-million-dollar company, and one of the investors was Baron Rothschild. It took a full year before another geologist," Esbeth tilted her head and looked up at a cobweb along the edge of the ceiling, "Clarence King, tracked his way to the Sierras and found traces of the diggings. One of the gems he uncovered was even partially faceted. That brought the whole business crashing down in what's been referred to as the Great Diamond Hoax."

Tillis let his head rest back on the back of the couch and looked up at the ceiling where Esbeth had been looking. "Is this yarn actually going anywhere?"

"Patience, dearheart. That's just some of the set-up for our story. All the backers, it turned out, were innocent. But a fellow named Cooper eventually confessed to orchestrating the whole thing: buying rough, industrial diamonds in London by bulk, and helping the so-called miners salt the field by drilling holes and dropping a stone into each hole. Weather packed the soil back into place by the time the backers ever got to the field."

"And you think Hank Spurlock…"

"If you're going to finish the story for me, I needn't bother."

Tillis had leaned forward again. He caught himself and sat back.

"You've got to remember the climate around here when our little version got started. A lot of time had gone by since the California diamond hoax, not that a lot of people were informed anyway. There had also been a so-called gold fever ripple down in the valley before it was flooded. And, as recently as nineteen oh-six, diamonds were discovered as near to here as Arkansas, at Murfreesboro. By international standards, the Arkansas find was small, but it did open minds to the possibilities. Any questions so far?"

"Yeah, does this class have a recess?"

"If you need a bathroom break, just hold up fingers."

"You don't want to know what finger I'm thinking of."

"Do you want to hear this or not?"

"Go ahead."

"If this sort of attitude continues, you're going to forfeit any right to call *me* cranky." She glared at him, but he was done talking for a while.

"What I'm going to say now enters the realm of hypotheses, based on a few known facts and a few givens."

Tillis' mouth opened, then shut.

"About fifty years ago the valley folks were moved up into the highlands and resettled. The Spurlocks were dominant up here, and their sway was usurped somewhat by the Hoels and Granites. Ten years later, Bill Hoel is complaining about his land not being near as good as what he had below. The soil wasn't as good for grazing, he said, and the labor to maintain it was too high. He was ready to sell some of the twenty-two thousand acres he'd been given. About that same time, Hank Spurlock located diamonds, or so the story goes, on land in the area. I have it on reasonably good authority that his find was on the Hoel property."

"Who?"

"Don't even press that button. But now we get to the tricky part. Hank Spurlock disappears, but leaves a legacy story about the diamonds, and all the Spurlocks—Hugh, Denny, even Donnie now—have been charged with saying nothing and striving to get back Hank's diamonds."

"If there were any."

"Oh, I think there were."

"Salted ones?"

"I think that too."

"How're we going to ever prove any of this?"

"I don't think you can."

"You think Bill killed Hank and took over the mine? Is that why the property went off the market?"

"If I was a full-fledged officer of the law, I'd maybe look into the diamond markets. Most of them are in Amsterdam or Antwerp. You could see if anyone bought rough diamonds forty or more years ago."

Tillis let out a slow puff of breath.

"Or you could see if someone sold the diamonds back, or if there's diamond production, if someone's selling diamonds at all that come from there."

"You know that'd be a needle in a haystack, even if I was still in a position to do anything like that."

"Yeah, I thought of that. Most of the diamonds sold at that time came through DeBeers. But who's to say you could locate whoever sold or bought diamonds to someone like Bill. And if he'd been halfway clever enough to do that, he might've gotten his diamonds elsewhere. India and Russia had thriving businesses going by then, and were as likely to have the rough, industrial diamonds as DeBeers, since they were focusing on D Flawless stones by then."

"You've done some homework. But it doesn't help much, does it? That's all you have, nothing more concrete than that?"

"I do have one little tidbit, not worth a lot, but it's a scrap."

"What's that?"

"Do you remember when books in libraries used to have cards in the back?"

He nodded.

"The library here shifted their card catalog over to a computer at least five years ago."

"But you found a book?"

"No. But there was a book, one written by Asbury Harpening, one of the backers of the Diamond Hoax, who sought to clear his name. The library had a copy, but it's missing."

"Like most of the history here."

"But when the books were converted to the computer system, all the cards were kept. This library's small enough it rarely throws away anything."

"And?"

Esbeth reached down into her purse and brought out a small card with names written down in a list on one side. "Once I'd sweet-talked her a bit, Florence helped me find this. The last person to check out the book was Old Bill Hoel himself."

"That's it? That's all you have?"

"I guess the library could zing him for the price of a new copy, if they wanted to. It took a few days to get a similar copy here on interlibrary loan for me to see just what was in the missing book. But it's the tiny bit of glue that tells me Bill might be behind more of this than you've unearthed."

"Okay, then. If what you say is true, and the whole diamond mine thing was a hoax to inflate the value of his land so he could sell it high, then he certainly didn't take it off the market because he found a real mine. Why then did he suddenly not want to sell it?"

"Yeah, I pondered that a bit too. But think about this. What if he located a whole new source of labor?"

Tillis gave a small jerk, as if he'd been stung by the idea. But he didn't seem quite as surprised by the idea as Esbeth expected. His eyes widened for just a moment, and he looked at Esbeth. "That could explain a lot of things."

"Seemed so to me."

"But we can't prove a thing. Can you imagine, given his clout, what'd happen if I stormed in there and tried to do anything based on what you just said?"

"It is kind of thin for that, isn't it? That's been my

dilemma. Now it's yours too, if it hasn't already been on your mind."

"Still, it's something, if just a scrap, like you said. Is there anything else?"

Esbeth shook her head, tired from the storytelling and wishing more than ever she'd whipped up that pot of coffee.

Tillis said, "You realize that all this may make you the first historical detective?"

"At my age, that's no surprise. But if you'd read your history, you'd know it's no first. *All* historians are detectives of one sort or another."

Tillis stood slowly, as if he'd become part of the sofa. But with each step he took toward the door he seemed to energize again, until he had the bounce of a dog in the back of a truck about to be put on the scent. Maybe he was getting a sliver of hope out of all that.

He stepped outside and Esbeth looked past his shoulder at the sky. They were both surprised that the threat of storm that had been there had skipped around the town, and that the sky was now a partially overcast and pensive pale blue. The edge of the sky, where the sun was nearing the horizon, was taking on a coppery hue.

"You mind hearing one more thing from someone as old and as crusty as me?"

He turned and looked at her, and took an extra step down the porch steps until their eyes were close to level. "Go ahead and say it," he said.

"I think there's something about this one that you needed, something that rattles you to your deeps. And it comes at a time when that's just the wake-up call in life you craved."

"Are you talking about …"

"No, not her. Though she'll be part of it before it all settles. You wait and see."

"You know what?"

"No." The sun poked past a cloud and she had to squint. "If you'd lived back in Salem, Massachusetts you'd have probably had a pretty toasty time of it." He reached up to tip his hat to her, then realized he wasn't wearing one, so he touched three fingers above his right eye, gave a short wave, and turned to walk down toward his parked truck.

Under her breath, Esbeth muttered, "I'd have probably given those old witch hunters back then all they wanted of it, too."

TILLIS' TRUCK PULLED away, and Esbeth was ready to rush out to the borrowed car and take off. But first, she made herself go inside and heat up some water to make a cup of instant coffee. While the water was heating, she changed into jeans, a worn but respectable white linen blouse, and comfortable shoes. She watered all the plants and checked the windows and doors. The preparations only heightened her own growing anxiety. She made herself sit still at the dinette and drink her coffee, and she even rinsed out the mug. Then she took the keys out of the drawer where she'd kept them out of sight of the Ranger, and she went out the walk to the car as if walking her last mile.

The car was a 1960 white Thunderbird that had seen better days. Well, Esbeth thought, so have I. When you borrow, you don't get much ground for grousing. Her own car had been a twisted knot that was hard to look at as she'd visited it at the wrecking yard to get the last of her possessions and the odd map out of the glove box. The only good thing about it was that she hadn't been in it at the time.

Someone would have to do some real talking to convince her that her car being smashed hadn't been a message to her to lay off, that her nosing had ruffled at least one set of feathers.

The paint on the old T-Bird had been worn thin, either by the Texas sun or too many washings. Inside, the upholstery had been sewed up enough times to look like the loser in a knife fight. She got in and opened the window. No air-conditioning—that figured. She started the car, and the engine rumbled with the rattling, loose roar of being six months past the need for a tune-up, on top of a partial muffler. She put the car in gear and pulled away from the curb. It had been a while since she had driven, and even with an automatic transmission her first few stops and starts kept her head bobbing. But then she settled down to a steady five miles under the speed limit.

"Go around," she yelled out the window. "Indianapolis and Daytona are to hell and gone from here."

Her face was flushed from either the wind or the state she was usually in while driving, full passive-aggressive attack. Driving was a painful and stressful ordeal for her. Only something pressing could get her out on the road with so many over-eager drivers. It'd be all right if she had the roads to herself. Was that a lot to ask?

"Get over in your own lane, or get a smaller car, and hang up that cell phone."

The chief reason Esbeth had been so willing to leave the world of cars and driving behind not so long ago was her fear that it brought out her real personality, and at its full crankiness. And it wasn't just her. Others were affected too, like the guy buzzing by now, who she was pretty sure wasn't waving to her that she was number one.

She was almost exhausted by the time she got to the edge

of Fearing and cut out onto the highway, heading over to the town of Hoel's Dam.

With an open road in front of her, she, for a moment, pressed on the gas and the old car gave a clumsy but eager lurch, like a hound grabbing at a scent. She eased off on the gas and the roar reduced to a loud, steady burble as the wind swept in the window and tugged at her white hair. It was a conflict for her. One part hying to the sense of urgency, the other governed by the wish to get there in one piece, and with the car intact at that. As it was, even at the more regular speed, the steering wheel rattled all hard and jittery in her hands, like a skeleton trying to pull itself free from a body.

She pulled into the edge of Hoel's Dam at last, and was physically exhausted after driving just the short distance. A long trip would have been the end of her, she figured. She did battle with the little dribs and drabs of traffic in town until she pulled up in front of the Victorian home that had served the Spurlocks all these years. A small cloud slid in front of the sun, and for a moment the house was vaguely sinister, but that could have been her thinking about Thirsty Mills being killed right beside the porch.

Esbeth banged on the front and back doors, and walked all the way around the house. She didn't see Denny's classic Dodge anywhere.

She had just gotten back to the front of the house after passing the spot where they'd found Thirsty when a noise made her look up.

A green truck screeched to a stop behind the car she'd borrowed. Logan Rainey hopped out of the door, slammed it shut, and came hurrying toward the house.

"Is he in there?" he shouted.

"No. And I guess this means he's not over at your house either."

Logan's jaw tightened and he spun without answering and ran back to his truck. He was in it and peeling away before Esbeth realized it.

For a second, she stood in the sun and felt a bit dazed; then she plodded back toward the car. She knew where she had to go now, and was saying to herself, "I wish just once I could be a step ahead, instead of half a step behind."

THERE WAS A line waiting all the way out to the parking lot at the Bluebonnet Cafe. But Tillis figured as long as he was in town he ought to give it a try, and he was able to squeeze past the line and get one of the open spots at the counter. Between meals like Donnie's breakfast and the lunch he ordered, he was going to have to start thinking in terms of exercise and diet, though the thought of exercise made him grin and think of Gala.

He was cutting his first bite from a chicken-fried steak, and sweeping it through the edge of the mashed potatoes and gravy, when someone tapped on his shoulder. He looked up, and Logan's face was bent down close, and it was nothing pretty to see. Any attempt Logan was making to mask his emotions was an utter failure. Tillis could read combined bits of panic, anger, fear, hurt, and a revolving door of other flickering insights into Logan's mood he didn't want right now.

"What?"

"I need to talk to you."

"Go ahead."

"Outside. Now."

"Can I…"

"No. Come on."

Tillis let out a long, slow breath and lowered his loaded fork back onto the plate. He rose and took out a bill big enough to more than cover lunch and tip, and then he followed Logan out the door, past the line of people still waiting, and through the sunny parking lot, until they stood in the shade of a live oak tree along the far end of the lot.

Logan waited until what looked like a young cattle ranch hand had helped his pregnant wife down from the high side of his diesel pickup truck cab and got her moving toward the line. When they were out of hearing, Logan's head snapped to Tillis. "Karyn's missing."

"Oh, come on. She's around somewhere."

"No. I mean it. She's gone."

"She'll come back."

"I don't know."

"Why do you say that? What'd you do?"

"I…well, I'm not very proud…"

"What?"

"I locked her in her room."

"Logan, you can't do that, even if she wasn't eighteen."

Logan's face flushed the brightest red Tillis had ever seen it. "Don't you tell me what…oh, hell. It doesn't matter. Just help me get her back, so I can talk to her."

"You know, the reason they wrap dynamite so tight is that being repressed is what gives it the kick."

"Can you spare me any retread farm wisdom you might've picked up from Eldon? Can't you see I need your help here?"

Tillis started to speak and stopped himself. He examined the faintly hysterical look on the face of his friend, who normally shared very little of his inner feelings. "How'd you find me?"

"That deputy. She knew where you were."

"Well, I didn't tell her."

"She knew just the same. I thought she might."

"Why do you say that?"

"You really think you're the only puppeteer around here pulling strings?"

"What do you mean by that?"

"Look, I know I was out of line earlier the way I talked about her. I didn't mean or intend any ethnic slurs."

"But you made them, just the same."

"And I'll take the rap for that. But don't you think your perspective might be compromised a bit, Tillis?"

"What am I missing?"

"Well, how she knows where everyone is all the time, especially you, and how Eldon jumps when she talks."

"That's…"

"Very unlike Eldon," Logan said.

Tillis looked away and said nothing. He'd had some mixed thoughts about Gala himself.

"And Tillis…"

"What?"

"I've got to…got to tell you something else."

"Go ahead."

"I'm the one who called Tim Comber to tell him about your fooling around with the deputy and the gambling. I hope I didn't screw things up too much for you." He was staring at the spot on Tillis' shirt where he would normally be wearing a star.

Tillis stared off into the top of an old and stately live oak tree across the street for a few seconds, before he looked back at Logan and said, "If it makes you feel any better, you weren't the only one."

THIRTEEN

"ARE YOU GOING TO get out of the car?" Donnie hiked back along the fence line after backtracking to cover the tracks where the car left the road.

"I'm deciding." Karyn sat in the passenger seat with the doors open on both sides. The car glittered dark green in the sun like some giant beetle.

It was hot, and Donnie could feel the sweat causing his shirt to stick to him as he bent to open the trunk. He got out the metal detector and the bolt cutters he'd brought. "Least you could do is carry the backpack with the water."

When she didn't answer, and stayed sitting in the car, Donnie slowed and bent forward until he could drop the tools to the ground with as little noise as possible. He had pulled the car all the way in at the corner of the Hoel estate, where the fence line turned and ran up into the tallest hills on the property. The vegetation was sparse here, and he'd had to use a mesquite limb and be careful of its thorns as he wiped out the tracks of the Dodge that led back to the patch of chaparral where he'd tucked the car. Where he walked now was loose dirt and sand, too dried for growing anything but occasional prickly pear cactus, yucca, a solitary mesquite, and strings of the hardy buffalo gourd vine. Occasional tumbles of rock here and there looked like great spots for rattlesnakes, and he watched for those as well, glad he'd slipped on his Red Wing boots this morning.

He turned and went back to the car to lean in on the passenger side. She sat with her arms folded, staring straight ahead.

"Look, we came out this far," he said.

She didn't say anything, nor did she look at him.

"You were fine at the library, even insisted on coming. What is it?"

Her head turned to him slowly, and though her father hadn't caught up to them yet, her expression was one worthy of Logan. "I'm having second thoughts. Diving at night by the dam was one thing. Stupid as that was, it's nothing compared to this."

"There's nothing stupid here. We're just going to check."

"The other wasn't very smart, Donnie, but this is illegal. You're talking about trespassing on someone's land, someone who specifically doesn't want you, of all people, on it."

She didn't have to point out all the posted No Trespassing signs that stood out with their fluorescent letters at regular intervals along the fourteen-foot-high fence with its razor-coiled top. If ever a property had "Stay out" written all over it, it was this one.

"I've told you, this used to be Spurlock land."

"Until the River Authority bought it up when they had to recompense Bill Hoel for his valley land, and he wouldn't take a cash settlement. I've heard the whole thing, Donnie. That doesn't change anything. It's still his land, and he's fussy about it. I've heard there're guards and everything. This is the kind of thing Esbeth Walters was warning us against. It's okay to dig into the history, but you're crossing the line here."

"I wish you wouldn't bring her up."

"I wish she was here to talk to you."

"Come on, Karyn. I just want to check, look around a bit. You know I have to do it, with or without you. Don't make me do it alone. Help me take just a short look, then we'll get off."

"You'll promise that?"

"I told you what Dad said. What he figured out by reading between the lines of the journal made him think the first pick was underwater. But his second choice was up here on the former Spurlock land."

"I haven't even seen any journal. You have, and I have to believe what you say. But have you stopped to think some of that might be the ranting of a lunatic?"

"Dad was no lunatic."

"No, but what got under his skin and maybe caused his death was listening to whatever his dad had to say. You never even met your Grandpa Hank Spurlock. What's to say he wasn't a little off? Why do you have to do anything, just because he said?"

"What're you saying? You think there's a vein of madness in my family?" There was some of the glitter of that old obsessive light in Donnie's eyes before he looked up and away from her. High on one of the fence posts, above the sharp wire, a mockingbird stood gray and black and white in the sun with its chest thrust out and tail cocked up at an angle. It made a haunting and repetitive cry.

"You've got the money from the insurance. What do you care about a bunch of diamonds? Can't you leave all that alone, consider the whole thing over?"

"It was a charge. It's all I was ever asked to do by my family. I believe Dad was killed because of it."

"It's what's killed everyone else in your family. You're what I care about. I don't want to lose you."

He looked back at her, at the shine of tears on her cheeks. "Look, it wasn't your father who was killed. Will you just do this? Come with me, look around. If we see nothing, or learn nothing, we get off the land and never come back. Will you do that one thing for me?"

She looked at him without blinking, though there were small wells of tears at the bottom of her eyes and her head was making tiny jerks. "You know I will. But just this once. Please? I understand a quest, but this's got to end. Agreed?"

He held out a hand. She wiped at her eyes and reached for it. "Yeah. You've got it. But just this once. Okay? I need to at least check, or I don't feel like I can ever sleep again."

TILLIS GOT BACK in Logan's truck and slammed the door, grateful for the air-conditioning Logan had left on while he waited. "She's not there."

"How did you expect that old coot to help us?"

Tillis turned to Logan. "You know, you've got some other problems to work on when this locking your eighteen-year-old daughter in her room business clears up."

"Don't you…"

"Give you a lot of crap about your parenting skills? Hell, Logan, you've been so damned wound up you haven't noticed that most of your people skills in general have gone to hell on a roller skate. How the devil did you get in this shape?"

"I …"

"There isn't a single excuse you can make. So get off that. Let's just focus on Karyn here."

"You've been a bit fast and loose yourself. Cost you your star."

Tillis' eyes narrowed at Logan. Whatever was on his face made Logan blink and clamp his mouth shut. "Just tell me that you care more for getting in the last word than you do about finding Karyn."

Logan didn't even try to speak.

"Okay." Tillis felt the warm heat rippling across his face ease a bit. He gave Logan new directions, and Logan eased the truck away from the curb in front of Esbeth's house without another word or glance.

THE SUN WAS BLISTERING hot in Esbeth's borrowed car that had no air-conditioning. Sweat had soaked through the back of her blouse, where it pressed against the cracked vinyl seats. The car rattled and jangled through the back roads, as if at any minute it might give up the whole business. It may have been maintained well once, but it had been let sit a long time.

She had never been up this way before, but had heard about it, so she wasn't too surprised to come to the green posts of Old Bill Hoel's fourteen-foot-high deer fence. She went slow by the front gate, and saw no one there, though she did spot an armadillo and a porcupine beside the road, both of which would have to be buried in pizza boxes.

Then she was surprised, and pleased, to see a roadrunner trotting along in its distinctive high gait on the other side of the road. She always thought it good luck to see a roadrunner, and this one had a small snake in its mouth, which was even better. Not that she was superstitious—far from it. But it made her think the world was working right, if only this tiny natural piece of it.

Esbeth wasn't sure what to expect or look for, so she kept a slow pace as she went along the long stretch of fence, watching for any little indication. It was too much to hope that she would just spot the car. If she had been the one looking to get into the Hoel spread, she would have sought a spot across the road to hide her car. But Donnie was too direct for that, and much of the area across the road from the fence was too wide open, except for occasional tree-lined drives leading back to other, smaller ranches. She even saw "Hurley" on one mailbox and remembered that Pudge Hurley had his horse ranch out here, somewhere across from the Hoel Spread.

Her slow pace was taking a toll on the car. Steam was starting to come out from the edges of the hood as she started up the sharper slope where the corner of the property climbed up into the rocky hills. That couldn't be good. She was one of the many people who, if she looked under the hood and didn't see something visible hanging loose or otherwise wrong, was out of ideas about how to fix a car. But even she knew what she'd see under the aged T-Bird's hood this time. It needed water, and, in her haste, she hadn't even brought any along for herself.

Paying attention to the car almost made her miss the spot. But she looked to her right as the corner of the property line came up, and at first there was nothing. Then she peered closer, saw the grass bent back funny, like a cat's fur when you've rubbed it the wrong way.

She drove on for a few hundred feet, then made a turn-around in the edge of an old lane where there was a wider gravel stretch on the other side of the road. That would leave as little trace as possible. She eased up until she could pull the T-Bird off to the right of the road. It tilted at an angle, with its right wheels down part of the way into a ditch. She had to struggle with the weight of the door to get it open and herself pried out of the car. Then she tied a spare handkerchief to the door handle, went around to the front, and opened the hood. Steam rolled out from around the radiator cap. It looked very much like a disabled car, which, in fact, it pretty much was.

Esbeth tugged on a pale green ball cap she used for gardening. It didn't fit all that well, and perched on top of her topknot of stiff, white hair. But it kept some of the sun out of her eyes. She trudged back to the spot where she'd noted the attempt at covering tracks. When she got there, she nodded. If she'd been going at regular speed, she probably would've missed it. A small holly-like agarita bush had been crushed, but was propped back upright with a small forked stick to look almost as it had before a tire had pressed it down. She could see where someone had worked with a branch like a broom, and someone who wasn't perfect at it. That, she figured, would be Donnie.

She skirted the repaired bit of flora and went along close to the fence, following back from the green corner post. The ground rose steadily, dipped, and rose higher. Behind the second swell, tucked away in the chaparral, she saw the antique green car that had once been Denny's and now belonged to Donnie. No one was in it. She took out a handkerchief from her pocket, wiped her brow and neck, and forced herself to keep moving.

She was watching for footprints, although the ground was too hard in most spots, when she came to the place where a small door had been cut in the chain link fence. The bolt cutters that had done the job lay along the outside of the fence, and the flap that had been opened had been closed by two bits of wire, wound from the inside to call as little attention to the hole as possible.

"Lord love a duck," Esbeth muttered. She reached for the wires holding the door closed and began to undo them. "And I thought at my age there was nothing left to learn the hard way."

THE USUAL NOISE of a hospital hallway spilled in through the partially-closed door, but it was otherwise quiet where Selma stood in the dim light of the pulled drapes and looked at her two boys. They'd been given a room together and, though Rocky had been awake, he was sleeping now, and Stone had been given a strong sedative after being brought down from the ICU not too long ago.

Out in the hallway on a chair, the deputy Rudy sat, soaking up taxpayer dollars, though it was pretty clear to Selma that neither boy was going anywhere for a while.

Though they were both still as out as the cross-eyed mackerels to which she had referred earlier, she spoke to them as if they were awake, as if it would make any difference.

"Sandy's out in the car. We're packed up and out of here, and I'm selling what there is of the ranch to get the best mouthpiece I can for you, but it doesn't look good. I might as well tell you that. They may be able to pin Thirsty's death on you, probably will, and will no doubt try to pin Denny's on you too."

Stone's formerly handsome face was wrapped in gauze, and there was still some question if he had any brain damage from a seeping skull fracture they'd had to go in and work on. Rocky was never going to be much brighter than he'd been.

"Can't hardly run a spread without you two. Maybe Ol' Hoel had the right idea after all. I know I wish I'd thought of it. Lot of us knew, but wouldn't say. None of it all's gonna matter now. Everything's gone topsy-turvy on all of us with change. Hard to believe that when the Texas Rangers were first formed, that their whole job was to run the Indians and even the damned ol' Mexicans off of here. Now look at 'em."

She glanced toward the closed door. "Gotta keep my language down or I'll have every spic, wop, mick, kike, and chink in the place thinkin' I'm a bigot." She chuckled to herself. "Folks can't hardly talk plain no more, but I can to you two.

"I'm sick and sad and disappointed, boys, with myself more than you two. I love you both, but I don't think we'll be able to get you off, though we'll spend what we have to trying. Me and Sandy and Pebble are going away—not too far, just far enough away that I don't wake in the night with no more cold, damp dreams about the likes of Morgan Lane, nor none of the rest of all of it. I guess I'm the only halfway smart one left of us, and I sure don't intend to stay here and let the area wear me down a day more. If I was spiritual at all, I'd say the place is cursed. But I don't much care. I'm beaten down all I care to be, and I'm out of here."

She looked at each of the boys a last time, then went out of the room and softly closed the door behind her.

"WAIT RIGHT HERE." Tillis hopped out of the truck and started in a run across the sheriff's department parking lot. Logan sat in the truck, with the engine idling, watching him.

Halfway across the lot, he saw Gala tossing her bag into the back of her gold Chevy Tahoe. He spun and jogged up to her.

She turned, and he saw she'd already taken off her tie, hat, and gun belt.

"Out getting exercise? How admirable," she said.

"Esbeth in there?" He was panting slightly.

"No. Why?"

He looked over at the building. "You going to be around later?"

"Can't."

"Why?"

"Just busy."

"Doing what?"

"I'm just busy, Tillis. I have other plans. What's the matter? Why am I having trouble getting through to you?" She looked up into his face.

He looked back down at her, feeling like it was some poker game, with neither of them trying to share a thing.

"Just dense, I guess." His face burned with a warm flush. He was mad, first at Logan, then at himself, then, maybe, at her. He wasn't thinking as clearly as he'd like; he knew that.

"What is it?" Her words were chipped ice this time. "Why don't you say what's on your so-called mind?"

His breath was just about back to normal. "I would really like to believe you're everything you say you are."

"And you can't?"

He glanced back at the truck, where Logan was waving through the windshield for him to come on.

"Tillis, you don't have all that many bridges left. I'd be careful with your matches, if I were you." She slammed the tailgate and walked around to the driver's side, and got in without looking back.

He had to hop out of the way, as the Tahoe snapped out

of the parking spot to throw a bit of gravel on its way out of the lot.

He walked back to the truck more slowly and got back in.

"Now what?" Logan's voice threatened to hop an octave. "We've checked the library, and half a dozen other places. Have you got any idea what you're doing?" He clenched the wheel like he wanted to tear it in half.

Tillis had his window open and arm on the sill, looking more comfortable than he felt. He was thinking about the old white car he'd seen outside Esbeth's house. "There's one other place that makes sense." He gave Logan more directions.

To Logan's credit, he just gave Tillis a sharp glance, then drove.

They pulled up to the small house with the uncared-for lawn, and Tillis was out of the car and walking briskly toward the door before Logan could speak. He piled out of his side and sought to keep up.

Tillis, though walking quickly, was thinking that all this was so much like one of those Chinese puzzles where you open the man, find the smaller man inside, open it, find an even smaller one. But there was never a short cut. You had to follow all the steps, even if time was no longer on your side.

The door finally opened a good two or three minutes after Tillis had pounded on it twice, after Logan, sensing some of the urgency, had pounded too.

Floyd Bettles blinked at the bright light coming from behind them. He was in a nightshirt, though it was midday.

"What is it? What is it?" He saw them looking at his nightshirt. "I take naps. You woke me. What is it? Who are you?"

Tillis nearly said he was a Texas Ranger. But he wasn't just then. Instead, he said, "It's about Esbeth."

Floyd looked about in a distracted way, then said, "You gents want coffee?"

"No," Logan said.

"Sure we would," Tillis countered.

Floyd looked at Tillis, nodded, and padded off to the kitchen.

"What're you doing? I thought we didn't have much time?" Logan whispered as they went on into the living room.

"First you give the rug, then you pull it," Tillis said softly.

"Do we have that kind of time?"

"It won't take all that long. He comes from that older school, where being host to us might make him a touch more beholden. We may need any edge we can get."

A few minutes later Floyd came in with a mug in each hand. He held one out to each of them. Tillis sat in the rocker, while Logan stood over by the window that looked out over the back yard. Floyd went back to the kitchen to get his own mug. None of the mugs matched. Tillis' mug advertised farm equipment. He couldn't make out the writing on Logan's mug.

"You have a car, don't you, Floyd? It's an older T-Bird, isn't it? White?" Tillis sipped at the instant coffee. It wasn't very strong, and was slightly bitter, so maybe its weakness was a blessing of sorts.

"How would you know that?"

"I've got an interest in any cars almost as old as I am."

"What's this about? Why d'you want to know about it?"

"I already said. Esbeth."

"What makes you think …"

"Where's your car, Floyd?"

"I don't drive much anymore."

"But you do have a car. She might be in trouble. Did Esbeth borrow it?"

Floyd glanced around behind him at nothing. Though he held his coffee mug, he hadn't taken a sip so far.

"She would want us to know. We're friends."

Floyd looked down.

Logan snapped a little louder. "Come on, you've got to…"

Tillis held up a hand and Logan stopped. Tillis said, "We aren't going to tell anyone what you told her about the diamonds, Floyd."

"She told that?"

"No, but you just confirmed who did tell her. But trust us, Floyd. Neither Logan nor I intend to tell anyone. I mean that."

"They'd kill me, like they done Denny."

"We don't know that. But I want to help Esbeth, and Logan's daughter may be in trouble."

"My life isn't gonna be worth spit."

"Floyd, tell us. Where did she go?"

Floyd's head drooped, but he still looked reluctant, and stubborn.

"Her life may be in jeopardy," Tillis said, pitching it a little stronger than he thought he needed.

Floyd's weathered, long face lifted. "She said…she said my old heap might have to take her as far as Old Bill Hoel's place. You gotta know I tried to stop her."

"But you loaned her the car anyway."

"She's a sweet lady. She'd never tell on me. I hope I haven't let her down."

Logan was already heading for the door while Tillis stood up. "You haven't, Floyd. Let's hope you've helped her."

DONNIE WAS AHEAD of her, and she let him be. Though he carried the metal detector, the pack on her back felt as if it were full of bricks. The sun beat down on them, and the way Donnie stopped and stared every now and then on the climb told her he was watching for snakes. They'd seen only one diamondback so far, and it was far enough away that Donnie could comment calmly that he thought it had ten or twelve buttons. She'd seen enough snakes to know he was talking about the rattle, but that didn't mean she wanted to see one up close just now.

Rocks were all around in profusion; most were sandy, reddish-yellow-looking rocks, with occasional darker slabs of what might be shale sticking up at odd angles out of the ground. Cacti and scrub weeds added a bit of dusty green to an otherwise dreary setting. But Donnie seemed to be getting more excited.

"You see how this path kind of weaves up like a big S? That's it, just like in the journal."

Karyn didn't feel she should share any of her thoughts about that damned journal just now. The dive at night, in the black water, had scared her like she'd never been scared before. But that was over. She couldn't help now feeling a worse sense of creeping willies at being on someone's land, someone who hated everyone named Spurlock, from all she'd heard.

"And if we can see the three peaks, we can even get a triangulation."

Karyn's long red hair felt heavy, as it clung to her. She stopped and took the pack off her back, lowered it to a flat rock shaped like a big yellow t-bone steak. The light breeze coming up the hill behind her made the damp back of her shirt feel cool. At first that felt good; then she gave a brief shudder and reached for the pack.

"It's here. It's here. Come're, Karyn and see—just like they said."

She sighed to herself and trudged up the last few feet to where Donnie had disappeared over the ridge. When she finally pulled herself up over the rim, she dropped the backpack, which didn't seem near as heavy now that they were here, and bent to take out a bottle of the water. She took a deep drink, and though it wasn't cool, it was as good as she'd ever had. She held out the bottle to Donnie and walked past him to see his perspective.

The top of this hill opened into a flat, rounded table, with a ridge of smaller points that rose around its edges. It did make the whole thing look like the dead top of a volcano, and in the distance she could count out the three peaks of other hills Donnie had said would be visible from here.

Donnie rushed over to a pile of loose scree and rubble along one edge. He dug beneath the loose rocks on top until he found something. "And look." He held up the broken oak handle of some kind of pick or shovel. "This is where I think they camped and mined." In this climate, old oak spokes of stagecoach wheels had lasted for years, and, buried like that, there'd been no reason for Hoel to find something like a broken pick handle.

In spite of herself, Karyn felt the same hope welling up in her she'd experienced during the first part of their dive. In her calm moments, all she wanted to do was get on with her life, and that included being with Donnie. But it was hard to deny the bubbling excitement of maybe being truly rich. Just as that thought got a firm hold, she dashed it away by thinking that this wasn't Donnie's land, and even if they did find something, that didn't mean it was theirs.

Donnie, though, had the metal detector out and was carefully sweeping the whole surface of the hill. He had the headset on and was intent on watching the dial.

She looked around for a shady spot and saw none, so she went over to where there was a slim darkness along the edge of one rim of rock. She lowered herself into it, and though the sun fell full on her face, at least her hands and waist were in a bit of shadow. From here, she could turn her head and look out across some of the miles of the estate. Except for the rocks and other hills, there wasn't much to see. There was the sound of birds, many out of her sight, and a few flying from cover to cover. High in the distance she could see three dark birds with deep-vees in their wingspans, circling and circling in a thermal. A tiny wisp of smoke led down to a spot, where if she leaned she could see a small cluster of buildings far away, low between distant hills, like a small village out where she knew there were no villages.

Donnie had covered most of the hill, and she could see his frown as he swept his way back, checking even along the sharp spikes of the ridge that rose around the hilltop. She'd already asked him how he expected to find diamonds with a metal detector. But he wasn't after diamonds yet. He was after the box.

She had to get up and move once while he swept where she sat. She moved to a spot that was even a bit more shady, though it wasn't much cooler than where she'd been.

He made another thorough sweep or two, with sweat soaking through his shirt, turning it dark. Then he finally took off the headset and put down the metal detector. He took the pick handle he'd found earlier and began to dig in several random spots with a new desperation.

Karen leaned her head back and looked up at a single spray of white wisp of cloud in all the blue of the sky. It was so still. Too still. Over the top of the sound of Donnie's digging, she heard nothing. Where were the birds she'd been hearing a few minutes ago? She'd heard the scurry a minute ago of a lizard, then nothing. The air around them seemed so suddenly still, and all too silent.

"Donnie."

He kept digging.

"Donnie." Louder this time. He looked up.

"What?"

"Listen."

"I don't hear anything."

"That's just it." But as she said it, she heard the scratching, slow steps, climbing the side of the hill, coming closer.

Donnie started to put the pick handle down, then he turned it like a club and started to ease his way over closer to Karyn, staying in a crouch as he did.

There was a snap of a twig, then another soft rustle of brush. Donnie held a finger up to his lips, though he didn't have to; Karyn was frozen to the rocks where she leaned, and icy fingers had begun to slowly crawl up and down her spine.

LOGAN DROVE HIS game warden truck hard, hands pale-knuckled white on the wheel at the ten and two position, the light truck sliding through the outside gravel of some of the back road curves, straightening as he goosed the gas pedal while giving the road a straight-ahead stare. They were racing along the tall fence with green posts along Bill Hoel's property, on the same road where earlier Esbeth had putted, when Tillis yelled, "Logan. Stop."

"What?"

Up ahead the gate was being opened and a car was waiting to come out.

"Can you get this off the road? Back there, where we saw that stand of live oaks."

"Why?"

"Just do it."

Logan spun the truck in a U-turn and went back to the spot, eased the truck off the road at a long gravel lane. He went down a ways, then turned and came all the way back until his truck was nestled in the shadows of the trees, pressed as far over against the fence there as he could get.

"Now what?"

Tillis waved a hand for him to be quiet.

They sat and waited. In a minute, a car went zipping by.

"That was Eldon Watkins," Logan said. "In his personal car. Why'd you have us hide from him?" He looked over at the expression on Tillis' face, then said, "Oh, shit. It's like that, is it?"

"I'm afraid so. We can go now," Tillis said.

"How long have you suspected?"

"Almost from the first."

KARYN MOVED CLOSER to Donnie, and gripped his hand. She could feel a small tremor in him now, though he held the broken handle like a club firmly enough in the other hand. They both stared at the spot where they'd come over the lip of the ridge themselves moments ago.

They could clearly make out shuffling steps now. Donnie let go of her hand, gripped the oak handle with both hands, and moved closer to the rim, with the handle poised back and ready to strike.

Karyn wasn't ready for the green ball cap on top of a white head of hair that popped over the edge, nor was Donnie.

"Good grief, Esbeth, you scared me out of a year's growth," Karyn said, as soon as she recognized her.

"What about me?" Esbeth puffed. "I lost at least a year of retirement time by climbing up here."

"No one made you. You shouldn't even be here." Donnie lowered the handle and glared at her.

Esbeth stood huffing, and looked around at the metal detector lying on the ground, and at where Donnie had dug his random holes. "So this is where the famous diamond mine was," she said.

"What do you know about that?" Donnie was as defensive as Karyn had heard him so far.

"I know there never was a diamond mine. Old Bill Hoel salted an area, probably right where we stand, and all to fool Old Hank Spurlock."

"That's not true."

"Let her talk, Donnie. Shouting her down doesn't prove much, at least what you want to prove. Esbeth, you're absolutely dripping. Can I get you some water?"

"It would save my life."

Karyn got her one of the plastic bottles from the pack, and they waited while she drank almost half of it. Donnie sulked and waited.

When she lowered the bottle, she looked at Donnie and said, "In all likelihood, he gathered the diamonds back up and sold them back to where he got them—cheap industrial-grade stones for the most part, but enough to stir up interest and an increase in the value of his property—that is, until he decided not to sell after all. It's all turned into some kind of cruel joke on the hopes of the Spurlocks for three generations."

"That's just lies," Donnie shouted. "Why don't you go back down where you came from? Why're you up here bothering us, anyway?"

Esbeth glanced around. "I came, hoping to get you down off here before there really is a problem. But it looks like I'm too late for that."

All Donnie's anger washed from his face. He was looking past Esbeth, while Esbeth could see some of the men popping up on the far side of the rim.

Karyn reached for Donnie's hand, and he seemed as eager for hers. He lowered the hand holding his makeshift club, and opened his fingers and let the broken wooden handle drop to the ground. Each of the more than a dozen men they could see held an automatic weapon, and their dark Latino faces looked eager for the chance to use them.

The one Karyn fixed on seemed to be the leader. He was closest to them, and appeared to direct the others into place. The men surrounding them slowly climbed over the lip of the rim and moved closer. The leader had a face to remember— the skin of it was as dark as the others, but looked like it had been pulled off his skull, crumpled like a piece of stiff paper, and then put back in place, badly. And he didn't look happy.

He said something to the others. Karyn glanced at Donnie, then Esbeth. "Did you understand that?"

"I think they're trying to decide what to do about us. He's telling them not to shoot, yet."

Karyn felt her own knees buckle, and she leaned against Donnie, and though he looked calm, she could feel him quivering now that she was against him.

Esbeth said something in halting Spanish, and the man with the wrinkled face tilted his head a quarter inch while he stared at her. Then he spoke to the others.

"What'd you tell him?" Donnie whispered, though the guards were all close enough to hear even that by now.

"I said they have us for trespass, at worst. They ought to let Bill Hoel decide what to do. That one," she indicated the man with the strange face, "is Estaban. He's the leader of this group."

Some of the men with guns argued back. It didn't look good to Karyn. Something had the men stirred up, and one or two were waving their guns and had the look of people who would rather act than think.

"*Basta,*" Estaban yelled, and he waved and started off. The ring of other men formed around Donnie, Karyn, and Esbeth and started herding them off the top of the hill.

"Looks like we got lucky," Esbeth said. "They're going to wait."

"How come I don't feel lucky?" Donnie said.

Esbeth nodded. "Yeah, it's only a relative kind of luck, at best, and is temporary, at worst."

"THERE."

"I see it. Is that Floyd's car?"

"Yeah. Hold on a minute." Tillis got out of Logan's truck and walked along the side of the road where the fence led up to the corner of the property. He'd barely gone ten feet when he saw the grass bent the wrong way as Esbeth had. He waved for Logan to follow. He took off along the trail Esbeth had made following the one Donnie had tried to hide.

Logan pulled off the road and drove along the fence line while Tillis trudged ahead. Then Tillis paused and climbed back into the truck when Logan caught up with him. They drove through the brush until they spotted the dark green Dodge tucked off in the only slightly lighter green brush.

"There's the little sonuva … pea thrasher's car."

Tillis took a deep breath and turned to Logan. Whatever he saw there discouraged him from speaking. He reached and opened the glove box, began to dig around.

"What're you after?"

"This." Tillis held up a box of 9 mm ammo. "Do you have any spare clips for your piece in here?"

Logan blushed an even deeper red than he had a moment before. "There's something we maybe better talk about."

"I'm not sure how much time we have. And if you've got a spare civvies shirt, I'd get it on. I don't think your uniform shirt'll help where we're going. I've seen armed men on the other side of the fence, and they seemed stirred up, ready to do something rash. Ditch what you can of the uniform, but you'd better bring along your sidearm."

Logan tugged off his uniform shirt, which gave Tillis a twinge of jealousy at how fit Logan had stayed. He rummaged around in the extended cab of the truck and came up with a flannel shirt with the sleeves cut off as a ragged-edge short-sleeved shirt now. "This do?"

"Yeah, I don't expect the fashion police, or anything. Look, see over there where the fence's been cut and wired back into place. They're inside."

"Esbeth too?"

"Probably. She's not the type to sit back and wait." Tillis took his own gun out of the small of his back and jacked a shell into the chamber, eased the hammer back down, and flipped on the safety. He looked over at Logan. "What?"

"There's ... there's something I should probably tell you."

"Go ahead."

"You know how I've hunted all my life?"

"Is this the short version?"

Logan frowned at him, and it was the kind of frown someone might make while passing a kidney stone. "The last time I went out hunting, I shot at a squirrel with a .22. I missed, hit the tree, but bark flew up and hit the squirrel. It didn't kill it, but the squirrel came down the tree and limped off, holding one back leg in the air. Another squirrel came out and ran along beside it."

"And?"

"I felt just awful. The whole thing made me feel mean. I went around for a week feeling mortally sad about the whole thing."

Well, this was something. Tillis had seen Logan kill men, dress out deer as slick as anyone, and live the life of the outdoorsman's outdoorsman. This wasn't good, wasn't good at all.

Logan took out his sidearm, a 9mm Browning, and held it flat in one hand, looking down at it as if wondering which end to hold.

At first, Tillis didn't know where to begin. He glanced at the fence, where the door had been cut, then looked back at Logan. "I think there's something probably admirable in all that, Logan. But this is about Karyn. You going to have trouble if someone's trying to hurt her?"

Logan slid the gun back in his holster and looked up, not happy, or eager, but resigned. "Let's go."

Tillis was bending back the cut section of chain link to

go through when Logan caught up. Tillis paused. "Let me ask you something. How can you feel that way about a squirrel, and act the way you do about Donnie?"

"The squirrel isn't trying to screw my daughter."

"I've got a late flash bulletin for you on that, Logan. Neither's Donnie."

"I don't believe you."

"She's, in all likelihood, as virgin as the day she was born, and maybe not altogether happy about that. But the Spurlock boy hasn't done a thing, yet. He's trying to be honorable about it."

"Why didn't he say so?"

"Oh, come on, Logan. You know the kid. And you're not all that easy for even me to talk to sometimes. He wouldn't tell you if his pants were on fire. He only told me because he loosened up for a moment when he didn't feel directly threatened."

Logan didn't say anything, but Tillis thought there was just a shade more hop to his step as he went through the gap in the fence and they both entered Old Bill Hoel's spread by its new back door.

They'd only gone a few hundred yards, with Logan on point, when Logan signaled back for Tillis to stop. It was a bit too close to some of the times they'd shared in Korea. Tillis kept quiet, but eased up until he was beside Logan.

"Up there, ahead. I saw a flicker of something." Logan nodded.

Tillis was watching a bush off to their left wiggle in the opposite direction of the small breeze.

"These guys have automatic weapons," Tillis whispered. Now something was moving to the far right.

Logan and Tillis eased closer and turned so their backs were almost touching.

"There," Logan whispered.

But he didn't need to, since all of the men stood up at once, with their weapons pointed. There was at least a dozen of them, and Tillis quickly picked out Jorge's angelic face leading them.

He heard, rather than saw, Logan's hand shoot down for his sidearm.

Before Tillis could say, "Don't," one of the Latinos started firing his automatic weapon.

Tillis and Logan both dove for cover behind the nearest clump of rocks. Logan had his gun out and was firing before Tillis could grab his arm and stop him.

"Wait." The shooting had stopped, and Jorge was yelling at his men.

A couple were impatient, or excited by the blood lust of the moment. They had crawled closer and began to shoot again.

Over the sound of shots and ricocheting bullets, Tillis could hear Jorge screaming at them. Logan rose enough to fire a couple shots back before Tillis could pull him back to the cover.

The shooting abruptly stopped. Logan was panting.

"For a guy who didn't want to shoot anyone, you're sure on the prod," Tillis muttered.

"Why're they shooting at us?"

"I told you, there's a lot of tension here. These guards seemed all wound up, expectant."

"But why?"

"I'm not sure. Maybe you can ask. Here comes their leader."

Down the trail they'd been following walked Jorge, his

automatic held low, but where he could swing it up and shoot if he had to. He stopped when he was a dozen feet from them. His eyes glittered at them in black intensity.

"*Lo siento*. The men were no supposed to shoot. I stop them. You trespass. Let's go now. You follow me." He waved for them to stand and go with him.

Logan stayed low, as did Tillis.

"You trust him?" Logan whispered.

Tillis was remembering the smile on the toe of Jorge's boot. "No."

He heard soft footsteps coming up the trail behind them now. "You keep an eye on him." Tillis swung around to watch the other direction. He was just in time to see Gala come up the trail. She wore jeans, boots, and a silk blouse of the same dusty green as the cacti around them. Her right arm was down at her side, and she was holding her automatic pistol in it.

Gala looked down to where Tillis and Logan were huddled close to the outcropping of rock. "Well, don't you two look cozy."

She spoke in Spanish to Jorge, and a lot of it was too fast for Tillis. Jorge answered. Then they went back and forth a bit. What Tillis could make of it was that Gala was insisting Jorge let them go, that she'd escort them off the land. He claimed she was trespassing too and should put down her gun and come along.

Tillis turned to look at Jorge, to see how he was taking it, and was just in time to see his hands tighten on the gun and swing it up toward Gala.

She had her gun up and fired before Jorge had the automatic level. One of his eyes, the one that remained, registered surprise as the gun dropped and he tottered backward slowly, then fell.

Gala dropped to the ground and the shooting around them broke out in earnest this time.

She crawled up to them and shouted, "Back this way."

Then she turned and took off low. They scrambled after her, keeping as close to the ground as they could.

After they'd gone a few yards along the path Gala had used getting to them, Tillis saw one of the guards tucked into a knot on the ground. They kept up with Gala until she was through the fence. She waved toward the truck, and Logan didn't need detailed instructions. He got in and had it fired up while Gala and Tillis clambered in. He started to back it up, but Gala said, "No. Forward. Keep close to the fence. You can get through up that way."

"Was that other guard …"

She interrupted Tillis. "He'll have a headache, but he's fine."

"Can't say as much for Jorge."

"It was his call to make, and he made it," Gala said.

"Karyn?" Logan asked.

"They have her, the other bunch, and Esbeth and Donnie too. But they'll have this whole side sealed off now."

"What's got them so trigger-happy?"

"Keep driving up along this fence line, as fast as this truck'll go. I'll tell you when." She glanced at Logan, then looked at Tillis. "This's been building a long time. How much have you figured out?"

"Let me guess. There're two factions out here, the guards and hit men loyal to Bill Hoel, and a whole population of formerly illegal Hispanics that have been cooped up for at least the last generation or two here on Hoel's place. The guards can't come from the families here, or they might have split loyalties. Sound close so far?"

Gala patted him on the leg, something Logan didn't miss.

"That fence. It's not there to keep people out, it's there to keep people in," Tillis said.

"Very good," Gala said. "I'll reward you later."

Logan glanced at Gala. "Then what's all this crap about diamonds?"

"It's just about that," Gala said, "a short-time ruse that was snuffed the minute it wasn't needed."

"Let's see, you probably even found where the diamonds were bought and returned." Tillis didn't look at her; instead, he watched the green poles whiz by as the truck rattled along beside the fence line.

"Antwerp. The deal took almost all the spare cash Hoel had then. So I could find out just when it happened. The Hoels didn't own the bank. Once I had the date, the travel came next, and tracing the tickets Bill bought led to Antwerp. It took over a week to find someone who remembered selling the diamonds, and their return a year later. Hoel took a bit of a loss on the deal, not counting the travel."

"But finding a new source of labor's what really put the ranch back right, isn't it?"

Gala patted him on the thigh again. "I'm so proud of you."

"Why isn't the INS on it?" Logan asked.

"La Migra tried, and were stymied or bought off," Gala said.

"You seem to've done a lot of digging for one person. Did you find out all that on your own?" Tillis asked.

"How much farther?" Logan interrupted.

"Better slow down, we're almost to it."

"To what?"

"Okay, stop here."

The edge that ran along the fence line ran out in a few more feet. If they'd kept going, the truck would've shot over the edge of a cliff that led down to the lake.

"What now?" Logan looked at Gala.

"There's a place along the other side of the cliff here where we can get in," she said.

Logan didn't move right away. "We should call for some kind of backup."

"Who? The Rangers? Or Eldon? Think about it." Tillis was already at the corner of the fence line, following Gala as she scrambled over the side.

Like Tillis, Gala kept her gun tucked at the small of her back. Tillis' left jeans pocket bulged with spare ammo, but it didn't slow him as he followed her careful steps down along the lip of the cliff, where they could only keep their footing by hanging onto the bottom of the fence. Logan brought up the rear this time, and Tillis didn't hear as much huffing from him as he seemed to be making himself.

Another few feet along the fence line, Gala came to a spot where a shallow depression had been scooped out beneath the fence. A fine black rope was attached to the nearest post and coiled beside the hole.

Gala slipped through first, and Tillis followed. When he stood, he looked around, then examined the hole as Logan was coming through.

"That's not new," he said. "How long have you been expecting things to pop loose out here?"

"There's been some tension building for years. As you were so clever to realize, there's quite a Latino population here on the Hoel place, even though you don't see but a few of them come in and out of town for supplies. Other than the handful of guards who're loyal to Jorge and Estaban, which translates as loyalty to Bill, a lot of the others would like to have a normal life. But the ones born here can't make too much of a beef, or Bill could make it tough on all the ones who don't have citizenship."

"The late Jorge, you should say," Logan corrected. "I still want to know why someone official isn't looking into this?"

"Someone is. Come on, we'd better get moving if we're to see what's happening to Karyn and the others." She turned and hurried off down a trail she seemed to know well.

Tillis had been worried about Logan. But the shooting had seemed to help—the need for action over words. Being around Gala had helped too—her being so calm under pressure. Logan had accepted her now, in a way that had been harder for him before. Tillis glanced at Logan's face— nothing but grim determination.

Let someone else worry now.

FOURTEEN

"ARE YOU *ESTUPIDO?*" Bill Hoel's voice was a crackling near-scream. He hobbled forward to stand leaning on his knuckles on the dining table, giving him what Esbeth thought was a simian look.

"They're trespassers," he shouted. "We take them to the front gate and firmly send them home. That's it. *Fina.* Do you get it? How many times have I told you?"

"They kill Jorge."

"These three?" Hoel waved a hand at Donnie, Karyn, and Esbeth, all still sandwiched between four of Estaban's fellow guards, where they had been made to sit on chairs around the dining table.

"Some *otras gringos.*"

"Where're they now?"

Estaban answered in Spanish, but Esbeth could make out that three men had been forced out the hole this one made. Estaban was pointing at Donnie.

Esbeth had never seen Old Bill Hoel before, something that a lot of the people in Hoel's Dam could say. Now that she had, she was surprised. He seemed barely able to hobble across the room, his bowed legs were so bent from horseback riding or arthritis. This might not be the best time to sense his calm power either. He was so angry that small sprays of spittle sprayed from his face with each bit of bad

Spanish he shouted at his men. If she wasn't so worried about the situation for the kids, she'd have had more pity for Bill than anything. On top of everything else, he seemed to be having a pretty bad day. She knew she might feel even more sympathetic if she wasn't having a somewhat snotty day herself, having just been marched in near double-time to a Jeep and then hauled to the ranch house.

Another of the guards came running into the room, stopped when he saw Bill's expression.

"Now what?"

Again, Esbeth had to piece what was happening together from the scraps of Spanish she could make out from the conversation that went way too fast for her. But it seemed that some other Hispanics on the place were rising up and giving the guards a hard time now too.

"Where did they get guns?" Old Bill Hoel wanted to know of Estaban.

His shrug was over-elaborate. "Not many have. With others it is rakes and, you know, sticks. They can do no much." His English was probably how Bill's Spanish sounded to them.

Hoel spun and pointed a shaking finger at Donnie. "It's you. Everything's been fine until you come along, a Spurlock. I mighta known. The whole lot of you've been the curse of my existence."

Please, Donnie, Esbeth thought, don't say a thing. Be your usual clammed-up self. It was, of course, too much to expect.

Even with Karyn hanging onto his arm, the boy shot up out of his chair, knocking it over behind him with a bang that caused three of the guards to raise their guns. "You killed my grandpa, my uncle, and my dad. How can you call us a curse?"

"Oh, sit down and shut up, boy. I only met your precious dad once, and that was when he was younger than you are. I wouldn't waste a flyswatter on him then, much less a bullet now." Old Bill leaned closer, glaring at Donnie with an intensity that would have made Esbeth sit back down. But Donnie stood his ground and looked ready to climb across the table swinging, if he wouldn't have been crushed to the table by two or three gun butts if he tried.

A crackle of shots outside broke the momentary tension.

"What the hell's that? Gunfire? I thought you said they didn't have guns?" Bill swung to Estaban. "You. Get out there and find out what's going on, and stop it. Then I want you to get these people off my place as quick as you can, and I won't be too upset if they pick up some splinters or gravel when they land."

He spun and hobbled over to the window to look outside.

One of the guards set Donnie's chair upright, and another grabbed him by the shoulders and slammed him back down into it.

More shots sounded outside, these closer to the house.

Estaban left two of the guards and hurried out of the room with the others.

"You think this's over," Donnie shouted, "but I'll never leave you alone. I know you at least caused the deaths of Grandpa and Uncle Hugh."

Esbeth thought there might be truth in what he said, but she joined everyone else in the room in wishing he'd revert to the clammed-up version he'd been earlier.

Old Bill Hoel spun and glared, his head as grim as Death's head itself. "The only thing's ever killed a Spurlock yet is his own stupid greed. And you, boy, don't seem any different or better'n the samples I've seen so far."

"DOWN," TILLIS CALLED out, and Gala and Logan each tucked low near the base of one of the trees.

"First guard we've seen, and he's fifty yards off," Logan said. "Why aren't there more guards along this line of the fence?"

"He's gone now." Gala stood. She waved a hand around them. "Pecan orchard. It runs along here for a mile, and goes almost a mile in. It's close enough to the lake for water to be pumped up for irrigation. Let's go now."

She started off at a trot.

Tillis kept an eye out for more guards. "You picked this approach for a reason. Why aren't the guards as thick here?"

Gala kept her voice low. "We're closer to the ranch house coming in this way, and to a couple of the villages on the grounds. Besides, the guards don't like to come in here."

"Don't like to come into a pecan orchard?"

Gala waved a hand at a tree they were passing. Bits of ribbon still clung to it where something had been, but had been torn away. "You know how my people are."

"I know I've seen wreaths of plastic flowers along the highways wherever a Hispanic has died in a car crash. Is this a…"

"Yeah," Gala interrupted, waved an irritated hand for them to be more quiet. "It's a graveyard, of sorts. But the guards are supposed to keep them from putting up memorials. Still, you'll see ribbons around some of the trees here and there."

They ran in silence for a while. But Tillis and Logan couldn't help glancing around at tiny scraps of color, and dirt that might've been recently turned. There was even a small mound they passed as they ran that had to belong to a small child.

They were all quiet for another mile or two. It was hard to tell how far they'd run so far. Tillis was trying to measure it by the amount of sweat running down into his eyes. He rubbed at the corners of his eyes with his fingers and kept going.

"It's not right that Karyn's in the middle of all this," Logan said.

In the distance, they could hear shooting.

"Not to mention Esbeth and Donnie," Tillis added.

Gala still led the way, and they ran in single file. Every bit of the Texas vegetation through which they passed now seemed to possess either thorns or something sticky. Their jeans were covered with scratches and small burrs—from the little gray beggar's lice to the bigger sand spurs. Twice they'd had to go out around a snake, and Tillis noted a scorpion that Gala had casually crushed with a boot step.

"How far are we?" Logan asked.

"This is the closest way to the house, coming in the back way from the lake side. But you've got to remember, this is one big spread." Gala still didn't seem to be panting, and that just inspired Tillis to run a bit harder to keep up. His shirt was soaked through, as was Logan's, he could see when he looked back.

"Who're we trying to link up with?" Logan asked.

"Well, it was Don Cinco Hernandez. He'd been a servant out here forever, but he's dead now. He led the Cincos. You know, like in Cinco de Mayo. Now the bunch of them are led by a few of the younger, angrier men. They've been trying to muster strength to make a break. But Hoel keeps guards around the clock along the far fence, and another smaller ring around the house."

"Must cost him a fortune."

"He probably couldn't afford it, if he paid all the Latinos who live here real wages."

"Why hasn't someone kicked their way in here before, straightened things out?" Logan was huffing, though not as much as Tillis, but it didn't keep him from pumping Gala with questions.

"They've tried. But Bill has way too much clout."

"How many guards are there?"

"Fifty or sixty, maybe a few more."

"And we're going to go up against all of them, just the three of us?"

"There're the Cincos, don't forget."

"How many men do they have?" Logan asked.

"It's not just men. Even the women have been preparing, and some of the children, saving up supplies, arming themselves until the time is ripe."

"I sure hope they don't think today is it."

"Sshh. We're getting too close now." Gala slowed, and Tillis, for one, was glad for the more reasonable pace.

Tillis eased closer now that Gala had slowed, and asked, "Is that who's keeping the firing going, the Cincos?"

"Probably they're just running skirmishes for now, trying to draw the guards out of position, spread them out. It's what we've got to hope for, if we're to get into the house."

"How long you think this shooting can go on, without drawing the attention of some kind of law?" Logan said.

"Think about how far we are from anything, and we're heading into the heart of Hoel's land, farthest from anyone who could hear or care. Besides, who pays attention to a bunch of shooting outdoors in Texas, anyway?"

Gala held up a hand and started to ease up around a ridge of rock covered by cactus that crested the hill they'd been slowly climbing.

Tillis reached to his back and slid out his automatic, slowly eased off the safety.

Whatever Logan saw on Tillis' face made him get his own gun out, and begin moving to cover their left flank.

Tillis eased carefully to Gala's right while she took her time getting to the crest and looking over the top. As soon as her head was above the rock, the chatter of an automatic rifle broke the quiet, and chips of rock and cactus sprayed up into the air while Gala ducked low behind the rocks.

"That's not good," she hissed. "There's a line of them, and they're advancing up the hill on us."

"Where're your Cincos now?" Logan said. He kept moving forward until he was near the cover of a rounded boulder.

Shooting started on both sides of them, while Tillis scurried low and ducked in beside Gala.

"You know, all these years Old Bill's holed up out here, and no one could've ever come in on him if he just kept his nose clean. Those kids being lured onto the place's what started all this. Is that the way you saw all this play out?"

She turned and looked up at him, her face dark and shiny with a light film of sweat. She looked fierce. He'd never seen her look more attractive.

"All I wanted was to get as many of these people out of here before any shooting happened."

"It's kind of late for that."

"Not my fault."

"I'm sorry," he said.

"For what?"

"For doubting you a time or two."

She gave his chest a small shove. "Go shoot at something," she said.

He started scrambling off to her right, saw movement behind a sage, and fired into it. There was a scream, and a short burst went off into the air, chipping off leaves as whoever was behind the bush fell. He could hear Logan out on the other wing returning fire. Even in the blur of the moment, and concentrating on each step and bit of movement around him, he suddenly felt a rush of warmth for his old friend. It was as if Logan had been away on a long trip and had just come home.

A guard stood pointing his weapon in Gala's direction, and Tillis fired two shots without raising his pistol higher than his hip. The man snapped back into the brush as if he'd been pulled by a cord.

Gala was pinned down now in the center of the fire. Estaban must be among them, and directing them to get the one who'd shot Jorge. Tillis saw one of the men sprint forward while firing.

Tillis wheeled, went into stance, and laid down a series of shots that met the man as he ran and snapped him double. He rolled to the open dirt and didn't rise. Tillis dropped to the ground himself and scrambled to the small cover of a patch of scrub mesquite. He yanked the clip from the gun and started shoving in new shells from his pocket. He looked up, and there, to his left now, Estaban stood up from cover not fifteen feet from where Gala crouched as she returned shots over the top of her ridge.

Estaban dropped his automatic and took out the big .45 pistol he wore on his hip.

"Hey," Tillis yelled, and loud as he could. *"Pendejo."*

Tillis shoved the clip back in and jacked a shell into the chamber as Estaban spun at him. He was still raising his gun when he heard the shot, but it was from Gala's gun.

Estaban's gun hand slowly dropped, while he fought to raise it. But he crumpled to his knees, then fell to his side.

"Thanks," Gala yelled.

"No problemo," Tillis yelled back.

But, unlike the movies, where the loss of their leader causes troops to retreat, seeing Estaban fall only pushed the remaining guards to new heights, and there seemed to be more of them than Tillis had counted on. From every side he saw men come scrambling out from behind cover and open up with their automatics.

The cold realization suddenly slammed home that this all might be too much. There were too many of them. He glanced to Gala and to Logan, as if soaking up all he could before they were all swarmed over and killed by these angry, armed men. He seemed to see each tree and bush and leaf with the stark clarity of someone taking his last look at the world. Ahead of him two men rose at the same time, with gun barrels pointed his way.

Tillis dropped flat as a line of bullets lifted an entire small tree off the ground and tumbled it and its thorns across him. But lying there, in the chatter of the intensified shooting, he heard, or felt, something else. He lowered his ear back close to the ground. That was it. Horses.

He slithered out from under the fallen mesquite, and pulled its stickery limbs loose from him in time to stand and shoot down a man who ran directly toward him. He saw the hole appear in the man's shirt, then the automatic tumble from the fingers, but the man still took a couple more steps before collapsing.

Past where he'd stood, Tillis could look down the slope behind the men firing at them. There were the horses, cutting through the brush like only Texas field horses can do, and on top of each horse was a man wearing a white hat.

"Rangers. By God, it's Rangers." He was yelling now. Shots came clipping in a line toward him, and he had to take a rolling tumble forward to dodge where they were headed. But when he rose, firing, the Rangers were closer, and shooting as they came up the hill, as fearlessly as he could hope for.

He saw flashes coming from one patch of cover and fired into it, and the shooting stopped. Some of the guards had stopped their charge and had spun to shoot back behind them now. Tillis saw Logan rise from his cover and take out one of them.

Several of the guards stopped firing, and broke and ran off to dive for new cover.

The horses were scattered through the brush, and the men on them were still firing at the guards as they made it the rest of the way up the hill. The lead horse, a big paint, came up around the back of Tillis' spot and stopped; the rider dropped off, tied up the horse, and scrambled up beside Tillis. It was Tim Comber. The other rider who had come up with him fell sideways off his mount, but held the reins.

Tim called back, "You okay, Pudge?"

"Come're and tie up this horse while I patch up."

"You brought Pudge Hurley out here with you?" Tillis said.

Tim winked. "Had to deputize him. He was able to get us

mounts. His place's just across the road. We waited until we heard shooting before we came in."

He went back and took the reins, while Pudge sat and whipped out a blue handkerchief, then started tying a tourniquet around one thigh above where blood was making his jeans shine damp in the sunlight.

"Now if that ain't just it," Pudge was shouting and laughing above the gunfire. "Now I'm the one-legged man in a butt-kicking contest."

Tim Comber tugged Pudge over until the three of them were able to cover each other's backs.

"I don't know when I've felt better about seeing those white hats and so many stars," Tillis said. "Isn't that Billy Joe Jarrett out there, and Gus Thomas?"

"And Diamondback Johnson, Gil Bradley, and Mel Fiddler," Tim said. "When you're gonna deal in mavericks, I say dig to the bottom of the barrel."

"How'd you free up the wildest bunch of all the Rangers for this?"

"Hell, when they heard about it, I couldn't keep them away. And I wanted you to know you aren't the only wild-eyed maverick wearing a star. There're others just as high-maintenance, and just as worthwhile keeping."

Pudge said, "I think I saw Mel take a hit back there."

"But he's still on his horse, you noticed that, didn't you?" Tim was laughing.

"You Rangers are one crazy bunch, I'll say that for you." Pudge winced, and leaned forward to tighten the handkerchief around his leg.

Tim handed him a short stick to slip in the knot and twist to tighten it.

"This getting shot isn't all it's cracked up to be in the pictures," Pudge said.

A burst from an automatic zipped past them. Pudge flattened himself, and came up spitting dirt.

Tim Comber rose and fired until his clip was empty. He dropped back to the ground while popping out the spent clip, pulling a fresh one from his belt, and shoving it in. He reached and slammed the flat of his hand on Tillis' back. "Isn't this a hoot?"

"If you say so." Tillis rose and fired three controlled shots, and the automatic fire coming at them stopped. He dropped back down. Tim was smiling at him.

"You know I couldn't fire you. I just know what a live wire you can be when you want to stir up something. I did know you were going out of your way to get me to change you to an unofficial status, and you couldn't very well ask on your own behalf for a vacation in the middle of an investigation. But even I didn't think you'd come up with this. I didn't have anything official to stand on before, and I'm not so damned sure I do now. But something's going on. I knew I could count on you for that."

"What brought you out here?"

"I was keeping an eye on Morgan Lane."

"And he's out here?"

"Somewhere."

Another horse rode up behind them, and Gus Thomas hopped out of the saddle and scurried up to them. "You okay, Lute?"

"Just taking a meeting," Tim said.

Logan and Gala both rose and came running over at the same time, firing as they did. Logan dropped down beside them, panting, and held out an open hand to Tillis, who reached in his pocket and got out a handful of shells for him.

"Haven't hit any squirrels, have you?"

Sprays of automatic weapon fire from two directions saved Logan from having to answer. It sent them all ducking low and scooting into a snug circle with their backs together in a way that would have made General George Custer proud. Gala popped up, fired, and one of the guns shooting at them stopped.

Logan was snugged in tight on the other side of Tim Comber and asked, "Where's this Don Cinco I've been hearing about?"

"Depending on which way you came in, you might've passed him," Tim said.

"What d'you mean?"

"He's dead I suppose, based on all that's going on here; probably buried out here on the place somewhere."

"The loss of leadership was supposed to stifle the Cincos, was it?" Tillis asked.

Tim waved his gun barrel toward all the chaos going on around them. "You can see that there's another plan that didn't quite come together."

"Seems to've worked for the Cincos, though I doubt it's what Old Bill wanted," Pudge said.

"Yeah, he hadn't counted on them having as much firepower or being as mad as they got. Someone was slipping them weapons and prepping them a bit." Tim tried to give Gala a meaningful glance, but she was bent over Pudge, holding his tourniquet stick in place while he reloaded his gun, what looked to Tillis to be a big replica of a single-action Sam Walker Colt.

"I guess our timing couldn't be better," Tillis said.

"Depends on how you read that. But, yeah, we're sure here when the powder keg's lit. They weren't as organized as they might've been, but whatever started things out here seems to've gotten the Cincos off the blocks." Tim hopped up, snapped off a couple quick shots, then dropped back down.

"We've got to get to the ranch," Logan said. "Karyn."

Tillis glanced to Pudge.

"You can have the borry of the horses, if that'll help," he said.

Tillis just nodded. He pointed toward some distant movement, and Gus rose and fired that way.

Tim turned back to Tillis. "If you're gonna do anything else unofficial or unorthodox, you'd better get it done before I get there."

He squinted at Gala, then Logan. "Don't any of you get hurt. Our job, for the moment, is to calm these factions and keep them from killing each other—or, at the least, protect the more innocent ones from these guards. You go on and take point in the house situation, and we'll be right behind you."

"Wish I could ride with you. My horse is the roan there, Bucko. A damned good steed," Pudge said. "Don't know when I've had so much fun." He winced, then fainted and fell back flat on the dirt.

"Get going now." Tim turned back to where the automatic fire was picking up again.

Tillis, Gala, and Logan crouched low and ran over to the horses. They led them off a few feet until they had more cover, then they all mounted, and took off riding.

ESBETH WAS LOOKING around the room in which they were virtual prisoners. Old copper pans hung along one wall, and the curtains matched everything else. There was a woman's touch here, but it'd happened a while ago. She tried to imagine Old Bill living out here, surrounded by just his help, getting crustier by the year.

He swung back from glaring out the window and looked at them, still surrounded by a pair of guards. The deep, weathered lines in his face seemed beyond ever smiling, and he had two or three days' worth of stubble. With hobbling, bowlegged steps, he went over to a cabinet that held plates and mugs. He opened a drawer and took out a very large single-action Western pistol, a .45 or .44, at least. Esbeth caught a glance of the end of the barrel, and it looked big enough for mice to crawl up inside. He limped in his unique way back to the table, holding the gun down low at his side, his face as full of hate as anything Esbeth had ever seen. He looked like there was something he wanted to say, but he was too full of bile to get it out. He spun and lumbered out through the door that led to the kitchen.

A few minutes later, he came back into the room with some rope and a silver spool of duct tape. The look on his face now was that of a trapped animal. He'd made some decisions, and not very good ones, Esbeth decided. But she was in no position to argue with them.

Bill tossed the rope to one of the guards, and nodded to Esbeth and the two kids. They got busy while he stood holding the big gun.

It was at that moment, as the tape was being pressed over her mouth and her wrists and ankles were bound to the chair, that Esbeth knew for a heart-of-stone fact that Bill Hoel had gone over the edge, that the years of living like this and fighting a constant battle with the growing resistance, as well as the past, had finally made him crack all the way. Until now, he could have probably calmed things down somehow and counted on all the favors ever owed him to straighten everything out. But that's not the way he was able to see it now. For the first time, Esbeth sincerely feared for their lives, and she could see everything she felt reflected back from the bleak, widening eyes of Karyn and Donnie over the tape that sealed their lips as well.

FIFTEEN

TILLIS LED THE WAY UP the hillsides through the thorny brush and sometimes along open stretches of worn cattle paths. Bucko was a sure-footed horse, and was cautious, to a fault. Several times Tillis found himself urging the horse forward, especially when he looked over and caught Logan's expression—that raw mix of eagerness and despair. Tillis could only imagine what it felt like, having a daughter in the middle of this and not knowing what was happening to her. The sounds of sporadic gunfire came alternately from each direction.

He gave Bucko a nudge with his heels. Tillis had the most horseback experience, although Gala seemed to have no trouble keeping up. Logan had ridden a number of times himself, but still forced himself to trail behind and keep a wary eye on their surroundings as they went up and down hills toward the ranch house. From what they could hear, it was an area of more intense gunfire.

As they neared the crest of a hill, Tillis pulled up behind a snug stand of mesquite and sat his horse. Gala slowed and held out a hand for Logan to go slower and be quiet.

They all slid off their horses and brought them close to tie them along a drooping bigger mesquite branch. Tillis ducked low and eased around a patch of prickly pear cactus and up to the top of the hill, with Gala following close behind.

He eased to the crest and peered over. Below them, the

hillside spread out into a flatter area, with corrals and riding areas beside a barn. Behind that, another hill ran up in a gentle, grazed slope to the ranch house.

A ring of guards surrounded the house, each staked into a position where he could cover a lot of ground. Varied-size groups of the rebellious Cincos, some carrying automatic assault weapons similar to those of the guards, others with mere hoes and other garden implements, were making attempts to break through at several points around the defensive perimeter, but hadn't penetrated yet.

There was a scurry of noise behind them. Tillis and Gala spun and stared at Logan, who restlessly kicked his way through a corner of the cactus toward them. He crouched down low and eased the rest of the way to them.

"We're taking too long. Karyn's down there. Remember?"

Tillis just nodded and looked back at the fighting below.

"The area around the barn's the only weakness," Gala said. "Behind that, there's a bit of garden and some sheds for cover."

Off to the far right, the gunfire accelerated in a fierce flurry. Tillis glanced that way and saw the first of the white hats swinging off their horses and taking cover as they took on the thickest part of the guards.

Gala turned to Tillis, saw his face. "I bet this kills you, not being able to join in."

Tillis turned back to the ranch house.

"I'll slip down first, make sure there's a clear line for you, and be right back. Can you stand still for that?" Her eyes darted back and forth between Tillis and Logan.

"We'll have to," Tillis said. Logan just looked off at the ranch house.

She slipped away and was out of their sight in seconds.

"One of us oughta be down there on point, scouting. Why her?" Logan said.

"She's got a better chance than a couple of gringos. Besides, she's very good at this sort of thing. Take a look out there. See if you see her anywhere, or hear a thing."

"Where'd she get that kind of training?"

"Watch her moves," Tillis said. "Some of them are the same ones you learned at Quantico."

"She's no Marine," Logan said. "The old Tillis'd be down there on point himself."

"I am the old Tillis. The younger Tillis might've done a lot of damn fool things. This version's trying to learn about trust."

"I just hope you aren't fooling with your education by putting Karyn at risk."

"Gala knows about the urgency."

"It's that old woman, isn't it?"

"Esbeth?"

"Yeah. Is she the one making you think you oughta open up a bit?"

"If she is, Logan, you could sure use a dose yourself." He held up a hand for Logan to be still and get lower. One of the guards below, on this side of the perimeter, was sweeping the hill with a rifle with a telescopic sight.

A few seconds ticked by while they crouched low and listened to the sound of shots being fired. Then Tillis eased back up to watch the action from the ridge. Logan slid up beside him.

The guards Tillis could see below looked uncertain in their movements, like people instructed to handle most situations by quieting anything that might attract outside attention. They didn't look ready for this, though some of that could be a leadership issue. He'd seen Gala shoot down both Jorge and Estaban, Bill Hoel's "hands of darkness." The presence of Texas Rangers on the property for the first time seemed to add to the confusion. But, instead of making the guards crumble and run, it seemed to make them only fight harder, for the moment.

"I'm doing what I can about myself," Logan mumbled, for the first time anything like contrition in his voice. "All I can think about is Karyn, and here I am up hunkered down with the likes of you."

Tillis sighed, and crouched low as they watched the fighting below.

KARYN COULD FEEL her tears trickle down her cheekbones, then shoot across the slick, silver tape across her mouth to splash down on her blouse. She blinked hard, trying to make herself stop. It wasn't helping a thing.

The guards stood near the two doors to the dining room, and when they looked at her there was no pity on their faces. Outside, she could hear more of the pops and strings of crackling Bill Hoel had said was gunfire. Some of it sounded like it was coming closer. But that just made her feel worse. Quick glances to Donnie and Esbeth hadn't helped, so now she stared across the room at the old china cabinet. She tried to think of nothing, but there was the never having been physical with Donnie, the idea that she had hoped she would one day have kids and a family life of her own, her trying to remember when she'd last told her father she loved him, things like that. When they dove deep into that black lake in the middle of night, and in a thunderstorm, she thought she'd been as scared as she'd ever been in her life, as she ever would be. But she'd been wrong. Right now, if she was down at the bottom of the darkest depths beside the dam, where she saw those thick, black shapes of who knows what, she might try to sport with them right now, like a dolphin. She felt herself trembling, and tried to stop, but couldn't.

Footsteps clomped back into the room. She looked up, and it was Bill Hoel. There was something gaunt, ghastly, and scared about his face. He went over to the window and looked out. When he turned back, there it was again. Where he'd seemed to be blustering and strong before, now he was crumbling.

"*Esta* Martinez," he shouted to the two guards. It was the first he'd spoken in a while. It made no sense to Karyn. She was too scared to feel anything else—not anger, or pity, or even hate. She only felt fear, that of someone young who was almost certain she was going to die sooner than she'd ever thought. Life seemed sweeter than ever before, and further removed.

The guards didn't seem to respond. Maybe Old Bill was used to yelling to his regular two bodyguards, the one with the twisted face and the other one she thought he'd tried to say Donnie had killed. Now Hoel was shouting strings of words in broken Spanish. She could only make out a word here and there. Hoel yelled something about "fuerza delta," but that made no sense to her. His garbled Spanish was hard for her to understand, and, at the moment, it didn't seem to mean all that much to the guards either. But Karyn saw something in Esbeth's eyes. She seemed to be getting something. Not that it would do any of them any good.

"Oh, to hell with it," Old Bill Hoel finally shouted. Pops

of gunfire punctuated his yell. He spun and headed back out to the kitchen with what looked like painful, bow-legged steps.

In the silence in the room after he'd left, she sat and tried hard to remember her mother's face. But she couldn't, no matter how hard she tried. Her mind was blank, and that made her cry again. Only they were angry tears this time.

TILLIS HEARD A small rustle and had the gun pointed to the green wall of vegetation, when Gala eased through the thick of the low mesquites and chaparral that ran up the side of the hill. She'd only been gone a few minutes.

"We'd better leave the horses tied here and go in on foot," she said. There was a small scratch along one cheekbone, and one of the knuckles on her right hand was swelling. But Tillis didn't ask, and she didn't offer. "We can get through, but not by riding."

"You find out anything about what's going on here?" Logan asked.

She looked at Tillis. "Not any more than that someone killed Don Cinco."

"I meant about Karyn," Logan said.

She shook her head. "Bill Hoel's at the house, and this whole business seems to have caught most of the guards by surprise. She's probably in the house too. I don't see any way Bill's men could have gotten anyone out to the road in all this." She waved a hand toward where the firing was thickest. "We've got just a few minutes to get through here. We'd better get moving."

"You see Morgan Lane?" Logan asked.

"No." Her head snapped to him; then she looked to Tillis.

"We thought we caught a distant glimpse of him. That's all," Tillis said.

"Headed this way?"

"I couldn't tell." Tillis looked to Logan, and he shook his head too.

"Well, let's get moving." Gala spun, and was gone. They took off after her, as fast as they could, to keep up.

After some brisk scurrying and jogging, they went past the first of the downed guards by the barn, and then slipped by another in the garden. The eyes of one of them were open and staring at nothing. Tillis didn't need to ask what'd happened to them. They'd been in the way, but now they weren't.

ESBETH HAD BEEN letting her head droop, but suddenly looked up and over at the two guards left to watch them. She was just in time to see one slowly raise his hands, still holding his automatic rifle, into the air above him. Someone stood behind him, and she caught just enough of a glimpse to think it was Tillis. From the other side of the doorway, Gala slid around, her gun pointed at the other guard, who spun and realized he had no chance. He slowly lowered his weapon to the hardwood floor. Then he straightened and raised his hands.

Esbeth could see for sure now that it was Tillis coming in through the door with his gun raised. His shirt clung to him, and was torn in a couple of places and marked by dirt in others. He looked grim and ready. He tucked his gun into his belt and eased to the table, then went to Esbeth first and pulled the tape off her mouth with a quick snap. He bent to untie her ropes. As soon as he was done, he tugged his gun back out. Esbeth tried to nod toward the kitchen, but her neck was stiff with tension.

She spoke in a hoarse whisper, "There's something you should know. Old Bill's around here someplace, and is off his rails."

He held a finger up to his lips and tossed the rope to Logan, who'd already taken the automatic from the guard he stood behind and had put a strip of tape across the guard's mouth. Tillis started to ease toward the door that led to the living room. Esbeth tried to shout, "The kitchen." But her voice just came out a harsh squawk that only made Tillis wave for her to be quiet again.

Gala had the other guard on the floor, and was finishing gagging him with tape and tying his ankles and wrists.

Logan finished his guard, put down the automatic. He rushed over to Karyn, and started freeing her. He stopped when he heard the voice coming from behind Tillis, though.

"All of you just stay right the way you are. Put the guns down on the floor."

Esbeth watched Tillis lower his gun and drop it, then turned to look at Bill Hoel, who stood in the kitchen doorway. He had his big revolver leveled at them.

"First one to move, the kids get it first. You understand?" The cracked voice was full of suppressed rage, but the gun didn't move at all, except for the finger that tightened in the guard.

Logan slowly lowered his pistol to the floor. When he stood, he managed to stand between Bill and Karyn.

"Get out of the way, you, so I got a clear line of fire."

Logan didn't budge. His shoulders squared, expecting to die right there if he had to.

Esbeth couldn't take her eyes off Bill Hoel, a man who for years had exiled himself from the rest of mankind, and for what, to keep his claws on a block of land that was barely fit for rattlesnakes.

"Move, I said." His voice had the hysterical, raspy edge of madness to it.

Esbeth watched Bill's hand tighten, the trigger finger starting to squeeze. She knew she had to do something. She shouted, "You've got nothing to lose at this point, Bill. You might as well clear the air about Hank and Hugh Spurlock. Folks are always going to wonder, unless you come clean." There was no reason for her to be talking at all, but that didn't stop her.

"You, shut up." But his hand loosened a bit, and he gave Esbeth his fierce glare. Karyn reached up to put her arms around her dad's waist.

Esbeth wouldn't let up. "I mean, that poor town's lived in a shadow all these years, not to mention Donnie here having this hang over his head all his life. You don't really want folks to never know just how clever you were, luring at least two of them to their deaths, especially since you still hold the Spurlocks accountable for the deaths of three of the Hoel clan back in that mess all those years ago."

"That's it. I mean it. You think I won't bust a cap on an old butterball like you, think again." Hoel was spitting with rage again, and his voice got up to a scream. He shifted the barrel of his pistol over, until it pointed directly at Esbeth.

It was what she'd wanted him to do, was why she'd butted in, but she felt herself swallow hard, and all she could see was the round, dark end of that gun.

"What about the one behind you, Bill?" Gala said.

"Don't give me …"

"Right here." Morgan Lane stepped the rest of the way

through the doorway, pointing a worn Army Colt .45 automatic at Bill's back.

Esbeth would always remember the moment as a big pause, when the world stopped and took a few deep breaths. But, in truth, everything happened fast, and in seconds.

Old Bill Hoel never hesitated. He spun, and Morgan's gun went off at the same instant. Hoel was lifted off his feet and the gun dropped from his hand as he tumbled across to the table, bounced off it, and came to rest in a pile at Esbeth's feet.

The blast was still ringing in the room, and Esbeth's ears were ringing.

Gala bent and picked up the pistol she'd dropped when Bill had them covered. "What took you so long? Where the hell've you been?" she said to Morgan.

"Whatever made someone his age think he could get the drop on me?" He looked down at the crumpled body of the old man in a level of scorn only he could manage.

Esbeth smelled the cordite in the room, and something else burning above that. But she couldn't move just then, even if the house was on fire. Her legs felt like jelly. Her breath came in short gulps.

Tillis went to Donnie and pulled the tape off his mouth and bent to the ropes that held him.

"Are you crazy, Esbeth? He could've killed you." Donnie's voice squeaked.

"She was saving Dad," Karyn said quietly. Her face was still flushed a different red from her hair, and she had soft hiccups from crying earlier. But now she looked as determined and eager to leave as any of them.

"I think you'd all better step lively now," Morgan said. "The Cincos have set the house on fire."

Esbeth caught Tillis looking from Morgan to Gala, then back again.

"You didn't mention Denny, Esbeth," Tillis said. "Any reason?"

Morgan stood there, the Army Colt hanging at this side, his eyes like some predatory animal's. It was now clear to Esbeth, as it may have been for a time to Tillis, that Gala and Morgan had been working undercover together all the time.

"What're you saying?" Esbeth's voice was dry and scratchy, when she tried to use it. She hadn't wanted to start this with the kids in the room. She tried to frown that message to Tillis, but he spoke anyway.

"That someone working on this might've thought the pace was going slow, someone on it for over a year might've tried to stir things up on his own."

"You're talking out your ass, Ranger." Morgan's restless eyes flicked around to each of them, never blinking.

Esbeth sighed. It took a moment more for it to seep through Donnie's thicker head.

He tried to rise. "*You're* the one who killed my father," he screamed. Understanding and rage mingled on his round, boyish face. Tillis held him harder by the shoulders and pressed him back into the chair.

"We'll straighten all this out later. We don't have much time for any half-baked theories. Let's go," Morgan said. He waved to the door with his gun. Smoke was starting to come in from the kitchen. Outside, they could hear gunfire getting closer to the house.

"That's a different gun for you, isn't it?" Gala said. "Didn't you used to have a 7.65?"

"You mean the one under my pillow? I'm surprised you'd

want to mention that right this moment." He was looking right at Tillis. "That came up missing."

"What they're saying makes sense. You didn't like it that I was called in either," Gala said. "You've been here too long, without showing any progress. You were having too much fun dragging things out with the small town, and weren't getting through to the Cincos, getting them to help themselves out of here. Did you really figure the mayor turning up dead would stir things up?" Gala was easing away from the table.

The talk wasn't to goad Morgan, but to buy Gala time to move any action away from the table. Esbeth could see that. But her glance to Donnie and Karyn found them more rapt than as scared as they should be.

"You had a good life, didn't you, Morgan? Your cover was sweet. You were making money. Your tastes ran to the exotic, to the very young. Did you make those personal porn film tapes of the two of you going at it, too?"

"Don't you go green-eyed on me now."

Esbeth rubbed her wrists and watched them talk with as detached a sense as she'd ever experienced. She felt like a lump of lead glued to her chair. There was Old Bill Hoel, dead and curled up on the floor. Outside there was shooting, screams, and all manner of chaos, but above that she could hear something cold and dripping in the kitchen, like a bent metronome. Behind that was a low, growing crackle, like a fire burning. Time seemed slowed, focused, and yet elastic and unreal. Tillis was lowering, lowering, getting closer to his gun all the time. But Gala had more to say.

"For that matter, I'm beginning to doubt Bill Hoel was even the one to eliminate Don Cinco. Maybe it was someone motivated to put down the Cincos' chance of freedom, to keep things the way they are around here."

Morgan's piercing eyes swept around to each of the others in the room, taking a quick straw poll to see how he stood. When those laser beams fixed on Esbeth, she could see no emotion in Morgan's face, no emotion at all. But she could see awareness.

Everything seemed to be happening too quickly for Esbeth, but that could be because she wasn't quite over looking down the barrel of Bill Hoel's gun.

Donnie started to scream something. Tillis clamped one hand around his mouth, while still trying to bend low enough to pick up the gun he'd dropped earlier. Morgan made his move.

His gun snapped up in a blur of blued-steel, and a shot rang out.

Esbeth had never seen anyone move as fast as Morgan, nor could she figure out the hole high in the center of his chest as he snapped back and crumpled against the door jamb. Across the room, Gala was slowly lowering her gun, with a wisp of smoke trailing from its barrel.

Tillis let go of Donnie and rushed over to him. Those penetrating eyes were already frosting over. But Morgan could make out who was there. He struggled to lift his head and could barely get out the words, "You'll never really know now, will you?" Then the eyes went out like campfire embers in a rain, and his head dropped back against the wall. Although he'd barely been able to whisper, Esbeth and the others hadn't missed a word.

"Okay, everyone. Let's go," Tillis shouted. He went over to help Esbeth up out of her chair.

Donnie stood on legs as wobbly as a newly-dropped colt. One minute he was upright, the next he hurried to the corner of the room and bent forward, retching. Karyn started to go to him, but Logan held her back. He went himself, and held out his handkerchief to Donnie.

Logan held the boy's shoulders, then helped him stand upright. Donnie wiped at his face, and turned with reddened face and watery eyes.

"Is all this over for you now, son?"

"It's … it's over. Yes, sir, it really is."

Gala spun and hurried ahead into the house to make sure the way out was clear.

Logan let Karyn come over to Donnie. He eased away and came over, picked up Tillis' gun, and leaned close to him as he handed it back. "You think Morgan's gun really came up missing?"

Tillis shrugged. "He played that awfully quick, like a card up his sleeve. He was a gambler, Logan, and it was a bluff that didn't take."

"You'll bet your life on that?" Logan said.

Tillis gave a not-very-convincing shrug. Logan turned and headed back across the room.

"Logan?"

"Yeah?" He turned back to Tillis.

"It'll be okay with me after this, if you go back to caring about squirrels."

Logan smiled over at the questions on the faces of Donnie and Karyn. He looked back to Tillis. "What do you think I'm doing?"

Logan went over and bent close, talking quietly with Donnie and Karyn, then got them turned and started out of the dining room. Tillis reached to help the still-shaky Esbeth up out of her chair.

Logan put his arms around Donnie and Karyn and kept them moving. Tillis held Esbeth upright as they went through the house. They all stopped at the side door that led out to the patio. Gala had searched the way, to make sure it was clear of guards, and was waiting for them there. Flames covered most of the other walls now, and portions of the house were beginning to crumble and collapse.

Outside, they could see the last of the guards retreating down the road that led to the front gate. Mounted Rangers on each side kept them moving, while small waves of the Cincos, some of them in worn and time-dated dress, rushed across the open places, trying to help in the fight.

"Looks clear enough," Logan said. Most of the shooting had stopped, or was too far from them to matter now. He started outside, with Karyn and Donnie tucked under either arm.

Gala came back to help with Esbeth. Tillis was looking out across the ranch, watching the white hats on horseback. His look was one of longing, and it seemed to Esbeth that he'd have given a lot just then to be on one of those horses with them. Gala reached and touched Tillis on the arm.

"I'm not the one who killed Denny. It was Morgan. Do you believe that?" Gala looked up into his face.

"Yeah, if you say so. What about the gun?"

"Well, I did know he'd had a gun like that, though I wasn't absolutely carved in stone that it was the same gun. You know how I knew he had it. I could have told you about the gun earlier, but I didn't. Does it matter all that much?"

Tillis looked out at the Cincos, who were doing more

cheering than fighting now, and many were running toward the house.

"Well?" Gala was watching his face closely.

"I suppose not." He looked down at her. Esbeth thought his voice had the hollow sound she associated with people who staggered out from the thick fighting in a war. But he did manage a tired smile for Gala. "No, I don't suppose it does at all."

The action seemed to be drifting away from them, except for the crowd of Latino women and children that swelled in size as they ran toward the flaming house, cheering and waving as the small group inside emerged.

A breeze coming up from the lake swept the smoke in the other direction and gave Esbeth her first breath of clean air, as Tillis and Gala helped her totter from the house.

ESBETH WAS PHYSICALLY and emotionally exhausted. She felt them guiding her up the hill, and then Gala helping her up onto the horse to ride, hanging on behind Tillis. But everything else still seemed hazy and unreal, no matter how hard she struggled to focus. So much had happened, and in not very much time. She clung to the back of the saddle, picturing herself falling to either side and lying there like a puddle. The horse's flanks pitched lightly from side to side with each step, accompanied by the slight creak of leather from the tack. Cowboys probably either enjoyed this sort of thing, or, at the least, were so used to it they didn't even notice. But Esbeth had all she could do to concentrate and just hang on, only occasionally glancing around.

She could make out Gala and Donnie, and Logan and Karyn, paired up on the other two horses. Tillis led the horses down to the driveway, now that most of the fighting was over. Then there were people everywhere, as the crowd of poorly-dressed Hispanics swarmed up to them along the drive as they headed for the front gate.

The people cheered, and reached out to touch the ones they called their liberators. The smell of burning scrub cedar and mesquite filled the air, and in the distance Esbeth could hear a few shots being fired. But these were in celebration. The crowd made way for them, and Tillis nudged Bucko into a faster trot. A woman holding a small child stepped close to touch Esbeth as the horse rushed by. Tears ran down both her cheeks. A man with a smear of dried and darkening blood across his forehead held up a tired hand and managed a smile at Tillis. Esbeth bounced and clung closer.

"Where are all these people from?" she shouted.

Tillis turned his head enough to yell back, "They're from here, though I don't suppose the Census Bureau ever got the chance to list them."

There was a lot more she wanted to ask. But she had all she could do, hanging on and watching, as they headed to the front gate. When she caught glimpses of Donnie's and Karyn's faces, they looked as tired and as confused as Esbeth felt. The crowd of people began to thin out as they got farther from the burning ranch house. Ambulances, fire trucks, and state trooper cars were coming up the drive, headed in the other direction, toward the burning ranch house. Tillis eased Bucko off onto the dirt beside the drive. He just waved at them and kept going.

"You back to being a Ranger again?" she asked. The scraps of her own mental fog were clearing a bit in the breeze from the jostling ride.

"Seems that way."

She leaned closer, so she wouldn't have to shout above all the noise of sirens and distant yelling. "With your instincts, I wonder that you didn't know more than I did about what was going all the time—you cut yourself off from being official for just this sort of mess, didn't you?"

"You and the Lute could nod heads over that, if it mattered," he said. The words were almost lost in the breeze and the sound of the horse's hooves.

By leaning out past his shoulders, she could see the congestion that was waiting for them just outside the gates to the Hoel spread. State trooper cars and EMS vehicles lined the road as far as she could see in both directions.

She could make out a knot of the former guards who were handcuffed and in a clump, waiting to be loaded and taken away. Texas Rangers were helping the uniformed state troopers load them into the backs of the state patrol cars.

Tillis led Bucko and the other two horses over to the fence just past the gate. He climbed down and tied the horse's reins to the fence, then reached to help Esbeth down. She was afraid she'd be too much for him, but his arms were strong and firm as he eased her to the ground. Her feet wobbled for a few steps, but she moved closer to the others as they dismounted, and she seemed to gain a little strength from that.

Logan and Gala were tying up the other two horses, and Donnie and Karyn were stretching after their bouncing ride, when a tall Ranger in a white hat pulled away from a group of Rangers and state troopers and came striding toward their group, with Pudge Hurley limping along as fast as he could to keep up.

"This's Lieutenant Tim Comber," Tillis told them.

"Gus and Mel are our only wounded," Tim said, "except Pudge over there. Mel and Gus are both up and helping out, and Pudge was barely hurt at all."

"Barely hurt?" Pudge's face was pale and lacked any of his usual blustery confidence. He limped over to his horses, and began checking them over to make sure they'd come out better than he had. One leg of his jeans had been cut away, and white tape covered his thick leg from thigh to shin.

"It's practically a flesh wound, Pudge." Comber turned back to Tillis. "Where's Morgan?"

"Dead," Tillis said.

"And Bill Hoel?"

"Same."

"Well, hell, Tillis."

"I think I can help explain," Gala said. She stepped up and stood beside Tillis. Esbeth, Donnie, Karyn, and Logan eased closer too.

"Senator Martinez is on his way by copter," Tim said to Gala. "I'd guess you'd know about that."

She looked at Tillis, but didn't say anything.

"I had a hunch it was something like that." Tillis nodded.

"And Morgan was his other agent on this," Tim said. "I wish you'd brought him out, too."

"I liked him better as the bad guy," Pudge said.

"Then I guess we got some good news for you, Pudge." Tillis glanced at him, then turned to Tim.

"He's the one who killed Dad," Donnie interrupted. He pushed closer, his round, boyish face both excited and sad, with Karyn clinging to him, and Logan keeping a gentle, re-straining hand on one of Donnie's shoulders.

Tim narrowed one eye at Tillis. "What exactly happened to Morgan?"

"He drew down on Gala."

"And Bill Hoel?" Tim looked at Gala.

"Morgan shot him," Logan said.

Tillis took a breath and, above the noise going on all around them, gave Tim the short version of what'd gone on back at the ranch house. Gala and the others chimed in, helping the story along, while Tim nodded. Their small cluster of people and horses tucked over by the fence was like a tiny island, with their heads close, while the chaos of news crews arriving and ambulances coming and going continued.

Tim looked down for a moment, absorbing everything, then looked back up at Tillis. "I suppose my instincts told me more than I let myself act on. But, Till, you've gotta know that Old Bill Hoel must've been using up every bit of clout he had, though I take responsibility for acting the way I did, when it trickled down to me."

Esbeth didn't know what was behind what sounded like an apology to her, but she was pleased to see the Lieutenant smile when he told Tillis, "Hell, maybe he heard of your bulldog reputation for solving cases, and that shook him to his rotten core."

"It's more likely he heard of Tillis' unique style," Logan said.

Tim nodded. "All that's past us now. I suspect there're gonna be more than few red faces back in Austin."

"More than when the Indians lived where Austin sits, do you think?" Esbeth said. "But I imagine the INS is in for some of that too, not to mention the local law."

"Where is Eldon, by the way?" Gala asked Tim.

"He's been asked to stand down on this. The Captain's

on his way and wants a talk with him. Eldon's got quite a bit of explaining to do."

"Speaking of which," Tillis spun and headed the few steps over toward the fence, where Pudge stood rubbing down the horses he'd loaned them. He grabbed Pudge by the shoulder and spun him around. Pudge flinched, but stood his ground.

"You mind explaining how you could live right across the road from Bill Hoel all these years and not know what was going on?" An angry red flush ran all the way up Tillis' face from his neck to his cheekbones.

"Easy, Till," Tim said. He walked over to stand where he could slow down any scuffle that might start. "I got a bit out of him a few minutes ago, once I pressed the right buttons. A very few people had rough ideas at best—not enough to act on, some of them thought."

"That's right," Gala said. She moved in close beside Tillis. "I hate to take the side of some of the locals. But the real problem here only started fifteen or twenty years ago, and crept up on the community without most of them knowing anything for sure, maybe just suspecting. Hoel only turned this into some kind of captive workforce camp a few years back. At first he paid wages, extremely low ones, to all the illegals he could get to move onto his spread; then he hired more guards and put up these fences. He's lived out here like a hermit and, with the newspaper in his hip pocket, he could keep a low profile."

"But people had to know," Tillis persisted.

"My guess is that Pudge did, or at least guessed a bit." Gala looked at him, and there was no admiration in her glance. "It probably wasn't gambling Denny and Pudge disagreed about. It was how to deal with Hoel. I think Denny guessed, or maybe suspected, but being mayor of a little town like Hoel's Dam didn't amount to squat. The county sheriff was the one who needed to act, and Hoel had him in his pocket. Pudge probably tried to keep Denny from stirring up anything until they knew more. Denny's the one who went to Martinez, and who went back to him when the first agent sent in didn't seem to be getting anywhere very quickly. That's probably the real reason Morgan popped Denny."

Pudge's face shifted from embarrassment to anger. "I'm not the only one. Other folks had a suspicion or two. But Old Bill lived out here alone, had real power like none of us could even dream about, and even if we did butt in, it was to save what?"

"They're just Hispanics, and illegal ones at that," Tillis shouted, "even though a whole generation had been born here in America, just like you. Is that what you're saying? A whole community that's learned to keep its mouth shut about one thing can about everything. You're a people without a past, or a present, and you're proud of that somehow?"

The horses took a step back at Tillis' tone, and Esbeth had never seen the Ranger so close to the edge. She figured at any moment he was going to haul off and punch Pudge, and Pudge must've thought so too, because he cringed back with the horses.

Gala reached and put a hand on Tillis' arm. "I'd slow down just a minute there, Tillis. How long have you lived here?"

"A few years."

"And you're a professional lawman, a detective, and a natural-born snoop. Did you know anything was going on out at the Hoel place?"

"No. I guess …"

She didn't let him finish. She spun to Logan. "And you? You're a game warden, and must've covered quite a bit of the county. And you've lived here a lot longer than Tillis. Did you know anything was going on?"

"Well, I …"

"I didn't think so." She looked over at Pudge. "I'm not making excuses for you, or the prejudice that's inherited and comes so natural to folks like you and a lot of your neighbors, who've lived out here all your lives. But this problem was buried deep enough it took some digging out. Are we all agreed on that?" She glanced around at the others, and settled on the lieutenant.

"She's kinda cute when she's angry," Tillis said to Tim, his voice calmer. All of his temper seemed in hand now.

"Why don't you get those horses over to the other Rangers, Pudge? That is, if we still have the loan of them." Tim's eyes were shaded by his white hat, but Esbeth didn't have to see them to guess at his expression.

Pudge nodded slowly, avoiding most of the faces around him. He clamped his mouth shut and didn't say anything, which confirmed to Esbeth that he was wiser than he acted. He gathered up his horses and, with a brief sideways glance at Tillis and Gala, walked them away from the small group.

"Now what's the matter?" Esbeth was looking at Donnie. For the first time she'd ever seen him show any emotion other than irritation, he was crying silently, and struggling not to the whole time. Logan had his arm around the boy, and was talking to him in a low voice.

"It's about his father," Karyn looked up and said. Esbeth noticed that her eyes were welled up too, but it was more like the happy tears she'd seen on the faces of the liberated

Cincos. "Knowing what his dad was really killed about helps, I think. He's glad … we're all glad it wasn't just over some stupid diamonds."

Logan gave Donnie's shoulders a squeeze. He could have said a lot about families not communicating well, but his glance at his daughter covered that.

In the distance, Esbeth could hear another helicopter approaching. There had been the Starflight copter, then a couple of news media ones. This one sounded like one of the big government jobs.

"That's probably Martinez," Tim said to Tillis. "I've got a few questions for him, myself, especially about all the guns that've showed up out here in the hands of the resistance." He glanced at Gala, but she offered nothing.

"This Martinez?" Logan said.

"Yeah?" Tim Comber turned to him.

"Hasn't he been mentioned as a future presidential candidate?"

"Well, he won't make it on a gun control platform," Tim said.

"You've all heard of the Delta Force, haven't you?" Esbeth stepped closer. Her voice was raspy, but she had a bit of her earlier feistiness back. She'd had plenty of time to think while wrapped up like some kind of Christmas present, and her years of following every scrap of news had given her a chance to make some sense of Hoel's rambling tirade.

"The covert counter-terrorist group out of Fort Bragg, North Carolina?" Tim asked.

"That's the one. They're a top outfit, or so I hear, tough enough to make Navy SEALs look like lightweights. Wasn't Martinez some kind of hotshot military intelligence guy once, even a member of Delta Force, way back before he was in the State Legislature, and then in the Senate?" Her eyes swept Tillis too, this time.

"Now, Esbeth," Gala said.

"Let her talk," Tim said. He leaned closer. "Yeah. Martinez was sure enough in the Delta Force once, and probably still has some connections. Where're you going with this?"

"Old Bill Hoel didn't miss many tricks. Even while he was slipping loose from reality a bit, he had suspicions about who was behind all this. He thought Martinez had gotten to one or two of those Delta Force people when their stint there had ended. He wasn't guessing. He knew it. My own guess is that Old Bill and Morgan had already come to some kind of deal, the same kind as the sheriff'd made. The way it plays out is that Gala was the next wave Martinez sent in, when nothing was happening. The INS, La Migra, had been compromised, as had the local law, and now it looked like one of his own covert people had rolled over. So he sent in the best he had." Esbeth nodded toward Gala.

Gala glared at Esbeth, but didn't say anything.

"Martinez heads a Latino relief fund too, that helps illegal immigrants. Though I'm not sure the donors know some of that might go for weapons." Esbeth didn't flinch in the look she was giving Gala.

"I doubt if they'd object as much as you think," Tillis said.

"You've heard of the fund?" Tim asked.

"I've may've even made a donation once." Tillis watched Gala's face, but her expression didn't change.

Tim turned back to Esbeth. "And you think Morgan shot Bill Hoel to keep him from talking?"

She nodded.

"Did Gala shoot Morgan for the same reason?" Tim asked her, but glanced at Tillis.

Tillis paused before he spoke. He could've said a lot of things. He could have said it was self-defense, which it was. He could have gone into how Morgan had learned the inside guts of the area and had manipulated people because of that, regardless of a human life here and there. But when he spoke, it was the way the locals spoke. "Gala shot Morgan because he needed shooting."

Tim tilted his head at Tillis, not sure how much he was being kidded. Then he looked toward Esbeth.

"I don't have anything to say about that, just now," Esbeth said. The sound of the bigger helicopter landing began to drown out her words. "All I know is that some horrible wrong is just starting to be made right."

Tim glanced at Gala, then back at Tillis, who just nodded, a careful smile easing onto his tired face.

Lieutenant Comber looked around at the others. Donnie and Karyn stood close, with arms around each other, and with Logan's arm around the boy. He turned back to Gala. "I want to talk to you later, after I'm done with Martinez. I don't suppose you'll take a powder on us, will you?"

"No. I plan to stay around here, maybe find me a warm man to hold me on cold nights. If the sheriff's spot opens up, as it just might, the area'll have a whole new bunch of voters, and maybe the county will be ready to consider a Hispanic sheriff."

"A lot of these folks were born here in this county. If only some of them register to vote, you may be in good shape on that," Tillis said.

Gala nodded slowly and looked around at the swarms of people around them.

Tim Comber shook his head and turned to hurry toward the helicopter, where the doors were open and men in suits were deploying for the arrival of what might just be a future president.

ESBETH SAT IN a not-entirely-comfortable squat on the shaded ground, with her back to the pole of one of the small tent-like canopies the Rangers had assembled to provide a bit of shelter from the harsh sun, while they processed the people, injured or not, who were pouring out of the Hoel compound onto the road. The heat had picked up, and there was almost no wind. The first of the media vehicles had arrived, and reporters with camera crews were hustling through the growing crowd.

Beneath her, Esbeth was prodded by jagged chunks of gravel along the edge of the mashed-over tall buffalo grass. She'd given up on making sense of much of the running around at this point. Donnie and Karyn sat to her left, neither saying anything, though pressed close and holding hands, while Logan stood beside them, his legs slightly spread and his arms crossed across his chest.

The swell of reporter noise grew, and Esbeth looked up to see Tillis and Gala leading a man her way who was wearing a dark suit in this heat. Other men in suits were keeping the reporters back while Tillis pointed and the man looked directly at Esbeth.

"Oh, good grumpy goose grits." She pushed to get herself to her feet, and Logan reached over to help. She was standing, though not without a slight wobble for a second, as the senator came up to her and stopped.

His dark Latino face was clean-shaven, except for the gray-speckled, mostly-black mustache. His eyes were as intent as those she'd seen in Morgan, or Gala. Yet, up close, as he stepped nearer, they seemed more like the tired, patient, wise eyes of Don Cinco. She braced herself to hear something like thanks on behalf or the Democratic Party, or some such. Instead, he stepped close and whispered so only she could hear, "I have just a moment or two to listen. Talk to me."

"Why me?"

"I understand we owe you much, and you don't seem all that happy."

"My car is squashed, it's likely I'm going to lose a job that's helping with a pretty limp budget, and I haven't yet found a great source of pie out in my neck of Texas. Why would I be cheerful?"

"All these people liberated?"

Esbeth glanced at some of the faces, tired to elated, of the freed Latinos around them. She fixed on Senator Martinez, took in the cut and fabric of his dark tailored suit, stiff white shirt collar, and red tie for just that hint of aggression. He wore just a hint of subtle cologne, one she didn't recognize. It was nothing you could pick up at Wal-Mart. She seemed to hear every slow tick of his Patek Philippe watch, with its maroon crocodile band. The darkish skin of his cheeks was freshly shaved and his breath was minty fresh. Sometimes, when she was making out her annual income tax check, she thought about the men in Congress, sitting in leather chairs that cost more than all the furniture in her living room, using ashtrays that were worth more than her flatware. Many came from privileged homes, had been to prep schools, and had from there been whisked through one Ivy League brain

factory or another. Still, the assembled group of congress-
men held the highest ratio of criminal activity of any occu-
pation in America. Like many of her fellow citizens, some
of the awe of the highly-placed official had fallen upon tar-
nished times. Yet she knew enough of Martinez's past to
know he'd come more by the path of hard knocks than most,
had paid his dues in the Armed Forces, had even been
Special Forces, and had been on that prestigious Delta Force.
That and his sincere and open expression decided her.

She leaned closer and said in a low voice, "You know, the
world we live in has gotten to be a pretty tough place in which
to live. And not all of it is on the other side of the globe. I
guess it takes special kinds of people to address that kind of
bad—ones able to flex past some rules and procedures."

"I like the way you use no talk of breaking eggs to make
an omelet, or of fighting fire with fire."

"I'm too pooped to even lean on the hinge of a cliché."

"And saddened?"

"That too."

"Why?"

"You know." She gave a curt nod in Gala's direction.
"Back there in the house, one minute she was saying Morgan
shot Denny to stir things up, the next minute she was
accusing him of wanting things to stay the same so he could
milk more money from the community, maybe even come
up with the diamonds. That's when I knew for a stone-hard
fact who was really doing all the fancy footwork."

"And?"

"My guess, if I was forced to make one, had to do, in part,
with Gala being female. I know that only men are accepted
into the Delta Force, so you must have gotten her from one

of the other groups, the spooks or those stiff-chinned sorts in the Hickey Freeman suits. You, being the fair sort of guy you are, wanted to show that women have a place in all the branches, even for the kind of work you know better than most people should. But you picked someone as ambitious as you, and just as willing to step around rules, even laws, to make things happen."

"What would you do, if you were me?"

"Bad is bad, no matter how you dice it up or package the end result. You play that way, and you're no better than the terrorists."

The senator hung his head a second before panning up to lock eyes with her. "I knew that already, and that I'd have to act. Thanks for giving me the chance to fix things myself."

Esbeth felt her own mouth hang in a sad frown as the senator turned and gave a short nod to the two men in suits standing behind Tillis and Gala. They stepped forward and had her by the arms, while Tillis reached around and took her piece. He looked about as uncheerful as Esbeth felt, maybe worse.

Gala's eyes opened wide, froze for a second on Tillis, and then fixed on Martinez.

"I let you go, everything I do is a lie," he said. "Morgan didn't shoot that mayor. You did. I never authorized that."

Donnie was trying to struggle to his feet, with Karyn holding him back and Logan helping, with his hands on the boy's shoulders.

Gala's mouth opened, then closed.

"Oh, come on, Gala," Esbeth said. "The poor boy's had quite of day of it, thinking he'd finally faced his father's killer and seen him killed. Help out here."

"Screw all of you," Gala muttered. But she stared at Tillis.

"I only met that Morgan fellow for a little bit, but I'd heard he was a gambler who never bluffed. You think he hadn't already sent hard evidence to the senator here, in case you crossed him?" Esbeth's voice had the most edge in it that she'd shown so far.

Gala's snarling face swung to Martinez, who nodded slowly, and a bit sadly. "Enough. Plenty enough. He was always one to hold an ace up his sleeve. You would know that."

He glanced over at Esbeth, whose voice sounded as tired as she felt. "Tapes. Right?" she said.

Martinez nodded and turned his attention back to Gala. "Right. Part of it was videotapes, in the usual 'Don't open unless I'm killed' package, which I watched just before coming out here myself. I did that, thinking I'd find Morgan alive when I landed, but I wasn't as surprised as I should have been to find him dead. One tape confirmed his alibi for the time the town's mayor was killed; the other shows you taking an automatic pistol from under Morgan's pillow. Actually, it shows a lot more than that. There's more, too. Like I said, enough. I'll get copies to the Ranger, though I doubt he'll enjoy them much."

Gala went into a sudden frenzy of twisting and wrenching her body, trying to get free of the men who held each arm. It nearly succeeded, and would have, if they weren't both as well-trained as she.

Tillis flinched, as if the struggle hurt him as much as her. But Donnie was suddenly still, and Logan could loosen his grip on the boy's shoulders. Seeing Gala so aware that she would no longer be free, the mad desperation that went with that loss, seemed to calm him, put him at peace with his father's death for the first time. He'd certainly been through enough to welcome some sense of closure.

The men in suits led Gala away. She still struggled.

Senator Martinez sighed. He stepped close to Esbeth again and spoke too softly for the others to hear. "You certainly are something. Though I was warned of that. You let me know if you ever want some work in this line."

"Count me out on that." Esbeth's voice had grown choked and fuzzy. "That cloak-and-dagger stuff is not up my alley at all. The only thing shaken here is me, not a martini. I don't have the heart for this biz that turns people inside out." She nodded toward Tillis, whose face was washed as pale as someone who had been gut-shot. "I get no joy from seeing people hurt, no joy at all." A single tear started its struggling way down across her wrinkled left cheek.

Martinez's face wrestled toward a smile and halfway made it. Then he gave a short bow of his head to Esbeth, and turned to follow the men and his former agent, who were headed toward the copter.

While Karyn moved close to put an arm around Donnie, Esbeth stepped closer to Tillis. "You wouldn't have slept well," she said.

"Like I'm going to anyway," he said, turning to watch the men lead Gala away, his eyes sad all the way to the cold bone of his skull.